C000113554

NOTE FROM THE AUTHOR:

Dawn Of Man is a work of fiction,
however much of it is based on cutting edge
work being done in the fields of
Alternative Archaeology and History
While certain locations have been alluded to,
the story itself is the author's attempt to explain
some of the unexplainable things in our diverse history.
Open your heart to what has been and let your imagination
soar...

Mesinva Shekarra Ceresse (live and love in peace and harmony)

<u>DEDICATION</u>

For my father Frederick,
a man who understood so much and asked so little.

Special 10th Anniversary Forward:

In 2010 I created this world, using inspirations from diverse cultures spanning across the planet and grounding the technology used by the characters in real-world science. I endeavoured to create a world that would stimulate the mind and make the reader think, "hmm... I wonder..." When I wrote The Exodus, things like alien life visiting earth were still considered fringe science. Ancient Astronaut Theory and other radical ideas were still fresh and not widely accepted. What a wild strange journey we have taken, to see today the idea of off-world visitations is common and even becoming mainstream news. Ancient Astronaut Theory has gained more and more depth and is much harder to dismiss. We have learned so much, yet still have barely scratched the surface of our potential as a species. If there is one lesson I hope you take from this adventure, it is that nothing is impossible when we cooperate and work together as a whole, rather than as separate parts. Humanity in the 2020s is truly at a crossroads, let us choose to walk into the future with peace, curiosity and wisdom; with our history so badly eroded by the ravages of time...

Can we really be so sure of our origins?

AN EXPLANATION OF SIRIAN TERMS

FIKAN - KILOMETER

FIKA - METER

SARA - SIRIAN ADVANCED RESOLUTION ARRAY (AI COMPUTER)

ISTS (ISTiS) - INTER-SHIP TRANSIT SYSTEM

MFARD (MICRO FABRICATION AND REPAIR DROID)

S.I.V. (SIRIAN IMPERIAL VESSEL)

S.I.V. JOVUS - MESHREW-SEBA (EVENING STAR) CLASS

S.I.V. HELIA - SARET (WISDOM) CLASS

S.I.V. SOLARAN – SAQR (FALCON) CLASS

S.I.V. VOLSHEEN TAONEEWA - AL-GHAṬṬĀṢ (ALBATROSS) CLASS

SIRIAN ESCORT SHUTTLE - TAEER ALTNAN (HUMMING BIRD) CLASS

PREFACE

Mars, 522,000 BCE. Atlanka City, part of the Sirian Imperial Alliance sits on the Martian landscape on a sandy white beach, beside a majestic sapphire blue ocean. A peaceful place of trade, learning, and exploration until disaster strikes. From the depths of space, hurtling towards the planet, a seemingly uncontrollable and massive asteroid is on a collision course. Only Persephone, Director of the Sirian Institute of Science has the courage to take control and avert disaster. From the deepest part of the solar system, where the S.I.V. Jovus, Solaran and Helia, three of the Empire's most advanced Star Ships attempt to destroy the asteroid, to the bowels of Atlanka City, where Persephone and her sister Josephine must try to outsmart a dynamic artificial intelligence, bent on stopping their efforts at all costs. The Exodus is an emotional rollercoaster, that takes the reader from despair to the deepest moments of human love and compassion. It highlights the absolute best of humanity in the direst of situations; from the S.I.V. Solaran being struck by a fragment of an asteroid, to the Helia rescuing the Solaran from a repair dock, before Mars is obliterated. The Exodus is sure to inspire readers of all ages. We have so much we cannot explain, so many monuments that are nameless. So much of our history is lost in time. To understand where we are going, we must be able to see clearly, who we have been...

SOMETHING STIRS

524,000 years ago on what we now know as the planet Mars, then a moon of Earth.......

Persephone and Josephine stood on the farthest dock of Atlanka City as they watched the last transport take off. The dock was now silent, the only sound that could be heard were the few birds in the air. Atlanka was a Mobile Star Base, built to resemble an immense flat bird. Atlanka had been retired to Mesira over 2,000 years ago due to space frame age and torsional stress in the Main Engines. She was deemed unfit for further service and was decommissioned to be a permanent metropolis on Mesira. The City's Mobile Infrastructure had fallen into disrepair and Persephone's team had only barely managed to get the Transit Systems online. Nobody knew if her Engines would engage. It was dusk on Mesira, the sky crimson with ribbons of orange dancing in the distance. The mid-afternoon sun shone low in the sky; it was the City's last day on Mesira. The dock, which was a gently brushed gold, was fairly ordinary for a Sirian Star Base. It was a Transit Station that serviced all incoming and outgoing transports. Persephone was short for a Sirian woman, her features were delicate and refined. Her hair was a brilliant strawberry blonde, the colour of a thousand breakings of the dawn. Josephine, a taller more strongly featured brunette was the farthest thing from intimidating. She and Persephone were sisters and both were scared to death. They stood watching the sunset for what would be Mesira's the last evening. Josephine stared up at the incoming asteroid. "Seph, do you think it'll work?" Persephone gazed up at the harbinger of their doom. "It has to Jo, we're out of time". Both women clasped hands and closed their eyes as they felt the Transporter engage. Taven was in the Centre seat, "let me see it". Two rectangular plates on either side of the forward section of the Bridge retracted and slid into the wall. Two brushed silver cylinders slid out and locked into place. Plasma energy coursed over the cylinders and two teal arcs of lightning struck between them as the Main Screen electrified with rippling currents of raw energy. Then there it was – large, ominous and completely unstoppable; it made Taven's blood boil. Taven sat back in his chair, "this is it, hang on!"

two weeks before...

Atlanka rested on the shore of a fairly large bay, the white sand glistened in the late morning sun. The City shone like a golden beacon out over the water. It was a fairly ordinary day, vehicles floated along the streets, and people went here and there. All in all, it was a day not unlike any other, on a thousand worlds in the Sirian Empire. The Sirian Council Building was in the centre of the City, it was shaped like a great hollow circle. Outside were a series of holographic fountains and landscaped gardens; a woman walked past the inside of the front doors and headed down a hallway. The hallway was brushed gold in colour with amber accents dotting the corridors. The hall was tiled in sandstone marble with columns every few feet. Computer Touch Panels dotted the halls and there were a few plants scattered around here and there. Persephone was walking down the hallway leading to the Third Minister's Office. She wore a light orange turtleneck sweater with a white skirt that fluttered at the knee. Skirts, in general, had gone out of widespread usage a long time ago, but she found something comforting about them and she felt more at home in them than she did in slacks. "Seph!" - "Seph!?" The voice called from behind her, a voice she knew all too well. She turned her head, and a smile crept along her lips with a giggle she just couldn't resist. "Yes Taven, what is it?" Taven was a well-built gentleman, quite handsome in all respects. His hair was chestnut-brown; he was tall with broad shoulders and strong arms, a typical military man - one Persephone found to be both irresistible and a joy to tease. Taven looked positively out of breath, "thanks for finally stopping; do you have any idea how hard it is to find you sometimes?" Persephone looked at the wall, "you know, you could just ask SARA?" Taven rested his hands on his knees and caught his breath, "I tried that and SARA couldn't find you." Persephone looked at the Badge on her wrist, "oops, I think I turned it off." Taven shook his head "you are an evil, evil woman". Persephone leaned closer and patted his cheek, "mmm-hmm, I know, that's why you love me," She rustled his hair and beamed a smile. "Now what's so all-fired important that you had to make me late for an appointment with the Third Minister?" He put his hands in his pockets and shrugged, "well, are we still on for dinner tomorrow?" She looked him in the eyes and tried to be sincere (only half succeeding) "well, of course, I don't go to all the trouble of making plans, then cancel at the last minute". Taven looked like someone who' just had the weight of the world taken off of his shoulders. "Phew, it's been worrying me for two days now". Persephone grabbed his nose between her first and second finger and wiggled it, "come on, you know me better than that; don't be so silly, I'll see you tomorrow evening" she grinned. Taven wrapped his arms warmly around her giving her a gentle hug, "okay, I'll see you then, sorry I made you late."

Persephone began to walk towards the Third Minister's Office, she looked back over her shoulder flicking her fingers in a goodbye motion, "oh that's perfectly fine Tav, I'll make sure Sorvan knows who to blame, tootles," and with that, she turned the corner. As Persephone walked into the office she caught the scent of lilac, she closed her eyes and inhaled deeply, letting every part of the smell saturate her senses, she enjoyed the moment. "Mmm," she thought, the office was a brushed gold colour with inlaid brown marble ringed in amber. In front of her was a brushed gold desk and some variety of potted plant. Sorvan was quite the Horti-culturalist but occasionally he suffered from a black thumb. Not able to bask in nostalgia for long, she shook herself back to reality and walked into the room. "Minister, you asked to see me?" She kept a fairly rigid pose and listened. Sorvan was a tall and firmly built man who commanded presence around him. He was far older than Persephone, grey lines dotting his hair and crow's feet hanging around his steel-blue eyes; but for all his stern appearance, he was as soft as a rose petal. "Seph, when are you going to drop the stiff back and learn to relax?" She grinned mischievously, "oh I don't intend to, I know how much you enjoy the attention". Sorvan chuckled and showed her to a couch "have a seat, my dear," he motioned to the end of the couch.

Sorvan sat down across from her, his legs crossed in a gentleman's fashion; he was wearing a dark blue two-piece suit with a white shirt unbuttoned at the neck. He gazed warmly at Persephone, "I asked to see you because you're the best scientific mind on the Planet". Persephone blushed, "well, one of them anyway." Sorvan sat forward, "Seph, we have a problem," suddenly Persephone's mood changed from jovial to worry, it was something about the way he said it, the undertones in his voice made her back shiver. "This is no normal visit is it?" He shook his head "I'm afraid not". Sorvan picked up a small hand-held device much like a remote control, its panel blinked on as his hand made contact and a series of symbols lit up brightly in amber. Sorvan pressed a couple of glyphs and a pair of slits in the wall about thirty-two inches apart recessed and retracted into the wall. Two silver rods slid out and locked into place. Energizing in teal forks of lightning and connecting with charged plasma, the Holographic Screen formed and solidified. Sorvan pointed the remote at the screen again and the image changed from a display of appointments and dates for Sorvan's calendar to an image of something that made Persephone's back grow ice cold. "We've picked this up on Long-Range Scanners, we estimate just over two months until it becomes a serious threat". The edges of the screen crackled with directed energy as an image began to play. It showed a large asteroid rolling in the vastness of the Solar System. Persephone brushed a lock of hair away that had fallen on her face, "is this on course for us?"

Sorvan sighed heavily, "it appears so, we're tracking it but for the moment it's not a threat, we should have time to recall a series of transports from Siria Prime". He got up off the couch, "in the meantime, I would like you and your team to start to draw up a plan for destroying it." Persephone's head dropped, "my people are Scientists, the planning won't be an issue, but the application of those plans is a job for the Engineers." Sorvan stood in thought for a moment, "do you have any ideas?" Persephone leaned forward, "a large team will only get bogged down in idea debates, I should keep the group small and focused". Persephone's head dropped, then she looked up and an idea struck her mind, "I'll need the Jovus". Sorvan stood for a moment in contemplation "I think that can be arranged." He tapped a Communications Badge on his left wrist, "Captain Taven, please report to my office". Taven's voice crackled through the Intercom, "on my way sir".

Taven moved through the halls of the concourse like a Star Ship on autopilot. He wore a standard light brown uniform with brown pants. The rank of Captain was clearly visible on his shoulders. It wasn't unheard of for a Captain in the Sirian Fleet to be summoned to the Third Minister's Office, but it wasn't a normal occurrence and it made him uneasy. His mind raced with ideas of what the Third Minister needed to see him about. He turned the corner and headed towards the Third Minister's Office. Standing at the door, he straightened his jacket and shook the thoughts from his head. Tapping the door chime, Sorvan heard the bell and got up "ah that must be him". He walked over to the door and lightly touched the amber unlock control, "ah, come in Taven, I believe you know Persephone", Taven's head nodded, "yes we're quite well acquainted". Sorvan nodded his head, "yes I know, please have a seat". Taven sat down near Persephone, he could see her discomfort; it hung over her like a dark raincloud ready to burst. "Taven we have a situation that's arisen and Seph's asked for your ship and your crew's assistance". Taven looked to Persephone then back to Sorvan, "she has? Is everything okay Seph?" Sorvan again touched the gold remote and the screen spread and crackled to life, teal energy sizzling along its borders.

"I have already made Persephone aware of the situation, but you should know what you're dealing with", again the ominous looking asteroid appeared on the screen and seemed even more foreboding than before. Persephone had a shiver roll down her spine, Taven's jaw grew tight and his brow wrinkled with intense thought.

Taven pointed towards the screen, "do we know its course and trajectory?" Taven was obviously worried. Sorvan clicked off the screen and it sizzled and flashed out, "yes it's on a direct course for Mesira, Seph's asked for the Jovus to assist her in determining the best course of action for deterring or destroying this thing." Taven looked at Persephone's face, she was almost trembling but attempting to keep her composure; the tension in the room was very high. "She knows full well that my ship and my crew are always at her disposal". Persephone's head turned and a golden strand of hair caught the light from the window, "thank you Taven." Sorvan rose to his feet and shook both Taven and Persephone's hands "then the best of luck to both of you".

Taven nodded, "thank you Sir." Sorvan lightly touched Persephone's shoulder and touched the door controls. As the door slid up, Persephone walked out into the corridor followed by Taven. Taven stopped just outside the door; Persephone noticed him halt and walked up to him. "Well, that explains why my Ship has been hung up in dry dock for the past month, while they upgrade just about every system on board." Persephone shook her hair out of her face, "you think it has something to do with this asteroid?" Taven's head dropped, "put two and two together and you'll always come out with four, I'd bet on it." Persephone rubbed Taven's shoulder. "I'm going to go pack, I'll see you on board okay?" Taven nodded in acknowledgement and grasped her hand before letting go and walking away. Persephone stood for a moment and watched him go, shaking her head, she walked across the atrium and out onto the street. It was a warm mid-spring day in the City. Cars floated down the street and people were out walking. Persephone walked down the road, passed a tree and onto the Main Transport Hub's Pads. Tapping her destination into a golden pedestal beside the clear pad she stood on, the Transport System started.

Teal lightning struck above her head and semi-transparent ribbons of teal energy encircled her from the top down; spinning faster and faster, two white beams of light shone in the torrent at her sides, scanning across her until they met in the middle and crackled with a resounding clap of thunder. Persephone emerged from the transporter in her apartment building. She walked down the hall which was much like any other Sirian structure, with chocolate marble floors and brushed gold walls. In this building the lighting was from sconces along the wall and between them hung many framed pictures. The soft amber light made her feel warm and calm. She walked up to her door and tapped the entry key, as the door slid up, she walked in. Her apartment was functional, it served her needs very well. As she came in she looked around, her living room was just inside the front door. A black leather couch and chair were arranged with a black glass coffee table. There were grooves on the wall where the Holographic Screen slid out. It served as both a computer interface and as mild entertainment. To the left of the living room was the kitchen. Brushed gold counters, a cooking surface and a refrigerator were among the most common in any Sirian household. A matter replicator was embedded in the wall with a control panel beside it. Many Sirians never cooked for themselves, it was somewhat considered an obsolete task. Persephone enjoyed it, she found it infinitely more rewarding than reconstituted matter. Along the wall to the back of the living area and kitchen was a massive window that looked out over the ocean. Down a hall to the right was her bedroom, a side table and small dresser for odds and ends furnished the room. Most of her clothing was stored digitally in the City's Main Database; one of the best innovations of the past several hundred years she thought - never having to clean your clothes, simply deposit them back into the storage system and they always come back brand new. Set into the wall was a long and fairly deep vertical rectangle which shone with amber light inside. Persephone smiled and walked over to it, she ran her finger along the top of the unit, "SARA, I'm going to be gone for a few days possibly a week, I need a set of clothes for that timeframe." SARA's voice was chipper and happy, "please specify your needs; casual, business or formal?" Persephone bounced on her heels while she thought, "umm, business." SARA's voice filled the room, "thank you, I have selected an assortment of clothing, I am materializing your requested items now." As the system hummed and her clothes crackled with light thunder and came into existence, she grabbed them from the unit and placed them into a travel case she had pulled out from under her bed. As she packed the last of her things, she closed the lid and engaged the magnetic locks. Pulling the handle up and placing the case on the ground, she dragged it behind her, "thank you SARA, please return to Power Saving Mode." SARA's voice softly echoed through the apartment, "powering down, have a pleasant trip Persephone, I will see you when you return home." With that Persephone walked out of her door, down the hallway and into the ISTiS. As the door slid down in front of her, she tapped the control key sequence for the Main Shuttle Hanger.

Normally she would simply use the ISTiS to transport aboard; however, the Jovus' Transport Systems were offline pending final inspection. It wasn't a long trip and she always enjoyed the quiet of a Shuttle, she found it much more preferable than the rapid transit so many in the City were accustomed to using in their everyday lives. She felt somehow at home, going where she wanted of her own accord. "There's something to be said for determining your own path;" the thought graced her mind and she smiled as she walked into the Main Hanger. It was a cavernous place, a large open space towards the back of the room provided ample space for several shuttles to dock and launch simultaneously. The room was a typical Sirian design, mostly brushed gold with columns supporting the structure in key places. Along the floor several mountings for Shuttles sat in rows, some were empty. Others had a Shuttle either being maintained, repaired or waiting for use. Hers was Transit Shuttle seventeen, she looked around the room, she wasn't all that accustomed to using propulsive transport since she spent most of her time in the City. She scratched her head and called out to SARA, "SARA can you give me a directional indicator to Shuttle seventeen?" Several rows down, a teal bolt of lightning arced down and struck one of the Shuttles, it now glowed and pulsed with brilliant teal energy and Persephone knew where she needed to go. Walking up to the radiant Shuttle, she tilted her head up slightly, "thank you SARA, please discontinue." The Shuttle's warm glow vanished and Persephone tapped the Door Controls. The door to the Shuttle parted in the middle and slid into the superstructure. Persephone ducked and tossed her bag onto one of the crew seats in the Aft section. "Why do they always have to make these things so small", she couldn't help but catch herself talking to the Shuttle. Sitting down in the navigator's seat, she slipped an earpiece into her right ear - "Atlanka Docking Control, this is Shuttle seventeen. I'm ready to get underway." A man's voice crackled through the Intercom, "Shuttle seventeen you are cleared for departure, please adhere to the filed flight plan, your Shuttle will be returned via remote operation once you have successfully docked with your Ship." Persephone reached over her head, "thank you Control, Shuttle seventeen out." Taking the earpiece out of her ear, she scratched the outside of her earlobes. She hated having to wear those, they always made her ears just a little itchy. Tapping the controls and leaning over to select a few icons on the Passenger's Console, Persephone looked down at the display. "SARA begin start-up sequence, interlock with Atlanka Flight Control, program exit trajectory and rendezvous course with SIV Jovus, Aft Docking Bay." SARA's voice filled the small ship, "Hello Director, Engines initializing, setting systems to flight mode, loading preprogrammed flight plan; error, please disengage docking clamps." Persephone giggled, she had completely forgotten. "Okay, try it now SARA." SARA's voice once again surrounded her, "interlock established. firing Ventral Thrusters, the Main Engines will activate in ten seconds."

Persephone leaned back in her chair and watched as the Bay sank beneath her and then panned across her screen. Within seconds, she was clear of the Bay and caressing the sky heading for orbit. Persephone's bags were light, she didn't expect the project to encounter any serious opposition, after all, it's just a big rock she thought.

The Jovus was an older Ship, her Engines were well used and her Space Frame was well beyond its years for any kind of deep space exploration duties, still, she found service as a Scientific and Medical Relief Vessel. A brushed gold colour, her hull was an engraved artistic masterpiece. Her Engines were as wings on a great hawk, as they swept forward they embraced the night sky. Her Warp Engines shone brightly from the Dorsal Running Lights. Her Aft Ion Engines were a deep amber, glowing as she hung in space at station-keeping. Her windows were a soothing amber, while she may have been considered as obsolete, she was still a sight to behold. Under one of the running lights just forward of the Tail, just where it met the Hull, Persephone took a look; yes, the glyphs were still there. A little chipped from all those years in space, but they were still very much there. In bold hieroglyphs, she read, S.I.V. Jovus. Taven clearly took great pride in her care and a personal interest in keeping her running at optimal efficiency. Persephone noted the work crews installing additional Plasma Wake Control Manifolds on her Starboard and Port Engine Housings, it was clear that this mission was to be made with the utmost haste and the Ministry wanted the Jovus to have her Engines back at full capacity.

The Shuttle was dimly lit, but reasonably comfortable for the job it did; a brushed gold and marble interior was intricately woven with Amber Computer Panels and Readouts. Persephone touched the Comm Panels on the Shuttle as she flew underneath one of the Jovus' massive Wings "Shuttle seventeen to S.I.V. Jovus, requesting docking permission". A familiar voice came through the system in response - "Shuttle seventeen you are cleared to dock, please reverse thrust to allow the tractor beams to lock on"

She was certain, "Josephine...Jo is that you?" An astonished voice responded "Seph"? Persephone's face beamed happily "will you meet me at the Airlock"? The excited voice responded, "are you kidding, they'd have to tie me down and lock me in the Brig, I'll see you shortly".

Persephone's Shuttle was guided in by a bright teal bolt of lightning which arced up and surrounded her shuttle with a lightning wire frame. The beam lowered the shuttle down and as it reached the floor, 4 plates slid open revealing 4 magnetic locks. As they clamped into place, a slow whirr could be heard as her shuttle's engines shut down. Persephone got up and grabbed her flight case then tapped on the amber Airlock Control Panel. The Rear hatch of the Shuttle pressurized and the door slid open. "Seph" an excited woman raced towards her and gave her a huge hug, almost knocking her off her feet, "I'm so glad to see you." Persephone was half in shock "I had no idea you were on board the Jovus, when did you arrive?" Josephine rested a hand on her hip and explained, "I transferred from the Serus last week, the Jovus was short-handed and needed a Science Officer with an Engineering background." Persephone was delighted, "if they just needed a Science Officer, they got way more than they asked for". Josephine giggled "no kidding, I probably know these systems better than the Chief Engineer." Persephone was happy, if this project was a little uncertain before, it couldn't possibly fail now with both she and her sister working on the problem.

"Have you taken a look at the data and telemetry from the Long Range Scans we took of the asteroid"? Josephine gestured towards the Inter-Ship Transit System commonly referred to as the "ISTiS". It was a Short Range Matter Energy Transporter that was used for inter-ship movement. It was far more efficient than power lifts or turboshafts and used less power, and power at the moment was at a premium on the Jovus. With all the upgrades her Reactors were being stretched pretty thin so there were measures in place so they didn't get too stressed, in theory anyway. Josephine nodded as she and her sister walked towards the ISTiS, "yes and once our retrofit is completed, we'll be underway; Taven has asked me to bring you to his office". Persephone remarked, "I noticed the Plasma Upgrades to the Warp Engines, I hope that's not the only upgrade the Ministry is providing you". Josephine's face lit up like a kid in a candy shop, "I never thought I'd see the Ministry put such a huge retrofit onto a Meshrew-Seba Class Exploration Cruiser, they're considered obsolete, but the upgrades they're giving us rival our most current Defence Cruisers and enough firepower to strip the atmosphere off a small moon." Persephone was caught off guard by the idea, "I'd like an inventory of those upgrades, if you don't mind." Josephine handed her a tablet "I thought you might, come on, Taven's waiting."

The ISTiS was always a strange feeling, no matter how many times Persephone went through it, she always felt like she was missing a couple of atoms when it was over. She just shrugged and thought that ignorance is bliss and wished she didn't know the physics and mechanics behind how it worked. She let out a slight laugh, Josephine looked at her thoughtfully "what?", Persephone smiled "nothing". Josephine giggled "ever since we were kids, you have never liked these things", Persephone's face loosened and she smiled, "well I just like to keep all my molecules where they belong, I suppose I'm spoiled having a vehicle in the City for so long". Josephine gave her a little push out the door as it opened "you are spoiled, come on." Taven sat behind his desk staring at progress reports, it all made his eyes hurt. Sometimes being in charge was downright painful; he longed for the day when all he had to worry about was shining his boots and sticking it to the man, now he was the man getting stuck and his boots were scuffed. Taven's office was off the Back Starboard Quarter of the Main Bridge, it was a place for the captain to find quiet, work or just plain hide from the crew at times. It was sparsely decorated, a curved piece of art sat by the window and on Taven's desk was a small brown bald cactus. Taven had many talents, but plants were not his strong suit. The room itself was a standard design for a Meshrew-Seba Class Vessel, brushed gold walls and deep brown marble floors, the lights themselves were a soft amber, very much like the rest of his Ship. The door chimed and slid up as Persephone and Josephine walked in. "Well, I must be living right to have the loveliest and the second loveliest women in all of creation to darken my doorstep." Josephine flipped her hair with a smirk, "why thank-you..." Persephone looked at her sister and shook her head with a smile. Taven chuckled "Seph welcome aboard, I see you have already met the newest thorn in my side". Persephone ran a finger around her ear, "she's been one in mine for years Tav, it's only fair you get the same treatment". The three laughed, it was a good release of all the tension that had been building, "please, ladies have a seat". Persephone pulled out the tablet Josephine had handed her and began to read.

===Upgrades Inventory===

Transversal Plasma Wake Stabilization Manifolds
Recursive Ion Drive Retrofit
Directed Energy Pulsar Astrogation Dish
Plasmatic Ion Distortion Shielding MK XI
Phased Plasma Energy Beams
Quantum Flux Torpedos
Triple Quantum Sublayer Refractive Sensor Array

The tablet read like a war arsenal, "are we going to war or is this a scientific mission?" Taven got up from his desk, his hands clasped behind his back, "the Ministry is concerned with the size of this asteroid and they're giving us the firepower to deal with it ourselves once we have an angle of attack, that's why you're here. We need to know its composition so we can fine-tune the yield on the Weapons Systems". Persephone bit her upper lip slightly, her brow knitted in obvious concentration, "well if it takes more than this to blast it apart, we have something to worry about because this is some of the most advanced defensive weaponry we have". Taven walked up between the chairs and rested his back on the desk. The general public is unaware for the moment, but the ministry is arming our defensive satellite network with High Yield Bitanium Warheads, just in case we fail. Persephone and her sister looked up, "they're that concerned?" Persephone let the comment slip. Taven looked warmly at her "yes, yes they are but not to worry, we have the Vorn sisters on the job, and that's good enough for me. Now then, as much as I'd love to chat, I'm up to my neck in status reports." Taven looked to Josephine, "why don't you show Persephone to her quarters, I'm sure you both have some catching up to do and if I don't get unburied from this mountain of paperwork, we're not going anywhere".

Josephine showed Persephone to a room on the Starboard Side of the Main Hull. It was a reasonable size with the usual brushed gold, much like the rest of the Ship. There was a blonde wood desk with an amber readout and Control Panel on the top. Behind the desk, a small unit was shimmering in light amber. Persephone made a conscious effort to avoid using the Food Replicator in her apartment, she wasn't all that enthusiastic about having to use one here. In the corner, a single bed lay peeking out from behind a door to the adjoining bedroom. All things considered, it was a fine room and she wasn't picky, she didn't plan to stay long. "Well Seph here you are, I'm still on duty for a few hours. Why don't you put your things away and get a little sleep, it's pretty late by Mesirian time and I'll take you to breakfast when my shift ends". Persephone nodded, "sure, that sounds wonderful. We can go over the progress of the upgrades and start to get a preliminary idea of what we're going to do with this monster when we find it". Josephine gave her sister a long hug and held her shoulders, "I'm glad you're here, if there's anybody who can fix this it's you," Josephine walked towards the door and stepped into the corridor. Persephone nodded to her sister and the door slid shut. She was so tired she didn't even notice the locking mechanism on the door. She walked into the adjoining bedroom and sat on the bed removing her shoes, she rubbed her aching feet. She had mixed feelings about this mission but she knew how important it was that she not fail. She ran her fingers through her hair and took her clothing off. She walked back out to the living room and dragged her suitcase into the bedroom. Unlatching the magnetic clasps, she opened it and took a silk nightgown out of the case. Slipping it on over her head, she took a hairbrush out and brushed her hair. Persephone pulled the covers back and laid down; sliding her feet under the sheets she pulled the blanket over herself and her eyes closed. She wondered what would happen in the coming days, nothing spectacular, surely nothing critical, after all, it's just a big rock.

FLIGHT OF THE JOVUS

Persephone awoke to the sound of the Standby Alert Klaxon blaring, something was very wrong. Josephine chimed the bell and walked in, "sorry Seph, I'm afraid breakfast will have to wait, we just got a report from one of our Outer Tracking Stations"; Josephine looked very worried. Persephone was still half asleep, she found it hard to focus as she rubbed her eyes and yawned, "what's so important?" Josephine struggled to get the words out, Persephone cocked her head sideways and looked at her sister with a cheeky smile, "well come on, out with it before I fall back to sleep." Josephine regained her composure, "we don't have two months, we have two weeks". Persephone eyes opened wide and she was suddenly very much awake, "two weeks?!"

Josephine nodded, "yeah, we have to go...now, Taven's doing a final check to see if we can get the Jovus moving". Persephone shook her head, "but the ship's not ready, the upgrades aren't finished and the Engines haven't even been started". Josephine agreed "I know but we'll have to finish en route, Fyar is in Engineering trying to cold start the Main Core, I just hope the Engines hold up under the strain." Persephone shook her head, "are you nuts? The core is two centuries old, it can't take the stress of a forced plasma induction, not to mention it's just had a complete overhaul, and we're not even sure if the new Plasma Distribution Network is installed properly, it needs to be tested first". Josephine shrugged her shoulders, "I know, but Fyar's one of the best in the Fleet and he knows his ship back to front, if he can't get us moving, we're finished." Persephone's shoulders slumped, "I sure hope your right", Josephine gazed into her sister's eyes, "I have to be because we just ran out of time".

Persephone threw on her clothes, then she and Josephine made their way quickly to the Bridge. Taven was already deep in thought and trying desperately to get the Ship underway; "Captain to Engineering, Fyar where the hell are my warp Engines?" A frazzled voice crackled over the Comm system, "One damned minute Captain, I can't get the plasma flow balanced, I need a Level Ten Certified Plasma Operator". Taven looked at the two women - "Josephine I need you to get down to Engineering to co-ordinate with the Chief, get those Engines online! Josephine stiffened "on my way, Sir." Seph you're assigned to Science Lab Three, I suggest you begin your work with all due haste, it looks like we just ran out of time." Josephine stepped into the ISTiS and headed straight to Engineering. Main Engineering was the largest room on board. The wall directly across from the door held a large teal disc with six fingers of white light streaking out from the centre. In the middle of the room sat the Main Console. It was a typical Console, black glass with Holographic Inputs available through Plasma Control Rods. Near the door and to the left of it, was a single stair and platform surrounded by a gold railing. On the platform sat a large wrap-around Console with four displays along the wall, each showing the status of a different system. Fyar, the Chief Engineer, was clasping his head in thought, sweat was beading just under his hairline and he had a migraine the size of Siria Prime itself. He was trying desperately to get the Jovus' Engines started; "Jo, over here I need you," he waved her over. Josephine moved swiftly over to the Main Panel, "what can I do to help?" Fyar pointed to the Main Engineering Readout, "I'm going to try a controlled Ion saturation to the Primary Drive Coils, I need you to watch the Plasma Flow, when I say now, I need you to shunt the Drive Plasma into the Primary Manifolds; now we find out just how good the Techs on your outpost really are." Josephine stood ready, although she was primarily a Scientist, she had extensive experience in Warp Mechanics, Plasma Flow Dynamics and Stellar Drive Systems, so she wasn't really out of her league. All of a sudden from behind her she heard "NOW!" Josephine quickly made the corrections to the Plasma Flow and the entire Ship and Star Dock was rocked by a sharp jolt. The Engines screamed under the stress, the Power Board lit up like a Christmas tree and the whole Ship groaned in agony. Gradually, the Engines got their bearings and quietened down. Fyar came over to Josephine, sweat glistening from his brow, an obvious nervous wreck but with a smile creeping along his face. "There she's got her second wind, not bad for a Ship that's two centuries old. After all these years she's still got the same fiery spark." Josephine grinned "Fyar you're in love". He winked as he tapped the amber Comm Panel on the wall next to the Main Engineering readouts, "Fyar to Bridge, Engines are online sir. Warp Power at your discretion, I recommend a low factor so I can fine tune the injectors then we can increase speed." Taven's voice crackled over the Commlink, "well done, I'm putting your entire team up for a commendation once we've completed our mission, that was one hell of a start-up." Fyar beamed, "thank you Sir, we couldn't have done it without Jo." Taven's voice sputtered back - "Jo, if you're finished there, Seph could use a hand in Science Lab Three, I believe you two have an asteroid to blow up." Josephine perked back up, "on my way." She made a quick glance at Fyar, "no rest for the wicked eh?" Fyar snickered as she passed by, "would we have it any other way?" Josephine retorted as she left Engineering, "oh no, that would be too easy!" Josephine walked into the ISTiS, as she spun on her heels she called out, "Deck 12, Science Lab Three." The door slid down and the transport sequence began.

Josephine walked into the Lab to find Persephone bent over a Console mumbling to herself, she was wearing a pink two-piece suit with a skirt that fell to the knees. The room itself was not unlike a hundred others on board the Jovus, except this one had Status Consoles and Programming Interfaces dotting the walls. In the centre, a circular Control Desk took command of the room and Persephone was clearly somewhere lost in thought. Josephine walked up behind her sister, "boo!" Persephone jumped and spun around. She glared at her sister, "Josephine

Alvareda!, how can you even think of jokes at a time like this. Josephine laughed and retorted, "just because there's some big rock that we need to blow to bits before it smashes into Mesira, doesn't mean I have to stop teasing you. It's my solemn duty as your older sister to get under your skin; besides, your just mad because you never catch me". Persephone crossed her arms and nodded her head, "you just wait someday, somehow, I'll get my revenge." Josephine put a hand on her hip and grinned mischievously at her sister, "believe me, dearie, I'm looking forward to it, but your revenge will have to wait until after the current situation, now then about this rock. We've got the Engines online which means that if we screw this up, it's all your fault, so we'd best get started on a way to blast this thing before it hurts anyone."

Persephone leaned back over and tapped a few controls, "I've been considering using the Plasma Beams to drill into the asteroid and then firing Torpedoes into the holes on time-delayed fuses. It would give us the benefit of being able to manually detonate them at a predetermined depth, the only trouble is I'm going to need to conduct extensive scans of the asteroid before we can finalize our plan". Josephine looked deep in concentration, "hmm, it sounds like a logical course of action, but there's just one problem. If we use the Beams in drilling mode, that's going to put our Reactors over tolerance, they're stretched pretty thin as it is. If we start channelling massive amounts of directed energy into the Forward Banks, it'll overload the Main Energy Distribution Net". Persephone looked up - "we should bring Fyar in on this, we'll need two Engineers overseeing the Power Systems, I don't want any slip-ups. The slightest miscalculation and we could find ourselves floating home." The Comm System sparked to life, "Bridge to Sci-Lab Three" Taven's voice was strained, Persephone could feel his stress level from halfway across the Ship as she tapped the Comm Panel. "Seph here, how goes our mission to leave Space Dock?" Taven's voice came back, "we're just completing final checks, I'd like you both on the Bridge, we're not sure just how stable the Power Systems are and the Bridge is heavily shielded." Persephone and Josephine both straightened up as Josephine responded, "on our way". The Comm channel closed and Josephine looked over to her sister, "that face, what's troubling you?" Persephone brushed a lock of hair away from her face, "it's Taven, I'm concerned. I've never seen him so stressed, I can hear it in his voice." Josephone rubbed her sister's shoulders, "He's carrying the literal weight of the world, he's strong, he'll be fine." Persephone nodded as the two women walked towards the ISTiS, as Josephone tapped their destination into the panel Persephone found herself admitting to something that seemed to come from deep within, "I care about him." Josephine clasped her sister's hand in support, "everyone knows that Seph." The transport sequence began and the two women vanished in a hail of twisting teal energy ribbons.

The two women walked out of the ISTiS and onto the Main Bridge, it was much darker than before, the entire ship was on night mode for power reasons. All non-essential systems had been shut down, which included all replicators and recreational facilities. Persephone couldn't say she was sorry to hear that the replicators were offline, except nothing was more disgusting than military rations; she wished she had a sandwich. Taven walked over to Persephone, "Seph I need you to monitor the Sensors and Power Stabilization Subroutines, Jo I need your expertise once again at the Engineering Station. I need you to co-ordinate with Fyar, I want to get out of here without blowing the Engines off my Hull". Persephone and Josephine stiffened and both said at the same time "right". Taven couldn't tell who said what it was so quick, which in itself he found rather amusing. Persephone had never spent a day in the military, yet she reacted like someone who was trained for the task at hand, she truly belonged here and he was happy to have her expertise on the Bridge. Taven sat down in the center chair, the Helm and Operations Station was to the Forward Starboard and Port side of the Main Bridge, directly in front of him was the Main View Screen. To his immediate left was Science and to his right Engineering and Damage Control, behind him and to his left was

Weapons Control and to the right was Communications. The Bridge itself was a golden colour although you could hardly see it, the entire room seemed to glow in amber from all the panels and controls lit up around it.

Lieutenant Tezra sat at the Communications Console and opposite her Lieutenant Second Rank Jasmine, they were both from Siria Prime. Tezra was a light blonde while Jasmine was slightly darker with hair the colour of ebony. Both women were slim and well built, they wore standard Sirian military uniforms similar to the Captain's, but the neckline was slightly different as they were female Officers. They both wore brown belts with handheld tablets. Jasmine's hair was tied back tight into a ponytail, while Tezra's was in a very neat-looking bun. "Taven to Fyar what's the holdup Chief, you promised me Warp Power twenty minutes ago." Fyar's voice crackled back, "just a couple more minutes, I want to make absolutely sure we're not going to be going nowhere fast," Taven sighed, "two minutes Fyar." The Engineering Room was abuzz with frantic preparation. Fyar was double and triple-checking everything, he'd served as Chief Engineer on the Jovus for over twenty years and he was not about to lose her now. These were his Engines and his responsibility. He moved back to his Engineering readout and tapped the Comm - "Jo, do you see that plasma abnormality in Starboard Coil fifty-four?" Josephine's voice came over the system, "checking, yes I see it, correcting now, check your Panel you should have green lights right across the board." Fyar double-checked his findings, "yep, everything looks good here, thank you, Warp Power available". Taven's voice came on, "thank you Chief", his voice then switched to Ship-Wide. "This is the Captain, we're about to engage the Warp Engines for the first time. We don't know how well the Inertial Dampeners will compensate for the initial jolt, I advise everybody to put down what you're doing and hold onto something, I don't want any injuries, our Sick Bay is understaffed, Taven out"

The Helm Officer sat forward of Taven, a rather brash young man, he and Taven had gone through the Sirian Defence Academy together. He was an extremely gifted pilot and had saved the Jovus from many close scrapes. He had sandy colour hair and wore a uniform similar to Taven's, except that his had an integrated Mental Control Port, its function was to augment the pilot's tactile inputs in a crisis which sped up response time and made corrections faster. His name was Zozen, but on the Jovus he was known as Clinch. His ability to fly so close to something he could almost scrape the rock or paint off the surface was something of a legend on board. In his own words "the Jovus may be old, but that's no reason she should manoeuvre like a whale or not have the ability to fight as she was designed to." That attitude resounded all over this Ship, her crew much like her Captain saw far more in the Jovus than others who were not walking her halls and corridors. There was something almost electric about the air on board, it made you feel alive.

Taven sat up "Clinch, take us out of Space Dock, Aft Thrusters to half then go to twenty-five percent Ion thrust, as the Main Drive Coils clear their Moorings." Taven turned his chair, "Tezra put our departure on the Main View Screen". He turned again, "Jasmine what's our weapons status?" She tapped a couple of buttons and responded "we have a full complement of Quantum Flux Torpedoes and the Plasma Banks are fully charged, just try not to give me too much to shoot at? I don't want to make Fyar actually have to work for his pay", she beamed a cheeky grin. Taven smiled, "I'll have to make sure I let him know"; Jasmine grinned and nodded as she turned her chair. Clinch swivelled slightly "Main Driver Coils have cleared the frame, Secondary Ion Generators are coming online now." Taven turned back to the Main Screen as its Silver Projection Rods slid out from the wall. Teal electricity crackled and arced then spread out as the screen's Holographic Matrix formed, "reverse angle." Taven commented, "it's a thing of beauty," the Space Dock began to shrink behind the Main Ion Engines' amber glow. Clinch piped up "we're clear." Taven looked at Josephine, "here goes nothing, initiate". The

Jovus shook slightly as her Main Driver Coils powered up to full capacity, the teal Initiator Strips on the Wings blinked from the closest to the farthest, then there was a streak of blinding teal light that screamed back across the Wings. Ribbons of teal energy encircled the nose, cascading down the hull until they reached out to the Wingtips. Spinning faster and faster, they dove into the now pulsing Initiator Strips and the Jovus tore off into the blackness of space, bolts of teal lightning trailing after her and the sound of a hawk's call echoing in the blackness

DEVIL IN THE DARK

The Jovus streaked through space like a soaring teal hawk, lightning bolts streaking the night sky as she moved through the solar system. As she soared passed a particularly large rock, hanging in the blackness between Jupiter and Saturn, she was seen as simply a blinding streak of energized teal lightning. Her Engines had held and her power systems were still functioning normally, albeit a little more stressed than they were. The Ship's mood had returned to upbeat, everybody was confident and the Bridge was buzzing with the normal day-to-day happenings on board a Sirian Star Ship. Josephine and Persephone were in the Ship's Dining Room, which was on the Starboard Ventral side of the Jovus just back from the Wings. Persephone looked out the window at the cascading bolts of lightning streaking by, as the ship flew faster than she had in over a decade. She took a bite of her salad and looked at Josephine, "how long do you think we can hold Warp six?" Josephine dabbed her mouth and took a sip of coffee, "until Taven says otherwise, or until the Engines burn out, whichever comes first." Josephine took another bite of her meal, Persephone wasn't exactly sure what it was, but it didn't smell too appetizing, "you're still worried aren't you." Josephine remarked, after studying her sister's face closely. Persephone gazed at her meal and poked it with her fork, "why do you say that?" Josephine sat back in her chair and crossed her arms, "because you're my little sister and I've been watching you since you were born, what's troubling you?" Persephone leaned forward, "have you taken a really close look at the power readouts". Her sister leaned forward and took another bite, "I scanned them to double-check everything why?" Persephone waited for a lower-ranking crewman to pass by, "the Forward

Plasma Emitters are charged but they are not online, they are only drawing enough power to keep the Capacitor from draining." Josephine nodded as she chewed "mmm-hmm and that's more or less standard procedure, why, what's worrying you?" Persephone leaned a little closer, "in order to bring the Forward Banks online, I'm going to have to shunt power from just about every system on this Ship to counterbalance the power constraints; that means no Shields, the Ship will have to be flown manually as I have to take the Sensor Grid offline and the Warp Engines will have to be shut down while keeping the Main Core online." Persephone's voice got low, "I don't think I need to explain to you how risky that is. With the amount of power we're channelling through the Forward Emitters, one wrong move and we could blow out power conduits across the entire Ship or worse, rupture the Reactors." Josephine's mood soured, "I see your point, well, we'll just have to make sure we get it right the first time, I don't intend to float home". Persephone whispered, "either way if something goes wrong, a lot of people are going to get hurt or the Ship will explode", her sister gazed down then back up, "what do you suggest?" Persephone looked around the Dining Hall, "let's continue our discussion in the Lab." As she and Josephine got up, Taven walked into the room and up to them. He seemed quite happy with his Crew and his Ship as he smacked his hands together and rubbed them briskly as he approached, "well now, that wasn't quite so bad was it?" Persephone tossed her hair behind her head, "that was the easy part, the hard stuff is next", Josephine gestured to the door, "we were about to return to the Lab, would you mind joining us?" Taven seemed a little unnerved by the forlorn look on their faces and graciously accepted the invitation, he knew that Persephone was particularly troubled and decided to try to brighten her spirits. "Seph, when this is all over, I'm still buying you dinner." Persephone looked up and grinned, "you'd better, a huge menacing asteroid is nothing compared to the wrath of Persephone". Josephine grinned and raised her eyebrows, "ooo, you've been warned..." Taven motioned to the door, "shall we?" Josephine ran up behind Taven and leaned in to speak into his ear, "so you finally asked her out eh?" Taven nodded his head in an agreeing manner. Josephine slapped him on the shoulder, "oh, may the Five Gods have mercy on your soul". She beamed a smile from ear to ear and shook her head happily as they walked into the ISTiS. As the door slid up, the three of them walked in and Taven tapped the Control Panel with the sequence for Science Lab Three. It took little to no time to reach the Science Lab and as Josephine and Taven walked in, Persephone tapped the door control and sealed the three in the room. She motioned to Taven to sit down, "I'll get right to the point Tav, we're walking a very thin tight-rope on power. As I have already explained to Josephine, just to get the Main Weapons online, I'm going to have to shunt power from almost everything except Life Support and the Ion Engines. That means Clinch is going to have to pilot the Ship manually on nothing but Visual Scanners, the Ion Drive and two Thrusters." Taven sat back, "that's not so bad". Persephone put a finger to her mouth to quieten Taven, "this is a very risky thing to do. I would be hesitant to put this kind of load on a Meshrew-Seba Class Cruiser even if it was fresh out of the Shipyards. This Ship is centuries old, her equipment is aged and worn, she was never built to handle the kind of power load we're asking of her, it's a miracle she's been this accommodating thus far". Taven rubbed his chin then responded, "well I did pull Fyar off of the Kamatis, her Captain owed me a favour, so I took his Chief Engineer. He's the best in the Fleet, there's nobody better qualified to keep us flying." Persephone crossed her arms and shook her head, "Fyar's an amazing Engineer but this Ship has limits and we need a plan "B", the Jovus can only give so much."

Taven looked at her face closely, gone was the light-hearted and sassy woman he had come to know so well, replaced by someone who was almost too serious. He slumped back in his chair, "what did you have in mind?" Persephone leaned over a nearby Systems Access Terminal and punched in line after line of code. Taven had never seen her hands fly across the controls so fast, she truly was the best they had. His admiration was cut short when the screen near his head crackled and arced to life. Displayed on it there was a schematic for something, but he couldn't make out what. He gazed at Persephone with a rather perplexed look on his face, "umm, that's amazing, uh what is it?" She pointed to various locations on the schematic, "in order to avoid the current power crisis we need a buffer, something to modulate and regulate the power flow to the Main Emitters, that should keep the power at a constant drain and avoid spiking, which could cause Power Conduit explosions or in the worst-case scenario, the Reactors themselves could ignite and possibly rupture. Taven studied the diagram, "I can see why you've been so worried, you're certain this is necessary?" Persephone's head sank as she took in a deep breath, "I wouldn't be suggesting it if I thought it wasn't and if I didn't think your Engineering crew couldn't pull it off before we get there". Taven smirked "Fyar's going to hate you, he just got this Ship running smoothly." Taven let a grin slip as he tapped the Badge on his wrist, "Science Lab Three to Main Engineering." Fyar's voice crackled over the Intercom "Engineering here, what's up Boss?" Taven got up and gestured at her diagram, "Seph's sending you a schematic of some changes to the Main Power Distribution Net, the Reactor Cores and the Main Plasma Array." There was silence then Fyar's voice came back "ingenious, I never would have thought of something like that". Taven remarked both to Fyar and himself, "can it be fabricated and installed before we reach the target." Again there was a brief silence before Fyar responded, "I think so, it will take a couple of hours to fabricate the components and install this, but there's one problem." Taven put his hand on his face and shook his head, "it's always something." Fyar's voice was broken by a crackle of static, "if things were easy, we wouldn't be out here in the first place; getting back to what I was saying though, in order to put this in, I'm going to have to remove the entire Secondary Sensor Array and the Tractor Emitters." Persephone looked at Taven with a long face, "I don't think we have a choice". Taven thought for a moment then responded to Fyar, "go ahead and make the changes, we'll deal with the mess later, for now just get that Power Conditioning Modulator installed and keep us running, Taven out."

Taven looked questioningly at the two women "is there anything else I should know?" Persephone's face darkened, "just that if anything goes wrong, people, a lot of people are going to get hurt. You should have the medical ward on full standby alert indefinitely". Taven tapped his Comm Badge once more, "Science Lab Three to Main Sickbay". A hastened woman's voice came over the Comm System, "Sickbay here, Chief Medical Officer Adelaide Zokan speaking, what can I do for you Captain?". Taven thought for a moment then responded, "I want you to prepare Sickbay for massive casualties, and get any staff you have prepped and ready to go at a moment's notice". The woman on the other end let a small laugh slip, "they already are, Sickbay is fully prepped and my entire staff has been briefed and is standing by". Taven looked perplexed and asked, "are all of you women three steps ahead of me?" Adelaide didn't get a chance to respond before Josephine piped up, "of course we are, that's why we're the master race!" Both Adelaide and Persephone burst out laughing, Josephine added after they had all enjoyed a good laugh at Taven's expense, "in all honesty the reason we're usually three steps ahead of you, is because most often we know what you're going to say before you say it. It's what comes from being a well-organized team". Taven looked at Josephine and grinned wickedly, "keep talking like that and I'll have to fire you...or promote you, either way, you're in trouble". Again the room was filled with laughter, Adelaide's voice perked up on the Comm System, "well I have a few things to attend to, try not to give me anything to do please??" Taven responded, "no promises Commander". Josephine got up from the chair she'd been sitting in, "well if you'll excuse me, I have an inspection to perform. I also want to check in on Fyar to see how he's progressing and if he needs a hand. Taven nodded, "very well, off you go." Josephine walked out the door and as it shut behind her, Persephone's body went almost limp, it was painfully clear to Taven she'd been holding all her fear and doubt back and the strain was becoming overwhelming. He came up behind her, resting his hands on her shoulders and massaging them slightly. She closed her eyes only for a moment before she spoke "mmm, don't do that." Taven lifted his hands and responded, puzzled "I'm sorry, I thought it would help." Persephone turned to face him and ran a finger through his hair, "normally I'd welcome the gesture, but we're in a dangerous situation and as uncomfortable as the stress is, it actually keeps me focused". Her palm rested on his cheek and brought his head back up, "we'll have plenty of time to get to know each other better when this is over, okay? For now keep this on you at all times," she leaned forward, kissed his lips softly and told him, "may it keep you strong and safe and give you courage when yours wavers." She rested her hand on his chest and held him briefly until Tezra's voice crackled over the Comm System.

"Bridge to Taven," Taven's head dropped and his forehead touched Persephone's hair for a moment, he drew a breath of air into his nose and patted Persephone's back as he broke away. Taven responded, "what is it Tez?" Tezra's voice was slightly shaken, "please return to the Bridge as quick as you can, we have the target on Short Range Sensors. We'll be coming up on it in less than five minutes." Taven looked into Persephone's eyes, he didn't need her to explain, he knew she felt as nervous as he did. Not wanting to break away from her gaze but knowing he had to, he rubbed the bottom of his nose, "we're on our way". Persephone looked at Taven, grasping his hand as he turned to leave the room and holding him for a moment. Her head dropped as she said exactly what she was feeling, "Taven, I'm scared". Taven put his index finger under her chin and pulled her head up, "me too." He ran his fingers through her hair and pulled her close for one last strong hug before they walked out of the Lab; moving down the hall, past a small potted tree and into the ISTiS. As the door slid down behind them, Persephone stiffened her back and gripped her emotions tightly, "Bridge!". SARA's voice filled the small room, "transport sequence in progress." Ribbons of colour danced around them and as the door slid up,

Persephone and Taven stepped out of the ISTiS and onto the Main Bridge. Tezra turned around almost immediately and looked straight at Taven, "I have it on visual Captain, but you're not going to like it". Taven straightened his tunic and looked forward. Take us out of warp and match speed with the target, in an instant the Jovus went from a streaking teal ray of arcing lightning bolts to a glimmering amber hawk amongst the blackness of space. As she secured from warp, her Starboard Wing dipped slightly and her Hull caught the light of the sun, she echoed a radiant light where there had been none only moments before. The Initiator Strips pulsed back across the wings once more, then blinked twice as the Warp Engines shut down and the Ion Engines took over attitude control. Back on the Bridge, Taven was seated in his chair, "alright, let's see it." It was then all their fears became realized and Taven couldn't avoid the slip of the tongue as he stood there in awe. "By the Five Gods, how big is that thing". Persephone's hands flew across the controls and she seemed unsure of her findings. Taven looked over at Persephone rather impatiently, "well?" Persephone couldn't believe her eyes and had to re-check her findings. "Taven that "thing" is over two-thousand Fikans in diameter. It has more mass than Mesira and is almost half the size of the planet." Taven got up to look at the console readout himself, he really did have to see it to believe it. He walked over to Persephone's terminal with his hands clasped behind his back and read the horrific report for himself in plain amber and white. Taven couldn't believe his eyes, he had to know, he looked at Seph who was right beside him. "How much more mass are we talking about? It registers as a mass greater than four times that of Mesira, I can't be sure, it's almost off the charts." Taven caught himself as he almost lost his balance, he knew what he had to do but he also knew that it was likely his Ship couldn't handle the strain and a lot of people, his people, were about to be seriously injured or worse. He shook the feeling and sat back down in his chair. "Seph, I need a complete materials analysis, I want to know what that asteroid is made of and exactly how much pressure we're going to have to put on the systems in order to carry out our mission. Josephine, as of now you're permanently assigned to Seph as her assistant and as her liaison to the Jovus. Seph, pull whatever manpower or miracles you need to, the entire staff of the Jovus, as of this moment is at your service including myself."

Persephone walked over to Taven and whispered, "Tav that's really not necessary." Taven tugged on a lock of hair behind her ear and she bent down so he could whisper. Taven's voice was intentionally low, "take a look outside and then look around the Bridge, these people are frightened and quite frankly so am I; even if the manpower isn't necessary, I need to make it look like we all need to help if for no other reason, to ensure my crew stays focused and alive." Persephone nodded, she knew all too well he was right. She gazed over the Bridge and decided to make use of her authority to get started and boost morale. "Tezra transmit a message to Siria, include a full transcript of our Logs and everything that has happened up to this point, please send it the moment it's ready." Tezra nodded and went to work. "Jasmine, I want a complete diagnostic of the Weapons Array and when you're done, run it again just to make sure nothing has been overlooked then bring myself, Taven and Fyar the results." Jasmine nodded "I'm already on it." "Clinch, keep us five-hundred thousand Fikans from that asteroid, no closer and no farther, if you have to steer to avoid hitting debris, I suggest you dazzle us with your renowned piloting skills." Clinch nodded, "you got it". "Bridge to Engineering", Fyar's voice crackled through the Comm system, "Engineering". Persephone took a breath, "Fyar I need you to meet us in Science Lab Three, we have a much bigger problem than we thought." Fyar immediately responded, "I'm already headed in that direction, I'll see you there". Persephone pointed to Taven, "you're with me." As they were about to enter the ISTiS, Persephone popped her head out "oh and Tezra, I'll need an open Comm-Link to the Bridge and Main Engineering. Also a Data Transfer Link to both Siria Prime and Atlanka City." Tezra turned to face Persephone, "data or audio/video?" Persephone thought for a second, "both, please route them to SciLab Three", Tezra turned back around, "you'll have access by the time you reach the lab". Persephone smiled, "thank you." With that Persephone stepped into the ISTiS.

Shortly after she and Taven materialized outside SciLab Three, she couldn't help but notice the smirk on his face. "What are you grinning about?" Taven attempted to hide his grin but failed miserably, "oh nothing." Persephone looked closely at him and shook her head "okay, it's an awful funny nothing though." Taven smiled "it's just that, for a moment you sounded like a Captain, not a Scientist." Persephone put her weight on her left foot and looked out a window close by at the sun which was now off in the distance. "Well, it's not so different, Military Personnel or Scientists, they all take instructions, mine, however, are usually working on unravelling the mysteries of the universe and developing new tech, whereas yours is a much more immediate style of command, but command is the same no matter what form it takes. Taven nodded, "very true." As Persephone and Taven walked towards Science Lab Three, Persephone remarked as they were coming up on the door to the Lab. "By the way, your crew is amazing, they know exactly what they're doing. I don't need to be in command. They know exactly what to do and when." Taven snickered, "still you seemed to enjoy giving orders, I think you could get used to it." Persephone's jaw dropped in shock and she smacked his shoulder, "that is the most ridiculous thing I have ever heard, well okay maybe just a little." As they walked into Science Lab Three, Josephine and Fyar were standing around the Centre Console and they did not look happy. Josephine looked at Persephone, "you should see these readings for yourself, I can't be sure because I don't have your scientific expertise but if I'm reading this correctly, we are in serious trouble." Persephone walked over to the monitor and tapped a few controls, as she read the results her eyes closed, it was what she had feared. "Iron Ferrite, Titanium, Fistrium and I can't even begin to imagine what those two are", Persephone shook her head at the console, "it's not going to be enough, we don't have the time or power surplus to do this." She sank into a chair her head falling into her hands. Fyar eyed the results and rubbed his chin, "there has to be a way".

Josephine had been oddly silent and Persephone suddenly realized that the wheels in her head were turning; she had this wild look in her eyes. She raised her thumb and forefinger to her chin in thought and at last said, "unless..." Fyar's ears perked up at this, "what are you thinking of Jo." Josephine spent the next ten minutes tapping controls almost as fast as Persephone had on the Bridge; at long last she called the others over to the station she'd been working on. On the display in front of them was what looked like a Plasma Beam that had been modulated into the shape of a spiral, almost like an antique drill bit from before plasma drilling had been invented. Taven looked a little puzzled, "for those of us who aren't geniuses and who are three steps behind the master race, what are we looking at". Fyar looked at Taven and mouthed the words, "master race?" Taven shook him off, "never mind, I'll tell you later." Josephine began to explain the technique behind her idea, "up until now we've been planning to use the beams as we would with anything else such as an attacking Starship, fire and forget. Well, that's not going to work here because of the super-dense nature of this asteroid. We need a way to enhance the beam cutting potential, while still maintaining the power levels on the Ship and in the beam at peak efficiency." Taven was listening, even if he was only half understanding; he knew the other two were deep in thought. Josephine continued to explain, "I was thinking of how to increase the cutting efficiency and my mind started to drift. I suddenly remembered something my grandfather used to have in the garage back on Tykis VI, he let me hold it once and told me it was very old, just like him. It was a steel drill, a physical boring tool used back on Siria centuries ago, it had been passed down through the family as an heirloom for generations. I started to think how I could adapt that design into our Plasma Beams and I came up with this, it works by shearing rock away from the centre of the beam and carving as it penetrates."

Taven was noticeably impressed, "that's one hell of an inspiration, it definitely sounds like it could work." Taven still saw concern, "okay so there's something you're not saying that I'm not going to like." Josephine rubbed her finger behind her ears, "mmm, nope you're not. In order for the spiral Plasma Bank to hit at the optimum range, we will have to get very close to the asteroid." Taven knew he didn't like the sound of this, "just how close are we talking?" Josephine struggled to get the next statement out, "less than fifteen-thousand Fikans." Taven's jaw just about hit the floor, "is there no way to extend the range?" Josephine shook her head, "I don't like tempting fate any more than you, but unless I get fifteen-thousand Fikans distance or less, I can't make this work." Taven's fingers tapped the table in thought. At this point Persephone piped up, "there is another danger to this plan, at less than fifteen-thousand, it leaves absolutely no margin for error, Clinch will have to dodge debris that will be coming off the back end of the asteroid while still keeping the Forward Banks locked, not to mention he'll be pretty much flying blind, with the Sensors offline, he'll have to fly manually by visual Sensors alone. There's a very high probability we'll be hit by a piece of debris." Taven rubbed his chin, "what do your calculations say Seph?" Persephone plunked in a couple of algorithms "according to this sixty-eight point six three seven percent, give or take a tenth here or there." Taven looked up, "I don't like those odds, we need to bring them more into our favour, there has to be a way. Fyar, I want you Persephone and Josephine to co-ordinate with Clinch, he likes a challenge, if he pulls this off they'll award him the Sirian Medal Of Valour." Taven made a motion towards the door and just as it opened Fyar called after him, "and if he doesn't pull it off, what then?" Taven was blunt which was unlike him, "then Fyar we will be a stain on the asteroid's surface and this will become someone else's problem. See that it doesn't, I want options people". With that, the door slid shut behind him.

Persephone pressed the Comm Badge on her wrist, "Seph to Tezra" a chirp followed "Tezra here, what do you need boss", Persephone weighed carefully the next choice she made. Finally, she decided, "how many Starships are currently within twenty light years?" Tezra's voice was silent for a few moments then responded, "I see three listed, SIV Helia, A Saret Class Support Cruiser, SIV Solaran and SIV Koltanastra, both are Saqr Class Rapid Assault Vessels." Persephone bit her lower lip, "alright, dispatch a request for assistance and see who responds." Tezra came back on the channel, "transmitting now, I would estimate any assisting vessels will arrive in six to eight hours if we assume they are travelling at maximum warp." Persephone sighed a slight relief, at least soon there would be three possibly four ships to work on this problem instead of one. Fyar looked over to her and observed, "Seph you're exhausted, why don't you get some rest, you've been up for twenty-seven hours straight, nothing is going to go wrong in the next five hours that you can't get a little shut-eye." Persephone shook her head, "no-no, I have too much work to do", Fyar looked over at her sister, "Jo please take Seph to her quarters, she's no help to us if she's too tired to think." Josephine walked over, "come on Seph, let's go get a cup of coffee and we'll sit and talk for a bit before you get some rest." Persephone blinked as she looked into Jo's eyes, "I don't suppose I can talk you two out of it. I'll have you know this qualifies as mutiny", Jo smiled, "good thing for me your not my real boss. Now come on out you go, Fyar has things under control here." Just before Persephone walked into the ISTiS, Tezra's voice crackled over the Comm System, "Seph, the Helia and the Solaran are enroute to assist. The Koltanastra is on covert patrol and can't break their cover, they send their regrets." Persephone nodded, "tell them we look forward to their arrival." With that, she and Josephine walked into the ISTiS and the door closed behind them.

It was early in the morning when Persephone's door chimed and Josephine walked in. The room was only barely lit and Persephone was in the corner nursing a coffee with a tablet on the table. Her hair still hadn't been brushed yet and she wore a white silk nightgown, she looked far away. Persephone had been up already for just over half an hour getting ready for the day ahead. They were expecting the S.I.V. Helia and the S.I.V.

Solaran later that morning, Persephone had been busy drawing up a plan of how they were going to go about drilling into this behemoth. It was a daunting task, the sheer density of the metals and the possibility of refractory material made her uneasy, if the beams became reflected when they struck the asteroid even in the slightest degree, the whole Power Distribution Net could collapse. The Jovus was the one in real danger since her power systems were on the brink of total collapse as it was. She honestly didn't know how Fyar was holding it together, Persephone for one was glad for the help and was thankful that the two ships were arriving to take the heat off of the Jovus. They were both far more recent launches, but the danger remained even with the latest technology. A wrong move in working with this rock could be disastrous. The Solaran had been launched earlier that year and still had the smell of being just out of Space Dock. The Helia was a different story, she was a little older, slow and bulky, she resembled a rather fat owl. Her wings were immense and her Twin Ion Engines put out enough power to move a small Star Base. That was to be expected though as she was a Support Frigate, a Ship dedicated to the healing of the sick and wounded and assisting stranded vessels in need. She was the most recognized in the entire fleet and her Ship and Crew had been decorated several times for valour. The Solaran however was a warship, considerably smaller than the Jovus, she was designed like a diving falcon. Her Wings elegantly swept back and her Forward Bridge slender. Her Centre and Aft Ion Drive were just a thin line of amber. Unlike most Sirian Star Ships, her Hull was completely devoid of any windows, this was due to the Phase Shift Cloaking Technology employed by her Refractive Dampeners. When on patrol or outnumbered, Saqr Class Star Ships could become completely invisible and undetectable. Even their Engine emissions were masked, it was a technology developed during the last great war with the Vortakans. As a Defence Ship, she was fast and incredibly manoeuvrable, her armament was equally impressive as she was equipped with Phased Plasma Cannons, Beams and Turrets, Quantum Flux

Torpedoes and Mines. She was also equipped with one of the only Bilateral Capacitance Modulating Coils in the Fleet. She was truly a sight to behold, the first Ship in what is sure to be a very long line of next-generation defence vessels. Persephone's only thought was to her crew, most of them had served under fifteen years none more than twenty. They were military tacticians, not scientists and sitting on that kind of power can at times make you a little too comfortable with it, she hoped for everyone's sake that they had learned humility. Josephine could see Persephone's eyes transfixed on her computer screen, then suddenly she looked up to the stars and over at her sister and smiled slightly "Hey Jo, I was in the middle of a complex calculation and I didn't want to lose my place".

Josephine walked towards her with a hand on her hip, swaying the opposite arm jovially, "oh? Which problem is it for, the, we need to blow it up problem or the not blowing ourselves up problem?" Persephone giggled, "both actually, I'm working on the intermix ratio for the Weapons, and the more I read these reports the more convinced I am that the Jovus should take a supportive role and let the Solaran do the work". Josephine sat down beside her mulling over her results, she noted several large spikes in the Jovus' power net where they had already redlined. She put down the tablet and thought for a second before she responded, "I see where you're having concerns." Persephone nodded, "she's just too old and her systems weren't made for this power load, it's too much to ask, we have the assistance of the other Ships, we should use it to the best of our ability." Josephine sat back in her chair and crossed her arms, "what did you have in mind?" Persephone picked up the tablet and pointed to several long lines of amber text. "You see here and here, these areas on the asteroid look to not have as much debris and they are also, if my scans are correct, the softest parts on the surface. A ship is going to have to cross-navigate that entire region and get to within fifteen-thousand Fikans of the surface, the trick is avoiding all that debris. I think the Solaran is best suited for this task, she's quick, smart and heavily shielded."

Josephine nodded, "that's a logical plan but what about the Helia, I doubt you would have requested her if you just wanted extra medical staff." Persephone grinned, "indeed, while the Solaran is dodging bits of flying rock, I'm going to have the Helia positioned off the Starboard Bow with her Tractor Emitters in repulse mode. Josephine nodded, "it sounds like a well-conceived plan, I don't see much that can go wrong with it, except for you, know us blowing up or getting hit by a rock, it sounds fine." Persephone scoffed, "grrr, your such a pessimist". Josephine shrugged, "I always hope for the best, life however enjoys being difficult at the worst times." Taven's voice came over the Comm System "Taven to Persephone, I hope I didn't wake you".

Persephone tapped the Comm Panel on her desk, "no, Jo and I have been reviewing our plan for dealing with the asteroid, do you have news of the Helia and Solaran?" Taven responded happily, "they're almost here, they should be dropping to sublight in less than five minutes." Persephone let out a sigh of relief, finally the first thing to go right. Her moment of peace was short-lived, however, as Josephine piped up, "we're on our way to the Bridge Tav, see you shortly." Josephine looked over to her sister "I'll see you on the Bridge?" Persephone nodded, "I'll be there, I just need to get cleaned up." With that, her sister walked out the door and Persephone jumped into her clothes. Persephone walked onto the Bridge in a full Science Officers uniform, it was itchy and her neck was uncomfortable, but she wanted to fit in with the rest of the crew. She gazed at the View Screen already tuned to the position the Ships would exit warp. Taven leaned forward in his chair as if straining to see something against the blackness of the galactic night. "Maximum magnification Clinch, I think I see something." Josephine squinted, "remind me to have your eyes checked." The view screen zoomed in closer and suddenly two faint streaks of teal lightning could be made out. Taven stroked his chin "standard magnification, hold us steady from the asteroid at five-hundred thousand Fikans."

Suddenly two bolts of teal lightning came soaring at the Jovus and two Sirian Star Ships emerged from warp. Almost in a strange unison, Persephone watched their wings blink in as the Warp Manifolds depolarized and they blinked twice to signify shut-down of the Main Driver Coils. Taven got out of his chair and looked back "Tezra, can you please extend my gratitude to both Captain Tyra of the Helia and Captain Romal of the Solaran, also please extend an invitation to both of them to a conference on deck six in the Wardroom in about an hour. It's time we finished what we started, Seph...Jo go prepare your briefing."

ZERO HOUR

An hour came and went. Persephone and Josephine were standing outside the door to the wardroom with tablets in hand. They knew what lay beyond and this was the moment, we go forward, this was the only way. Persephone's chest heaved heavily as she touched the door panel and thought "this is it, the fate of Atlanka rests on the decisions made here." She walked into the wardroom and the door slid shut behind her and Josephine, both women were tense with adrenaline. The wardroom was dimly lit as was much of the Ship, The Jovus was processing a massive algorithm for power flow and as a result, much of the Jovus was in grey mode, three-quarters of the Ship's Systems were offline and only the Primary Systems remained unaffected. Even the lights were almost off; the sun beamed into a nearby window with an almost blinding radiance. Taven noticed her squinting as the light shone in her face. As Persephone raised a hand to shield her eyes, Taven moved towards the window and gently tapped an amber control key near the bottom of the panel, the window tinted and the once glaring sun on Persephone's face turned to a soft golden glow.

Persephone lowered her hand to allow her eyes to readjust, then exhaled heavily and walked over to the table. Three Star Ship Captains made for a very imposing-looking entrance, but she knew them all far too well. Captain Tyra was a woman of many accomplishments, she and Persephone had worked together before to develop a vaccine for an outbreak of Surandan Nucleotic Fluenzëita. She was a very muscular and tall imposing-looking woman, dark as a moonless night with amber eyes that shone like a blazing fire. Typical of a Surandan, their whole race was more or less similar in appearance, most with very light hazel eyes and very dark skin tones. They made for excellent Diplomats and Physicians, they were said to have one of the best minds for intellectual forethought and problem-solving in the galaxy. Tyra, for all her imposing looks, was kind and an easy woman to talk to, she seemed to have endless patience and what some would call an unhealthy capacity for forgiveness. She was the very embodiment of a healer.

Captain Romal on the other hand was a military man, Persephone had taken the liberty of obtaining both Captains' service records when she requested the assistance for the Jovus. Romal was a brilliant tactician and a cunning warrior, his role in at least three major defensive engagements against the Vortakans had been pivotal. He had handpicked his Crew from the best and brightest the Defence Academy had to offer and they were some of the most brilliant minds in the Fleet. The Solaran like her Captain and Crew had led a short but distinguished career in the half-year since her launch, her combat commendations spoke for themselves and her manoeuvring was considered to be among the best in the Fleet. Persephone's eyes had caught the attention of one final detail among Captain Romal's records and achievements. There was an incident during the battle of Kuma III where he was ordered to withdraw. He chose to disregard that order and instead flew straight into the atmosphere of a class "T" gas giant. His Ship was heavily damaged but the Vortakan listening outpost was destroyed, the manoeuvre was officially declared a resounding success, but behind closed doors, he was given a very stern warning from the Fleet Admiral in charge of that sector. He was reminded that his Ship and his Crew were far more valuable than one listening outpost and was chastised accordingly. Persephone was hopeful that he wouldn't make the same mistake twice, the stakes here were much higher than one Ship and one Crew.

Persephone had barely noticed her daydream when she snapped back to reality. She walked towards the table motioning for her sister to follow, the two women stopped beside a bare wall with a single control key. Persephone nodded to Josephine and her sister tapped the control key. Two plates widely spaced apart recessed into the wall. Two silver cylinders emerged and locked into place, energizing with teal plasma, the screen crackled and energy rippled from the edges, it then spread and projected an image of the Plasma Beam modifications, Torpedo Guidance, Yield guidelines and power load readouts for the Jovus, the Helia and the Solaran. Persephone began her report as she pointed to the Beam adjustments, "as you can see we've had to come up with a completely new design for implementing Fractal Plasma Directed Energy Technology". She noted the spiral patterns on three separate diagrams, "these models illustrate the direction we've taken with our theoretical models, by all our simulations, these modifications should give us enough drilling pressure to cut into the rock far enough to fire three Quantum Flux Torpedoes into the fissure, which we will detonate at a depth of one-thousand Fikans." The resulting collateral shockwave should reduce the asteroid to nothing but particulate matter no more than a Fika in diameter."

Josephine stepped forward, "the power requirements of these modifications are extreme and the entire plan is not without risk." She nodded at Tyra, "that's why the Helia is here, if anything goes seriously wrong, she's been equipped with Phase Pulse Tractor Emitters and should be able to snatch any of the Ships out of harm's way if the need arises." Persephone touched her sister's shoulder and then tapped a sequence in on her tablet. The image on the screen flickered and changed to a schematic of the Helia. She motioned to the six Tractor Emitters that were spread across her Hull. Persephone looked at Captain Tyra, "your job is to fly cover and interference, your Tractor Beams are to be set on repulse mode. You're to push the debris out of the way as best you can in front of and behind the Solaran, while she makes her attack run." Tyra twirled a lock of hair around her finger and looked deep in thought, "with the amount of debris trailing the asteroid, we won't be able to sweep away everything, some of it is going to be missed". Persephone looked at Captain Romal, "that is why I asked for a Saqr Class Star Ship, she's quick, smart and should be able to avoid any debris left over." Romal looked uneasy and was a little too quiet. Persephone crossed her arms noticing Romal's unease, "is your Ship and Crew up to the task?" Romal snapped back to reality and clasped his hands together. "Yes, although we've never had to dodge such vast amounts of material, usually the only thing we need to dodge is weapons fire". Persephone's gaze tightened, "if you have any doubts Romal, I need to know now, not later" Romal shook his head and smiled, "just because we haven't had to do it before, doesn't mean my Crew isn't up to the challenge, we're all professionals here, it will be done". Persephone nodded in approval and turned to Taven, "the Jovus will serve as the command ship for the fleet, it will coordinate our strike and serve as a platform to provide backup support only in the worst-case scenario. Our job is to destroy what the Helia's Tractor Beams miss, if we do this right, there shouldn't be that much for the Solaran to contend with in there." Taven spoke up, "Is everybody clear on what we need to do?" Romal and Tyra looked at each other, then at the rest of the group. Tyra was the first to speak up, "I think so, your plan seems straightforward enough, dodge rocks, drill big rock, blow up big rock, go home, sounds simple to me". Persephone couldn't help but let a small giggle out, Tyra's simplicity was downright comical. Taven rose from his seat, "if there's nothing else, I believe we have three Ships to prepare for this task. Thank you and may fortune favour us all."

Tyra and Romal rose from their chairs and walked over to Persephone and Josephine's location. Persephone tapped a command sequence into her tablet and looked up to both Captains Tyra and Romal. "I've sent a copy of the systems changes to both of your Ships", Tyra nodded at Persephone, "we've got this, with all this planning we can't possibly fail". Tyra walked up close to Persephone and looked her deep in the eyes, "I see in your future, yes, a good meal and a half hour's rest". Tyra looked over to Taven, "Captain, I believe you're quite familiar with this woman, I strongly recommend you take her to lunch". Taven got his mouth open but nothing more before Tyra pounced on him, "ah ah, don't make me make that an order!" Persephone giggled out loud as Tyra turned to her, "what's so funny?" Persephone blurted out through uncontrolled laughter, "you're a Captain, you can't order him he's another Captain." Tyra leaned over to Persephone, "shhh, what he doesn't know won't hurt him", both women began to laugh as Taven simply grinned and shook his head. Taven reached over for Persephone's hand and grasped it, "come on Seph, before you get me in any more trouble with my boss, besides we never did have dinner, so lunch it is". Tyra looked over at Romal, "have you got those systems specs sent to the Solaran?" Romal was tapping a pad and looked up, "I just finished getting the verification from my Chief Engineer that he received Seph's transmission and is making the modifications." Tyra nodded in approval, "good, because you're buying me lunch". Romal shook his head and snickered, "okay, let's go, I'm sure we could all use a break." With that Romal and Tyra walked out and Taven put his arm around Persephone as they left the room. The lights dimmed the rest of the way, the window brightened and the door slid shut. All that could be heard was the gentle hum of the Jovus' Engines.

Persephone stared out the window, she had barely touched her lunch. The lounge was dim, the only light came from the tinted windows and the strips of amber light that lined the Ship's interior walls at the midpoint. The lounge was not unlike many in the Imperial Fleet. A fairly large room, with long rectangular windows that curved into semicircles at the ends. The floor was a dark chocolate marble with golden pillars in various places around the room. The pillars themselves were ribbed in spirals, with a falcons head adorning the top and claws at the bottom. The tables were a brushed gold much like the walls. The chairs were a comfortable, sandy-coloured fabric with brushed gold legs and arms. Inset into the wall across from the windows, towards the exterior, were three Food Replicators and a half-circle Bar. The Jovus, while a functionally designed Star Ship did cater to its

Crew's needs as best as it possibly could. Taven and Persephone were seated near one of the large windows along the Outer Hull, the asteroid clearly visible from where they sat. Persephone looked long and hard at it. She had trouble understanding why something so incredibly beautiful, must also be so destructive. The two just didn't seem to fit, she poked at her lunch with a fork not having much of an appetite. Taven leaned forward with a Plasma Torch he had smuggled out of Engineering and with a doctor's precision, lit a candle he'd been hiding at the base of his chair throughout lunch. Persephone felt the warm golden glow on her face and closed her eyes, "mmm". Taven rested his hands together, "not exactly the romantic meal I had intended, but, it'll have to do." Persephone smiled warmly as the light from the candle danced on her skin, "it's the thought that counts Tav, I know you wanted more but it's perfect just like this." She reached out and ran her fingernails around his ear then rested her hand upon his. Taven nodded towards the window and the asteroid hanging almost motionless beyond, "think we'll pull this off?" Persephone bit her lip for a moment in thought, "you want the awful truth?" Taven shrugged, "sure, let's hear it." Persephone put down her fork and intertwined her fingers, bringing them to her chin she took a deep breath. "We have a forty-three percent chance of success, what's really worrying me is I cannot get a clear Sensor reading of the debris coming off the tail, something is obfuscating the readings and it's troubling me. As it moves closer into the system, the amount of matter trailing off the back of it will increase exponentially." Taven brought out a tablet and handed it to Persephone. "I had Jo do some intensive scans, I probably shouldn't have used the Standby Reactors, but like you, I don't like not knowing what we're in for." Persephone read the report "it's more or less what I already know, what I really need to know is the density and composition of the core of this beast, so I can calculate the shearing pressure on the Tractor Beams." Persephone put the tablet down and scraped her fingers through her hair as she let it out of the ponytail it had been in all day. She gazed out the window and whispered, "you don't want to give up your secrets, do you?" Taven leaned forward and grinned, "you know the best ones never do". Persephone looked back to Taven as a lock of her hair caught the sunlight and fell across her eyes, she smiled radiantly at him. Taven returned the glance, he held out his hand and for a long moment, their fingers intertwined together as they held each other's hand. He was just beginning to unwind when the Comm Line chirped. Taven tapped the Badge on his wrist, a voice shrouded in static seemed to fill the void in the room, "Captain, we just received confirmation that both the Helia and the Solaran are ready to engage on your command". Taven smiled a big smile, "they're ahead of schedule, how's Fyar coming with our preparations?" Tezra's voice was upbeat and positive, her optimism was infectious, "he was done half an hour ago". Taven chuckled, "when is he going to stop surprising me, thank you Tezra. Persephone and I will join you on the Bridge momentarily." Taven looked toward Persephone as he stood up and extended his hand to her, "the first thing to go right in two days." Persephone nodded as she grasped his hand and stood up, "indeed." They made their way out of the lounge and down the hall, Persephone gripped Taven's hand firmly, he knew she was uneasy about this but her emotions were glacial. He didn't know if he should be impressed or concerned but he knew that inside, she was shaking. They entered the ISTiS and they were treated to the curling ribbons of colour in the matter stream. They rematerialized moments later and stepped onto the main bridge.

The Bridge of the Helia was a deep golden tone, amber ambience split by steady flashes of teal light. The ship was on Alert Status One, most of her Subsystems had been rerouted to Energy Allocation and Emitter Stability, so her main lights were dimmed quite a bit. Still, the amber displays, which were prominent around the Bridge gave off an almost luminescent feel. The Ship's layout was not all that different from the Jovus, almost all Sirian vessels were of a similar modular design, it kept things simple for the Engineers when the Ships needed parts or replacement units. The Helia's Bridge, however, was quite a bit larger than the Jovus, she was designed for heavy casualties and her Medical and Scientific Facilities rivalled those on Atlanka City, she truly was a mobile hospital in the vastness of space. Captain Tyra was standing near the Operations Console twirling a lock of hair around her index finger. Deep in thought, she was caught off guard when the plates on the Forward Wall retracted and the silver rods slid out for the Main View Screen. As the plasma energy connected the top and bottom of the screen, the holographic system engaged. Captain Taven was on the Screen, "I was just informed that both you and Romal are ready to begin. My compliments to both of your Engineers, you're both quite ahead of schedule." Tyra moved to her chair in the centre and sat down crossing her legs as she responded, "we're just trying to get the job done Taven, now let's blow this rock and go home". Taven nodded, "you'll get no argument from me", Taven looked back to Tezra, "end transmission". Taven sat in his chair and took a commanding posture, "Tezra, I need a data burst link and an open Comm channel with both Ships. Seph, I need you to monitor all three vessels and try to get a scan of the debris in the tail as we draw closer." Taven looked to Josephine "Jo, I want you down in Engineering co-ordinating with Fyar, I intend for us all to survive this insanity in one piece." Taven gazed forward, "Clinch we'll undoubtedly have to dodge a few bullets ourselves, I'm going to be counting on your reflexes to keep us away from any large pieces, the Helia should take care of the rest." Taven looked around, "Is everybody ready?" There was a unanimous group of nods from around the Bridge. Taven couldn't help a but feel a rush of pride surge up his spine and flood from his face, "I'll buy everyone a round of drinks at Vorla's Pub when we're finished here." Clinch spun around grinning, "make mine a double boss." Taven smiled and took a deep breath, "Ion Drive to seventy-five percent, take us to ten-thousand Fika's off the Helia's Starboard Wing and take up an inverted chevron formation." The Engines of all three Ships ignited and from a bright amber, they changed colour to a vibrant teal as they made their way to the asteroid. Slowly entering a horizontal inverted chevron formation, the three Ships danced in the night sky, like birds floating on a summer evening breeze. The Solaran was leading the charge, as she would be heading into the asteroid, the Helia was no more than twenty-five thousand Fika's behind her, off to the side and behind slightly. The Jovus brought up the rear and she was to stay ten-thousand Fikans away from the point of entry. The three Ships manoeuvred with such grace and elegance, that even the asteroid seemed to acknowledge their beauty. Onboard the Helia, Tyra gave the order to Extend the Tractor Emitters. With a slight glint to the Hull, a loud clunk could be heard as the covers retracted and slid into the superstructure. Six Tractor Beam Emitters emerged from beneath the surface, they pulsed with a teal glow as they powered up. Rippling currents of plasma energy arced over them as the system locked into place.

Onboard the Solaran, Captain Romal was leaning over the Tactical Display, double-checking several last-minute readouts as the Ship was manoeuvring into position. The Solaran was a combat vessel, her Bridge was small and she lacked any of the Exploration or Scientific Suites the other two Ships possessed. The Bridge itself was of an oval design, Romal's chair sat in the centre of the Bridge, flanked on either side of his seat and towards the Aft area of the Bridge sat two semi-circle Consoles with a companion set on the wall across from them as well. In front of Romal's seat was the Conn, a fairly large rectangular Console supported on the sides by two large bird's legs with talons at the base. Towards the front of the Bridge along the wall, were several black panel displays and readouts. The Solaran was dimly lit as a matter of course, her systems demanded much power from her Reactors and the lights were not a huge priority. He looked over to his Tactical Officer and while no words were exchanged, both men nodded in approval. Romal sat in his chair and tapped a command sequence into his Holographic Interface. From the arm of the chair, a small display rippled to life. Romal pulled his stylus from his pocket and he tapped a few more controls into the Holographic Interface.

Romal looked forward and prepared to finish the job he'd started, "initialize View Screen, Alert Status One!, Arm Weapons, Deploy Shields". The panels on the wall retracted and the Screen Emitters slid out and locked into place. The view screen crackled and rippled to life, displayed on it were tactical readouts and trajectory analyses. The status lights on the Bridge which were inset into the edges of the ceiling began to pulse a vibrant teal and the lighting strips that lined every Sirian Star Ship pulsed the same brilliant colour with the sound of a hawk's call filling the ship. It was a single burst audible alert that was standard equipment on every Ship. The Solaran's left wing dipped briefly in an almost majestic fashion and the Barrel Ports on the Wings slid open. Six barrels on each Wing slid out, locking into position. On her tail and under her beak, large circular panels retracted and slid into the Hull, half-circle Plasma Beam Emitters lifted out and locked into place. Energized with cascading ripples of teal electricity, they illuminated the darkness. Two smaller circular panels retracted on both the Dorsal and Ventral sides of her Wings and slid into the Hull. Four double-barrel Turrets slid out, locking into place with a large thud, the Barrels began to glow a radiant teal. On the underside of the ship, two large circles slid into the Hull and a pair of Torpedo Tubes could be seen. Romal looked to his Communications Officer, "signal Captain Taven that we're ready to engage". The Comm Officer responded, "he says you may begin at your discretion." Romal looked forward, "then, by all means, take us in." The Aft Engines of the Solaran and the Auxiliary Ion Drive atop her back shimmered a brilliant teal as her Engines accelerated and she pulled away. She moved away from the Helia and into the trailing edge of the asteroid. Romal watched the View Screen with intent and a single bead of sweat ran down the side of his face, it was all up to him and his Crew now, he couldn't afford to fail.

SACRIFICE OF ANGELS

The Solaran pitched, rolled and turned in a delicate ballet of movement, teal lighting arced from her Wings in all directions and a flurry of Plasma Bolts streamed from her Forward Cannons toward every rock in her direct path, shattering them into a trillion tiny pieces. Romal sat in his chair intensely monitoring the situation as his Ship danced between the debris, "distance to target?" The question wasn't really aimed at anybody, but as usual, Sorn his Operations Officer responded "twenty-thousand Fikans to target". Romal sat back a moment and tapped on his chair with his finger, "okay, we've crunched the smaller ones, now comes the hard work. Set all weapons to drill mode and load six Quantum Flux Torpedoes into the Forward Tubes, full Yield and the safeties on". Romal sat forward again, "steady, let's do this right". A voice from behind Romal suddenly blurted out "that's it, fifteen-thousand Fikans". Romal nodded as he stood up "all batteries, fire on target". The Solaran seemed to vanish into a hail of teal, and arcs of lightning from the Helia streamed past her hull as the two Ships began to work more and more closely. Tyra was standing behind her Helmsman carefully watching Romal's progress. "She certainly does live up to her reputation as the most manoeuvrable class in the Fleet doesn't she?" Trell, her Helmsman spoke without breaking his gaze, his lips cracked a smile reminiscent of a kid in a candy shop, "she sure does". Tyra smiled and tapped his shoulder gently, "don't you get any ideas now". Trell looked up, "I wouldn't dream of it". Taven sat aboard the Jovus watching the ballet on the screen and the progress the two ships were making. "Seph, how deep are they?" Persephone was entrenched in thought, she was bent over the Starboard Science Station scratching her head and tapping keys.

"five-hundred Fikans so far, a little slower than we'd anticipated". Taven stood and moved up beside her, "is it going to cause any problems with the mission?" Persephone shook her head, "I'm not sure, you see this mineral and this one at the seven-hundred and sixty mark, I can't read them at all and this one doesn't appear completely solid. I'm getting reflected readings and a lot of EM static interference. It almost looks like one of those filled cookies you eat as a kid." Taven looked at the readings and weighed his judgements carefully, "do we abort?" Persephone rubbed the side of her head, "without more concrete proof of what the interior structure is comprised of, I can't give you a scientific recommendation, but if you want my personal opinion, I suggest we continue, we've come this far let's see how it plays out".

Back on the Solaran, Romal was watching the tactical readouts when he noticed an anomalous reading from the Starboard face of the asteroid. "Analysis of fracture" his Science Officer Sera piped up. "Major destabilization of the starboard side of the asteroid, it looks like an entire layer is ready to come loose." Romal stood up and moved up beside her, "no no no. Can we complete our objective before it dislodges?" Sera looked up at him from her Console, fear cresting over her delicate features, "I don't know". Romal nodded, "I didn't come this far by not taking risks, Ion Drive to full power, continue firing." The Solaran pitched and twisted between the Helia's dancing arcs of pulsing teal lightning in an almost heavenly duet. Romal looked around the Bridge "depth?" Sera called out "six-hundred fifty Fikans, we're almost there". Suddenly a cloud of white vapour burst forth from the asteroid, enveloping the ship. As the Solaran was shrouded in a mist of dust, Romal's eyes squinted trying to see through the cloud, "what do the Sensors say?" Sera was frantically pushing buttons "nothing, my readings are reflected, I'm getting ghost images everywhere, I can't scan through the mist". Sorn suddenly called out, "Captain, the asteroid!" Romal spun around on his heels and was horrified by the massive chunk of debris that was almost on top of them.

Romal grabbed the back of Sera's chair, "full axis rotation, hard to starboard!" The Solaran began to flip on her main axis but just as she hit the midpoint, the asteroid impacted her right Wing, shearing it off of the Fuselage. Conduits exploded in every corridor, a beam crashed down on the Bridge destroying the Primary Science Station and knocking Sera and Romal to the floor. Sparks flew everywhere, fire raged from ignited plasma. Romal strained to get his senses back as he yelled, "damage report?".

A shaken voice came from behind him, "our entire right Wing has been torn off, we're heading straight into the asteroid". Romal struggled to stay up amidst the shaking Ship and the screaming of metal being stretched and torn. "Can we use Reaction Thrusters to steer clear of it?" The voice answered once more, Romal couldn't make out from where though, as the bridge had been engulfed in a thick cloud of smoke. "No sir, the entire Power Grid has been destroyed. A sharp pain tore through Romal's head, his eyes dipped and then rolled into the back of his head as he fell unconscious. Tyra was sitting with her back to the Main View Screen signing a status report when Trell, in an almost panicked voice yelled out, "Captain, the Solaran, she's been hit!" Tyra spun around, "by the Five Gods" is all she could get out. "Primary Tractor Emitters, emergency reconfiguration to Tractor mode." Andara, her Science Officer, punched icons frantically on her console "thirty seconds for the change, the Solaran is drifting dangerously close. Taven squinted as the blinding light hit his screen, sparks showered the Jovus as her left-wing dipped by about thirty degrees. He covered his eyes as the blast subsided. A massive boulder was on a direct collision course for the ship, "Clinch, evasive!"

He couldn't say more, his focus shifted momentarily as he looked over to Persephone, who was holding onto the chair nearest the Science Station, her eyes betraying her calm look. His focus snapped back as Clinch responded "I'm already on it!" The Jovus spun ninety degrees and pulled up in a sharp manoeuvre, so fast that the Inertial Dampers barely compensated for the shearing forces being exerted on the Ship's Hull. Taven looked up, and the full force of the situation hit him. The Solaran was drifting straight into the main portion of the asteroid, only trace amounts of the white mist remained. Persephone had moved from standing behind the chair to sitting in it, Taven hadn't even noticed her move. As she tapped controls, she yelled out amidst the chaos "thirty seconds to impact". Taven hit the Comm Control on his chair "Jovus to Helia, please tell me you're about to grab the Solaran?."

Tyra pointed at Lazarus silently saying to connect the Comm Channel "we're already on it Taven." Tyra looked at Andara, "time?" Andara called back "twenty seconds, it's going to be close." Tyra hit the Inter-Ship Comm "Tyra to Sick Bay, Rachel respond!" Rachel ran to the panel on the wall as the Ship shook from a secondary explosion from the Solaran's damaged Warp Conduits. She lost her footing and fell into the wall. As she regained her balance, she ran her hand across her forehead brushing her hair out of her face as she hit the Comm Panel, "Sickbay, what the hell is going on up there?" Tyra responded, "the Solaran's been struck by a large piece of the asteroid, her entire Wing has been ripped off. Rachel's jaw dropped, "any idea on casualties?" Tyra's voice was shaky, the situation was clearly doing a number on her nerves. "No idea, but I want to prepare for a worst case scenario. I need that Medical Bay ready to receive mass casualties immediately." Rachel nodded at the wall "we're already set down here", Rachel spun around at the nurses on the floor who were looking at her somewhat perplexed. Another secondary explosion shook the Ship and Rachel grabbed the wall steadying herself. As she took command of the situation, she walked across the main Medical Ward, "okay, I want this room prepped to receive patients an hour ago, I need Medical Wards Two through Six ready to receive casualties from the Solaran, MOVE MOVE! Rachel hit the broadband Comm Control on the panel beside her "this is the Chief Medical Officer, all medical personnel on or off duty, you are to report to your designated emergency stations immediately, this is not a drill." Rachel pointed to the two nurses nearest her, "you and you, you're with me".

Andara looked at Tyra, "five seconds". Tyra sat forward, "standby." Andara tapped two controls and turned, "ready!" Tyra squinted as the Solaran passed a rock, "grab her!" From the spanning golden Wings of the Helia, two forks of teal lightning shattered the night sky. Arcing toward the Solaran, they entwined her in a web of teal electricity, snatching her away from the asteroid mere seconds from impact. The beams crackled as pulses of white light ran up the bolts of lightning and into the Helia's Tractor Emitters. Andara smiled as she turned her chair "we have them!" Tyra nodded, "secure the Solaran in towing position." Andara nodded "right away" and spun her chair back around. Tyra tapped the Comm Control on her chair "Captain to Sick Bay, Rachel, the Solaran is secured and being towed into position. I need you and a medical team to meet me in the Main Transport Chamber in two minutes." Rachel's voice crackled across the Comm System, "right away". Tyra looked to her Executive Officer, "Cicero, you have the Bridge, make sure the Solaran's Emergency Systems receive power to engage, I don't want to walk into a raging inferno." Cicero nodded, "anything else?" Tyra gazed at the Jovus, hanging motionless on the screen. "keep an eye on the Taven, he and Romal are good friends and went to the Training Academy together, he might not take this well and has been known to act impulsively." Cicero nodded, "it will be done". Tyra pointed across the Bridge, "Andara, Kiana you're with me." The three women stepped into the ISTiS and seconds later were struck by a bolt of teal lightning, swirling ribbons of teal energy encircled them and a pair of white lines scanned across the group. As they touched, they electrified and a rumble of thunder could be heard. Rachel was waiting for them on the other side as they stepped out of the ISTiS and into the hallway. Tyra motioned towards the door at the end of the hall, "come on." As they walked towards the door Rachel looked over, "has Taven responded yet?" As the door slid open Tyra looked at her, "no, and that's what concerns me." The group which consisted of the four officers and a team of Engineers and Medics walked onto the Transport Pads. Tyra called out, "SARA, initialize." The group was enveloped in the transport sequence and shortly after emerged into something they could barely recognize as a Sirian Ship. Scorching painted the halls, all the lights were blown out and the only thing running were the Emergency Beacons. They made their way to the Bridge passing seared panels and people. Rachel looked around, a tear strayed from her eye but she fought back. As they approached the Bridge they walked past the breach in the Hull where the Wing had been torn from the fuselage. Tyra stood in awe at the destruction, "oh my." Rachel placed a hand on Tyra's shoulder, as Tyra looked back she nodded. They walked down the rest of the corridor, several bodies were near the Bridge. All had been burnt beyond recognition. Rachel looked around and saw several black panel displays that were charred and blown outward. "they must have been nearby when the system erupted." Tyra shook her head, "poor souls." As they came up to the Bridge, the door groaned and opened a crack. Tyra motioned to Kiana, "give me a hand". The two women reached into the door and forced it open. Rachel coughed a little, not all the smoke had dispersed. Rachel pulled a tablet from her jacket breast pocket and a small antenna rose from the side, an amber light blinked from the top. She began to scan the area. "Amazingly they're all alive, Sera's in bad shape but if I get her back to the Helia she'll be fine." Rachel motioned to the Medics behind her to circle the Bridge. Tyra moved over to Romal and shook his shoulder, "Romal...Romal!" Tyra tapped his cheeks to try to bring him around, his eyes fluttered open. Tyra knelt down beside him, "Romal, what happened?" Romal struggled to get out the words, "we failed", Romal fell back unconscious. Rachel tapped her tablet and moved towards Tyra "they're stable for transport". Tyra tapped the Communicator on her wrist, "Tyra to Helia, Bridge Crew secured for transport directly to Sickbay." The entire Bridge shimmered in a blinding teal light, bolts of teal electricity struck in every corner of the Bridge, ribbons danced around each person and everyone left alive on board the Solaran was transported aboard the Helia.

Taven watched the screen as a Tractor caught the Solaran barely before she impacted the asteroid, his eyebrows knitting together in obvious frustration. "Seph, how deep did they get?" Persephone looked up "nine-hundred fifty Fikans, they were almost there." Taven's head dropped as he rubbed the back of his neck, as his head rose he had a different look, a resolute one that Persephone hadn't seen before and which scared her just a little. "Clinch set course to follow the Solaran's trajectory", Taven called down to Engineering "Fyar, I'm going to do something you'll probably regret, bring the weapons online." Fyar's voice crackled through the Comm System "please tell me you're playing an elaborate joke?" Taven's voice weighed heavy "we're going to finish what the Solaran started, be ready." Fyar's voice crackled back "oh this is a bad idea, weapons preheating and coming online now."

Persephone moved over to Taven's chair, "can I speak to you for a moment, in private?" Taven nodded and got up, they both moved over to the corner of the Bridge and Persephone spoke in a hushed tone. She looked at him closely as she spoke "are you insane, this Ship's power is so incredibly stretched, there's no way she can withstand what you're thinking of doing. Even if, and I stress, if you manage to evade the debris in the tail of the asteroid, the second you fire those weapons you'll fry half the systems on this vessel." Taven looked around a little and then responded to Persephone, "if I do nothing, the people who lost their lives on the Solaran will have died in vain. I cannot, I will not dishonour those men and women in such a manner." Pesephone stood her ground, "you're not thinking clearly, you can't help the survivors if you're dead." Taven stood, toe to toe with the woman he loved, at odds for the first time and he didn't much care for the feeling. "I appreciate your insights and I do value your input, but I know this ship. The Jovus may be old but she's still got some fight in her yet, and Fyar's the best Engineer in the Fleet, we'll be in one piece". Taven started to move away but Persephone placed a hand delicately on his chest in a way he hadn't been expecting, her eyes welled with emotion as her gaze bored into his very soul, "don't do something you'll regret." Taven leaned down and kissed her gently, he whispered in her ear, "I would never take an action if I thought you would be hurt." Taven nodded to Persephone and she stepped out of the way. Persephone thought for a moment and stepped back into Taven's path, she kissed him strongly, and with one last gaze she whispered, "on fate's wings, we fly". Taven walked back over to his chair and stood stiff as he spoke. "We all just watched what happened to the Solaran, we know the risks and the risks if we fail to stop this, here and now. Most of you call Atlanka home, and I've known all of you for many years. I could simply make this an order but I won't, this asteroid has to be stopped. However this Ship is well beyond her years for such a task, so we won't proceed unless everybody agrees". Clinch turned around and with a seldom-seen solemn, look he rested his hands on his legs, "Captain, I think I speak for the entire Crew when I say, let's blow this thing and go home!." Taven looked around as his entire Bridge Crew nodded their heads at Clinch's bold statement. Taven's gaze caught Persephone's as her eyes stared deep into his, "I hope you know what you're doing". Taven's gaze penetrated deep into her soul, "so do I." Taven sat and tapped the Inter-ship Comm Channel, "Captain to Engineering," Fyar's voice crackled back "Engineering here, are you guys ready up there?" Taven shifted in his seat slightly "now how did you know what I was going to do?" Fyar's voice responded "I know you very well Sir, Ship's systems are secured, although I can't speak for the Power Distribution Net if we overload, but, I suppose we'll handle that when it happens. Engines set to fifty percent nominal output, weapons are hot and awaiting your command." Taven breathed a sigh of relief as Fyar's voice crackled back over the Comm once more "please don't leave me with too much of a mess to clean up," Taven smiled "I'll do my best, Bridge out."

Taven leaned forward, "is everybody clear on what we're doing?" He looked around as his Crew nodded in agreement "okay then, for the Solaran...Engage!" The Jovus' Engines ignited in a brilliant teal flash, her Cannon Ports slid open and her Gun Barrels slid out from the Wings, locking forward and beginning to glow a bright teal. Most of the debris had already been either blasted or moved out of the way by the Helia's Beams so their path was reasonably clear. Clinch sat at the Conn, his hands flying across the controls, the air on the Bridge was dead silent, you could have heard a pin if one had been dropped. The Jovus glided elegantly through what was left of the debris, every so often pitching and turning to avoid the larger pieces. Persephone's voice shattered the silence on the Bridge "we're in range!" Taven stood up from his chair and clenched his fist "fire!" A firestorm of teal bolts sprayed from the Gun Barrels of the Jovus. Tearing into the asteroid, a teal rain of superheated plasma preceded her every movement. Persephone's voice rang again "fifty Fikans to target depth." Suddenly the piercing call of a hawk rang out, Taven yelled overtop of the deafening noise "report!" Persephone struggled to be heard "power levels are spiking, the Reactors are red-lining, if we're going to do this, it has to be now. twenty-five Fikans to target depth." Sparks sprayed the Aft stations, reports came in from the lower decks of fires breaking out from blown Power Relays, Taven hit the Broadband Comm Channel. "Captain to all hands, drop what you're doing and get away from any console unless you are at a secured station and you're a required Officer. Enough life has been lost today and I don't intend to lose a single Crew member from this ship." Four people on the Bridge surrounded Taven as the Captain's chair was the safest place in the event of an explosion on the Bridge, Persephone was among them. Taven reached for Persephone's hand as he tapped the Comm Panel "Torpedo Bay load forward tubes, four Quantum Flux Torpedoes". A shaken voice responded "ready". Taven again tapped the Broadband Comm, "all hands brace for impact". The ship lurched as an explosion rocked the entire superstructure from the aft section, Taven for an instant looked down at Persephone who was clutching his shirt.

Taven looked at Clinch "fire!" Clinch's finger hit a bright red control and a tone sounded, Four brilliant white balls exploded from the Bow of the Jovus. Taven watched the screen as they flew away from his Ship, "Clinch, get us out of here". The Jovus spun ninety degrees, Taven screamed over the deafening noise, "put it to the floor!" the Jovus broke free of the gravity of the asteroid just as the four Torpedoes flew into the interior, not ten Fikans away, the asteroid vanished in a brilliant explosion of pure white, a shockwave of hyper-accelerated debris and plasma ringed out from the asteroid. Taven watched as it approached, there was nowhere to go, and nothing could be done. They could not escape, their Reactors were on the verge of exploding and all Taven could think of was Persephone and his Crew. He tapped the Comm Panel to Engineering "Fyar, code twenty-six, Emergency Reactor Shutdown, dump the Core!" Fyar called back, "Core Ejection Systems not responding, I'll have to cut the feeds." Taven grabbed Persephone and held her tightly, "make it quick." Fyar ran across the Engineering Bay, dropping to the ground underneath the Main Ion Drive Core, he ripped three panels off the wall. Scrambling for a plasma torch, he severed the power feeds to the Main Drive. The Reactors in the pit below Engineering were enveloped in a blaze of teal plasma fire, three of them ignited and began to melt, the fourth clunked as it shut down. Every light showered sparks around the Bridge, Taven could hear several explosions from the hall behind him. The ship was rocked over and over by internal explosions, Taven looked around all he could think was, "please, hold together." The wave was mere seconds away from the Jovus' tail, Taven squeezed Persephone, shielding her head under his arms. Moments later the Ship was rocked by the massive wave, what few Power Conduits were left undamaged exploded throughout the Ship. Persephone buried her face in his shoulder, she cried out as fear gripped her. The Ship came out of the ring seconds later powerless, motionless, listing to the side and adrift.

Tyra had just arrived on the Bridge after ensuring that Romal was stable as the Jovus emerged from the plasma ring. She had felt the explosion buffet the Shields but since they were at full strength she didn't realize the scope of the damage until she saw the Jovus adrift on the Main Screen. She pointed to Andara "Tractor on the Jovus, now!" Taven picked Persephone up off the floor and sat her in his seat. He moved to check on the rest of his staff around the Bridge as a grid of energized plasma enveloped his Ship. He knew they were no longer in any danger, the Helia had them in a Tractor Beam and they were being pulled away from the asteroid. He breathed a sigh of relief. Tyra's voice crackled over the Comm, barely registering and almost totally garbled "Helia to Jovus, Taven, please tell me you're okay." Taven raised his head "my Bridge Crew is fine, shaken but uninjured. I don't know about the rest of the Ship we've had a lot of explosions over here and we're cut off, please transport my Crew to the Helia for assessment." Tyra's voice came back covered in static, "understood, we'll be transporting you and Persephone directly to the Bridge, prepare for transport." The Bridge of the Jovus shimmered in a teal glow, lightning arced from every corner and ribbons of energy spun around the entire Bridge Crew. As the Ship rippled away, dancing colours replaced the Bridge of the Jovus. Taven and Persephone flew through the matter stream and as the rainbows melted away, the Bridge of the Helia faded in. Tyra moved over to Taven and gave him a warm hug gazing into his eyes, "what were you thinking?" Taven, realizing the full scope of what had just happened choked on his words. "I had to do something, those people, they're my friends. I couldn't let their sacrifices be for nothing." Tyra squeezed his shoulder, "you don't need to explain, I understand." Andara's voice came from behind them, "Sickbay reports no fatalities from the Jovus. Mostly first, second and third-degree burns, some bumps and bruises and a few broken bones, nothing serious." Persephone turned and began to shiver, her voice shaken, she placed a hand on Taven's shoulder and he turned to face her. She nodded towards the screen "look". Tyra, and the entire Bridge Crew looked on in astonishment, the asteroid had survived, it seemed smaller with significant debris around it but continued to spin, pressing forward. Taven's head sank, Tyra put a hand on his shoulder "there's nothing more we can do, let's regroup. The Council will need to be apprised of the situation. We need to think of another strategy, we did our best now it's out of our hands." A tear rolled down Taven's cheek and Persephone wiped it away as she led him off the Bridge. Tyra sat back down as the Helia prepared to tow both Ships back to Atlanka, "Andara are both Ships secure?" Andara hit a few controls and responded "both the Solaran and the Jovus are secured for Warp tow." Tyra spun around to face the view screen "Trell set course for Mesira, best possible speed." Trell tapped the Conn Panel bringing up a destination list, tapping the entry for Mesira he responded "ready". Tyra sat back in her chair and said to nobody in particular, "when it rains..." She looked at Trell "let's go home, Initiate." Trell tapped a control on the panel and a set of amber indicators began to fill up indicating the Warp Drive charging. The teal Initiator Strips on the Helia's Wings flashed from the breast to the Wing tips, a burst of teal energy ran back across her wings and energy ribbons danced around her massive form. From the nose they encircled the hull, spreading out across her Wings spinning until they dove into the Initiators. Lightning arced from her Wings as she tore off back into the Solar System. All that could be seen was a trail of arcing lightning bolts and the asteroid that threatened to destroy everything.

THE ROAD HOME

Space in it's infinite night, a single light streaks silently just inside the boundary of the solar system. Along the Dorsal Wing, the heiroglyphs S.I.V. Helia illuminate the darkness and just as fast are gone again. Tyra had been pushing the Engines a little harder than she probably should have, but things had not gone to plan. The Helia was limited in her speed because of the combined weight of the Jovus and the Solaran being towed. Taven was walking the corridors aimlessly with no real destination, he enjoyed a good walk, it focused his thoughts and calmed his nerves. Today though, he found it difficult to centre himself. His thoughts kept drifting to Persephone and his crew. He had endangered them all. They had lived and suffered no greater than shaken wills and some minor injuries, but still, he was haunted by that moment. He knew that he never should have given the order to pursue the Solaran's assignment. He knew that he should have listened to both his conscience and the woman he had fallen in love with. He stopped near a window along the breast of the Ship and watched the lightning arcing behind them as stellar dust slipped by like shooting stars.

Persephone sat with Josephine in the Helia's lounge, twirling her hair between her fingers and sipping a cup of tea. Josephine put her cup down "that was close, a little too close if you ask me". Persephone tapped her fingers in thought as she sighed, gazed out the window and brushed a lock of hair away from her face. "You've known Taven longer than I, has he ever been prone to such rash actions?" Josephine nodded her head and tucked her hair behind her shoulder; she took a long sip of tea and closed her eyes a moment. Josephine looked at Persephone, "once, I had been assigned to the Jovus several years ago briefly to assist with a relocation project. It was during a scientific mission to study an unstable moon; we were categorizing DNA samples and retrieving them for transport to a similar planet to save the ecosystem from certain extinction. He had sent Clinch and I to gather the last few animals from the southern continent. There was a massive eruption from a lava vent on the surface just as we passed it and lava hit the Starboard Engine and half the Wing. The entire Tail Assembly melted away, we lost control and impacted the surface. The only reason we survived the impact at all is because of Clinch's piloting. I would have been dead right there if he hadn't kept the nose up and skidded us in on the belly. Metalli-Reflective ash and particles were thrown into the stratosphere and the planet began to break up. Taven took the Helm himself and dove the Jovus into the planet's atmosphere. He dodged at least twenty eruptions; I've never seen that Ship move so fast. I watched as her golden Hull screamed towards us, I felt the ground beneath me give way. I grabbed Clinch's hand and thought this is it, be merciful. I opened my eyes for a moment and just as we fell, I watched everything around me wash away in colour and moments later I fell onto the deck in the Main Transport Chamber. All I remember after that is watching everybody around me lose their footing and hit the floor. I blacked out, when I came to, Taven and Adelaide were standing beside me. Adelaide sat me up and Taven grasped my arm, all he said as he gave me a big hug was "I thought we'd lost you". Persephone's eyes were wide, "you never mentioned any of this in your mails, why?" Josephine smiled "I didn't want you to worry, I know how much of a mother hen you can be". Persephone sat back with her arms crossed and her face wrinkled, Josephine just snickered. Persephone met her gaze, barely hiding her smile, "well cluck cluck", Persephone couldn't hold it in anymore and giggled as Josephine put her cup down. "He doesn't act that way without reason, and I've watched it haunt him for months afterwards.

He's a good man and the best Captain I've had the privilege of serving with". Josephine sat back with her arms crossed and thought a minute "he's probably weighing it all right now, maybe you should go see if he's okay." Persephone pointed at herself "me? I'm sure there are other people he'd rather talk to". Josephine shook her head "you still can't read the signs, can you? You never could see the simple things in life. Just go to him, trust me, he needs you; especially now." Josephine looked up at the door at the edge of the room and saw Taven pass by. Josephine smiled, "speak of the devil, look who's out for a walk". Persephone began to get up "okay, here I go". Taven was contemplating the many unpleasant possibilities that could have befallen both himself and his Crew, the stars helped, it made him seem not so alone. A soft voice whispered behind him, "Taven?" Persephone lightly touched his right shoulder, he let his head hang a moment and turned to face her. "Seph, I could have...I didn't but I could have." Persephone put a finger over his lips, "shhh, we're okay, nobody's dead". Taven took her hands in his "I got lucky, really lucky". Persephone gazed at their hands and looked up into his eyes, "no, your Crew is phenomenal and you put the lives of those on your Ship first, it's the mark of a good leader". Taven gazed into her eyes "how can you be so sure?" Persephone drew closer "because, I know you", with that she leaned forward and kissed him, drawing her hand tenderly across his cheek and into his hair. They broke for a moment before Taven wrapped his arms around her waist and returned her embrace. As their lips parted he gazed into her eyes, they shone beautifully in the Helia's soft golden light, "see I did get lucky". Persephone beamed a smile and rested her head on his. "What do you think will happen next?" Taven drew in a deep breath "we'll need to bring this to the Council of Thirteen, they need to decide the next course of action". Persephone looked up and kissed his cheek "by the way, thank you." Taven moved her back slightly "for what?" Persephone brushed a strand of hair behind her ear, "for saving my life". Taven pulled her close "you're welcome, let's just hope that the Council has more ideas because I'm fresh out".

Tyra walked up behind Persephone "well I see you two are finally getting some quality time." Taven put his arm around Persephone, "hi Tyra". Taven looked back to Persephone and grinned "you know she's been telling me to ask you out for months." Persephone looked at Tyra "really? Not too bright is he?" Tyra grinned "nope, can't see what's in front of him half the time, it's why I'm forever saving his ass." Taven chuckled "how's Romal?" Tyra put her thumb up behind her "that's why I'm here, he's just regained consciousness and wants to see both of you." Taven nodded in approval "lead the way." Tyra leaned over to Persephone and whispered in her ear "you'll have to tell me everything later". Persephone giggled under her breath, "oh I have stories!"

The Main Sickbay on the Helia was a cavernous circular room; tall strings of amber light lined the walls and stretched up to a central sphere of white light. Romal was laying halfway around the room. He was covered in a soft fluffy golden blanket, and above him a large computer panel blinked amber indicators of all his vital signs. An Intelligent Reactive Status Display that the doctors could access at a moment's notice displayed necessary information above him. The system was standard on all Saret class Ships and the displays around the room made for an almost musical ambiance. Rachel was standing at the base of Romal's bed lightly tapping a tablet, a stylus in her hair and her top jacket buttons loosened a little, she was obviously deep in thought. The door slid open as Tyra, Persephone and Taven walked in. Rachel looked up and grabbed for the stylus behind her ear, she walked over tapping icons as she went and looked up as she approached Taven. Taven nodded towards Romal, "how is he Rachel?" Rachel tapped the stylus on a blank part of the screen in thought. "He's lucky, his wounds looked much worse than they were, but if that beam had been any closer..." Tyra crossed her arms as she choked on the next sentence, "how many did we lose". Rachel slipped the stylus into a hole in the tablet, turned the unit off and slipped it into her jacket pocket. "seventy-five fatalities, twenty-five injuries on the solaran, mostly people who were exposed to space when the Wing was sheared from the Superstructure. The twenty-five who lived were in adjacent corridors, they suffered mostly asphyxiation and third-degree burns. The seventy-five were in corridors and rooms along the outside of the vessel. When the wing was sheared off they were all exposed to hard vacuum, death was instant, they didn't feel any pain." Romal's eyes fluttered open, "Rachel, Tyra?" He began to sit up and winced in pain, Rachel rushed over with a hand behind his back "whoa there, you're not going anywhere anytime soon. You've got blunt force trauma from a falling beam, it sent you flying into the deck plates. Most of your ribs are bruised from the impact. You're lucky Captain, had you been two fika's to the right you'd have been under that beam". Romal caught his breath and waved his three visitors over, he winced again as a sharp pain washed over his face. Rachel tapped an icon on the bed's upper frame and a drawer slid out, she picked up a handle with a golden rounded nozzle on the front. She slipped a rectangular teal-coloured square into the base of the handle and pushed it into Romal's arm. It made a buzzing sound as Romal's face eased, it seemed his pain was abating. Romal nodded his head to Rachel "thank you". Rachel rubbed his arm, "that should last for a few hours, call me over if the pain returns, I'll let you four talk". Romal reached for Tyra's arm, "on behalf of my entire Crew, thank you for saving our lives". Taven walked up behind Tyra and grasped Romal's upper arm firmly in a caring manner. Taven looked at him and he knew he had to ask, even though he didn't want to, "what happened". Romal grabbed Taven's hand, "have a seat". Taven half sat on the bed beside Romal, "go ahead".

Romal gazed upwards as he began, "we'd just hit about five hundred fikans depth, I'd noticed a particularly large destabilization on the asteroid's surface some moments before, but I thought we had enough time to complete our goals and get out before it shook loose. What I didn't anticipate was the mist, this white cloud billowed out from below the surface. It blinded the Sensors, engulfed the View Screen and while my crew and I were distracted and trying to analyze the cloud and get our Sensors back online, that piece of rock I'd noticed before had come loose and we didn't see it until it was right on top of us. I tried to veer away, we almost got our full rotation but we weren't fast enough. It hit the Wing, sparks flew everywhere, there was fire and I couldn't breathe. I watched my best friends succumb to smoke inhalation within seconds and I thought we were all dead. I crawled to the Conn and tried to get us out of the way of the asteroid with Maneuvering Thrusters but all the systems were fused, I couldn't get any power to them. The last thing I remember is a brilliant fork of teal lightning striking my Ship and honeycombing the Hull, then everything going black."

Tyra took Romal's hand "we almost didn't catch you, a few seconds more and you'd have been just a fused pile of rubble on that asteroid, a thought that I find most disturbing". Tyra's eyes gazed long into Romal's before she caught herself, Romal clasped her hand with his other one, "well we're okay, at least most of us are." Taven who'd been keeping fairly quiet put a hand on Tyra's shoulder, she looked back and moved aside. "You know they're going to want an investigation into the events that led up to the damage and personnel losses right?" Romal sniffed a little "yeah, I know the procedure and the Council will be told the truth the same as you have been". Rachel drifted over from a couple of beds down the room "okay, times up guys, he needs to rest". Rachel brushed her hands on Persephone's back, "plenty of time to talk tomorrow". Tyra, Taven and Persephone all grasped his arm. Tyra looked up "get better soon okay?" Romal turned his head "I'm planning on it, hospital food is enough to kill anyone". Persephone giggled as Rachel retorted from the other side of the room "I heard that!" With that they left Romal to rest and Tyra took her leave to tend to Ship's business on the Bridge.

Taven and Persephone walked into the Aft Observation Area of the Helia. She had a very large bubbled seating area in the back between her Primary and Secondary Ion Drive Manifolds. Taven sat down with Persephone on one of the larger couches and they both stared into the vastness, as they watched the teal lightning arc into space. Taven reached for her hand, "so about earlier?" I suppose we should talk about exactly what happened.

Persephone looked down at Taven's hand "I think you know what happened, I love you. All I need to know is if we walk this path together or if I am alone.". Taven put a finger below her chin and tilted her head up "you've never walked alone".

Persephone's face lit up with uncontrolled happiness almost instantly. She beamed a smile at him, "so, you feel the same?" Taven returned her warm smile "I have for a while now, it wasn't until I almost lost everything on that bridge, that I realized how quickly everything can change." Persephone squeezed his arm lightly "life is change, my darling. What's important is that we stay true to ourselves." Taven pulled her close "you always have the best advice". Persephone snuggled up against him to watch the stars streak past, she was just starting to fall asleep when the Intercom Chimed. It was Tyra's voice "Captain Taven, Persephone, please meet me in the Conference Room on Deck Two. Taven looked up, he didn't need to but it was an old habit, "we'll be there shortly". Persephone got up and extended her hand to Taven as he got up "all these interruptions...next time we turn the Intercom off." Taven grinned, "isn't that a breach of some protocol?" Persephone snickered "oh only about a dozen or so, I won't tell if you don't." Taven took her hand and got up from the sofa "agreed". As they walked across the room the door to the ISTiS slid up, Taven tapped the sequence for Deck two into the panel and they dematerialized into the Ships transit system.

Taven and Persephone walked into the Conference Room to a rather unsettled image of Third Minister Sorvan. He regarded them both for a moment then sighed heavily. "I understand things did not go as we expected", Taven rubbed the back of his neck, "no, they did not. In fact, things are probably a lot worse now." Sorvan sat back in his chair "how so?" Taven motioned to Persephone and Tyra to take a seat, "the asteroid has been shocked, the rock itself is lightly charged with quantum particles and the wash from the Ion Engines has likely excited those particles. There's a very good chance that the asteroid's materials are being transformed into something that is far more volatile than simple iron. The main core is also unlike anything we've ever seen. Four Torpedoes barely made a dent". Sorvan sat forward "do you have any other ideas?" Taven sat back for a moment and thought, "all I can think of is sending a squadron of Phenomite Class Attack Fighters loaded with High Yield Plasma Cannons and Bitanium Enriched Quantum Flux Torpedoes". "it's a long shot though, it's a bit like chipping away at a granite stone with nothing but a rusty spoon, but it's all I can think of right now." Sorvan looked like he hadn't slept in days "alright I'll make preparations on this end, we'll have the squadron return onboard the Carrier S.I.V. Kem-akhet." Sorvan's eyes brightened slightly "I need a front man to plan the attack and lead the formation, any ideas?" Taven straightened up "I can be ready within two hours." Sorvan shook his head and smiled "no, not you, I have a different task for you. What about that hotshot navigator of yours, I understand his brazen flying skills are the only thing that kept the Jovus in one piece." Taven rubbed his chin "Clinch? he could do it in his sleep." Sorvan grinned, "then the job is his, tell him to report to the Operations Room on the Kem-akhet when she arrives in orbit. When you arrive in orbit, meet me in my home in quadrant C of the City. Suite 4206 in the main tower of that section. In the meantime make haste with your return, we're running out of time and options, I won't see this City destroyed, Sorvan out."

Taven watched as the screen blacked out and the energy ribbons around it sputtered and evaporated. He sat back in the farthest chair of the Conference Room. Tyra placed her hand on his shoulder in a comforting manner then tapped the Comm Panel nearby on the table. "Tyra to Main Engineering, Juice you're not going to like what I have to tell you." A rather frazzled voice came back over the Ship's Comm mixed with the ever-present static of the Ship's Internal Power Systems, "aye, and what's that then? Oh wait let me guess, you're wanting more speed from the Engines are ya now?" Tyra's head drooped as she grinned, raising it again she brushed a lock of hair behind her ear, "nothing surprises you does it?" Again a now irritated voice came back over the Intercom "not with you it doesn't, need I remind you that we've got two oversized turkeys we're draggin' along with us?" Tyra crossed her arms "I know we're weighed down but I think the Ship can handle it, bring the Auxilliary Reactors online and heat the Drive Plasma up, you may have to bypass a few safeguards, but I'm pretty sure we can get a little more out of her." Juice responded once more "I'll need your command authorization codes and some help to get the job done, can you join me in Main Engineering and bring Josephine with you." Tyra leaned over "we'll be down momentarily, as much as I want the extra speed, you're under orders not to compromise Ships systems, if it looks like the risk factor is beyond marginal your standing orders are to abort. I would rather get home a little slower than not at all." Juice's voice filled the room once more "aye, understood, you'll get whatever I can give ya, Engineering out." Tyra tapped the amber Intercom panel inset into the table once more and a bubbly voice responded, "yes Captain, Jo here, what can I do for you?" Tyra straightened slightly, "I need you to meet me in Main Engineering, we're going to try to coax a little more speed out of the Helia's Engines." Josephine's voice crackled back over the intercom "understood, on my way".

Tyra strolled out of the ISTiS and onto the Main Engineering Deck, around the corner she could hear Josephine and Juice talking, she couldn't help but eavesdrop on their conversation. Juice's voice was intentionally quiet "Captains, they always want the impossible and then some." Josephine couldn't help but giggle at his frustration, he was quite excitable but he'd been Chief Engineer on the Helia for thirty years and through both Tyra and her predecessor's commands. Tyra grinned mischievously and intentionally walked around the corner hoping to catch him like a deer in the headlights. Sadly he was facing the console and as she walked into the room she heard from his back, "hello Captain, come to try to teach an elephant to sprint have we?" Tyra grinned so hard she had to drop her head to keep from bursting out laughing. She tried desperately to hold it in, clearing her throat she walked over to Juice "you know you have the most descriptive way of putting things?" Juice turned around and leaned against the console "mmm hmm, but you wouldn't have me any other way, especially when you're making my life difficult." Tyra crossed her arms and simply looked at him. Juice was quite tall, Tyra figured he was at least seven Fikans two Fika's tall, he was a skinny man with salt and pepper hair dotting his balding head. He almost always had a slight beard that seemed to grow in during the day; it covered his leathery worn face. His skin was mostly of an olive complexion and he wore the standard Sirian Navy Engineer's Uniform, a brown vest over his tee-shirt, long pants and black boots. Almost his entire uniform was dotted with pockets everywhere, and he wore an old-style tool belt. He said it made him look distinguished, Tyra thought he liked it because it gave him a place to keep his tools handy. She shook off the thought realizing that her line of thinking was about to go completely downhill, she grinned. Juice crossed his arms "oh, and what's so funny?" Tyra shook her head "nothing, nothing". Juice turned back to his console "shall we get to work then?" Tyra nodded and motioned to Josephine to man the adjacent Computer Control Hub on the side of the room. Main Engineering aboard the Helia was a massive room, a testament to her incredible powerbase. The Main Plasma Focal Chamber was inset into the ceiling and encased in a gold/titanium based alloy. Its gentle hum gave Engineering a peaceful teal glow. Past the door, and beyond the core and control centre lay the massive Reaction Control Manifold. The vaulted ceiling gave way to immense Reaction Control Filters and Huge Screens inset into the wall in the back of the room, which read out constant data about the entire Ship and reported instantly if there was any failure in any place. The Main Engineering Console was a rather large and lengthy tactile panel set so that the chief could simply look up to see where any problem had arisen. To the left and right of the Main Console lined along the walls were the Auxilliary and Backup Systems along with Control Consoles which managed everything from Food Replicators to Weapons Systems. The Helia was one of the first Ships in her class, the Engineering rooms on subsequent ships had been scaled down to accommodate more rooms in the surrounding sections and additional Surgical Bays. The Helia herself had retained her cradle of power, and Juice wouldn't have it any other way. Tyra was checking the radiation and thermal gauges, she motioned to Juice "look at these, does this look like they're running a little hot to you?" Juice leaned over and read the display "they are indeed, do you feel like getting your hands dirty, Captain?"

Tyra grinned mischievously "for you my friend, always." Tyra waved Josephine over, "Jo can you take the Starboard Reactor Grid and double-check the readouts. Manage them if necessary, Juice and I are checking the Port Grid and surrounding Couplings." Josephine nodded in agreement "I'm on my way". Jo beckoned from the rear of the Engineering compartment, "Simmons, Taylor, Venz, you're with me." Josephine headed out the door with her assistants and the door slid shut behind her. Juice raised his hand in a gentleman's fashion "after you, Captain". Tyra smiled and headed for the ISTiS. Tyra remarked as they stepped in "you know you've been with the Ship for years and I've never figured it out, why do they call you Juice?" Juice stepped into the ISTiS and pressed a couple of icons on the panel, "my first Captain was a power-hungry maniac. He'd always call down to Engineering wanting more power for this and that. Finally one day I said, Captain, I've got no more Juice to give you, you're stuck with what you've got. The name just kind of stuck." Moments later, a teal bolt struck the pair as ribbons of energy rippled around them, Tyra watched as the room washed in a rainbow of colour and moments later the colours faded away to reveal the ISTiS near the Port Power Couplings. Tyra and Juice stepped out of the ISTiS on the lower decks, Tyra simply remarked "mmm hmm, now I understand."

The lower decks on a Sirian Star Ship were dimly lit at the best of times. The illumination was kept low due to the heat generated by the Main Core. This class of Ship had two Gravity Well Generators putting out more energy than a small star. Tyra and Juice walked along the corridor, dim amber lights lined the hallways and amber flashes echoed through the dim light from control panels along the wall. Tyra and Juice stopped about five metres apart from each other and began tapping a few control keys. Tyra rubbed her chin, "Yes, just as we thought, Sub Core Processor Khepri is having some coolant issues. Primary Reactant Injector Port twenty-seven is also a little sluggish." Juice drifted over, tapping a few more controls on the pad he read another readout. "Yeah, I see the problem. The Secondary Plasma Conduit is clogged. I'll run a systems purge, it should flame out the blockage and restore full coolant pressure. It will take about five minutes or so." Juice tapped three controls in ascending sequence on a square pad underneath the Main Control Screen. A door slid open and an amber horizontal keyboard slid out from the wall.

Juice fixed his eyes forward and began his repairs. Tyra leaned up against the wall and crossed her arms. "You know I've been in the Sirian Defence Force for the better part of twenty-five years. The Helia is my second command and in all that time I've only run into five people with your accent. It's very uncommon, what part of Siria Prime are you from?" Juice's gaze didn't waver as he responded, "well that's your first problem, I'm not from Siria Prime, I'm from Siria Minor." Tyra straightened a little as she was obviously surprised, "Siria Minor, as in the third moon?" Juice nodded "aye". Tyra rubbed her neck "I knew there was a settlement there but they keep to themselves". Juice once again nodded "indeed, for the most part, the bulk of Siria Minor's populace is a little backwards, they are mostly farmers and merchants. Very few people from there leave the planet and even fewer join the Imperial Navy." Tyra turned towards the Secondary Systems readout, "it looks like the coolant pressure is rising." Juice tapped a few control keys on the primary screen "it is, but not enough yet, I'll continue with the purge and I'll re-route additional coolant pressure from the adjacent systems."

Tyra returned to leaning against the wall "what's it like, Siria Minor, I've never been there." Juice's hands stopped typing and he looked at her "it's the lushest world you can imagine, sprawling golden cities separated by rolling green hills and crystal clear lakes." Tyra smiled "I think I know where I'm taking my next leave." Juice nodded and returned to his work. "let me know when you're going and I'll join you, I haven't been home in almost ten years." Tyra nodded, "great!" She moved back to the Secondary Panel "all systems are showing green, thermal and mechanical readouts are clear." Juice tapped the same square control pad this time in descending sequence, the keyboard slid back into the wall and the door lowered back down. He tapped four keys on both screens and they blanked out, all that remained were the flashing amber status indicators blinking in the dim light. Juice turned to Tyra, "we're done, I can do the rest from Main Engineering." Tyra remarked as they headed back to the ISTiS "how much more speed do you think you can give me?" Juice said as the doors closed, I think I can manage point six more." Tyra nodded, "I'll take whatever I can get." They were enveloped in a vortex of teal energy and then they were gone.

The door to the ISTiS slid up and Tyra walked onto the Main Bridge, "how are we doing?" Trell spun around from the Navigation Console, "on course Captain, estimated arrival time is in five hours at our present speed". Tyra sat down and nodded "moving at in-system warp for long periods always throws off my time a little, I'm used to using the Main Engines between stars." Trell grinned "well it may be boring for you, but it keeps me on my toes, no end of stellar obstacles and debris out there to avoid." Tyra's head tilted just slightly "I never thought of it that way. Well, I'll leave you to get us the rest of the way, I'm going to try to get some sleep." Trell nodded "pleasant dreams". He spun back around to face the Main Screen and brought up the Tactical Display and Hazard Warning Icons. Tyra rubbed her temples as she got up, she'd been nursing a headache for the past ten hours. She walked across the Bridge and as the ISTiS door slid up, the panel chimed awaiting a destination. She tapped four glyphs in and the door slid down as the transport sequence began.

Tyra walked out of the ISTiS and down the hallway, stopping just before a door on her left. She breathed in and began to rub her neck as she walked into the room. Rachel was sitting in her office at her desk; it was a nicely illuminated and adorned room. A potted plant was on the floor and Rachel's desk sat in the corner. Her desk, a dark chestnut wood had two black chairs opposite her. Two or three paintings were hung on the walls and a large window behind Rachel shimmered with space dust streaking by. She was turned around watching the arcing electricity trailing behind them. Rachel heard Tyra walk in and tapped a couple of controls on a panel next to the window on the wall, the window tinted darker and Rachel spun her chair around to see Tyra. Tyra still rubbing her neck, came in the rest of the way and sat down in one of the chairs. "Hey Rach, got anything for a headache?" Rachel got up and grabbed the tablet from her vest shirt pocket, "sure, how long have you had it?" Tyra knew she was going to get it the moment she said it. She sighed and told her "about ten hours". Rachel ran the tablet over Tyra's head a couple of times and simply said "uh huh". Tyra looked at her in surprise "no speech?" Rachel shrugged "would it do any good?" Tyra smiled "no probably not". Rachel rubbed her shoulder "come on let's see to that head of yours".

The two women walked into the next room and Rachel walked towards a medical station which was against the wall to grab an injector. Tyra went to sit down on a diagnostic bed in the middle of the room. She walked back over to Tyra and leaned her head to the side slightly. She put the injector up to her neck and pressed a button on the handle, a slight crackle and hiss could be heard. Tyra's shoulders dropped and her eyes closed. She sniffed and her eyes opened up "that's much better". Rachel rubbed her shoulders, you really should come and see me before you torture yourself you know? Tyra nodded "yeah, I just get." Rachel finished her sentence for her "get so busy that you don't have time, yes I know. Now go get some sleep, you've been up for twenty-two hours straight." Tyra nodded, "I was headed that way next". Rachel grabbed the injector off the bed and went back to put it away "good, see to it you get there this time, no diversions." Tyra got up and headed towards the door "thanks Rachel". Rachel was looking at a view screen of information and waved at her "yeah, yeah, now go get some sleep." Tyra walked out of the Medical Bay and down the hall, she stopped briefly to gaze out a window at the crackling teal energy bolts dancing off the Wings. With a heavy sigh, she walked into the ISTiS and tapped a couple of controls. She watched as the room bled away into a vibrant display of colour then back again. She was on Deck Twelve Officer's Cabins. She walked out of the ISTiS down a hallway with long horizontal windows going the entire length of the Deck. She walked into her cabin and took out the pin that had been holding her hair in place and shook her hair out. She slid into bed and tapped a couple of controls on her nightstand. As the lights dimmed and some soft piano-like music gently filled the room, she breathed in and closed her eyes and just like that she was fast asleep.

THE COUNCIL OF THIRTEEN

The Comm Panel chimed, Tyra's eyes fluttered open. She pulled the covers over her head and rolled over ignoring it. The Comm Panel chimed again. She groaned and rolled over tapping the Comm Pad "yes?" Trell's voice crackled over the speaker "we're about fifteen minutes out, I thought you'd want to be on the Bridge when we enter orbit". Tyra sighed "thank you, I'll be there shortly". The Comm crackled slightly then shut off. Tyra sat for a moment, "time" she said to an empty room. Lightning crackled down the wall slightly and flashed into a set of four symbols. Tyra got out of bed and headed to the washroom, "three hours, three measly hours. Just wait until I get my hands on that little"...the shower door slid shut.

As Tyra left her quarters she had a hair clip in her mouth. Rushing slightly, she was still half gathering her hair between her fingers when she walked into the ISTiS. She tapped in the control sequence to the Bridge and the system chirped acknowledging the transit request. As the materialization sequence started, she took the clip out of her mouth and held it in her hand. Watching the wash of colour cascade over her as she made her way through the ship's systems, she felt her eyes shutting. She suddenly realized that extreme fatigue and matter transportation systems don't mix very well. As the sequence ended and the energy ribbons spun back up into the ceiling and she let loose a very big yawn. Tyra walked onto the Bridge from the ISTiS, tucking the clip into her hair and finishing her ponytail, "Trell, status". Trell spoke without turning "thirty seconds from destination". Tyra sat down, Persephone came out of nowhere and handed her a cup of coffee "you look like you need it". Tyra looked up at Persephone "oh you're an angel, thank you." Tyra took a long sip and enjoyed the moment until Trell interrupted it for the second time today, "we're here". Tyra forced herself into focus, "alright cut the Engines, move us slowly towards the Dry Dock." The Helia streaked to a stop, the Warp Strips on her huge Wings blinked back in towards the Hull and finally twice to signal her Warp Engines were shut down. The large Ship carried under her Wings the Jovus and the Solaran, cascading bolts of teal energy surrounding both Ships, the Helia's Ion Engines lit up along her Tail and she slowly moved towards the Dry Dock area which was in orbit above Atlanka. Ever so gently she guided the Jovus towards the Dock. Tyra sat forward in her chair minding the screen. "Okay cut the Tractor Beam, inertia can carry the Jovus in". The crackling bolt of lightning faded and the Jovus glided into the Dry Dock, smaller bolts of lightning near the front of the Dock energized and white lines began to pulse along them. The Jovus was gently guided into position as clamps and extenders came out from the Dry Dock. Crew Access Tubes and External Energy Conduits locked in until finally, she was safe and secure and home. Trell on the Bridge breathed a sigh of relief, "she's in". Tyra as well breathed a little easier but their job was far from over. The Solaran was so damaged that putting her into a Star Dock was impossible, the Helia was going to have to take her into the atmosphere and set her down in one of the Planetary Maintenance Hangers, not an easy job with a disabled Ship.

Tyra looked over to Andara, "are the Tractor Systems ready for planetary delivery?" Andara was busily tapping away on her Console and responded without breaking eye contact with her monitor. "They should be, I'm just doing some final checking now. We can deliver the Solaran whenever you're ready Captain". Tyra sat back in her chair, "alright let's take her down slowly. Tuck the Solaran under the lower decks and make sure it's secured." Andara hit a few controls and pointed at another crew member who came over beside her and double-checked the position and co-ordinated the delivery procedure. Tyra tapped an amber glyph on the arm of her chair and the Comm System crackled to life. "Atlanka Docking Control, this is the S.I.V. Helia on final approach to deliver S.I.V. Solaran to Docking Bay Four on the southwestern quadrant of the mechanic's district. Please confirm preparations are complete for Star Ship delivery." A man's voice crackled over the Comm System "S.I.V. Helia, Antigrav Support Struts are online, full system automation and shutdown will commence as soon as you complete delivery. Planetary Tractor Emitters will lock on as soon as the Solaran is directly overhead, bring her home." Tyra tapped a secondary Comm Channel, "Docking Control, confirming receipt of instructions. we're on our way."

The Solaran was neatly tucked under the breast of the great golden bird, two bolts of crackling teal energy at nearly forty-five-degree angles encased her in a plasma energy grid. Electricity arced all across the Helia's Hull and a bubble of pulsating arcing lightning surrounded both Ships. Like a great owl taking shelter from a storm, the Helia gently dipped into the atmosphere, her Shields a glow of warm orange as she crossed through the thermosphere; before the Ship, a layer of white clouds was moving ever so slowly. The Helia slipped into the clouds, the white mist caressing the Shields sending ripples along the energy structure and leaving a wake behind her Tail. It was as if the sky itself was welcoming the Ship home. The clouds thinned and a vast ocean lay below them, sapphire blue with the occasional whitecap. In the distance was a large landmass, so enormous it stretched along the entire horizon. Green hills, snow capped mountains all set on the backdrop of Mesira's crystal clear sky. The Helia dipped down closer to the water, her air wake was so massive the waves beneath her parted as she soared over the ocean. In the distance, huge golden spires appeared on the coast. First thin and sharp as a needle, then taking shape to reveal sky-scraping towers. Atlanka lay in front of the ship. The original City itself was designed in the shape of an immense flat bird. Her Stardrive Engines stretched across her wings and her Ion Drive was tucked under the City, below ground. Atlanka was a port of commerce and trade, as well as serving as a repair and re-supply dock for the Sirian Imperial Fleet. The City itself had rested on Mesira for hundreds of years, her wings supporting the sprawling colony and beyond. Atlanka was a unique Star Ship design in the Sirian Fleet, there were only four others like her. She was designed to be a massive mobile installation capable of deploying and redeploying wherever she was needed. Atlanka as a Star Ship utilized a unique system of travel, her buildings and infrastructure were not originally part of the design. One of the crowning achievements of this class of vessel was the ability to erect the structures that were needed for any given situation on any planet upon arrival. She also carried massive Bio-molecular Pattern Storage Buffers, she could in effect dematerialize and store people in the City, reabsorb the matter of which the structures were made, then restore everything to its previous state upon arrival at her new location. But after centuries, the colony had grown significantly larger than the original size of the City when it first set down, and the internal workings of the Star Ship had fallen into a measure of disrepair. The Helia soared passed what was now the downtown core which serviced most of the business and commerce that came through Atlanka.

Flying past the City and turning slightly, she flew over grasslands and farms to what was a smaller suburb a few miles out from the main colony. Slowing to a fraction of her previous speed, she hovered over circular pits that were almost part of the planet itself. Tyra sat in her chair gazing at the screen, she leaned forward to Trell and whispered "the beauty just never gets old does it?" Trell smiled as he moved the Solaran gently over her Berth, "nope". Tyra sat back "okay, let's put the Solaran to bed shall we." The Helia slowly lowered over the massive circular chasm, as she did, pulsating arcs of teal electricity flickered on. All around the circle four bolts of lightning shot out like spokes on a tire, then angled up to encapsulate the Solaran. Tyra was running her index finger along the side of her armrest when the Comm crackled to life, "S.I.V. Helia we have the Solaran, please disengage your Tractor Beams; well done and welcome home." The Helia's Tractor Beams arced and sputtered as the Solaran was gently pulled down into the Docking Bay until the Tractor

Beams were flat against the ship. Four massive support braces emerged from the sides of the bay as interlocks slid open on the sides of the Solaran. The beams slid into place with a resounding clunk and the Tractor Beams holding the Solaran arced with a thunderous sound. Tyra got up, "right, let's get back into orbit, Trell I believe you know the way. I'm leaving the Bridge under your command, I have a meeting with the Council of Thirteen." Trell spun his chair around "I'll keep your chair warm" giving Tyra a wink. Tyra grinned while shaking her head and walked over to the ISTiS. Tapping two controls the door slid up and she strode in, turning and tapping another control inside the door, it started to slide down and she grinned at Trell "don't have too much fun". Tyra's body was struck with teal lightning as ribbons of teal energy encircled her. Scanning beams of white light moved across and as they connected a spark of lightning erupted from the lines and there was a resounding rumble of thunder.

As the energy ribbons twisted up into the ceiling, Tyra walked out of the ISTiS on the lower decks near the Medical Ward. She hadn't been back here since the Helia warped away from the approaching asteroid and she wanted to check in on Romal. She walked into the Medical Bay and Rachel was standing next to Romal tapping on a tablet. Tyra walked over to them with a hand in her hip pocket, "how are you feeling?" Romal smiled "Doc here says I've made just about a full recovery". Tyra motioned with her thumb behind her head, "we're back at Atlanka. The Council wants to see you and the others to discuss the events that transpired." Romal nodded "so I've been told. Are Taven and Persephone meeting us there?" Tyra looked over to one of the small windows along the wall, "they're already waiting in the City." Romal stood up, "well then if it's okay with Rachel we should be on our way." Rachel's head popped up from what she was working on, "you're cleared, but I want you to take it easy." Romal nodded and patted Tyra on the back, "let's go see the Council".

Persephone paced outside the Council Chambers, she knew that their time was running out and that they had no discernible plan to deal with this asteroid. Taven was sitting near Persephone and looked up at her. "Will you stop pacing? You're going to wear a rut in the marble." Persephone brushed a lock of hair behind her ear and sat down beside Taven. "We should be working on a way to combat this thing, not standing around waiting to tell the Council about why things happened the way they did. We're wasting valuable time." Taven nodded, "I know that, you know that, hell, the Council probably knows that; however, they need to know what has happened so they can plan and coordinate with the colony leaders and department officials if things get crazy." Persephone leaned forward and looked to her side at Taven. "You know any plan will likely come from us, not the Council". Taven patted her on the shoulder, "which is why I'm not the least bit worried." Romal and Tyra rounded the corner and walked over, Taven got up to greet Romal. "Good to see you up and around my friend, we were all a little worried there." Romal nodded, "I'm fine, Rachel says I'm over the worst of it". Persephone looked up at Tyra "are you ready?" Tyra breathed in a heavy sigh, "it's not every day you get called before the Council is it? Yes, I'm ready". Tyra walked over to the Council Chambers door and pressed the open key. The doors opened to a room surrounded by stained glass windows.

The table of the Council was a brown marble and semi-circular, the chairs were made of soft brown wood. Immense columns stretching to the ceiling lined the chamber leading from the door up to where the Council was seated, forming an invisible hallway. Taven led the group into the room. A large bell chimed and the Council Members took their places. First Minister Ben'veh addressed them. "Captain Tyra of the S.I.V. Helia, Captain Taven of the S.I.V. Jovus and Captain Romal of the S.I.V. Solaran, this Council session is to clarify events leading up to significant damage to both the Jovus and the Solaran. Now I've read all three of your reports on the incident and while I accept them, I'm still a little unclear as to exactly what happened on board the

Solaran before impact. Captain Romal your report states that you were drilling and your Sensors picked up a large portion of the surface of the asteroid and warning icons indicated a possible rupture and collision. Why didn't you abort when you saw that a significant piece of the asteroid was about to dislodge and was in the direct path of your Ship?" "First Minister, if I may respond candidly?" First Minister Ben'veh nodded. "Sir, I didn't get command of the Solaran by taking the safest road. Sometimes risks must be taken to ensure the success of the mission." The First Minister sat back in his chair and crossed his arms. "Seventy-five lives lost and half your Ship ripped away, I think you'd better have a good reason for that."

Romal began to recount events. "We were on the Bridge, drilling as you pointed out, I saw that the asteroid's crust was beginning to lose integrity. I double and triple-checked the depth calculations and even considered aborting, but felt that we had enough time to complete our task and get out safely. I know my ship, she's fast and my Crew highly skilled." First Minister Ben'veh shook his head, "what went wrong then?" Romal continued, "As I stated in my report, we were enveloped by a white mist, which I can only assume was released from the fracturing asteroid. It blinded our Sensors, we couldn't read a thing. Even our display barely functioned and then we saw it, almost on top of us. I gave the order to abort, but it was already too late, half into our turn, the asteroid hit with full force. It sheered the wing off and I lost ten Crew members who were manning plasma dispersion stations in the Auxilliary Engine Room and another sixty-five in adjoining corridors and sections. Now I have to somehow tell their families that they're not coming home and that they died for a reason." The First Minister interlocked his fingers and thought for a moment. Finally speaking he gazed at Romal, "while I can question your actions after the fact, I cannot place myself in the moment when you gave the order; so while I find no evidence of negligence on your part, I am ordering the Solaran or rather what's left of her to be transferred to your Second in Command pending a psychological review. If you pass the exam your command will be restored." The First Minister leaned forward and clasped his hands together "Romal, I know you and I know you would never put your Crew in danger without just cause. But this event has left you shaken, the psych exam is as much for our benefit as it is for yours. I'd also like you to see a Counsellor for a few weeks. This will take a toll on you, but we still need you and your experience." The First Minister struck a gavel onto a plate with a clack, "let it be done." He motioned to Romal, "you can have a seat, Captain Taven, you're next." Taven stepped forward in front of the Council. First Minister Ben'veh skimmed a few pages on the tablet in front of him. "Now your report says that you flew the Jovus into the mouth of this beast after watching the Solaran impacted by the asteroid and decided to finish the job they started?" Taven nodded "that's correct". First Minister Ben'veh rubbed his head "forgive me Captain, but that sounds incredibly foolish and reckless. You'd already seen a fellow Star Ship disabled by large debris, what were you thinking flying your Ship into the heart of that mess?" The Jovus is hundreds of years old and despite the upgrades you received before you embarked on this mission, you knew the state of your vessel." Taven cut the First Minister short. "Sir, may I speak my mind?" The First Minister was taken aback for a moment by the outburst, then nodded in acceptance. Taven spoke perhaps the strongest he ever had.

"I've served in the Sirian Navy since I was a very young man. I've been in battles and seen friends fall. Sir, when you witness what I did, when I saw the Solaran's wing ripped away, the explosions rock her side and see the Ship twist erratically out of control, you get angry. I had to do something, I was unwilling to let those people, Sirian Defence Personnel, people I'd worked with and called my friends, die without something good coming from it. So I took a chance, and we got lucky." Ben'veh put down the tablet he'd been referencing, "Captain Taven, this isn't the first time you've acted rashly. I recall you standing before us several years ago after a Shuttle accident almost claimed the lives of your Helmsman and your Chief Engineer." Taven stiffened, "I don't leave people behind Sir!" First Minister Ben'veh shook his head, "as noble as your intentions might be I simply cannot..." Persephone walked straight in front of Taven "Captain Taven was following my recommendation". First Minister Ben'veh was taken aback once again. "You suggested that Taven take the Jovus into such a dangerous situation?" Persephone brushed her hair out of her face, "yes, considering the risk to Atlanka and peoples' lives that are at stake here, I felt that the risk was warranted. I had rechecked the power conversion calculations and felt the Manifolds could handle the excessive pressure. I was wrong, I made a mistake and Taven's Ship was damaged in the process. It's not entirely his fault, he was acting under my guidance." Ben'veh sat back and crossed his arms. "Captain Taven, do you have anything to add?" Taven looked at Persephone as she bit her lip and stared back at him. "No First Minister, I think that about covers it." First Minister Ben'veh sighed heavily, "so be it. Captain Taven because you were acting under the guidance of the Science Directorate I'll forego any permanent reprimand. Director Persephone, while I doubt any blemish on your record will cause people to lose confidence in your leadership, I trust that you won't make a habit of such errors."

Persephone crossed her hands behind her back and stood straight. "I wouldn't be Director of the Sirian Institute of Science and Research if I did. While I cannot assure you I'll never make another mistake, I do my very best to avoid them. After all, we're only mortal." Ben'veh nodded "let the record show that Captain Taven's Ship was damaged through no direct fault of his own, and he is to be commended that no lives were lost in the explosions that rocked the Jovus." Ben'veh struck the gavel on the plate once more, "this session is terminated." The Council rose from their seats and made their way out of the room. The group walked out of the Chamber doors and Taven quickly grabbed Persephone's arm and tugged her off to the side. He stood for a moment with his arms crossed before he spoke. "Why did you tell them I was acting under your instructions?" Persephone shook her head, "because you were about to get a full reprimand and possibly lose your command and rank. I warned you long ago such impulsive decisions would be the end of you." Taven put his hands on her shoulders, "but now you have to deal with it." Persephone's hand drifted to Taven's arm, "yes, but they can't demote me or take away my job. Besides I'm a scientist, we make the odd mistake now and again." Taven touched her face, "you didn't have to do that." Persephone gripped his shirt and pulled him forward into a kiss. As they parted, she whispered to him, "yes I did." After a longer than usual moment, Persephone and Taven rejoined Romal and Tyra who were discussing the situation they now found themselves in. Tyra was leaning against a pillar, "well aren't we supposed to all meet Sorvan this evening?" Romal nodded, "so far as I know, shouldn't Clinch be here?" Taven shook his head, "no I sent him to Sirian Command Central to speak with the Task Force being assembled." Persephone stood near Taven rubbing her neck, "but what can twenty-five Combat Fighters do that a Star Ship can't?" Taven sighed "they're hoping the constant and variable direction of the weapons fire from strafing fighters will chip away at the asteroid enough so that it loses all cohesion and simply breaks apart." Persephone brushed a lock of hair out of her face, "I think it's time for the four of us came up with a Plan "B". I'm concerned our fighters will have no effect on it." Tyra straightened up, "do you have any ideas?" Persephone shook her head, "not yet, but Sorvan might. He's had a tendency in the past for coming up with bizarre solutions that most of the time actually work." Tyra called out to the air, "time!" Electricity arced from out of nowhere above them and struck forming four symbols in the air which pulsed for a few moments and then sizzled out of existence. Tyra put her hand in her hip pocket, "well we've got a couple of hours, I'm going to transport back to the Helia and make sure Trell isn't reprogramming the food dispensers to serve cold coffee again." Romal straightened up, "I'll head to the Solaran to check on repairs and I'll set up those appointments." Taven put his arm behind Persephone's back, "and we'll head to the Science Building to talk to some of Seph's people and see what they can come up with." Tyra clapped her hands together, "right, we'll see you guys in a couple of hours at Sorvan's home." The group split up, Romal walked towards the ISTiS, Tyra headed towards Solar Transit Systems and back to the Helia, Taven and Persephone walked outside and breathed in the Mesirian afternoon breeze. Always at this time of day, a warm breeze washed over Atlanka, she had landed on the coast a few Fikans from the shore on what was then a grassy patch of flat land. So much had changed, but the afternoon breeze had remained the same. Persephone walked over to a railing overlooking some of the lower buildings which were only a couple of stories high, then down to the street level. Antigrav vehicles floated down the road, an older form of transport considering the Integral Transport Network, the ISTiS. Even still, many people enjoyed the feeling of taking themselves where they needed to go. It was something that had endured for centuries, ever since the vehicle was first invented back on Siria Prime. She gazed over the City, tall gleaming amber towers in the distance, a glimmer of light sparkled off one of the City's Astrological Sensors. Persephone's head turned to gaze down the length of Atlanka, her face being caressed by the soft salty breeze of the ocean, her eyes closed and she stood motionless for a moment and simply let it wash over her. When her eyes opened, her gaze drifted towards the shore and her sight drifted down to street level and just beyond. Then it dawned on her, Taven was standing beside her, his arm around her back and his hand on the railing enjoying the moment as well, when she turned her head to face him. "Taven, this City is simply a giant moving replicator is it not?" Taven caught her gaze and instantly knew what she was thinking but asked anyway. "It's more complex than that, but essentially yes. What did you have in mind?" Persephone's gaze washed over the City again as she spoke, "well if we can't make the asteroid get out of our way, then we're just going to have to get out of its way." Taven shook his head "this city was never meant to take flight again, she's been here for centuries, and was in service as a Mobile Port for ages before. I don't even think her

Engines will fire and who knows what the Buffer System is like after so long without operation." Persephone's head turned again to face his, "it's an option and one I am perfectly suited to pursue, I think we have our Plan "B". Sorvan's not going to like this and it carries great risk, but if the fighters don't prevail, I think we have to give this serious thought." Taven nodded in agreement and they headed to the Science Ministry. The large glass doors of the Science Ministry parted as Persephone and Taven walked inside the building. Persephone headed for the front desk, the man seated behind it was surprised to see her. "Seph, we hadn't expected to see you back for a while yet. Is there anything you need?" Persephone put her forearm on the desk "hi Geldar, is the Science Team from Telonis IV still here giving their report on that pre-industrial civilization we were studying?" Geldar tapped some symbols on the keypad in front of him and scanned the monitor. "Yeah, they're scheduled to return the day after tomorrow". Persephone nodded "I need you to postpone their return and send them to my office, I have another task for them." Geldar nodded, "right away".

Persephone led Taven over to the ISTiS which was at the centre of two large holographic fountains, which shot water straight up from the floor, but the water never made the area wet. It was an illusion to the eye but a pleasing one. The Ministry, itself, was a smaller building, no more than ten floors. Its foyer was a gallery, surrounded by amber glass with round balls of light which seemed to float with no visible support. To the far left and right of the doors, stairs curved upward and the entire floor was a chestnut-coloured marble. Matching marble pillars adorned the path from the door to the receiving desk which was in the centre of the atrium. The ISTiS was in between the two sets of stairs, at the far back surrounded by fountains, which used no water and lights which never dimmed. The ISTiS door slid up, Taven and Persephone walked in and Persephone leaned forward and tapped two controls. She looked up at him and smiled as they both were encircled in ribbons of energy. The ISTiS door slid up and Taven and Persephone walked out and down a fairly long hallway with doors at offset positions along the corridor. Brown marble inset with sandstone was adorned the floor. Amber wall sconces passed them casting a soft light. They turned a corner and Persephone tapped an amber control pad in sequence. A loud click was heard and the door slid open. Persephone motioned to the chair in front of her desk, "have a seat, the Scientists might be a while". Persephone's office was quite spacious as was expected for a person of her distinction. There were four vertical windows along the wall behind her desk, all looking out over the City and towards the ocean. Her desk, a brown marble, was offset in the corner, a high-back office chair behind and two smaller chairs in front. A rather comfortable-looking leather couch sat in the opposite corner underneath one of several wall sconces which maintained the soft lighting.

Persephone sat down behind her desk and tapped a control pad. Two panels on the desk retracted and slid open. Two silver rods slid out and energized in rippling currents of plasma energy. The display emerged, and from the other panel in front, a keyboard rose up, both were full of amber symbols and blinked once as they locked into position. Persephone tapped a key on the board and a stylus popped out of the top of the desk. Sirian technology was highly based on arcing electricity, as such when working with Holographic Monitors or any Holographic Device, a stylus was needed as a hand would be delivered a most unpleasant jolt from the rippling energy currents. Persephone picked up the stylus and tapped on what seemed like random spots on the monitor, and then she placed it behind her ear and sat back in her chair. "Request interlink with SARA Core, authorization Ptah two six seven five. SARA was quiet for a moment waiting for Persephone's request. Persephone spun around in her chair and got up to look out the window, quietly in thought for a moment she considered what she was about to do. "Query, can the Ion Engines on S.I.V. Atlanka be primed and operated for a short duration without catastrophic damage to the City or the Vessel. Also please report on the condition of the Bio-Molecular Data Storage Housing and Matter Conversion Matrix. Persephone's monitor behind her flickered and symbols danced across the screen, then SARA's voice filled the room. "The Bio-Molecular Storage Housing has degraded past safety limits, repairs will need to be affected before the System can be operated without data loss. The Matter Conversion Matrix is stable but it will need to be re-initialized. The Main Ion Thrusters are operable but require maintenance, several fissures have developed in the Fuel Lines and Injector Ports, also Injectors six, twelve and forty-seven are clogged with debris." Persephone sat back in her chair and tugged at a lock of hair. "Not as bad as I thought, not great but still not bad. We might be able to pull it off." Taven sat forward and interlocked his fingers, "just what do you have in mind? You're not actually thinking of trying to move this City?" Persephone shrugged, "why not, it's a mobile platform designed to be moved at will to any location and set up with relative ease." Taven crossed his arms "this colony is centuries old and the Ship it rests on has over fifteen-hundred years in service. It was placed here as a permanent fixture, it was never intended to be moved again." Persephone sat up and put her hands on the desk, "Mesira was never meant to be obliterated by a massive asteroid either. The Council is relying on me and the Sirian Imperial Navy to safeguard the lives of everybody in this colony, which means I must pursue any and all options open to me. If that means I need to practice a little unorthodox thinking or attempt to move a fifteen-hundred-year-old Star Ship, then that's what I'm going to do." An indicator on the desk blinked several times, "ah good, my team is here." Taven got up from his chair "I'm going to let you handle this, I need to check in on the Jovus and see how repairs are getting along. I'll see you in a couple of hours." Taven got up and circled around the desk, he leaned over and gave her a quick kiss on the cheek then headed for the door. Persephone got up, bending over her desk and tapping a couple of controls and as Taven stepped out of the room, the team of Scientists walked in. Persephone walked over and shook their hands. "Welcome gentlemen, sorry to keep you from your return to Telonis, but I have a pressing need for your skills here."

The four men looked a little confused and stood waiting for an explanation. Persephone motioned for them to have a seat as she moved around the desk and sat down herself. "You are all aware of the issue currently being dealt with that is threatening the City, correct?" The four men nodded, Persephone pushed back from the desk and got back up, moving towards a blank panel on the wall, she grabbed her stylus and tapped three icons on the control keypad nearby, the wall retracted and a screen slid out slightly. Electricity arced from its corners with a loud crackle and sparking loudly, the screen blinked on. A technological representation of Atlanka was shown but suddenly Persephone gazed down and scratched behind her ear. She motioned towards the desk and tapped a control on the pad. "Please give me a moment, I neglected to summon the best Engineer I know." Persephone muttered under her breath, "must be the pressure." She tapped a Comm Panel on the front top of the desk and a woman's voice crackled over the Intercom. This is Commander Josephine, how can I help you?" Josephine had her head three-quarters of the way under the Aft Science Station on the Bridge of the Jovus, with a mechanic's beacon on her arm and a spanner in her hand. Persephone's voice responded through the Intercom, "Jo, it's Seph, I know you're overseeing the repairs to the Jovus, but can I borrow you for a few minutes in my office at the Ministry of Science?" Josephine clicked the flashlight off and placed the spanner on the floor beside her. She wriggled out from beneath the console and placed her hand on top where the panel sat to steady herself. As she got up, she looked briefly at the spanner on the floor and not at the top of the console access panel in front of her. Persephone heard a low thump, Josephine's voice echoed over the Comm Channels. "Ow!" Persephone shook her head "you okay Jo?" Josephine rubbed her head "yeah, I'll be there in a few minutes".

Josephine tapped the channel closed on the panel and motioned to two gentlemen across the Bridge. "Maddok, Simmons, I'm needed in the City, take over. I want that Science Station online before I get back. Oh and double-check on the Repair Crew on

Deck Five, they should be halfway through replacing the Plasma Conduits in that section by now". Josephine tapped the Comm Panel on Taven's chair, "Josephine to Engineering". Fyar had his hand wrist-deep in the Warp Core Control Matrix when the call came in; "Ugh, always when I'm in the middle of something". Fyar removed his hand and wiped it with a towel he had draped over his shoulder. He walked over to the Main Engineering Comm Panel and tapped a control, "Engineering." Josephine looked at the panel on the chair, it wasn't needed but it was an old habit; "I've been requested at the Science Ministry, I think Persephone is getting one of her crazy ideas. You have command until Taven or myself return." Fyar nodded at the Warp Matrix, "sure thing let me know what she's come up with." Josephine smiled "I'll make sure you're the first person I tell, Bridge out." Josephine walked towards the ISTiS, she tapped a control and the door slid up. She walked inside and tapped a control key on the interior panel. She said to nobody in particular, "SARA override normal functions, crosslink with the Main Transporter Array and send me directly to the Ministry of Science, Director's Office." SARA's voice filled the small room, "transport sequence in progress, stand by." Josephine was struck by a bolt of teal lightning and encircled by ribbons of energy as the transport sequence finished.

Persephone was seated at her desk. One of the Scientists was rubbing his face. Persephone adjusted the stylus behind her ear, "okay Ferus, out with it." He rubbed his forehead and sat forward slightly. "Well, normally we're anthropologists, what do you need us for?" Persephone pulled the stylus from behind her ear and tapped the display on her desk, keying in information as she went.

She read the results and sat back slightly in her chair. "It lists all of you as holding high-level clearance in Archaeology, Anthropology, Engineering and you specifically in High Output Engineering, Bio-molecular Storage Systems and Systems Maintenance is that correct?" Ferus shook his head "yes, that's true, but I haven't used my Engineering skills in over ten years, since I began working for the Ministry." Persephone tapped the screen a few more times. "It lists here that your previous position was as a Star Drive Maintenance Systems Specialist in the Sirian Exploration Division." Ferus again nodded "it was, I took the job with the Science Ministry because I got tired of talking to the Warp Core." Persephone couldn't help but let a giggle slip, she had just imagined Ferus petting the Warp Core and praising it for being a good little power plant. At the back of the room near the door, a fork of lightning struck and Josephine began to materialize. Persephone's eye was caught by it, "ah, here she is". Josephine's body was caressed by spinning ribbons of teal electricity as she entered the room, "okay I'm here, now what's so important that you pulled me away from my repairs?" Persephone tapped a control on the desk, the window tinted and the lights dimmed. The large display's energy ribbons made the room a gentle teal in colouration. Persephone tapped the bottom of her stylus and it grew in size to be more of a pointer. "Okay, we're all painfully aware that we're on a clock until this asteroid impacts Mesira. I've had my team, which was aboard the Jovus with me, working on what the problem was that caused our Torpedoes to blast the asteroid's surface off instead of shattering it. We've found two very unsettling things about this particular asteroid's composition. I was unable to ascertain the geological makeup of the asteroid at the time the Solaran engaged it, if I'd known what it was made of, I would have aborted the mission right there." Persephone leaned over the desk tapping keys on her keyboard, the image on the Main Screen shifted from one of Atlanka to one of the asteroid split into sections based on chemical makeup. She moved back over near the display, "this is the asteroid as SARA has evaluated it, and I know where our problem is. The exterior crust and sub-layer consist of Titanium and Iron, and the inner layer consists of random deposits of Iron Ferrite. All those materials are easily destroyed by our weapons; however, the layer beneath it was shrouded by Tevene Gas. That's why our Sensors couldn't penetrate it and it's also why the Solaran was enveloped in a white cloud that obscured all her Sensors. The material beneath the gas is Varium. Nothing we have will disrupt it, even our most powerful Molecular Disruptors will only reorganize the matter, they will not shatter it." Persephone tapped a control on the panel on her desk, the lights rose and the windows tinted back to clear. "We need a new plan, those fighters the Council is sending will be completely ineffective." Ferus crossed his arms, "well what are you suggesting since you obviously have some kind of plan already half-formulated." Persephone tapped the bottom of her stylus again and it retracted, she slipped it back behind her ear as she typed into her keyboard again and the schematic of Atlanka displayed once more. She sat back down at her desk and clasped her hands. "If we cannot get the asteroid out of our way, we must get out of its way." Josephine brushed her hair behind her ear and bit her lower lip, she knew exactly where Persephone was going with this and she knew the risks involved. She was not surprised now, that her sister had summoned her for this meeting. Ferus looked back to Josephine and saw her discomfort, he looked back at Persephone, "you can't be thinking...?" Persephone looked down briefly and breathed in deeply; she looked back up and assumed a strong position. "This City is a mobile Star Base designed for movement and redeployment. I have already assessed the condition of the critical systems, they are not in heavy disrepair, but I need a crew of professionals. Jo, I asked you here because I need your experience in Atlanka's Engine Room, but I also need the Jovus under her own power and out of Dry Dock within twenty-four hours. I know she suffered a lot of damage, just get her Engines online, that's your team's priority. I want you heading up the repairs to Atlanka's Main Star Drive, pull whoever you need from the Engineering District. Ferus, I need you and your team to assist Josephine, but I also need you to refit the Bio-Storage Cores and ensure everything is in the green. I want this as a viable option, if we need to uproot, I need this City airborne." Josephine rubbed her neck, "I'll have to get down into the old Engineering Room and manually pull every Ion Control Panel and inspect the Power Flow Matrices manually." Persephone looked towards Ferus. "While she checks out the Engines, I need your team in the main Bio-Core distribution area, checking system status and initiating system start-up. I want those systems hot if we need them." Josephine nodded at Persephone, "then if you'll excuse me Seph, I have an Engine to nursemaid". Ferus stood, "and we have to get started as well". Persephone stood and shook Ferus' hand. "I wish this wasn't necessary, I don't want to leave Mesira behind. This has been my home all my life, but I have over one million people to think of in the City, they're my first priority, let's get the job done." Josephine tapped the Comm on her wrist, "SARA acknowledge, override Safety Protocol Set 271, transport me directly to SIV Atlanka Engineering Core." SARA responded "Processing, Core access confirmed, transport in progress." Josephine was encircled in twisting ribbons of teal energy and dematerialized away. Ferus headed for the door "we'll give you a report on our progress in a few hours." He tapped a control and the door slid open. He nodded at Persephone in confirmation as he and his team left her office. Persephone drifted over to the window, she put her hand on the sill, and lightly touched a flower in the corner. She spoke softly to it. "I will not let any casualties come from this, enough good people have died, I will not permit any more, this time no mistakes!"

FAILSAFE

In the darkness of the unlit Engineering Room, a teal bolt of lightning split the blackness. Twisting ribbons of energy spun down from the ceiling and Josephine materialized into the Engineering Section just left of the Main Console. The Engineering Core of Atlanka had no appreciable lighting. There were random flashes of energy from light fixtures that had decayed over time and were malfunctioning. She looked around the room, the Main Engineering Console was offset from the middle of the room in the Forward Quarter nearest the Main Access Door. The only reason she could see it was because the panel was flickering in the darkness. The dim light from the computer panels played off the golden walls as they flickered and flashed. Clearly, this section had not seen any life for many years. Forward of the Main Console was a large area with four displays along the walls, two Secondary Consoles in the Centre Rear of the room laid out back to back, so that the Officers working on them could face each other. Beyond that, lay the Main Systems Monitoring Screen. Two of the four displays on the left and one on the right of the walls were flickering. Only one screen near the Right Centre of the room was functioning correctly. Obviously, the Trans-optical Connections had decayed over time and the system was suffering from gross disrepair. The Main Screen was half-covered in snow distortion and flickered and jumped occasionally. The Secondary Console on the right of the room was only half-lit, the other half was flickering randomly. Josephine stood for a moment gaping at the apparent lack of care this section had received, "what a mess!" The comment was to nobody in particular, but the scope of the visual neglect was overwhelming. Josephine brushed her hair behind her ears and pulled an elastic tie from her vest pocket. Tying her hair back into a rather messy ponytail, she again took one last look over the room. The Engineering Section itself was of an older design, one which she could barely see. It was evident that some damage had befallen the Primary Systems. The Main Screen reported leakage in the Fuel System and there were fissures in the Main Driver Coils, likely a result of intrusion by animals.

She looked around, there were several spider webs strewn along the walls and across the Engineering Section in general. She moved over to the Main Control Console and curiously found a Sirian Plasma Arc Pistol and a note on paper of all things taped to it. She picked up the pistol, removing the note she read it. "To whoever picks up this pistol, you're going to need it, you should be finding out why right about....now." Josephine heard a screech from behind her, she spun around to see a group of three rather large spiders eyeing her hungrily. She gasped just as they charged at her. She raised the pistol and fired several discharges rapidly, striking all three spiders. They were not dead, stunned heavily, but not dead. Josephine began to turn towards the console when she heard a chattering noise from across the room, then a squeal. She heard the sound of running feet. Unable to initially make out what was running towards her, she knew that squeal all too well and then she saw it. It was an enlarged Tero Rat, she fired the pistol but her uninvited guest darted out of the way. Still chasing towards her, she fired again as the rat dashed out of the way a second time. She followed its path, wanting a clear shot. She did not have the time she wanted, the rat found a place and leapt towards her; she discharged the pistol rapidly in all directions, frantic to hit the flying rodent before it hit her. As luck would have it, the rat was in midair about to hit her square on, and one of the discharges struck the rat right in the belly. The rat hit the floor, not three Fika's from her feet shuddering and convulsing. Josephine turned quickly towards the console, "I'll need it indeed, whoever left that note should be praised, or shot." She brought the Main Power Systems online and raised the lights in the Core. Erecting Security Fields over the access tubes leading to the Main Drive Coils and Fuel Assembly, she was then safe from any other unexpected visitors. She tapped a Comm Control on the panel. "Josephine to Science Ministry, Director's Office, oh Seph, are you still there?" Persephone drifted back to the desk from the window and tapped the Comm Panel. "I'm here, did you find the Engine Room?" Josephine eyed the pistol, "I did, and I found some rather insistent friends here who wanted to have me for dinner. Is the Ubrean Forest still densely populated with spiders and Tero Rats?" Persephone raised an eyebrow, "yes, why?" Josephine smiled from the other end, "just going to send my hosts home before they wake up, Atlanka Core Out." Josephine opened up the Transporter Controls and looked towards the now incapacitated spiders, "sorry fellas, this time you don't get your dinner." Josephine keyed in the coordinates of the Ubrean Forest's densest zone. She hit a couple more keys and tapped the console once more. The animals were transported out in a vortex of twisting energy ribbons. Josephine moved towards the Main Core Control Array and removed the lower systems plate to pull out one of the Felasadine Crystal Control Boards. She began to inspect Atlanka's Main Systems closely.

Persephone tapped the Comm Panel, "Persephone to Ferus, be aware Josephine had some furry companions waiting for her when she got to the Engineering Core, hold off going into the Bio-Core. I am sending a Security Detail to sweep the room and secure the area for you." Ferus had just walked out of the ISTiS onto the deck where the Bio-Core was, it was similarly lit, dim and ominous. These sections of the Star Drive had been powered down centuries ago. They were left on automated running and hadn't been used for ages. The City was fully capable of controlling and regulating its own functions by automation, of course, it was not able to repair any damage done by animals burrowing inside. There was the sound of tapping down the hall passed where he could see, and a loud screech came from one of the adjoining rooms at the end of the corridor. He moved towards the wall and tapped a Comm Panel - "furry companions?

I probably don't want to know. It sounds like we have some visitors down here as well, I've heard some odd noises from down the hall. We'll hold here until the security team gives us the green light." Persephone was still bent over her desk "thank you, work safely. You're down in the lower decks, that section has been unoccupied for over several hundred years, watch your back." The Comm chirped and Persephone tapped the panel a few times to switch channels. Taven's voice crackled through, "it's almost time for our meeting with Sorvan." Persephone straightened up, "thanks Taven, I've been monitoring the teams I sent into the lower levels of the City. I'll meet you at the ISTiS Terminal nearest Sorvan's building. Can you remind Tyra and Romal of the time as well?" Taven's voice once again sizzled in response, "Romal's here with me but I'll contact Tyra and remind her, she's probably lost in paperwork." Persephone tapped a control on the front of her desk and a drawer slid out, she quickly grabbed a pink scrunchie from it. She pulled her hair back into a ponytail, flipped it and gave it a tug, "I'm on my way".

Ferus was propped up against the wall waiting when the Security Team arrived. They wore standard Sirian Defense Uniforms, but overtop they wore tan-coloured armour. On their hips, they wore Arc Pistols as side arms and they carried Plasma Bolt Rifles as their main weapons. The squad leader walked over to Ferus and raised his targeting reticle which was an Enhanced Target Acquisition Device that was positioned over the squad leader's right eye, "we heard you have something of a rodent problem?" Ferus nodded, "I'm not entirely sure what's down there but since we're unarmed..." The soldier tapped Ferus' shoulder "not to worry, that's what we're here for". The soldier looked behind him to his squad, "alright guys you heard the man, time for a little exterminating." The soldier almost had a grin across his face as he said it. He and his team flipped down their targeting reticles and clicked a couple of buttons on their rifles. Their reticles glowed amber and their rifles had a teal stream of encased lightning that glowed from just under the Discharge Emitter. Amber light shone from one side of the rifle, piercing the darkness. It was obviously an Electro-luminescent sight, a low light illumination system designed for easy acquisition of targets in a low light environment. The team moved forward, near the first door the leader raised his hand in a fist, and then motioned towards the facing wall and the squad split in two. The leader moved to the opposite side of the door and reaching, began to slowly retract it open with his hand. As he did, numerous scraping sounds were heard. One of his team members laughed heartily, "woo hoo, this is where the fun begins. Pick your targets, boys, let's clear the room." A flurry of gunfire ensued, and the hallway echoed a brilliant pulsating teal. Almost mesmerizing, you could forget that it was caused by lethal bolts of plasma energy. As the last shot fired, the squad leader motioned to Ferus, "alright guys this room is clear, you can set to work in here. We're going to check the other rooms and finish up with whatever is left down here." Ferus walked over and grasped his hand, "thank you". The soldier just smiled, "Hey, it's what we do".

The room was of a similar design to that of the Main Engineering Core, the only noticeable differences were four large cylinders with wrapping view screens inset into the corners of the room. They were the Main Core Control Monitoring Stations, and there was a massive Control Array just in front of them in the centre of the room. Again like the Engine Core, there was a large display which constantly showed details pertinent to this system and its adjoining facets. The Main Console sat atop a slightly elevated area, which had brushed gold bars surrounding it. Ferus and his team walked into the room - it stank. The floor was littered with animal waste and now dead carcasses. Ferus covered his face with his hand, it didn't help but somehow it made him feel like retching less. He motioned to one of the other team members, "get Environmental Systems online, I want the pressure in this room reversed and fresh air pumped in. You two transport these dead animals into the forest, try to get as much of the waste out of here as you can while you do it. The Environmental System will take care of the rest." The team broke into three, it took a few minutes but without Ferus taking much notice, he was blinded by a cascading teal glow that filled the entire room as the animals dematerialized. Most of the debris was gone, the walls were still filthy and the floor stained, but otherwise, the area was clean. Ferus' immediate Second called over to him, "Ferus, I've got the Environmental Systems online, I can initiate a Plasma Wash over the Bulkheads and Deck Plates as soon as you're ready." Ferus motioned to the other two to join them on the raised control platform. The Ship intelligently sensed the location of the room's occupants, it patiently waited for them to leave the area to be cleaned. Then, a shower of rippling teal energy filled the room, carefully tuned to not hit the Control Area, it was like watching a midnight thunderstorm all around you. The shower ended and SARA spoke up, "plasma wash on Primary Deck has been completed, please vacate the Control Area for the final phase." Ferus pointed to the lower level and they moved to the lower deck. The Control Platform was bathed in a brilliant teal light, much brighter than the main wash due to the confined space it was in. When completed, SARA piped up again "full plasma cleansing of this room has been completed." Ferus took a deep breath of the newly recirculated air, "ahhh fresh air, well more or less. Alright I need you three on the Consoles, I want to know the integrity of the Storage Cores, and I'm going to go check the Main Transfer Control Matrix. Ferus walked over to the Main Monitoring Console and tapped a few keys. The lights raised and the Consoles sprang to life.

"There, now that's better isn't it". The comment wasn't directed at anyone but rather to the Ship. Ferus had always had a fascination with this particular class of Star Ship it was unique, there were few produced and they were scattered across the Sector. He'd only seen one other on a planet in the Kertan System. Kertan VI had the sister City to Atlanka, Vorala, and it was just as old. Ferus tapped a couple more keys and looked over towards the door on the right side of the room. He tapped one more icon and a loud clunk was heard and the door slid up. SARA spoke the obvious "Core access has been granted". This

City had a Vocal Access System, most Sirian vessels had a lower version of this system, still very functional but much less irritating. Ferus looked up "thank you". He walked over to the now open door and poked his head in; still slightly anxious about unannounced guests, he quickly shook off the notion and walked in. It was a silly feeling, if anything had been in the room, it would have been vaporized when the Plasma Maintenance System washed the room clean. The room itself housed an additional four large cylindrical Cores and a large screen on the far wall. Two vertical keypads lay beneath it, and a large indent below. Ferus moved over to the screen, after reading the information listed on the screen, he tapped symbols into the right keypad. A door slid up at eye level and SARA responded, "Primary Core access denied. Retinal scan authorization is required for core access approval." Ferus moved over to the newly opened panel, "request Atlanka Bio-Core Access". SARA responded, "standby, scanning". A green beam shot out from the panel straight into his eye, a shimmering white line moved up and down the beam twice before it retracted back into the panel. The panel slid down and the bottom indent slid up. As a massive keyboard slid out, SARA spoke once more. "Atlanka Core authorization approved". Ferus looked down at the keyboard, "thank you, now maybe I can finally get some work done". He looked up at the main readouts and returned to watching what his fingers were doing.

Josephine was in one of her normal positions, her body was half inside the wall, her left leg over her right, whistling contently while she poured over every last millimetre of the Engine Systems. Her hands were filthy, covered in muck but she didn't care. She was most at home in the Core of an Engine and she loved it that way. What she was seeing though was anything but good news, she would need to pull help down from the Jovus to repair the Main Drive Coils and there was another even more troubling matter. The Fuel Feed System wasn't just clogged, a clog was easy enough to deal with. A widespread plasma beam and the way would be cleared. What she was seeing she was growing more and more concerned over. There was obvious stress in the Fuel Storage Tanks, several showed signs of small fractures in the inner skin. Because Atlanka's Fuel Lines had been leaking and plugged with debris, this further complicated things as the reserve fuel for her Main Ion Engines was quite low. If she didn't stop the leaks immediately this ship would never fly again. She was trying to siphon off the tanks' feeds to conserve as much fuel as possible, her hand was between two release valves when she slipped and her hand caught one. "Ouch, Son of a...! Great this is the last thing I need right now." She wriggled out from the wall, as she got up holding her hand to stem the bleeding, she walked over to the Main Console and tapped the Comm. "Atlanka Engine Core to Tetra Municipal Hospital. I've cut my hand pretty good, could you send a nurse over to heal the wound." A man's voice crackled through the Comm, "understood Core, someone should be with you shortly". Josephine drew air through her teeth and the pain shot into her fingernails. "Doctors, always on their own time clock." From her left, she saw the ISTiS matter sequence start and Rachel materialized. With her medical kit in hand, she walked over shaking her head. "What have you done this time?" Josephine nodded towards the partially disassembled wall, "I was trying to siphon off the fuel lines to retain what's left in the tanks, the lines are leaking quite badly." Rachel pulled a Medical Regenerator from her kit and pressed it to Josephine's hand. Josephine cringed as her flesh knitted together, it wasn't a pleasant experience. Rachel looked at her while she healed her hand, "aren't you supposed to wear Dermabrasive Gloves when working on any parts in the Main Engine System?" Josephine winced "yeah, I know, I was in a hurry, the system needs to be shut off or we'll lose the rest of the fuel." "Well", Rachel removed the device from her hand and wiped the blood clean. "You've lost more time now than you would have had you worn the gloves in the first place, your hand's as good as new." She grabbed a pair of gloves and hit Josephine on the head with them, "now wear your gloves!" Josephine rubbed her palm, "okay, okay." Rachel nodded in response, "good, I don't want to have to come back down here again. " She walked over to the wall and tapped the Comm panel, "Rachel, ready to return to Tetra Hospital". A voice responded, "standby, initiating". The room filled with a warm teal glow and as cascading ribbons of teal energy spun around Rachel she dematerialized away. Josephine got up from the console she'd rested on, she began to walk back and stopped. Looking down at the gloves she'd been slapped with, she shook her head and grabbed them then returned to her work.

Persephone made haste down the hall towards the ISTiS, tapping the controls as soon as she was in range. She immediately selected the Lower Central Platform and as a lightning bolt struck her, a vortex of teal energy spun around her until she vanished from the room. The square glowed randomly with the comings and goings of people, it was at the corner of a reasonably busy street. Vehicles floated past and people walked by, very much like any city you would find on any planet in the Sirian Empire. Taven was standing on the street corner near a fountain when Persephone flashed in; she walked straight over to him and clasped his hand. "Our backup plan is in motion." Taven shook his head, "I still think you're out of your mind, moving this monstrosity is a task even when it's in shape to do so." Persephone nodded as they started to make their way up the stairs. "I know, but I need something to bring to Sorvan, he's counting on me to give him options." As Taven got to the door, he guided Persephone forward, "I just hope he doesn't shoot you down in flames, because I don't think we have any other options." Persephone again nodded as they walked towards the ISTiS, "we don't, and this is the only way to avoid disaster".

The two walked into the ISTiS. The building itself was fairly ordinary, it was a standard residential construct from a very plain databank of stacked housing. The front area itself was small except for two fountains on either side of the door and a short entranceway leading to the ISTiS. Taven tapped in their destination on the keypad and the door slid down, in a moment they were on the correct level and stepped out into the corridor,

It was like most other Sirian buildings. Between the apartments, there was a vertical rectangular window. Two lines of lighting ran down the corners of the roof, the floor was a sand-coloured marble. The walls were painted a soft light brown, amber sconces gave the hall a soft mood. Taven started to walk down the hall, Persephone tugged on his arm stopping him just short of Sorvan's home. "Taven", she brushed a lock of hair behind her ear and seemed to stop to think for a moment, she gazed up at him her eyes glossy, deep with worry. "What if this doesn't work, if we can't get this ship flying by the time that thing gets here, all these people - I can't risk their lives, I can't, I won't put them in jeopardy on the chance we succeed." Taven rubbed the back of his fingers down her face, "how much extra Crew space is on the Helia?" Persephone sniffed, obviously trying to manage her own uncertainty. "I don't know, it's a big Ship but this city and everyone here, we don't have time to call for transports." Taven put his hands on her shoulders as if to silently reassure her, "We put as many civilians and Scientists on board the Helia and Jovus as we can. We tow the Solaran out with the Helia and we pile as many people as we can fit into the Crew Shuttles for the city. If all goes well, we can all rendezvous on Vercor II in the next solar system." Persephone looked deep into his eyes, "what if I'm wrong?" Taven took her hand, "in the Command Academy I learned a great deal, but one of the greatest lessons I learned was always remain positive, even in the face of certain doom, and never be wrong. When you walk in there you're right and this is the way it has to be, there is no other way." He ran a finger through her hair, "purge all doubt from your mind, this is your call. You're Director for a reason, they trust you, now trust yourself." Persephone kissed his cheek, smiled and nodded in acceptance. "Let's get this over with". Persephone pressed the chime for the door and waited a moment, Sorvan answered. "Seph, Taven, I'm glad you could make it. I don't usually conduct affairs from my home, but this is far from a normal situation." Sorvan showed them in, his home was modest. A screen on the far wall entertained what was obviously his young daughter, a woman's voice hummed from the other side of the apartment. It was tan, as was most Sirian architecture, a carpet of deep brown covered the home from wall to wall. A plant or two adorned the floor while images of the family hung from the walls. He led them into the living area and shooed the little girl on the couch. "Celia, go play in your room okay? I need to talk to these people." The little girl nodded and as she passed Persephone she stopped briefly and looked up. "Miss, are you going to save the world from the big rock?" Persephone dropped to her level, "oh I hope so sweetie. Run along now." Sorvan noticed her straining to keep her emotions in check, she'd always been a soft soul but this was obviously causing her great emotional strain. Sorvan reached for her hand to bring her back up, "can I fix you a drink?" Persephone nodded, "thank you, I could use one." Sorvan moved over to a cabinet in the corner, taking out a crystal container he added without turning, "anything for you Taven?" Taven nodded, "whatever you have in mind for Seph, I think we both could use it." Sorvan nodded as he poured three small glasses. He brought them back to Taven and Persephone and motioned towards the couch. After a long group sip he sat back, "yes, I was made aware of the events on the Jovus, you took a big risk." Taven nodded, "if I hadn't tried, if I hadn't attempted to do something to give those lives meaning, what kind of leader would I be?" Sorvan nodded, "still there are those on the Council who would disagree. Lucky for you someone stepped in and saved your hide." Sorvan eyed Persephone, "a gutsy move for you regardless of your position, one I would not have expected you to take for a comrade who had made an error in judgement." Sorvan raised his hands, "regardless of his intentions, or is there something else I should know about?" Taven looked at Persephone then back at Sorvan, "it isn't a defence or political issue". Sorvan leaned forward and placed his drink on the table. "It becomes an issue when the Director of the Science Ministry assumes responsibility for something she did not do, now are either of you going to tell me the truth or would you like to continue this charade?"

Persephone sighed, "Taven and I have become, attached". Sorvan looked at Taven, then to Persephone, he again looked back to Taven and once again at Persephone. "Attached as in....?" Persephone nodded "yeah, that..." Sorvan burst out laughing a hearty belly laugh, "it's about time, do you know how long she's been eyeing you. I told her months ago to do something, but she was too scared. Well now it makes sense, and I guess I don't need this". Sorvan tossed a small crystal onto the table. Taven eyed it guardedly, Sorvan pointed at him, "take it, your secret is safe with me." He pointed at Taven once more, "you treat her proper, understand?" Sorvan leaned back in his chair, "now then, on to more important matters. The squadron is formed up and is prepping for interception. We hope to chisel enough material away that we can use the Helia's Repulsors to move this blasted thing before it can do any harm." Persephone took another sip of her drink and placed it down. " About that, you may want to recall those fighters. I have reason to believe they will be completely ineffective and could suffer damage or possibly worse." Sorvan looked rather shocked, "you suggested this and now you're telling me that it's a bad idea?" Persephone nodded and brushed her hair out of her face. Sorvan seemed more than slightly irritated, "care to tell me why?" Persephone rested her hands on her lap, "after we got back, I had the Team that was there with us start a detailed analysis of the composition of the asteroid. I know why the Solaran was hit so badly and why it couldn't evade the asteroid chunk that was slammed into it." Sorvan sat back and interlocked his fingers, "now you have my attention". Persephone continued, "the reason the Solaran lost all Sensor Telemetry and was suddenly flying blind, is because it was enveloped in a thick mist of Tevene gas". Sorvan sat forward "what, Tevene gas is extremely rare and not native to this solar system!" Persephone nodded, "and highly volatile. If the Solaran hadn't veered and collided with that asteroid when she did, the death toll aboard would have been a total loss. As you know, Tevene gas is pretty stable until it's exposed to superheated plasma, like our weapon's fire." Sorvan sat back and slumped, "my God, why do I get the feeling the other shoe hasn't dropped yet". Persephone took off her left shoe, held it in front of her and dropped it. "Because the asteroid's Core is pure Varium, nothing we have will affect it, not even the Bitanium explosives placed in orbit will stop it."

Sorvan leaned forward and held his head in his hands. After a moment to regain his composure, he looked back up, "do you have any ideas on how to slow this thing down, stop it, blow it up? I don't care, but it's got to move". Persephone bit her lower lip, hesitant but she spoke despite her fear. "I have one, I have a Team already in the lower levels of Atlanka working on repairs. Josephine, my sister is in the Engine Core trying to get the Engines fixed. Ferus and a Team of Scientific Engineers are in the Bio-Core restarting the Matter Conversion System. They could both use help to accomplish their tasks." Sorvan got up, rubbing the back of his neck with his hand, "you can't be serious, you're talking about moving this City?" Persephone looked up at him, "this is a Mobile Deployment Platform, it's designed to move." Sorvan walked across the room, "yes but it's centuries old, Star Ships this age just don't move, this City was placed on this moon because her service career was over and her Space Frame was no longer strong enough to handle warp speeds. Now you're asking me to restart a dangerously old system and place the entire inhabitants of this City into suspension?" Taven interrupted, "not everybody, we'd evacuate every civilian and Scientist we could onto the Star Ships in orbit and the transport craft Atlanka carries with her. We'd execute the move of the City with minimal staff and with as few people in the buffer as possible. I know it sounds risky, but if Seph has proven one thing," he looked towards her, "it's that her crazy ideas usually work in the end". Sorvan shook his head, "I don't know, this sounds very risky. I cannot make a decision like this alone; I must call an emergency meeting of the Council." Taven and Persephone rose from the couch to their feet, Persephone looked at Sorvan with the deepest sincerity. "Do hurry, every moment we waste making decisions is one less moment we spend preparing this Ship for transit."

Sorvan motioned to the door, "then as much as I hate to be a bad host, if you'll excuse me, I have some heads to knock together." Taven and Persephone walked out of the door and it slid down behind them. Persephone wrapped her arms around Taven, "thank you". She broke the embrace quickly and moved down the hall back towards the ISTiS. Taven looked over to her, "do you think the Council will approve?" Persephone's brow had tightened, a look he knew all too well when she'd dug her heels in. She looked at him as they reached the ISTiS, she pressed the icon to open the door and spoke. "Whether they agree or not this City is moving. I'll do it without their permission if necessary and most of my team will help me." Taven nodded as they walked into the ISTiS and the door slid down. Taven looked over to her, "you know they'll have your head?" Persephone gazed back at him "either that or they'll call me a hero, either way, it's fine with me." Persephone returned her gaze forward and spoke in a firm tone to SARA, "Jovus!" In a twisting vortex of teal energy, they were gone, and only the hum of the power conduits remained.

The Jovus was still in Star Dock, repairs being done on her Main Power Distribution Net. Most of the crew was either in Atlanka or had boarded the Helia for the return trip to the Sirius System. Persephone walked out of the ISTiS and onto the Bridge. "Taven do you mind if I use a secure channel in your office?" Taven motioned towards the Starboard side of the Bridge, "not at all". Persephone walked in and went immediately to the facing wall. Tapping three amber icons on the instrument panel, the wall retracted and a computer screen slid out. "SARA, give me the locations of Captains Tyra and Romal, Commander Josephine of the SIV Jovus, CMO Rachel of the SIV Helia and the remaining Bridge Crew of the SIV Jovus." SARA was silent for a few moments then responded "I have located the individuals you have requested." Pesephone sat down at Taven's, desk tapping a few keys on the keyboard she once again addressed SARA. "SARA, open a secure channel to all persons for simultaneous transmission." SARA responded "channel open." Persephone tapped a few keys in sequence "lock channel". Three ascending beeps signified a secure transmission. Persephone began what she hoped would be the only time she completely disregarded standard procedure. "Rachel, Jo, all of you, I'm transmitting on a secure carrier wave. I need to see this entire group on board the Jovus in one hour." Josephine's voice was the only one to speak "we'll be there". Persephone closed the channel and looked over at Taven, "you know, I don't think either of us has slept since we were on the Helia coming back." Taven nodded, "we've been too busy." Persephone got up and walked over to Taven. Wrapping her arms around him, she yawned "I'm going to try to get a half-hour of sleep, wake me before they arrive?" Taven rubbed her back "of course". Persephone smiled "mmm thanks Tav". She patted him twice on the shoulder and walked out of the room heading towards the ISTiS and then home. Persephone walked in the door of her apartment, she didn't bother to turn the lights on. She found the nearest couch and simply fell onto it. Within a few moments, she was fast asleep.

OPERATION ATLANKA

Taven was still in his office, he'd tried to catch a nap in his chair but sleep had evaded him. His mind raced with images and feelings. The thought of losing Atlanka City, his home for most of his life was so disturbing, that it made his heart sink with sorrow. He knew how Persephone felt, different reasons causing their shared heartache, but the sadness remained. He turned to gaze at the stars, Mesira's soft blue globe seemed to beckon him home. He got up from his chair and walked close to the window behind him. His office was one of the few areas on the Jovus that had not taken massive internal damage. Most of the internal superstructure of the Ship was in tatters, deck plates had heaved, conduit and piping dangled from the ceiling and wall after wall was blown out. Only his office and the Bridge had sustained less damage because they were heavily shielded from explosions. He stood in silent contemplation watching Mesira turn silently, eternally. He spoke to the walls and the plants, the desk and the chairs. Not that they listened nor cared what he said, but speaking seemed to ease his tension slightly. "I won't let you come to harm, not when I've safeguarded you for so many years. If I don't come home to you, I don't come home. Over my dead body will Atlanka City be destroyed." His outer monologue was interrupted by SARA, "Captain Taven, You asked me to remind you to wake Director Persephone at the time." Taven smiled at SARA's lilting voice, "thank you SARA, how are you handling all of this?." SARA's voice filled the room, "I am having difficulty processing the thought of having to move the city from its current location, I have become accustomed to the area and this place to me is familiar. It will be difficult to leave it behind." Taven turned and ran his fingers across his desk, "I know how you feel, please transfer control of the Jovus to automatic and initiate sleep mode until I return". SARA responded, "understood, low power mode has been activated, I will await your return." Taven made his way out of his office, the lights that were left were dim, he watched his step. The amber Control Pad of the ISTiS shone brightly in the dim light, he tapped a key and the door slid up. He walked in and touched four keys in sequence, the ISTiS hummed warmly. Then he vanished into a vortex of teal energy. Taven was transported into Persephone's building and onto her floor. The door slid up and he walked casually out of the ISTiS. He hadn't been to her apartment before this crisis but he knew where she lived. He had been looking forward to dinner and some personal time with her before all of this started; a thought that seemed so far away now, that he wished for the simplicity of that time again. At that moment, he wished for nothing more than no threats, no trouble and nothing to do except talk to and spend time with the woman he'd been intimidated by for over three years. In a way he thought, he had to thank the current situation, if it wasn't for being thrust together in this crisis and having to work so closely, he might never have had the nerve to tell her how he felt. Still, he had a job to do, as did she and if they and Atlanka City were to survive the next forty-eight hours, they both needed to be at their best, a large helping of luck would be appreciated as well. Persephone's apartment was unlocked, almost all but the most paranoid citizens didn't lock their homes. Crime was virtually unheard of, aside from the occasional crime of passion, it had been almost completely wiped out. Taven tapped three amber keys on the wall next to Persephone's door. As it slid up he took a single step in, it was quite dark. He took a quick look around in the dim light, he was about to look away when he caught a speck of light. Persephone's Science Ministry Insignia shimmered in the darkness. She was still out cold, he smiled and thought, "she must have forgotten to set an alarm, no wonder she asked me to make sure she was up". Taven walked over to her and knelt beside the couch; brushing a lock of hair that had fallen across her face away, he leaned forward and kissed her forehead. Persephone's eyes fluttered open, a smile crept across her lips quickly followed by a grimace and a yawn. "It's not an hour already?" Taven's beamed a large smile at the question, "almost, forty-five minutes actually, but I thought you'd want to be alert when the Team transported aboard". Persephone patted his face, "mmm hmm, you know me too well". Taven stood and reached for her hand, "I'm getting there."

Persephone stood and straightened her jacket. Shaking her fingers through her hair, she looked at him and grinned, "I bet you're scared senseless". Taven put an arm across her shoulder, "oh, I'm positively terrified my dear, shall we?" Persephone smiled and locked her arm into his, "yes let's". lowered his arm and they clasped hands as they walked out of Persephone's apartment, she stopped and stood for a moment gazing back at her home. Taven walked up beside her, "it'll still be here when we're done". Persephone turned her head, her hair gently falling against her back, "oh I hope so." The lights were still off and the shadows of furniture and plants echoed from the darkness, the door to Persephone's apartment slid down. She and Taven walked together down the hall. Taven put his arm around her waist once more, "whatever happens, we stay together." Persephone looked to the side, "always".

Taven and Persephone walked down the hall towards the ISTiS, Taven tapped two keys together and the ISTiS door slid up. The couple walked in and Taven called out to SARA, "SIV Jovus, Bridge". The door slid down and they were both consumed by a torrent of twisting teal energy ribbons. As they materialized on the Jovus SARA came online and remarked, "welcome back Captain, as per your instructions, backup power systems are coming online." Taven smiled, "thank you SARA." Persephone drifted over to Taven's chair and gazed down at it. So much had happened and it was weighing heavily on her. Taven found it hard to watch her struggle with a situation she had never dreamed of but he was so proud of how she had handled things thus far. At that moment, the Transport System beeped just as Tyra and Romal materialized into the ISTiS. Shortly following them were Clinch, Rachel, Josephine, Juice, Adelaide and a moment later Fyar, Tezra and Trell. Most of the Bridge Officers of both the Jovus and the Helia were here, and now Persephone had to make her case, dismal as it was.   Persephone greeted the group and ran a finger around her ear, tucking a lock of hair that was becoming annoying out of her face. "Taven, is the Conference Room on Deck Six repaired yet?" Taven shook his head, "no, we've been making propulsion a priority. Engineering and the adjoining sections are still a mess. Actually, most of the Ship is a disaster at the moment." A cold chill ran up Persephone's spine but she shook herself fairly quickly, "okay, we meet here, find a seat."   The group marginally dispersed across the Bridge. Taven sat in his usual place as Captain. Persephone at his side, she began her long explanation, going into vivid detail about the events on the Solaran, why it was affected and subsequently severely damaged and the dark prospects of the events of the next forty-seven hours, if they didn't take matters into their own hands. The group was stunned at the explanation, Tyra looked especially shocked.

Persephone was just finishing her explanation, as Tyra got up from the Helm where she'd been seated. She drifted over to the Main View Screen, normally full of stars as the Ship travelled from star to star, now devoid of all life, black and its edges charred and partially melted. Her heart sunk into her stomach as Persephone finished elaborating. "Nothing in the entire Sirian Weapons Arsenal, including experimental designs will be effective against this target. The asteroid's core is pure Varium with a liquid Tevene sheath over it. The most we will accomplish is stripping the exterior shell and flooding half the solar system in Tevene Sensor interference. Tyra's hand floated up to her chin as she gazed into the blackness before her. "So what do we do, abandon the city? There isn't enough space on my Ship to accommodate over a million people. The Life Support Systems can't create enough oxygen, even if we were to cram every room and corridor with evacuees. We would all die on the return trip to Siria Prime from asphyxiation. Atlanka's transport Shuttles only hold forty souls before their Support Systems become over-taxed, and they have very finite supplies of power to operate their systems. Overload them and the entire Shuttle would lose power. How do we evacuate so many, you can't be suggesting we leave them here to die with the City?" Persephone walked over to Tyra and gave her a huge hug, "never". She stared into her friend's eyes, trying to reassure her and only half succeeding, "that being said and let nobody think otherwise, we must find another solution. It's obvious that the asteroid isn't getting out of our way, so we must remove ourselves from its path of destruction. Clinch had been eyeing the Science Station and interrupted, "call me crazy but can't we simply focus all the Helia's Tractor Repulsors into a concentrated pattern and push it out of the way?" Persephone shook her head. "I considered that first, but the Solaran is a wreck and the Jovus isn't much better off. We would need all three ships to even begin to affect its course and the only operable ship right now is the Helia. Her Power Systems just don't put out enough force to alter the asteroid's trajectory, think of it like an ant pushing a mountain. No, we need a real solution, I have come up with one, but it carries extreme risk. There is also a high probability that the Council will not see the impending danger, and will seek other alternatives categorizing this as too risky. Rachel was moving back and forth in her chair and stopped, she leaned forward and crossed her legs, "what are you suggesting?" Persephone tapped a few keys on the Conn, the once black main screen sputtered and sparks flew out from the sides as it struggled to come to life. Arcs of energy finally split the air as the Main Screen powered on. An image of Mesira, Atlanka and what would be an exit trajectory out of the gravity well of both Mesira and Terra. Trell looked positively shocked, "you want to move the City?" Persephone tapped a couple more icons on the panel and an icon indicated exact movements. "It's the only way to safeguard everybody's lives in the city." Rachel pointed at the screen "the Council will never agree to this, not only is it risky as hell, but they'll view it as desperate and the Council never operates in desperation". Persephone nodded "I know, that's why I called you all here. You've all worked together for many years, some of you have known me for longer. I cannot do this alone, I need help but I'm confident that this is the only option available to us. I know Atlanka is old but I think she can handle one last adventure. This is not an official request from the Ministry, I'm acting so far outside the rules, I'm having to fight myself. Know that if you decide to help me you will be called for an inquiry at the very least, but most likely you'll lose your career and your commission. I'm asking as your friend please, help me save our home. Anybody who is unwilling to accept the consequences of this action or who does not want to risk their career, you're free to leave the Bridge. Nobody will think less of you if you do." Persephone cringed as she said the words, she needed every last one of them, and the loss of anyone would be absolutely devastating.

A tear got passed her emotional barricade, she watched the Bridge and waited. Not one of them moved a muscle, Taven reached up and touched her arm, "I think you have your answer". Pesephone's eyes betrayed her as another tear rolled down her other cheek. She looked at the floor for a moment to combat the emotional roller coaster she was riding, "thank you, thank you all. We'll probably never see the stars from orbit again, but we'll still see the sky from our home. Now, we have a lot of work to do and very little time to accomplish it. Clinch, Josephine, pull repair teams four, seven and twenty-six from the work on the Solaran. Take them to the Engineering Core under the guise of repairing the affected systems because people have been complaining of Power Flow interruptions. Rachel, Adelaide and Fyar, I need you in the Bio-Core. That system has to be perfect, I won't risk a single soul. The rest of you, pull the rest of the team off of the Solaran, and put them to work on getting the Engines on this ship online. When that thing hits, I want this ship out of range. Tyra, the Solaran's your job. I need her out of the Repair Pits and back in space. I don't care if you set her adrift five-hundred thousand

Fikans out of orbit, but I want her out of any possible shockwaves. Perhaps on the other side of Terra, so the atmosphere will deflect anything away from the ship. Tyra nodded, "We should pick who's going to crew Atlanka's Bridge." Persephone thought a moment, "I think we should stick to as few people as possible. Taven, do you feel up to the responsibility of commanding that Ship?" Taven looked around the Jovus, "Clinch when the time comes, I want you in command, your standing orders are to get to a safe distance and wait for instructions." Tyra piped up, "you'll need an experienced Command Officer for your Executive." Josephine grabbed Fyar "and the best two Engineers in the galaxy getting that old girl off the ground". Fyar looked at Josephine, "oh thanks for volunteering me." Josephine grinned at him, "no problem, don't mention it". Fyar looked forward, "oh don't worry, I will". Persephone giggled, Rachel called from across the room. "With all that power and the possibility of systems failing, you'll need your best Medic with you. Adelaide, when the time comes, I want you aboard the Helia, you're to take over my duties until I either return or the Ship docks at Siria Prime, whichever comes first. Tyra looked at Trell, "I'm trusting you with the Helia. Don't hurt my ship, she's your responsibility". Taven looked at Tezra, "I know you're assigned to the Jovus, but I want you on the Bridge of the Helia. Siria Prime needs to know what's gone on here, I'm trusting you to deliver that information." Persephone walked over to just in front of the Main View Screen. "The Council doesn't know about this meeting, and we need to keep it that way. I don't have their answer as yet and until they say yes, we're working under the assumption they'll refuse. Keep this under your hats and try to work without raising suspicion, but I don't need to stress that Atlanka must be airborne in forty-four hours or we're too late." The group nodded in understanding, Persephone tapped a key on Taven's chair and the Main Screen winked off. "Right, let's get the job done." Taven leaned over to her and said quietly, "one mountain scaled." Persephone leaned back over and responded, "that was the easy part, making this happen will need a miracle".

The Communications Station blinked and an alarm chirped indicating an incoming transmission. Persephone drifted over to the panel with Taven. Taven tapped a key and Sorvan's face appeared on a small monitor encased in the station. "The Council is requesting to meet with Seph immediately". Persephone tapped a key and responded, "I'll be there shortly". Sorvan nodded, "alright, don't be long". The screen blanked out and Persephone looked at Taven, "here it comes". As she headed for the ISTiS Taven said to her, "do you think there's a chance they'll understand." Persephone shook her head, "they're politicians, what do you think"? Taven looked at her with a defeated expression, "right..." She stepped into the ISTiS and the door slid down. Persephone called to SARA, "override standard transport procedure and lock on Council Chambers, Atlanka City." SARA was silent for a moment then spoke, "I have a transport lock." Persephone straightened up, "initiate". As she was struck by a bolt of teal electricity, cascading energy ribbons enveloped her as she dematerialized out of the Ship.

The matter stream was a wash of colour the entire spectrum danced like ribbons twisting in the wind. Persephone always loved that about the ISTiS, the wonderful colours during transport. As she admired the shower of colour, it evaporated giving way to the Council Chamber. Sorvan stood next to her, First Minister Ben'veh was seated across from them, most of the Council had been dismissed and it was just the three of them. Ben'veh rubbed his forehead, "Director Persephone, you have convinced Sorvan here of the impending doom. I, however, and the bulk of the Council remain skeptical. You are suggesting very dangerous solutions to a problem that has yet to be verified." Persephone's astonishment must have blasted through every corridor and room in the City as she spoke her mind, "what?! Are you and the Council blind? What part of indestructible and unstoppable did you fail to comprehend? How much more basic do I need to make this?! What counts as verification? When the spires of this city are vaporized by an explosion that will rip the planet in half?!" Persephone looked over to Sorvan, "you showed him the information on the data crystal I gave you, right?" Sorvan nodded, "yes I did, and they don't believe it's that severe". Persephone was fuming now, her rage was impossible to hide as she looked over to Ben'veh, "who told you that?" Ben'veh gestured in a very casual manner to her, "your staff on Siria Prime." Persephone's jaw dropped but she quickly recovered. "They are subordinates for a reason, they don't know what I do about Quantum and Hyperdimensional Physics. Aside from me smashing some heads together when I get back to the core worlds, I'm telling you right now, Those fighters will do nothing but make matters worse and I promise you, this City will be obliterated in less than forty-four hours if you continue to do nothing." Ben'veh folded his tablet up into its case, "I'm sorry, but it is going to take far more than the word of one emotionally troubled Scientist to convince me, I'm taking you off this assignment, I will assign someone with a far cooler head." Persephone was flabbergasted, "you can't be serious, you're pulling me now?!" Ben'veh shook his head, "take a vacation Seph, you obviously need it." Persephone retorted in clear shock, "WHAT?!!" Ben'veh looked directly at her, "that wasn't a request!" Persephone turned on her heels, "fine! have it your way!" She stormed out of the Council Chambers, Sorvan who'd been watching the entire exchange like a spectator at a tennis match didn't know which way to jump, as Persephone got to the door he chased after her, "Seph, Seph wait." Persephone kept walking, "why? Are you going to try to convince me I need help too?" Sorvan stopped dead in his tracks and called after her, "no I'm agreeing with you." Persephone halted midstride, Sorvan walked up from behind her, "the Council is wrong, I've seen the data and the composition of the rock. You're right, whatever you need, tell me. I'll help you, this is my home too." Persephone's fuming rage vanished in a fluttered heartbeat, astounded by his willingness to sacrifice everything, she was speechless, "you know what you're saying?" Sorvan placed a hand on her shoulder, "I've been around long enough to know how things work, and I've known you since you were a child. You don't put your back against the wall unless there is no other option. I know you, and I know you're doing this because you're certain beyond a shadow of a doubt." Persephone sniffed slightly, she hadn't expected support from him. She had always thought of him as a second father, he'd been there for her for so long. To hear him say that, she finally believed that the connection went both ways. "Can you keep the Council off balance? I need them to keep looking the other way".

Sorvan motioned towards a balcony, "this way, we can talk freely against the sound of the city". It was late evening, in the time it had taken to put the team to work and meet with the Council, two hours had passed. They were two hours closer to zero hour. As Persephone walked out onto the balcony, her hair caught the evening breeze and was tossed around behind her head, strands flew into her face and she brushed them away. Sorvan motioned for her to stand close, "I know about the two teams down in the bowels of the city working on repairs." Persephone's heart jumped, she didn't know what he was going to say next. Sorvan smiled warmly, "I made sure they got past the Sensor Grid without being seen. They're already ahead of schedule but I fear there is so much to do preparing the City for transit, we will run out of time." Persephone turned and put an arm on the railing, "then we need to prioritize our time to accomplish the most in the least time available." Sorvan nodded, "agreed." Persephone's gaze shifted as she watched the traffic move by and the sun set on the City. Sorvan's eyes glimmered in the dim light. "I suggest we get the Jovus' Engines online as quickly as possible, and then we take a skeleton crew aboard the Helia tonight and rip the Solaran from its moorings." Persephone shook her head to toss her hair out of her face, "how do you propose to get that massive Ship past the City without anybody seeing her?" Sorvan's eyes shone brightly as the City's streetlamps began to switch on, "ever heard of running silent?" Persephone tilted her head slightly, "with that Ship? The power curve is next to impossible to mask." Sorvan poked her, "not when you're the finest Scientist in the empire". Persephone thought, "the problem with reducing the

Helia's power curve during atmospheric flight, is the required energy to sustain the Antigrav Generators and the Thrusters needed to move the Ship." Sorvan nodded, "what if we powered down every system except for basic propulsion and the Antigrav Generators during our approach." Persephone bit her lower lip in heavy thought, running complex calculations on power curve requirements; she rubbed her temple. "That would ease the power signature, but we have two other problems. With the power that low, the Ship itself would be hell to handle; moreover, we have the problem of still being visible to the naked eye, much less the issue of the Ship possibly being too heavy to sustain flight while registering power that low." Sorvan leaned over the railing and watched the sapphire night sky envelop the vibrant colours of dusk. "What if we altered the Ship's mass using the Graviton Emitter on the Main Astrogation Deflector Dish? We should be able to envelop the Ship in an Inverse Polarity Gravimetric Field." Persephone looked over at him surprised at the solution, "an interesting approach, if the field is balanced to the opposite of the magnetic pole of Mesira, we might be able to sustain flight on magnetics alone, without needing the Antigrav Generators online at all. Ahh, but there's a problem. The magnetic field fluctuates across the surface of the planet, how would we balance and manage the field symmetry that quickly?" Sorvan stood for a long time and then had what could only be described as a Eureka moment. "SARA could do it, we could preprogram the approach course and let her use the Forward Sensor Bank to intelligently read the terrain ahead and make corrections faster than any of us could." Persephone tapped her foot, "that could potentially work. The Main Sensor Array uses a fraction of the power that the Antigrav Generators do. We only need it for the approach, once we're in position, we bring the ship up to full power, snatch the Solaran and make our escape." Persephone stood for a moment before she lifted her head, "SARA have you been listening?" SARA's voice softly rode upon the breeze, "I have Director, I believe your plan has merit." Persephone wasn't sure but she thought she saw a glimmer of light near the railing by her hand, as it coalesced a woman's face appeared, built from holographic particles. It was silver in colour with grey eyes and hair that looked like fine strands of platinum. Persephone wasn't sure but her instincts were soon proven correct. SARA continued from her now projected self, "please excuse my sudden appearance but I felt the situation warranted a face-to-face discussion." Sorvan looked at the face, now with its holographic hair catching the breeze, "SARA?" SARA smiled widely, "Hello my friend, it is good to see you." Sorvan was surprised, "you too, I didn't know you had a physical appearance." SARA responded, "I hadn't until recent events made me reevaluate my position and I realized that a face helps with communication, especially in times of stress. Persephone smiled at the thought and asked SARA, "are you up to the challenge of guiding the Helia in on low power?" SARA turned to Persephone and again smiled, "I am more than capable of performing such a function, you need only provide me with the details and I will take it from there." Persephone nodded, "thank you SARA, your support means a great deal." SARA responded, "I have no desire to see this part of myself destroyed nor the souls in my care harmed in any way. It is my primary responsibility to safeguard the people in this city and all other imperial ships, installations and colonies. You are all very dear to me and I protect you from harm as best I can." Persephone understood precisely what SARA meant and nodded her approval, "we'll pass you the information as soon as we have it." SARA nodded, "very well, I will await your instructions. Good day Director...Minister." Sorvan nodded and SARA's image faded, "well that was unexpected." Persephone looked over with both amazement and joy shining from her face, "indeed, but I think it's a good change and one we need." Sorvan looked back out into the now darkening cityscape, "It's a good plan, but where are we going to put the Solaran while we execute the remainder of the plan, I would rather not set her adrift in space. We risk the Vortakans seizing the vessel while we work to save the city." Persephone nodded, "the Vortakans, nobody has seen or heard from them in three centuries." Sorvan tapped his foot, "you didn't hear this from me, but our Intelligence Operatives have intercepted several Vortakan transmissions aimed at what we believe is uninhabited space. They suggest a military buildup of some kind, but there is no indication as to what or where they are massing for. It, however, has given the Sirian High Council cause for concern." Persephone nodded, "let's not risk it then. Wait, we're on a moon, there's a huge planet below us, which is, for the most part, uninhabited except for a few pockets of primitive life. Could we place the Solaran on an island in their ocean and burrow her into subspace? That way, she's protected and we know exactly where she is." Sorvan nodded, "that sounds like it would work perfectly." Sorvan turned to Persephone, "got any ideas on how to hijack the Helia?" Persephone grinned, "I'm already ten steps ahead of you." Sorvan smiled, "just a normal day at the office then?" Persephone tapped the Comm Control on her wrist, "Persephone to Josephine." Josephine's voice crackled across the Comm channel, "I'm here Seph, is your end secure?" Persephone shook her head, "no, do you think you can gather your tools and meet me on board the Helia, I need help with a project." Josephine was silent for a moment then her voice snapped through again, "from which toolbox?" Persephone smiled as she knew Jo understood the message. "Captain Tyra keeps one in her office off the Bridge, but I need you to bring yours and Clinch's as well." Josephine's voice broke the silence again, "on my way, I have what you need with me". Persephone motioned to Sorvan and they walked towards the ISTiS, "are you sure you want to do this? This is your last chance to change your mind? After this, there's no turning back." Sorvan nodded, "I'm sure, someone has to keep an eye on you". Persephone tapped the control on the wall and the door slid up, they walked into the ISTiS and Persephone tapped three keys on the panel. She turned to Sorvan, "we're taking a shortcut". She then spoke to SARA, "override standard transport procedure and lock on S.I.V. Helia Main Bridge". SARA responded promptly, "I have a lock, ready for transport.". Persephone straightened her back, "initiate". The room flooded with a teal glow and once again Persephone marvelled at the dancing ribbons of colour before the darkness of the Helia's Bridge burned through and stood in front of her, large and in this light very ominous. Tyra's office door slid open and Tyra walked into the doorway and leaned against the panel holding a toolkit on her index finger. "You mind telling me why you summoned me up here with a toolbox in hand?" Persephone grinned at her, "put the tools down Tyra, you don't need them, but I need you as Captain to summon your Bridge Crew. Josephine and Clinch should be with us momentarily." The corridor behind the Bridge that led to the ISTiS glowed with a soft teal for a moment. Shortly after, Josephine and Clinch came around the corner.

Josephine smiled and held up her tools, "someone called for the most amazing Engineer in the Fleet?" Persephone waved her over, "you forgot beautiful, funny, talented and most importantly modest!" Josephine grinned, "nice to see you too sis, now what kind of trouble are you up to this time?" Persephone pointed at Tyra, Tyra moved forward to the centre chair and tapped a couple of controls. The Comm Lines crackled to life, "S.I.V. Helia recalling key personnel." Several icons blinked across the Conn Panel as a wave of acknowledgements flooded the Comm Array. Within moments, the hum of the ISTiS echoed through the halls several times and the bulk of Tyra's Main Bridge Crew walked onto the Bridge. Persephone stood firm to address them, "we need to break the Solaran out of Dry Dock. As long as she remains there, the Ship is in grave jeopardy. Our task is to fly towards the city under silent running mode, past Atlanka and hover over the Repair Pits. We will then bring the Ship up to full power, lock on the Solaran and get away before anybody realizes what's happened. Hopefully, they suspect raiders or pirates using cloaking technology. The resulting confusion will allow us to complete repairs on Atlanka's Main Ion Thrusters in time and without being discovered. Now once we have the Solaran, we're going to take it to Terra; we plan to scan the ocean to find a secluded island to place her down on. Then using the Main

Deflector we're going to burrow the ship into subspace so that it's indistinguishable to the natives and also hidden from any potential poachers. We'll also have the benefit of knowing exactly where we put her. Setting her adrift means we'd have to tunnel through subspace to locate the ship and then pull her out." Persephone then noted, "SARA has agreed to fly the ship into the atmosphere and get us safely to the repair pits." Trell looked a little uneasy, "are you sure that's wise, handing the ship's controls over to the onboard AI?" A light shimmered across the bridge, bright and almost blinding at first then dimming and forming a shape, as it faded a tall woman emerged. Silver Skin, Platinum hair and grey eyes, just like in her projection but this time she was fully formed. SARA wore a long dress that fluttered around her heels, made from sparkling silver material with two wide straps that went over her shoulders. Tyra and the rest of the bridge crew took a step back as Persephone began to introduce them. "SARA, you know our friends. Everyone, this is SARA, just...in the flesh...kind of." SARA nodded in appreciation and moved to join the group, "it is good to see you all, you need not be concerned for your safety. I have already spoken at length to Persephone about what is needed and I will guide you to your target without incident." Tyra moved over to take a closer look, SARA smiled at her and put a hand on Tyra's shoulder. "it really is me, all of our long talks when you were struggling to find the right path." Tyra smiled widely and wrapped her arms around SARA, hugging her tightly, "Thank you for being here." SARA squeezed her back, "I am preserving myself as much as all of you, however, we do need to begin." Tyra broke away and clapped her hands, rubbing them vigorously, "well, you heard the lady! What are you all standing around for? Take your stations, we have a ship to steal."

LIBERATION OF THE SOLARAN

The lights across the Helia vanished, and her windows blinked out in groups. Her running lights which normally illuminated her Hull blinked off. To anybody else looking on, they would assume the Ship was going into standby mode but that couldn't have been farther from the truth. Aside from a low-level light at the bow of the Ship where the Bridge was, she was completely dark. A black owl prowling for a midnight snack, she began her descent into Mesira's atmosphere. Tyra was seated on the Bridge, on the edge of her seat, her nails almost digging into the leather trim. Persephone was at the Starboard Science Station while Josephine manned the Rear Engineering Console. Persephone was watching the "Z-axis" elevation, she looked over to Clinch. "Watch your dive angle, too fast and we'll emit condensation streaks. We're in no hurry here, take your time." The Helia moved like a silent stalker, and as the outer atmosphere coalesced, the clouds lay beneath her. It was a starlit night, normally a beautiful sight but on this occasion, Persephone had hoped for cloudy skies. Josephine had been watching the power levels from Reactor One, as it approached the yellow line she called out. "The power levels are coming into the detection zone." Tyra spoke without breaking her gaze forward, "SARA, are you ready to take over?" SARA moved to beside clinch at the helm and looked back to Tyra, "I can begin at any time." Tyra sat back in her seat, "alright, time to see if this crazy idea gets us all killed. SARA, the ship is yours." SARA reached out her hand and gently touched the Comm console, as she did her eyes illuminated a brilliant teal glow. A scattering of wild beeps screeched through the halls and echoed in the Bridge and the Helia began to lose altitude fast. Clinch called back to Josephine, "is it supposed to do that?!" Josephine called forward, "I have no idea, this isn't my brilliant plan, ask Seph."

Clinch looked over to Persephone, "well?" Persephone shrugged her shoulders as the Ship shook and convulsed, as it seemingly had lost all control and was plunging to the ground. They were less than one thousand Fikans from the water, Clinch yelled over the sound of straining metal "that's it, I'm enabling the Antigrav Generators and getting us out of here!" SARA touched Clinch's hand for but a moment and gazed down at him, her eyes shimmering with light. "It's alright, I'm in control." Persephone called out hastily, "look!" Clinch's jaw dropped, as less than five hundred Fikas above the water, the Helia hit the magnetic plate. She levelled off and soared across the ocean. "I don't believe it, our altitude is low but stable. We seem to be hugging the contours of the surface beneath us." SARA smiled and took a breath. Persephone beamed and nodded in relief. Tyra looked over to Persephone, "can we stop to grab my stomach on the way back up?" Persephone grinned, "you wouldn't want to leave that behind". Clinch hit a few controls on the Helm. " Atlanka City directly ahead." Persephone looked on, "we should be starting to veer west right about now." As she finished her sentence, the Ship tilted slightly and began a slow turn west. Clinch turned his chair to look at Persephone, "how far out are we going?" Atlanka City grew in size but slowly slipped off the right side of the screen. Persephone looked on, "about five-hundred Fikans, then we turn around and approach the Atlanka Repair Pits from the southeast." Josephine was minding the Engines but took a moment to check the time, "ten minutes to shift change for Atlanka Defence Teams." Persephone quickly turned her chair and began wildly tapping keys on the Science Console. Tyra looked over and was curious, "what are you doing?" Persephone spoke without breaking her concentration, "I'm configuring the Main Sensor Bank to deliver a massive ultrasonic burst from the Main Astrogation Dish Array. It shouldn't affect any person in the City but the burst should knock out any Monitoring Systems for a few seconds. With luck, nobody will know we were there until tomorrow morning when the crews find the ship missing." Tyra was impressed, "ingenious". Persephone turned briefly and grinned, "I thought so". She turned back around and returned to her programming. The great Wings of the Helia slid by the City without notice. Against the night sky, her darkened form stalked the ground silently, prowling along the terrain until she could not even be distinguished from background shadows. Persephone checked their course from her station, "not long now. Course reversal in five....four....three....two.............now!" As she said it, the Ship again tilted on her axis and turned slowly, patiently. The now distant spires of the City were a stark contrast against the black night. So far, they had escaped notice, but that was all about to change. Tyra watched with intent as they slid closer to the City, "cut the Engines, Reverse Thrusters, bring us in on inertia." SARA inhaled slightly and closed her eyes. The ship began to slow until she was silently moving over the landscape without a whisper. Persephone turned and winced to see through the blackness of the night. Most of the industrial areas were powered down at night, as nobody was working there unless it was an emergency. Persephone pointed, "there that's the one. Jo you know what to do." Josephine nodded, "ready on Full System restart". Tyra watched as they slinked over the Solaran's Repair Dock. "Alright, bring us to station-keeping. SARA, opened her eyes, "we're in position." Steady, alright Seph, you're on." Persephone tapped a few keys in ascending sequence, "Packet Storm initiated." Josephine called from the Aft Station, "initiating Engine restart, standby". The Helia hung like a giant black night owl waiting for a feast, her Wings silent against the night sky. Josephine called out from the Aft Station, "Generators at full capacity restart sequence in progress". SARA lifted her hand from the Conn panel and as her eyes returned to their soft grey, she looked down at Clinch, "I believe you know what to do from here." Clinch gave her a cheeky grin just as the night was shattered by the Helia's running lights, her windows illuminated in sections down her Hull, her Navigational Beacons lit at the tips of her Wings and her Main Ion Engines rose to a warm amber glow.

Tyra looked at Persephone, "lock on the Solaran, we're in it now." Persephone's hands flew across the panel, "I have a lock but the Tractor Beams won't engage, the Mooring Struts are still locked into her Hull. Tyra got up, "dammit! Clinch, do a quick scan for the coolant pressure tanks. They should be near the Main Struts and to the side. Clinch drew his hands across the amber panel, "got them". Tyra leaned over, "I want a narrow beam shot from the Forward Plasma Emitters. Don't touch the Solaran, but I need those Struts superheated." Clinch nodded, "firing". Two searing teal beams of plasma erupted from the Helia's Wings. The rails that held the Solaran in place began to groan and glow white-hot. Persephone's time program beeped from above her, "we have less than sixty seconds before the Sensor Net is back up." Tyra leaned over Clinch, "pour it on, I want that Ship loose. Seph, lock in the coordinates and set the Tractor Beams to cross-link." Persephone's hands danced across the keys, "set." Tyra watched as her tension grew, "come on baby, we're trying to save you." Clinch's display lit up, "structural weakness, The Main Braces giving way." Tyra spun around, "now get those Beams on." Persephone hit a large icon in the centre on the Main Panel and two forks of vibrant teal lightning shot out from both Wings. Pulsing with white lines, the tug of the Tractor System began to break the Solaran free. The Solaran groaned under the strain, shaking and quaking, she began to slowly raise out of the Pit she was in. Persephone was monitoring, "thirty seconds!" Tyra looked to Clinch, "the instant we're clear, I want full speed out of the atmosphere, tuck us behind the second moon and we'll hold there while we scan for a place to set down." Clinch nodded, "got it". Persephone called out again, "fifteen seconds". Tyra called behind her, "Set Ion Drive to flight configuration, Main Coils to one-hundred and fifty percent and bring Main Engines to full standby, we're going to do a burnout." Josephine was already halfway through the sequence before Tyra said a word, as she finished Josephine looked up, "ready to go." Persephone called out again, "five seconds!" Sorvan had been monitoring the progress of the Solaran, "she's clear!" Tyra spun her chair around to the Main Screen, "ENGAGE!". With that, the Helia's great Wings scooped up the Solaran and tucked it beneath her belly. She rose up off the ground, dust flying across several hundred feet from her Thrusters, her Bow lifted slightly and her Main Ion Engines flashed a blinding teal light and she tore off into the atmosphere. The Ship was quaking under the pressure, Josephine's hands moved at a blinding speed. "Tractors exceeding tolerance, if we don't break free of the atmosphere, we're going to lose her." Tyra called out amid the chaos, "I'm not losing that ship! Reserve power to the Emitters, Clinch, get us out of the atmosphere." Josephine hit a control and called down to Engineering, "Juice, take the safeties offline." A frazzled voice came back "what?!" Josephine responded, "I don't have time to explain, do as you're told. Take the Reactor safeties offline now!"

Juice's voice shook through the groaning metal screaming under the pressure throughout the Ship. "Safeties off, whatever you're going to do, make it quick." Josephine spoke out loud with each step, "ramping up Main Fuel Feeds to three-hundred percent, overheating Drive Plasma by thirty-five degrees. Flooding Main Drive Coils with coolant, releasing superheated plasma into Main Drive Reaction Chamber. Ramping up Engine output to two-hundred percent above normal." Josephine's Engineering Panel was cascading with blinking red indicators and warning lights. "Clinch, you should have the power now, but make it snappy." Clinch yelled above the klaxons and groaning metal, "the board shows green". Tyra leaned forward, "punch it!" The entire ship rocked under the power increase, lights flashed on and off, and the Helia's Engines became a brilliant red as she penetrated the outer atmosphere and escaped the planet's gravitational well." Tyra yelled over the noise, "are we there yet?" Josephine yelled back, Mesira's gravitational well is subsiding, reading background radiation ahead. Gravity drain is approaching zero, I'm reversing the Engines." Josephine tapped the Comm Panel on her station, "Juice, are you alive down there?" Juice's voice came back over the Comms, "are you trying to get us all killed?" Josephine grinned, "re-engage the safeties and take the Main Engines offline while I run a full diagnostic." Juice's voice crackled through the system "you'll get no argument from me." Tyra got up and patted Clinch on the shoulder, get us behind that moon." Tyra looked over to Josephine, "can I breathe now?" Josephine smiled as Tyra walked over to the Conn. "Was there any damage to the engines after all that?" Josephine leaned over the Helm momentarily and tapped a few controls. After she had checked a few readouts, she stood back up and gestured towards the Engineering Station, "not that I can see but Juice should give the Engines a full check as soon as we get the Solaran placed."

Tyra nodded and tapped her Comm Interface, "Juice, how are my Engines?" Juice was silent for a few moments and then responded, "I don't know what Jo did, but the searing on the Main Drive Coils is superficial at most. When we're done with this business, you've got to tell me where you learned that trick." Josephine spoke from beside Tyra, "once we get Atlanka moved, I'll tell you that story and many more over a hot pot of coffee at my place." Juice's voice crackled through the Intercom, "you got a deal". Tyra got up and moved over to Persephone who was still at the Science Station across the Bridge, "once we get behind that moon, you can access the entire Sensor Suite from Deck Two Section C." Persephone nodded, "let me make sure our passenger is fully secured and tucked in". Tyra smiled, "good work, both you and your sister, and indeed all of you. Now, if you'll excuse me. I'll be in my office trying to get the colour back in my knuckles." Persephone snickered, "stone white are they?" Tyra leaned over and whispered in her ear, "with this job, sometimes I'm surprised that my hair isn't the same colour."

Persephone grinned and Tyra walked across the Bridge and into her office. Persephone double-checked the Emitter Pads and Plasma Seals, SARA had reported some mild stress damage on the Port and Starboard Emitters. The Tractor Beams were functional, however, and operating at 100%, they could park in orbit and conduct repairs once they had secured the Solaran on the surface. Persephone looked at the screen, as they looped passed Terra's second moon Laana, a vast horizon lay before them. The sun was behind the curve of Terra's surface, as they began their pass over the northern pole, it peeked out from behind Terra and cast a warm glow over both the Helia and the planet below. The Helia caught the beams of the sun like a radiant golden owl, her vast Wingspan tilting slightly as she caught a magnetic anomaly in the atmosphere. Persephone smiled as she watched the Main View Screen, the view never got tiresome even near home. She got up and walked over to her sister, who had returned to the Engineering Station and had been managing the plasma flow from the Main Star Drive. Persephone leaned against the console, "so how did we fare?" Josephine tapped a couple of controls and hit a few more above her head, "all in all not too bad. Some buckling on the Starboard Engine and some stress damage on the two Main Tractor Emitters. I think Reactor four overloaded, we may have to do some internal reconstruction, it could have been worse." Persephone asked, "so that trick with the Engines wasn't some random idea you plucked out of your head was it? You've done that before haven't you?" Josephine looked over as she conducted some diagnostics on the Tractor Systems, "yes, three years ago on the Serus we came out of warp into what should have been a three-planet binary Star System and instead we got caught in a collapsed star's gravity well. We would have been crushed like an egg too, had I not dumped superheated Ion induction fuel into the Main Drive Coils, we almost didn't make it". Persephone crossed her arms, "how come you never told me this". Josephine looked at her and then back to her work, "you were always worried about me being in the Sirian Navy, I didn't want to give you ammunition to say I told you so." Persephone smiled and raised an eyebrow, "well, I told you so!" Josephine nodded, "you just couldn't resist could you?" Persephone shook her head, "nope, but in all seriousness, it's my job to worry about you". Persephone placed a hand on Josephine's shoulder, "after all, we're family". Josephine smiled and grasped Persephone's hand, "truer words were never spoken." "Listen Seph, I have maintenance to do and you should be on Deck Two, you need to find us a place to drop our package". Persephone nodded, "Sorvan's already down there. I saw him take off shortly after we started our pass over Laana. I should go see what he's come up with." Josephine looked to the side, "let me know when you find something hmm?" Persephone nodded, "sure thing." Persephone made her way across the Bridge to the ISTiS, walking inside she listened to the door slide shut. She let out a huge sigh, one mountain moved, now the next. Her moment of silent calm was interrupted by SARA's request, " what is your destination, Director?" Persephone rubbed her neck, "back to work, right, Deck Two Science Array." The gentle hum of the ISTiS enveloped her and she closed her eyes as she was bathed in swirls of dancing colour.

The ride to Deck Two took longer than usual. The Helia was running on half power because they had been performing shadow maneuvers near Atlanka City just before grabbing the Solaran. The other two Main Reactors had been shut down to minimize the Helia's power signature and had not been brought online yet. As Persephone phased in, she opened her eyes to a spectacle of dancing colours that swished away as the transport cycle completed. She took a deep breath, and made a move towards the door, as it slid up she walked out onto the deck. The deck was dark, lights flickered in the walls and the overhead lighting flashed erratically. Persephone looked down one side of the corridor then the other, noticing a Repair Team a few doors down the hall from her, she figured a Power Transfer Node had failed during their ascent. Her curiosity being satisfied she turned down the hall from the work crew and walked a few rooms away from the ISTiS. Touching an amber panel on the wall, the door she came to slid up and she walked into the room. The room was lit with both amber standard lighting and an amber glow from all the stations along both walls and the massive Center Console. Sorvan was on one side of the Main Science Array in the centre of the room. Bent over, he poked his head up as Persephone walked in. "Seph, come in I think I have a few options." Persephone tucked her hair behind her ear and walked over to where Sorvan was working. She looked over his shoulder and then leaned against the console folding her arms. "You know it's starting to look like the Jovus out there". Sorvan stopped for a moment and turned to her, "let's just hope that it doesn't end up looking like the Solaran before we're finished. I'd like to have at least one Ship come out of this intact." Persephone smiled and walked into the Semicircle Console, tapping a few keys near the top, a large monitor on the wall crackled to life and displayed a sensor image of Terra. Sorvan moved towards Persephone, standing at the Main Console next to her, "I've narrowed our list to three possible choices, I'll bring them up on the Main View Screen." Sorvan pulled a stylus from his vest pocket and tapped several controls on the console. The Main Interface was a Plasma Infused Holographic Interface much like the rest of Sirian technology. The planet shown on the Main Screen spun on its axis and zoomed in to show dunes and a dry desert. Readouts on temperature and climate scrolled on the side of the screen, as various images flashed across. Sorvan pointed at the screen with his stylus, "option one, arid climate and major desert. Benefits: No population, no possibility of water entering the structure and causing collateral damage." Persephone rubbed her neck, "yes, but one good sandstorm and the Ship would be half-buried. I don't want to be worried about the weather and trying to move Atlanka at the same time. Also, see these fissures in the Main Ventral Plating?" She brought up an image of the Solaran's current state of repair on the console in front of them. Persephone pointed to Hull fractures and several damaged areas along the underside of the Ship and along the Main Beam. "If sand gets into these areas, the gritty nature of it could cause just as much secondary damage as water." Sorvan nodded, "alright. Option Two: Arctic climate, similar benefits to Desert climate but cold will preserve her internal systems." Persephone tapped through schematics of the Solaran and shook her head. "I don't know, these Hull breaches near the Main Reactors could cause problems. If snow gets in there and melts, it could short out the entire Reactor Control Network and cause them to go supercritical." Sorvan nodded, "okay Option Three: Temperate island climate. This one's a lot riskier, but we don't have the problem of the Ship being buried by snow or sandstorms, we do however have the possibility of rain." Persephone's head fell, "once, just once, I'd like something to be simple." Sorvan seemed hesitant, "there's one other complication I should mention. There's an indigenous population about twenty-five fikans from the target area, not a serious threat, but should they run across the Ship and gain access..." Persephone rubbed her forehead, "okay, let's think about this for a second, we have a Star Ship in a vulnerable state, The dock for it is prone to rainstorms and water plus electronics is never good. How do we shield the Ship both from the weather and the people living in the area?" Sorvan stared at Persephone, putting his hands in his pockets he shrugged, "I've got nothing." Persephone turned back to the console, "me neither". She started tapping through diagnostic readouts, "wait a second, it says here that the Primary Power Conduits have been repaired." Sorvan reached over and tapped a couple of controls on her display, "they were the first priority once Tyra got the ship docked. I insisted that the Power Systems and the Engines were the first to be fixed." Persephone looked at Sorvan, "so does that mean the Engines are operable too?" Sorvan shook his head, "almost but not quite, the Main Plasma Feeds need to be secured and shielded but that's all." Persephone tapped a control or two and moved to an adjacent station, "what about the Main Fusion Reactors?" Sorvan pointed to the reports that Persephone had brought up on the screen in front of her. "The Reactors were repaired and certified ready for use." Persephone's face suddenly glowed as she smiled and turned her head to face Sorvan, "I think I have an idea". Persephone called out to the room, "SARA, what's the condition of the Solaran's Internal Security Grid." Silence followed for a moment before SARA responded, "The Internal Security Grid is intact." Persephone shifted her weight from her left foot to her right, "can the grid be expanded to encompass the Ship entirely?" SARA again was silent for a moment, "The Internal Security

System can be set to a Cascading Particle Mode, however this setting is not recommended." Persephone tilted her head, "why?" SARA responded "the field symmetry is indiscriminate, all bulkheads both internal and external will be shielded." Persephone tapped a couple of icons on the display, and a plate retracted as a keyboard slid up from the console. Persephone typed silently for a few moments. "SARA the Cascading Particle Field, can it be controlled remotely?" SARA was a little faster responding this time, "the field can be controlled remotely, if the command codes of the current Commanding Officer are input into a Sirian Control Network Terminal aboard an Imperial Vessel." Persephone grinned like a schoolgirl, "oh I know exactly how we'll do this." Her fingers flew across the keyboard, Sorvan watched perplexed at what she was actually doing. He only half understood some of what she said to SARA, but he was at a loss to figure out what she was concocting this time.

Persephone hit a few amber icons and called out to SARA again, "SARA pull up a current status schematic for the Solaran and put it on the Main Screen." The Main Screen flickered and crackled with energy. An image of the Solaran replaced the green fertile landscape of Terra. Red areas flashed, indicating major damage points. Persephone stood for a moment in thought before continuing. She spoke as she worked. She knew Sorvan was completely baffled by now, "see, we can form a Cascading Field using the Internal Security System, it'll cover every access point and all the damage as well. Now if I can just attenuate the field strength to both resist precipitation and entry - wait, I think that's got it." Persephone looked up tucking her stylus behind her ear. "SARA, restore the image of Terra's target island." As Persephone issued commands SARA responded almost instantly. "Okay now, pull a graphical image of the Solaran's current state from the Damage Control Records and place the Ship on the ground in that setting. Now initiate the field on the simulation to the specifications I have input into the Main System Command Buffer." The Solaran appeared on the screen on its belly, one wing slumped to the side. An amber light flashed from the inside near the Aft Section and a ribbon of teal electricity painted itself along the internal structure of the Ship. Snapping and arcing as the wake passed along the superstructure, the major Hull breach crackled as it was shielded. Once the simulated activation was complete, a teal shell encompassed where the breaches were. Persephone scratched her head, "okay SARA, real-time scenario using true variables. On the simulation initiate a major thunderstorm." The serene scene changed to that of a raging torrent. Rain whipped sideways, wind howling through the trees, lightning flashing across the sky. "SARA, run an internal sweep of the mock-up, is any precipitation getting through the shielding?" SARA was silent for a long moment. "There is a point zero zero six percent bleed-through". Persephone breathed a sigh of relief as she turned to Sorvan, who'd been remarkably quiet this whole time. "Okay that's one hurdle down, one to go". Sorvan simply shook his head "I was lost with Cascading Particles, I'm a Politician, not a Scientist." Persephone grinned and turned back to the Main Screen, "SARA reset the simulation to the moment of field activation". The serene image of softly rustling leaves and cotton ball clouds returned. "Okay SARA, now give me a random image of the indigenous life forms armed with wooden clubs. Now have them attack the field itself and the Hull. Scan for damage or weak points in the field." SARA played the image of a pack of barbarians beating the Ship and grunting. Persephone stifled a giggle, it was rather funny to see. SARA responded fairly quickly after running the readout. "No weaknesses in the field have been detected". Sorvan moved closer to Persephone, "you know, if they find the Ship, they're not intelligent enough to realize it's impenetrable, what we need is a little pest control." Sorvan called out, "SARA in the current design is it possible to electrify the Hull to give anyone who comes in contact with it a jolt?" SARA was silent in thought before responding. "Electrification of the field is possible; however, the power requirements will be raised by one-hundred and fifty percent for a full field effect". Sorvan looked at Persephone, "that means we're going to have to risk running the reactors at fifty percent power and leaving them online for the duration." Persephone shook her head, "I don't think we have a choice, we've already come this far, she's a tough ship. I think she can handle being left on her own for a day." Sorvan nodded, "I think this is our best bet as well". Persephone took her stylus out from behind her ear and tapped the control to tuck the keyboard away. She called out to SARA one last time, "SARA transfer the details of the Solaran Rescue Project to the Main Engineering Station on the Bridge with an alert priority for Josephine and end simulation." Persephone slipped her stylus into her vest pocket and turned to face Sorvan. "I'd better go tell Tyra we have a plan." Sorvan nodded in agreement, "I'll forward the coordinates of the target island to Clinch and issue an approach plan." Persephone nodded and began to make her way out of the room. She turned just as she was at the door, "I'll see you in a few minutes". Sorvan smiled and nodded then returned to his work.

Persephone walked onto the Bridge; Tyra was in mid-conversation with Josephine and vaguely nodded to acknowledge Persephone was there. Tyra leaned close to Josephine, "are the Second, Third and Fourth Reactors now online?" Josephine nodded, "The Second and Third are online and running at peak efficiency, but the Fourth is showing signs of core stress and damage to its Primary Control Systems. I'm keeping it offline until we can take a look and assess the damage". Tyra sat back in her chair, "it's a wonder we didn't lose power and burn up, I don't ever want to do a one Reactor tractored launch again". Josephine nodded, "no kidding, I'm surprised we got off as light as we did". Tyra motioned to Persephone to come over and looked up at Josephine. "By the way, where did you learn that little trick with the Engines?" Josephine paused for a moment before she answered, "it was before I became Executive Officer on the Jovus. About four years ago, I was Systems Engineer on the S.I.V. Serus and we came out of warp in the gravitational pull of a collapsed star. Stress was so severe on the Ship's frame, we lost four of our Actuator Strips the second we dropped to sublight. We barely had time enough to get our Shields up before the entire Hull was stripped away. Well to make a long story short, I had to get creative fast." Persephone interjected mid-sentence, "one of Jo's specialties as I'm sure you're discovering." Tyra looked behind Josephine at Persephone, "so, have you found a spot for us to put down the Solaran?" Persephone nodded, "Sorvan should be feeding the co-ordinates and atmospheric flight path to the Helm shortly." Clinch turned to Tyra, "it's coming in now, we're to land the Solaran on an island west of what looks like a main continental landmass, the exact location is being extrapolated." Clinch tapped a couple of controls on the console, "SARA please confirm target lock?" SARA's voice filled the Bridge, "the target is locked and your flight plan has been set." Tyra motioned to Clinch's Conn Panel, "whenever you're ready." Clinch turned back towards the Main Screen and entered the final command sequence into the Navigation Array; the Ships Directional Thrusters and speed were set to automatic approach. Clinch's hands lifted off the Main Panel, "that's it we're on our way".

The Helia, which had been tucked behind Laana avoiding the Main Sensor Array of Atlanka City began her turn, banking about fifteen degrees, she spun around until she was facing the horizon of Terra. Her engines rose in light level slowly at first, then peaking at normal, they flashed a brilliant teal and her nose dipped slightly as she started her descent. Tyra was watching the progress from the Bridge as her Ship slowly broke through the stratosphere. She looked to the Science Station where Persephone was watching the black of space fade away to a soft cool blue, "what's the status on our Heat Shielding?" SARA materialized beside Tyra and responded, "the head shielding should be activating momentarily". As she finished her sentence, the Ship's outer edge crackled with electricity and a bubble formed around the two Ships as they dropped further into Terra's now brilliant blue sky. Soft white cotton ball clouds greeted the Helia as she slipped through the atmosphere; passing through a particularly large one, the deep blue of the ocean lay beneath them. Josephine, who was still standing beside Tyra mused to nobody in particular, "it's not that different from home is it". Tyra shook her head, "no, but it's a lot bigger." The Helia dropped to about thirty-five thousand Fikas above the crashing waves of the ocean, her golden shape caught the rays of the sun and she shone like a beacon for a moment. Persephone smiled, "it's absolutely beautiful." A distant speck appeared on the screen. Tyra got up and moved over to the Navigation Console, "is that our target?" Clinch who was sitting back with his arms crossed nodded, "that's it". Tyra looked back to the Main Screen, "it's hard to believe we were right next door but never really explored this planet, such a shame." Persephone piped up from across the Bridge, "well if things go badly, we may have a very long time to explore this planet." Tyra looked at her, "shh, don't be such a pessimist". Persephone pointed to herself, "who me...? never!" Tyra nodded, "right."

She looked down to Clinch who had uncrossed his arms and was checking the target location for dense foliage or anything else that the Main Tractor Array would have to brush aside before they could set the Solaran down. "Not too far now, looks like we'll have to repulse two large trees out of the way, or at least most of their leaves and lighter branches." Tyra tapped his shoulder, "we'll be fine." The island now filled the screen, the Helia's altitude dropped to where she was around twenty-five hundred Fikas. The Solaran's broken Hull soared just above the tree line, as she reached the final few Fikans of her descent her Braking Thrusters raised from the Wings. They were designed as large rectangular Engines, they finished their ascent and locked into place. Glowing a blinding teal, they flashed in several bursts as the Ship slowed to a soft hover over a beautiful green landscape. Now almost totally still, her great Wings stretched over the trees, silent almost haunting the grasslands below. SARA ran her hand along Tyra's Armrest, "we have arrived." Tyra nodded and motioned to Persephone and walked over to her, "alright let's get this over with. Set Ventral Repulsors to twenty-five percent and target those trees." Persephone leaned over the Science Station; brushing a lock of hair out of her face, she tapped the control to raise the auxiliary keyboard. A drawer slid open on the console and a silver keyboard, backlit in amber, rose out and locked into place. Persephone typed commands into it and selected various screens from above her head with her stylus. Two plates on the Nose and the Tail of the Helia's underside retracted and slid open. Four more Tractor Emitters slid out and locked into place, coursing plasma energy rippling across the pads. She turned to Tyra, "okay, the beams are ready to go." Tyra pointed to Josephine, "alright, let's give those trees a gentle nudge." Josephine turned to the Engineering Console and activated the Ventral Emitters. Two forks of teal lightning shot out of the front of the Ship. Another two out of the tail, one was flashing and quaking erratically, violently hitting the tree and knocking several branches off. Josephine called behind her, "I'm having trouble with Tractor Array Four on the Aft Section, it looks like damage from an overloaded plasma coupling. That poor tree is taking a beating." Tyra raised her hand in a motion of frustration, "alright shut it down, we'll have to do this on three Emitters. Jo, run a full diagnostic of the Aft Array, I think that tree has suffered enough." Tyra moved back to the Navigation Station and crossed her arms. "Alright, since you don't want to play nicely, Clinch turn us ninety degrees horizontal axis. Swing the tail until the Fore Array has a clear shot." Clinch nodded, "turning." The Helia's great bulk silently spun above the trees. The Solaran glowed as its wing caught a fleck of sunlight amidst the afternoon sky. Clinch remarked to himself, "okay, we're coming into position now". Tyra walked to the Aft Engineering Station where Josephine was busy working. Josephine looked to the side, "well the second Aft Emitter is toast, it looks like the entire Control Relay is fused. The unit will have to be replaced. As for Emitters One, Two and Three, they look okay. Let's hope it stays that way." Tyra nodded, "well, we haven't got much choice, that ship's got to be landed and we can't simply float here". Josephine nodded. Tyra pointed to the Navigation Station, "alright Clinch, hold us steady, Seph, target and activate the remaining Beams and brush those trees out of the way. Jo, when we have a clear open space, begin the landing sequence for the Solaran."

Teal bolts of lightning rippling with pulses of white light shot into the trees like a sun-lit thunderstorm. Just underneath the tail of the Helia, the two trees directly beneath them rustled and creaked as they were moved out of the way. Tyra moved back towards her chair, "gently, we've done enough damage already." The trees slowly moved farther and farther apart until a sizeable hole was carved into the foliage. Josephine called out from the Aft Station, "we have a clear space, initiating the drop-off procedure." Slowly the Solaran began her descent to the ground. Her superstructure groaned as if to complain about being moved. As she descended, her remaining wing tilted slightly into the now-setting sun. She caught the light and sunbeams shot out from along her curved Wing as if to say I'm alright, I'm home now. The grass fluttered with the air movement and dust flew out from beneath her. As the Solaran touched down, the Tail sparkled catching the light. Josephine was watching the entire manoeuvre when the serenity of the moment was shattered by the piercing call of a hawk and blinking teal lights. The Engineering Station behind her erupted in a shower of sparks flying in every which direction. The Beams that so gently caressed the Solaran began to flicker and shudder. Josephine screamed against the noise, "son of a....!" Tyra fought her way to Josephine to steady her, Josephine called out "it's the Main Power Feed to the Auxilliary Plasma Junction, I knew something wasn't right with it. The power is spiking uncontrolled, if we don't disengage the Beams, we'll crush the Solaran like an egg." Tyra called across the Bridge, "Seph, shut them down!" Persephone was trying to steady herself against the buffeting, "I can't, the Main Control Array is fried, I can't even initiate a plasma dump." Clinch called from the Navigation Console, "Hull stress on the Solaran is passing tolerance, reading micro-fissures forming on all points, total structural failure in thirty seconds." Tyra looked blankly at Persephone, "if you have any brilliant ideas, now would be a good time." Persephone was all of a sudden back on the hot seat, she heard Clinch call out again, "twenty seconds until structural failure, if we don't do something quick..." Persephone called out, "I know, I'm thinking!" Suddenly Persephone's eyes lit up, "blast them off." Tyra was shocked by the suggestion, "you're not serious?" Persephone nodded, "no other choice, we can't sever the power in time and if we destroy that Ship, all the trouble we're already in... you don't want to face the Council and say, "I destroyed a Star Ship". Tyra nodded, "okay you've convinced me, how?" Persephone bit her lower lip, Clinch called out again, "ten seconds, major Hull fracture along the Secondary Support Beam. Projected collateral damage in seventeen sections." Persephone gently moved Tyra out of the way, "got it!" She moved over to the Helm and spoke directly to Clinch, "bring the Main Weapons online and shunt the plasma flow to the Forward Emitters." Clinch turned to face her, "are you sure?" Persephone nodded, "no, but do it anyway." Clinch tapped the panel, "okay, Main Plasma Banks charging....wait for it, okay, weapons are hot." Persephone's next instruction left even Josephine in disbelief. "Target the two Main Tractor Emitters on the Port and Starboard Wings with the Forward Plasma Banks and fire. I want those Emitters destroyed." Clinch shook his head in dismay, "Juice is going to strangle me with his bare hands, firing." Teal arcs of superheated plasma shot out from just beneath the Helia's great hooked beak, impacting the Wings on either side, they flashed with sparks for a few moments, culminating in a huge explosion and a shower of sparks that rained down on the Solaran. Clinch sat stunned, Persephone put a hand on his shoulder. "Juice will have to go through me first." Clinch nodded in appreciation. Tyra looked to Persephone, "is our plan still going to work given the additional damage?" Persephone ran another simulation, "according to SARA everything is still as it was with the Shielding, although I'm not sure if it will be totally effective." Tyra shrugged, "well what choice do we have?" Persephone nodded, "right, hard locking with Solaran databanks. Handshaking, transmitting Romal's authorization and Sirian Fleet Identification. Initiating Cascading Particle Flow." The Solaran's hull sizzled with teal energy ribbons, lightning crackled across her broken frame and a wave of teal washed over every crack and every breach in her Hull. When the field reached the tip, she looked like she was lit up from the inside out, you could see every window and every structural deformation shining a brilliant teal. Persephone breathed a deep sigh as Tyra grabbed her shoulder, Tyra smiled "it's okay Seph, it's done now." Persephone turned to Tyra and returned the smile, shrugging and lifting her hands into the air. "Why can't anything be easy?" Clinch was sitting back in his chair with his arms crossed and retorted from across the Bridge, "oh no Seph, if that happened, it would make our lives boring, can't have that now can we."

Persephone squinted and shook her head, "you would find something amusing about all of this wouldn't you?" Clinch raised his arms up, "that's my charm, a silver lining in every cloud." The door to the ISTiS slid up and Juice walked onto the Bridge, moving over to Tyra he joined her and Persephone at the Science Station. "Is everybody alright, my systems registered a Console explosion up here, but I couldn't respond until now because I was manually balancing the Engines to keep us in the sky." Josephine drifted over, "I was nearby but thankfully not close enough to suffer any injury." Juice nodded, "good good, the Solaran, how is she?" Persephone pulled up a general readout of the Ship's condition for Juice. "Buggar, did more damage did we? Oh, there's going to be hell to pay from the Council about that." Josephine crossed her arms, "it might have been a great deal worse had we not destroyed the Tractor Emitters". Juice's eyes went very wide and his overall attitude turned to a massive frown, "you did what?!" Josephine shrank away slightly as she explained, "if we hadn't, the uncontrolled energy wracking the Tractor Emitters would have crushed the Solaran; it was either the Emitters or an entire Star Ship; we figured that the Emitters were a small price to pay". Juice's expression changed from concern to astonishment then to controlled anger, " Do you have any idea how hard it was to procure those particular Emitters for this ship? I specially ordered them from Sorkana III and spent two weeks of my own spare time installing them." Persephone shrugged, "sorry Juice, we'll get you new Emitters, I promise." Juice slumped, "oh all right, I suppose an entire Star Ship is worth more than a couple o' lousy Tractor Beams. Just tell me before you blow any other components off my Ship please?!" Tyra nodded and brushed Juice towards the ISTiS, "okay okay, we'll make sure you know, but I'm not planning on any more destruction to the Ship." Juice sulked, "alright, I'd better go see how bad the surrounding damage is on the Wings. Hopefully, you didn't completely obliterate the mounting brackets." Juice walked into the ISTiS and tapped the control, all Persephone could see was his head shaking as the door slid down. Tyra walked back over to her chair and sat down, "he's not happy." Persephone gazed at the door, "nope, I don't think I've ever seen him so quiet". Tyra sat back, "and that's what worries me, he put so much of his own time into improving this ship." Persephone walked over to Tyra's chair, "it can all be fixed, nothing is final until you're dead." Tyra sighed, "I know." Motioning to the Helm briefly she calmly remarked, "take us up". The Helia's nose rose to the sun which was now deep in the sky, a wash of red struck the clouds as she began her ascent back up. Persephone watched the beautiful view on the screen and commented to Tyra. "You know if they've discovered what we've done, we're going to get it." Tyra didn't break her gaze from the screen, "oh yeah, and then some". The Helia flew off into the sunset, white stripes slipping from her Wings until she vanished into a cloud of cotton.

WHEN IT RAINS

Tyra watched as the crimson sunset of Terra's sky bled back into the blackness of space, its soft blue globe slipping beneath them. Persephone, who'd started to run a diagnostic of the Main Systems, and Josephine, who was wrist deep into repairs to the Main Engineering Console were completely engrossed in their work. When the Comm chimed all three were momentarily startled, Tyra slumped and looked towards Clinch. "Tell me that's not..." Clinch answered before she even got the words out, "it is, and hopping mad." Tyra rolled her eyes, "here we go, put him on". The Main View Screen crackled with energy, coursing ribbons of teal lightning streaked across the sides as the image flickered on. First Minister Ben-veh stood against a starlit background, his face pink and sweat glistening on his forehead. He was angry at the abduction of the Solaran from Dry Dock and what's worse is that not only was a Sirian Commander and her Star Ship responsible, but the Dock itself sustained significant damage from the forced removal of the vessel. Ben-veh's eyebrows knitted together, "have you lost your mind Tyra?! What in the name of the Five Gods were you thinking?!" His heartbeat obviously racing in a fit of rage, he stood silent for a moment with his eyes closed, he was trying to calm his nerves before addressing the issue. "As much as I would like to have you in my office and revoke your command status over this, the Ministry of Defence needs your Ship to paint a target lock on the asteroid, so our ground-based Torpedo Batteries have a clear path to the target." Tyra was puzzled, "what about the Fighter attack which was scheduled?" Ben-veh shook his head. "That idea has been shelved as it was deemed ineffective." Tyra who herself was now beginning to get more than a little annoyed shook her head, "there's no time for that, if you don't call in a Fleet of Transports now, they will not arrive from our transport facility on Siria Minor in time. You've got to make the call!"

Ben'veh shook his head in stout defiance, "the Council doesn't believe your doom and gloom scenario." Tyra sneered, "you mean YOU don't believe it." Persephone, who'd been working on trying to get the Main Sensor Array back to one-hundred percent spun around and got up from her seat. Her normally soft look now enflamed with passion, "you're a fool, even if, and I stress if you didn't believe Tyra, the fact that you doubt the rest of us as well is positively stupid and borderline criminal! We're telling you as a combined team of trained professionals, that you're WRONG!" Ben'veh pointed a finger at Persephone, "I wouldn't speak to me in that tone again, you're already on very thin ice." Ben'veh turned back to Tyra, "paint your target, confirm impact and then I expect you and your accomplices to report to the Council Chambers." With that, the screen sizzled and winked out. Tyra sat motionless for a few moments, then slapped her chair's arms hard while getting up, "Imbecile!"

Clinch, take us to the designated coordinates. Seph, find Taven and your sister and meet me in my office. I'll be lying down nursing a headache." Tyra turned back to the Navigation Console, "oh and Clinch, alert me when they're ready for us to transmit." Clinch and Persephone nodded. Clinch hit a few controls and the warm blue globe of Mesira slipped off the screen. The Helia softly dropped her Port Wing as she banked lightly to the left. Her engines flashed with a teal glow as she picked up speed and finished her turn. Her nose caught the sun's light and shimmered amidst the black night, her Starboard Thrusters puffed briefly and she completed her turn. Directly ahead now was the massive gas giant Jepatira. As they got closer, their nemesis became all too real, there it was, silently hurtling through space, seemingly unstoppable. The Helia's Engines dropped to a soft warm amber. She slowed, hanging just off the side of the asteroid to avoid debris being caught in Jepatira's gravitational well. Persephone's ride in the ISTiS was not nearly as fast as she would have liked, she emerged in a rush on Deck Three near the farthest section Aft. It was a dimly lit area, much like the Reactor Core Control Array that her sister had described when she was in Engineering School, but it seemed smaller, perhaps Josephine's overzealous enthusiasm had made things seem larger than life. Still, she appreciated the subtle changes in architecture. Small windows dotted the upper area of the wall, the normally brushed gold was instead replaced with a matte finish, and the Alert Status Strip which was ever-present on the upper decks of any Sirian Star Ship, was instead placed above the windows. The recessed centre in the ceiling was absent and instead replaced by soft square amber lights, which cast a virtual absence of illumination. Her eyes adjusted to the dim light momentarily, and she looked down the corridor first towards Port then Starboard. Seeing Taven and Juice kneeling in front of a rather large ominous construct she could only assume was the fourth malfunctioning Reactor, she made her way over. Taven had been working with Juice on getting the Reactor online. They hadn't been having much luck when Persephone walked up behind them and patted Taven on the shoulder. Taven nodded in acknowledgement and put down the Subspace Flux Spanner he'd been using; getting up off his knees he caught sight of Persephone and couldn't help but smile. Persephone returned the smile but was far more occupied with their current situation. "Taven, Tyra wants us to meet her on the Bridge. Has anybody brought you up to speed on what's been happening?" Taven looked out the small window and then back at Persephone, "I've been in the bowels of the Ship with Juice for the past hour or so. Other than dropping off the Solaran, I'm a little out of touch." Persephone motioned towards the ISTiS, "I'll tell you en route, Tyra's waiting". Taven nodded, "let's not keep her then". As they began to walk down the corridor, Persephone explained about Ben'veh's ludicrous plan and his refusal to call in Transports for evacuation. She was just finishing telling him about them being labelled thieves when Clinch's voice crackled over the

Intercom. "Bridge to Taven, we're at the target, please report to the Bridge." Persephone moved towards a dimly lit wall panel and tapped a few keys, "Seph here Clinch, we're on our way." Taven shook his head in disbelief, "I can't believe Ben's being so stubborn, he's jeopardizing the entire City just because he doesn't want to be proven wrong." Persephone and Taven walked up to the ISTiS and she tapped a control. As the door slid up she looked at Taven with that look. He knew it well, she'd dug her heels in. "Someone's going to make him see reason or see to it that he's not a threat. That someone is me!" Taven's eyes went wide, "you're not going to kill him?". Persephone shook her head, "no, but when I'm done with him, he might wish I had". Taven and Persephone walked into the ISTiS and Taven spoke aloud to SARA, "Bridge." With that, the door slid down, they were enveloped by teal energy ribbons and were whisked through the Transit System, to their destination.

The dancing colours of the matter stream were always lovely, strangely Persephone took little notice of them. Usually, the shimmering palette provided a calming sensation, now she hardly noticed it was there. The colours began to fade and then phase away, as the last of the ribbons wound up into the ceilin, she and Taven stepped out of the ISTiS and onto the Bridge. She looked around and caught Clinch pointing to Tyra's office. "She's in her office, nursing a headache." Persephone nodded, "I'm not surprised with all that's going on." Persephone and Taven walked over to the door and Persephone tapped the chime. Tyra was lying down on her couch with her hand over her eyes. It was dimly lit, the dark helped. She was just about to fall asleep when the door chimed, "ugh, come in." Persephone and Taven walked through the door, Clinch who had put the Ship into Auto Station-keeping Mode quickly walked up behind and joined them. Persephone's eyes took a moment to adjust to the dim light, "trying to conserve power?" Tyra sat up and rubbed the back of her neck in obvious discomfort. "No, SARA please return the lights to normal". The lights came up to their standard illumination and Tyra got up from the couch, stretching her arms out front she looked at Taven, "ahh, so has Seph told you what's been happening". Taven motioned to Tyra's chair in a have-a-seat fashion, "yes, I can scarcely believe Ben's being so stupid as to risk the entire City over a matter of pride." Persephone leaned against the wall with her arms crossed, "he's not, because I won't let him". Tyra's gaze shifted from Taven to Persephone, "well, how do you plan to stop him, shoot him?" Persephone shook her head, "no, that's not my style, you know that. Currently, however, I'm scratching my head, say where's Jo, I thought she was supposed to be here." Tyra looked back and forth instinctively, "she was, it's not like her to be late." Persephone nodded, "indeed, I wonder what's keeping her." Tyra hit the Comm Channel on her desk, "Tyra to Josephine, Jo, you were supposed to join Taven and Seph in my office." A moment of silence followed then Josephine's voice crackled over the Intercom, "I was halfway there when I had a brainstorm. Knowing Ben-veh's stubbornness and Seph's temper, I figured she wouldn't take no for an answer." Persephone crossed her arms, "oh, this should be good". Josephine continued her explanation, "obviously calling us in front of the Council is a sure-fire way to get all of us rounded up in one location. In Ben's current frame of mind, he's most likely to have us confined behind a Security Field, not good for the City, large flying space boulders care little for small Force Fields." Persephone scratched the top of her hand, "what did you have in mind". Josephine's voice split the air once again, "obviously none of us can be restrained or else the entire City is doomed, we need a way to incapacitate the entire Council and the Guards in the room." Taven had been listening intently, "how Jo, even if we managed to get past the Weapons Scanners and we were all armed, there are fifteen Guards stationed around the Chamber at all times, they usually do nothing more than stand there, but they are there and they are armed. We can't possibly stun them all and the Council, before someone gets to a Control Pad or gets clear of the room." Josephine's voice once again filled the room, "right, so we need a way to accomplish this simultaneously. Here's my idea, what if we use the Main Bio-Molecular Storage Array?" Persephone's eyes lit up, "you mean put them all into storage?" Josephine responded, "yes". Persephone twirled a lock of hair in thought, "it's a good idea but there's a problem, the Main Transfer Matrix is calibrated to store all persons in the City at once, I don't know if it can be set for a smaller zone." Josephine's voice crackled through the Intercom again, "there's one other hurdle, we're going to be in the room when it activates, so we need a targeted safe zone around us so we're not scooped up as well." Tyra nodded, "can you do it by the time we finish with painting the asteroid for Atlanka?" There was silence for a long moment, "I think so, I'll need Seph's help and maybe Juice too." Persephone nodded, "let's get to it". Tyra looked over to Clinch, who'd been standing in the corner opposite Persephone listening quietly, "are we ready?" Clinch nodded, "we're in position but we have yet to hear from Atlanka on their status." Tyra shook her head, "taking their sweet time, you'd think they didn't understand what the term emergency means". Clinch smiled and looked down, "I'm beginning to wonder." The Comm Panel chimed, Tyra shook her head, "their timing is impeccable." Clinch pointed to the door, "I'll be on the Bridge." Tyra nodded and hit the panel, "yes First Minister?" Ben'veh's voice crackled through the Comm System. "Tyra is your Ship in position?" Tyra nodded to the desk, "we're here, the Main Sensor Matrix is online and ready to transmit." Ben'veh's voice was sharp and unemotional, "good, we're beginning the Primary Firing Sequence." As the Comm Channel closed, a sharp sizzle could be heard. Tyra was growing uncomfortable at the prospect of returning, but she was the Captain and there was a job to be done. She shook herself of the feeling and got up from her desk. As she passed the window on the opposite wall from the door. She stopped and turned to look out, she was drawn to the starlit sky. Oh, how she longed for those boring foliage sampling missions or even Diplomatic endeavours. As she stood gazing out at the blackness, she could just make out Mesira's tiny blue sphere hovering near Terra. As she stared at home, a shiver ran up her spine, a result of the pressure she was under. Tearing herself away, she walked towards the door, straightened up and hit the control key.

As the door slid up, she walked back onto the Bridge, "Clinch how are we doing?" Clinch tapped away at the key panel, "we're holding station about five-hundred Fikans from the target. I'm having to adjust our attack curve fairly often. I'm not sure, but I think the gravitational well of Jepatira is having a negative effect on this asteroid, I could swear it's picking up speed. The sensors say it's not, but I don't trust them, it feels faster." Tyra moved over to the centre seat, "if that's true, what kind of effect would a major torpedo bombardment have on it?" Clinch stopped typing as he considered the thought. He turned his chair around and went completely pale. "If the torpedoes strip away all remaining non-super-dense material, it could conceivably decrease the overall area of the surface, which would have a serious impact on directional mass. We could be looking at a speed increase of over one-hundred percent." Tyra's jaw dropped for a moment before she leaned over and tapped the Comm Panel. "Helia to Atlanka City, First Minister, I seriously suggest you abort this strike. I have reason to believe that a torpedo bombardment against this target would strip material and shorten our window of opportunity. This thing is only thirty-six hours away from Atlanka at its current speed." Ben'veh's voice crackled back through the Comm System, "SIV Helia, we are handling this matter, just do your job." The channel abruptly closed with a sharp snapping sound. Tyra sat there, dumbfounded, she looked at Clinch, "did he just cut us off?" Clinch looked to the side, "apparently, should we abort?" Tyra sat in thought for a moment, "no, let's do this, any deviation from orders now would only weaken our efforts. Besides, it will give Seph and Jo time to get that algorithm interfaced with Atlanka's Primary Data Core, we need more time." Clinch spoke without gazing back, his eyes transfixed on the asteroid ahead, "this is a very bad idea." Tyra sat back in her chair, "may fortune smile upon us this day, lock target!"

It was early in the morning in Atlanka City, the sun was low in the sky. The blue globe of Terra could be seen hovering in the distance through the light clouds. It was going to be a beautiful day, one of the most pleasant Mesira could boast. Near the oceanic docks, the waves crashed against the shore in a soft lapping motion. Across the City and over a grassy plain, the Ubrean Forest rustled in the breeze, the wind softly blowing through the trees. A pair of Forkati Deer stood in a clearing, listening to the breeze. A gust of wind caressed their ears and they ran towards the trees. It was a day of complete tranquillity and peace, at least outside of the City. From the forest to the river, winding down the stream to the gleaming golden spires of Atlanka City, past the housing, under the Freeway Bridge, the Downtown Core sparkled in the morning sun. The Sirian Defence Force had a base in the City, a small Command Centre to organize Star Ship deployments and duty assignments. Ben'veh stood in the heart of the Command Centre. This was the central authority for the Sirian Military in this region. The room was monstrous, a golden hall lined with Computer Consoles and huge Holographic Screens. A massive Centre Console sat in the centre of the room with various people seated around it. Ben'veh was standing near the command area beside two pulsing amber consoles and a large display. "Confirm that we have a lock on the target via telemetry from the Helia." An Ensign nearby tapped a few keys on the Control Panel he was facing, "target lock confirmed." Ben'veh cracked his knuckles, "very well, deploy Defence Batteries." From seven different locations around Atlanka City, inconspicuous domes separated from the centre, peeling away and slipping into the structure. The shell of the domes lowered to reveal seven massive Quantum Flux Torpedo Chain Guns. These were designed for planetary defence against orbital bombardment. Slowly the weapons raised from their housings, catching a fleck of light, the massive weapons glinted in the morning sun. Finishing their ascent and locking into place, the massive Cannons sat motionless for a moment. Ben'veh who was watching the progress on a monitor nearby grinned, "excellent, activate the batteries and spin them up." The huge Cannons suddenly sprung to life, first aiming up and then swivelling to lock onto the asteroid. As they came to a stop, the Barrels began to spin rapidly, almost at a blinding speed. Ben'veh stood watching inside the Command Centre, "Barrel velocity?" The Officer who was to his left responded, "we're coming up on one-hundred percent, all weapons read as online and ready to fire". Ben'veh turned to look at the telemetry of the incoming asteroid, he squinted at it with hatred, "fire!" A stream of white bursts emitted at a blinding speed from the Chain Guns, from the Docks to the Ministry of Science. Across the City near the Star Ship Repair Docks and down near the Market Sector from all corners of the City, an intense barrage of white bolts shot out into Mesira's blue sky. Tyra was leaned over talking with Persephone quietly about their backup plan when Clinch hit a few controls and the screen snapped Aft. Mesira's small globe hung there and to the side, a mass of white left the planet and approached the Helia at incredible speeds. Clinch sat back in his chair, "here it comes". Tyra looked up as did Persephone, "my God." The screaming mass of torpedoes wailed through the blackness of space, the Helia was in front of them, her massive Wings soaring in the night sky, blocking out the sun slightly as she drifted in front during the torpedoes approach. Rushing passed the Helia and heading straight for their target, the mass of white torpedoes was seconds from impact. Tyra looked at Persephone, "are we at a safe distance, that's an awful lot of firepower?" Clinch piped up, "registering one-hundred and eighty Quantum Flux Torpedoes in the swarm". Tyra barely got the words out from sheer shock, "one-hundred and eighty?!" Clinch pointed to the display, "that's what it says". Tyra turned back to the screen, an intense flash filled the display and the entire Bridge turned a blinding brilliant white. Tyra covered her eyes from the blast as did most of the others. As the blast wave subsided, the asteroid remained, although now it was significantly smaller and debris was scattered around its remaining mass. Clinch leaned forward, "oh no, that's what I was afraid of." Tyra shook her head, "that fool". Ben'veh stared in disbelief, much of the asteroid had been vapourized or sheared off by the blast, but the large core remained. Infuriated at being proven wrong and not destroying the target with the first volley, he snapped at the Ensign to his left, "call up another volley, twice the yield and take the safeguards off." The young man turned to face Ben'veh, "off?" Ben'veh stared him down and barked in an overbearing manner, "you heard me! do as you're told or I shall find someone who can!" The Ensign stood up from his seat, "respectfully Sir, no, I will not do that. There is an Imperial Vessel at risk from the subsequent explosion." Ben'veh grabbed the young man by the shirt "I'll deal with you in a moment." He then shoved him toward a security guard. Ben'veh was furious, he looked at the asteroid on the screen and sneered with boiling anger, "I'm going to kill you." Ben'veh set the torpedoes accordingly and pressed the fire button. Another massive barrage spewed forth from Atlanka City, the sky became tainted with crimson smoke from the Sylthetic Ion Discharge from the Drive Coils of the torpedoes.

Clinch had his back turned to talk to Josephine about how best to circumvent the Security Net while activating the Bio-Transit System silently when Persephone got up from her seat, "by the Five Gods, what is that?" Clinch turned around, he had a stylus in his mouth from working on a tablet. As he caught sight of the view screen, the stylus dropped from his mouth and the tablet hit the deck. "my God." He quickly ran a scan on the incoming projectiles. "Registering three-hundred and sixty torpedoes, this is odd, they're travelling at double the speed of normal." Tyra got up and moved to the Navigation Console, "what?! That's not possible, the only way to increase velocity is to..." Clinch looked up at her, they both knew the next words to be spoken. He ran a scan on the incoming torpedoes. "Sensors are reading a one-hundred and fifty percent increase in yield, the safeties are off, I repeat safeties are non-functional. Torpedo impact is projected as one hundred and thirty seven percent, the profile is purely ballistic. Quantum Flux Warheads are fully active and reaching a point of critical mass. Tyra was scrambling to keep up, "that son of a, he knows we're hanging out here." Clinch looked up repeatedly while entering commands, "I guess when you're thieves your lives are forfeit." Tyra moved quickly back to her seat, "like hell! Seph, how long 'till impact." Persephone gazed at the monitor above her, she tapped a couple of controls, she could barely believe her eyes, "twenty seconds." Tyra's eyes bulged, "what?!" Seph nodded, "I know I know". Tyra spun around, "Jo get the Shields up!" Josephine entered the key sequence to erect the Shields and the console beside her exploded. She was thrown against Tyra's chair. Tyra got up, "Josephine!" Tyra motioned wildly with her hand, "Clinch get us out of here." Clinch hit the Main Core key and the keyboard slid up. Entering a new course, the Helia slowly dipped her Starboard Wing and began her turn. Josephine's eyes fluttered open. Tyra breathed a sigh of relief, "Jo, are you hurt." Josephine winced, "only my pride, get me up". Josephine called across the Bridge, "Taven throw me the Suppressor." Taven ran towards the Aft section and broke the protective glass on the Emergency Fire Suppressor. He tossed it to Josephine, as she began to spray the console and put out the flames, she called above the noise to the Helm. "Clinch bring us to two eight zero point seven four, if we're going to ride this, I'm going in nose first." Clinch responded, "two eight zero point seven four, executing." With the console reduced to some random smoke, Josephine went back to the Engineering Console. "dammit, we blew a relay. I can bypass it, but it's going to take a few seconds." Tyra called back "make it quick". The cluster of torpedoes now almost filling the view screen, Clinch called out, "ten seconds". Tyra's fingers dug into the leather arms of her chair. "Jo, now would be a good time." From behind her she could hear Josephine frantically pushing buttons. Clinch called out once more "five seconds." Tyra and the rest of the Crew braced, Josephine cried out from the Aft Engineering Station, "come on, work, don't do this to me now!" Tyra watched the swarm smash into the asteroid, Clinch called out, "impact!" Josephine squealed from the Aft Station, "yes!!!!" The Helia's Shields crackled to life as a massive plasmatic ring impacted the

Forward Section. Like a great wave breaking against a continent, the plasmatic ring forced itself around her Forward Sections travelling Aft. Her Shields screeched under the pressure, sparks flew from the ceiling of the Bridge. The entire ship rocked under the impact, pitching and tossing, dipping and dodging. The wave crested past the Wings, Josephine scrambled to stay on her feet, her gaze caught the readout above her. "Shields down to fifty percent, if we don't pass through within five seconds they'll fail". Tyra yelled to Clinch who was trying to hold himself steady amidst the chaos. "Full speed, push us through". As the wave approached her Tail the failure klaxons sounded and SARA announced, "Warning, Shield Failure Imminent, rerouting power to Internal Security System, Force Fields on standby." Clinch hit a few controls on the Main Panel and the Helia's Engines flared a searing bright teal, mixed with flecks of slight red as they overheated a little. She roared and pushed past the wave. As the last vestiges of the plasmatic ring slipped passed her Tail, a loud alert sounded, SARA was louder than Tyra had heard her in a long time. "Shields have Collapsed, The hull has been exposed". as she said that, the Port Side of her tail exploded in a shower of sparks and white flames. The Helia rocked to the side with the force of the explosion. Clinch held himself steady, Josephine was lucky to have been holding onto something. Persephone was tossed over. She shook herself off and got up off the floor. Clinch was holding onto the console with one hand and hitting controls with the other, "one moment, I'm compensating, we're out of it." Taven moved over to Persephone as the Ship returned to normal, holding her as she got up, he made sure she was okay. Realizing he'd let his emotions override his training, he moved back a step. Tyra got up and rubbed his shoulder, "it's okay Taven, nobody expects you to be a stone." Taven adjusted his shirt as Tyra gazed to the Aft Station. "Josephine, how did we do?" Josephine was bent over the console tapping controls. "The Shields failed at the last moment, we lost Engine Ports one through six on the Main Array, but the Secondary Array has taken over. All things considered not too bad, she's a tough Ship, almost as tough as the Jovus." Taven suddenly looked at Tyra, "I'd almost forgotten, we have to get her out of Dry Dock. If we don't, she'll be destroyed by the blast when the asteroid hits." Tyra motioned to Josephine and Persephone, "that's our first task after we get done with the Council. Persephone rubbed her head, the fall had given her a bit of a headache and she was still shaken when she looked at the screen. A wash of horror rolled over her face, she clasped Taven's hand hard. "Taven, turn around." Taven, Tyra, Clinch and the rest of the Bridge Crew looked at the screen. The asteroid that had been there, now was simply a massive ball of superheated plasma. Persephone's reaction was not the only one, Ben'veh who was watching the same scene from Sirian Defence Headquarters stood in disbelief. Absolutely dumbfounded that the asteroid hadn't been destroyed by the blast, he stood in awe of the sheer resilience of this particular rock. His gaze was only broken by the Sirian Sector Commander walking up to him. He was a very average man, dark brown hair and a light beard. His blue eyes were sharp as a knife, he was not in a good mood. "First Minister Ben'veh, I've just received a very disturbing report from our Automated Sensor Grid. You executed an unsafe torpedo strike against a target when there was an Imperial Starship within the blast radius, is that correct!?" Ben'veh was brought back to reality almost immediately. He'd been so focused on destroying the asteroid, he hadn't stopped to consider the lives he almost extinguished. "We lost the feed from the Helia a few minutes ago, how close was she." The Commander handed him the readout on a tablet. "Within five hundred Fikans, far too close." Ben'veh read the report, "is the Ship okay?" The Commander was flabbergasted, "the ship, is that all you care about? Do you care nothing for the souls on board? There are over five thousand people on board that Ship, you would exterminate them without a second thought, what kind of monster are you?" Ben'veh's back arced up and he became extremely defensive, "I'm doing what I must to ensure the safety of this City." The Commander pointed to the monitor showing the flaming ball of plasma, "yes, you're certainly doing a magnificent job. Even you have to report to someone, I'm taking this both to my superiors and to the highest levels on Siria Prime. A person like you is dangerous to leave in charge."

Ben'veh pointed to the crest on his robe, "yes but until then I'm still in charge, and you are to leave immediately". The Commander grabbed the tablet from Ben'veh and stormed out. Ben'veh motioned to the Lieutenant to his right, "get me the Helia, they have to answer for their theft." Aboard the Helia, Josephine was working at the Aft Station securing the rest of the systems and assessing the damage. Taven walked over to her, he'd seen an unusual shine on her hair. "Jo, stop for a moment." She turned around, "hmm?" Taven ran a finger through her hair and it was ringed in blood. "Jo, you're bleeding". Josephine touched the side of her head and blood stained her hand, "oh, so I am. I suppose I should go to Sick Bay." Taven took her hand, "I'll go with you." Persephone called after both of them, "Taven what's going on?" Taven turned to Persephone, "Josephine's got a nasty gash on the side of her head, probably from when she hit Tyra's chair. I'm taking her to Sick Bay to patch her up, I don't think it's serious." Persephone dropped what she was doing and walked over to her sister, "Jo, you okay?" Josephine nodded, "yes, it doesn't hurt. Then again that could be shock too, but I think I'm okay." Persephone looked up at Taven, "you'll let me know?" Taven squeezed her arm to reassure her, "of course. I wouldn't let you worry." Persephone smiled, "thank you." Taven took Josephine's hand once again and motioned toward the ISTiS. "Come on, let's fix that head of yours."

As Taven and Josephine vanished behind the door of the ISTiS, the Main View Screen crackled to life. Tyra was still dusting herself off and checking on her Crew, Ben'veh's face flashed into focus. "You will report to the Council Chamber immediately to answer for your actions." Tyra's temper overrode her better judgement, orders were one thing but this was absurd. "You cold-hearted son of a... you just about killed me and my Crew and you expect us to answer for saving one disabled ship without authorization, which of us has committed the greater crime...SIR!?" Ben'veh's face was cold and unfeeling. "You will report, or I will have your ship dragged back in disgrace and your entire crew will be locked up for the rest of their lives." Sorvan ran onto the Bridge, Tyra was fuming and in her anger, she didn't notice. Sorvan placed a hand on her shoulder and she stepped back slightly. "Ben, have you lost your mind, this isn't you, what's wrong with you. You'd freely murder people who you've sworn to protect and serve? You're sick, you need help. These people are trying to save the City not destroy it." Ben'veh's eyes turned to slits, "Sorvan, I should have known, your Council status is hereby revoked and your seat dismissed. You choose to ally yourself with criminals who would circumvent my authority? You will pay for it." With that, the channel closed and the screen flickered and turned off. Tyra's hands were clenched into fists, "I'm going to kill that bastard." Sorvan could see how angry she was, he moved over to her, trying to calm her before she did anything she'd regret. Always the perpetual peacemaker, his nature could not be helped, he was how he was. "Tyra, it's not your fault, something's gone wrong, he's lost his mind and he's sick." Tyra turned to Sorvan, "can I talk to you privately?" Sorvan pointed behind him, "office?" Tyra nodded visibly upset, "yes". Tyra and Sorvan walked into Tyra's office. She walked in with her hands at her sides still clenched in fists. She was motionless, standing in front of the window. Sorvan grew concerned when she didn't speak, Tyra wasn't known for her silence. He moved over to her, and as he did he saw the tears rolling down her cheeks. He reached for her, she was almost the same age as his oldest daughter and he knew how passionately she cared for her Crew. She struggled to get it out, "he almost killed us, if Josephine hadn't got the Shields up, we'd all be dead. My Crew, they're my responsibility, they're my family. In the blink of an eye...he could have killed them all." She broke into tears as Sorvan wrapped his large arms around her, the stress had taken its toll. Sorvan had seen Tyra in just about every situation possible, from emergency relief efforts to war-torn planets. While she was a passionate woman of deep feelings, in all that time he'd never seen her break down into tears. He held her for a moment before responding, giving her the chance to release the incredible pressure she was under. "But they're not, Jo got the Shields up and everybody's okay, except for you. Your Crew needs you now more than ever, their homes are about to be obliterated and you need to be strong for them. They look to you for guidance and leadership." Tyra looked up, "thank you". Sorvan released her and placed his hands on her shoulders. "Sometimes you just need someone to remind you that it's okay to be scared." Tyra dried her face and blew her nose. "I don't know what to do next, Ben's lost it". Sorvan nodded, "He needs to step down, he's not well". Tyra shrugged, "how?" Sorvan moved up to stand beside her and looked out the window, "doesn't Josephine have a working plan to store the Council and their Guards in Bio-Molecular Storage?" Tyra nodded, "she does". Sorvan rubbed his chin, "then it would seem your path is clear." He turned to face her, and she to face him, "don't let anybody second-guess you, make you doubt yourself or interfere with you. The lives of every citizen of Atlanka City are on your shoulders, while that may feel like a huge weight, I believe it's a responsibility you're more than capable of handling and I believe in you." Tyra smiled and looked down a moment, Sorvan was curious, "what?" She looked back up, "you remind me so much of my Dad." Sorvan grinned, "well I have two daughters near your age and a granddaughter, I know how these things work." Tyra straightened her jacket, "right, back to work." She hit her Communicator on her wrist, "Josephine, Seph I need you in Engineering Lab three in five minutes." Both women's voices crackled through almost simultaneously, "on my way, enroute." Tyra looked at Sorvan, "I don't get taken down so easy." Sorvan smiled, "and you never will". Tyra turned and walked out of her office and headed for the Helm. "Clinch set course back to Atlanka City, one eighth Main Drive thrust. Clinch looked at her, puzzled at the odd request, "one-eighth thrust, are you sure?"

Tyra crossed her arms, "if we're called into the Council Chamber before we're ready, you do realize what happens don't you?" Clinch nodded, "ahh, one-eighth thrust it is." Tyra patted Clinch's shoulder, "I'll be in Engineering Lab Three on Deck Two if you need me, otherwise, the Bridge is yours." Clinch nodded, "understood". Sorvan ran out of Tyra's office after her, "wait up, I'll join you."

CONTINGENCY

Tyra and Sorvan walked into the ISTiS from the Main Bridge and Tyra spoke to SARA, "Deck Two, Section Sixty-two B". A bolt of lightning struck and teal ribbons of energy danced around them until they vanished in a burst of teal energy. Tyra wasn't wasting any time, walking out of the ISTiS on Deck Two with Sorvan in tow they turned Aft. Passing several Medical Labs and Personnel Quarters, she and Sorvan came up to the door to Lab Three. Hitting the door chime, Persephone's voice came from inside, "come in, we're already here." Tyra tapped another control on the amber panel and the door slid up. Tyra and Sorvan walked into the Lab and could see both women at the far side of the room. The room was a soft golden glow, amber displays ran along the walls. Reports printing across several screens constantly provided a current status update for all Ship's systems. Josephine was bent over a console keying in commands, while Persephone was seated at a rather large circular Centre Input Panel. Tyra and Sorvan made their way over, Tyra placed a hand on Persephone's shoulder just to tell her she was there. "So what do we have so far, I know Jo had some of this planned out already?" Josephine turned to face Tyra, "we may have hit a snag, this plan was contingent on me still having Core access to Atlanka City's Main Computer Network remotely. It would seem Ben'veh's paranoia has reached new heights, he's pulled my access codes as well as Persephone's." Sorvan facepalmed, "Ben you stubborn old fool. I wouldn't expect mine to work either, he's just revoked my Council standing." Persephone bolted upright and twisted to face Sorvan, "he did what?!" Sorvan nodded, "I could scarcely believe I was talking to the same man." Persephone shook her head in disbelief, "I would never have dreamed...my God. Jo, can you get in through a backdoor port?" Josephine's hands danced across the console. She shook her head disappointingly, "no he's locked the servers in Synchronous Bit Transfer Mode and disabled remote network access. The only people who have access to Atlanka's systems now are those within the City." Persephone's head sank, "ugh, we'll figure this out." As Persephone racked her brain, suddenly the amber alert indicator flashed, Josephine began to scramble, "we've been discovered." Persephone's head snapped towards Josephine, "quick, sever the connection." Josephine hit several keys and her hand smacked the console, "I can't, they've hard-locked the connection from their end." Persephone knelt down and opened the Main Panel, "how do I cut the power? Jo? Josephine!" Persephone got back up, not understanding why her sister was silent, on the screen was the Sirian Fleet Commander.

Persephone brushed her hair aside, "Cernan, how can we assist you?" Cernan's gaze was stern, the epitome of a military man, never revealing his intentions until he was ready. "Director Persephone, Commander Josephine, I have detected your repeated attempts to circumvent Atlanka Security." Persephone and Josephine turned to face each other and responded in unison, "who us?" Cernan interlocked his fingers and leaned forward on his desk, obviously considering his next move carefully. His hand drifted to a control pad beside him, he tapped what seemed like random keystrokes and the display printed, "secured." He crossed his fingers once again and looked to the side as if uneasy about his next words. "I want to help you, I assume you're trying to regain some control over recent events. I know what happened on board the Helia, I voiced my extreme disappointment to the First Minister. He didn't care, he seemed far more interested in the condition of the vessel and had little regard for its complement. What can I do to help?" Persephone breathed a sigh of relief, Josephine did the same but far more controlled, likely due to her military training. Josephine tapped a couple of control keys and gazed into the Monitor. "Ben'veh's revoked my Core access, I can't even contact SARA for assistance." Commander Cernan reached over his desk and tapped some controls, an amber backlit keyboard raised out from a recessed area in his desk. His hands tapped lightly on the keys. Again his hand drifted back to the side of his desk and after two light taps on the control pad, the keyboard withdrew. "Done, your codes and your sister's are reinstated and locked with my own personal access code. Sorvan I'm sorry, I can't do anything about yours, they're Council property and I don't have direct access to modify the permissions." Sorvan nodded, "that's fine, I'm not the one who needs it." Josephine nodded a sigh of relief, "thank you." Cernan laid his hands flat, "is there anything else I can do?" Persephone leaned over, "can you ensure the teams we left in the Bio-Molecular Storage Core and Main Engineering are both on schedule and left to complete their work?" Cernan nodded, "I'll see to it personally, Atlanka out." The coursing energy surrounding the screen crackled and the screen winked off.

Persephone scratched her head, "well I never". Josephine pointed to the adjoining station, "let's not waste this opportunity." Persephone nodded, "right. What about the Targeting Sensors, can we temporarily force all the sensors except those in the Council Chamber into standby mode." Sorvan tapped Persephone on the shoulder, "I'll leave you ladies to it." Persephone looked back to him, "okay, why don't you check in with Rachel and Ferus, find out how they're doing?" Sorvan nodded, "alright, I'll be back." Tyra nodded to Persephone and Josephine, "I'll be on the Bridge if you need any help." Persephone nodded in acknowledgement, she and Josephine turned back to the Console they had been working at. Tyra walked towards the door and as it slid up, she walked out into the corridor. Josephine tapped a few controls and a plate recessed into the console, the plate slid back and a keyboard rose from underneath. Positioning her fingers, she began keying in sequences. Josephine pointed to the screen in several areas, "maybe, the trouble is going to be overriding the interlocks governing simultaneous pattern storage." Persephone set her own Console to manual input mode and began to work on the problem. She checked cross-sections of Atlanka's Computer Core, working area by area until she found what she was looking for. "There, Vector five six nine, section Mut, there's a circuit here that looks like it can be temporarily shunted to a nearby pathway breaking the Transport Protocols." Josephine looked at Persephone, "if we do this, we need to be absolutely certain we can undo it, this City still has to store the rest of the residents before we move it." Persephone put her hands in front of her and wiggled her fingers, "that's why they call me Magic Hands." Josephine rolled her eyes, turning back to her Console she brought up a few more diagrams. There's still the problem of the safe zone, I don't feel like being stored in a Buffer. Persephone looked up for a minute, clearly thinking, suddenly her eyes perked up, she'd had a brainstorm. "Does the Armory have some Personal Shield Generators?" Josephine stopped typing, "what on earth would you need PSG's for?" Then the light came on and Josephine started to get an idea of what Persephone had in mind.   Persephone turned to Josephine and crossed her arms, "just how good are you at small arms recalibration, I know you took advanced training in it?" Josephine stopped typing as well and turned to her sister. "I could make a Communications Badge sing a concerto in D Minor if I wanted to, why?" Persephone's face drew a satisfied smile, "think you could turn a few PSG's into Transport Repulsion Fields?" Josephine's eyes went wide, "you're serious?" Persephone grinned, "well just how good are you." Josephine's lips curled into a cheeky smile, "your challenge, dear sister...is accepted!" Persephone looked at the controls behind Josephine, "are we set here?" Josephine turned back to typing, "almost... just one more... there that's got it, shunt inserted; now that should prohibit the rest of the people in the City from being stored. I don't know how long it will last though, so we'd best not take too long." Persephone pointed to the door, "alright to the Armory." Josephine nodded, "let's go, if anyone gets suspicious, let me take the lead, I'll pull rank if I have to, the word classified is always a good fall-back." Persephone shook her head with a smile, "you would." Josephine walked towards the door, "of course I would." Persephone and her sister walked out into the hallway, turning towards the ISTiS, they walked down the brightly lit corridor. As they approached the door to the ISTiS, it opened abruptly. A young woman dashed out and bumped into Josephine, "whoa, Kiana slow down." Kiana dusted herself off and tossed her ponytail back behind her head. "Ben'veh is furious, he demands to know what the holdup is." Josephine looked at Persephone then back to Kiana, "holdup?" Kiana looked back and forth between the two women. "Tyra is returning to Atlanka City but only at one eighth Ion thrust." Persephone grinned mischievously, "cheeky Tyra, very cheeky." Kiana looked totally lost, "so what do I tell him?" Josephine began to share Persephone's grin, "tell who? As far as I know, we've had a major failure in our Communications Array, all systems are offline." Kiana raised an eyebrow, "no their n....oh, okay I get the drift, right, I'll have a team start repairs on the Communications Matrix as soon as I can, it may take some time." Josephine straightened, "thank you, Lieutenant, take all the time you need." Kiana shook her head and walked between the two sisters. She disappeared around a corner some distance down the hall. Persephone looked at Josephine, "you know he's going to try to roast us alive." Josephine flashed a smile, "you just have to know how to dance in the flames." They walked into the ISTiS and Josephine tapped the control key for the Armory. The door slid down and both women were enveloped in dancing ribbons of energy, two brilliant white lines scanned across them and as the transport sequence finished, the lines electrified and a resonating clap of thunder could be heard." Persephone and Josephine walked out of the ISTiS and turned towards the Starboard side of the Ship. In the distance, they could see a single guard stationed outside the Armory. Josephine stopped Persephone short of the door, "let me talk to him, I might be able to occupy his attention while you slip inside." Persephone nodded and Josephine walked in front of her, approaching the guard, Josephine's face turned to one of surprise. "Hey, Kordin, I haven't seen you in a while, how have you been?" Kordin's face lit up, "hi Jo, I've been stuck down here in the bowels of the Ship." Josephine put her hand on her hip, "well when do you get off, we should grab a cup of coffee and catch up?" Korvin tapped a key on the pad next to him, "about five minutes, can you wait?" Josephine brushed a lock of hair out of her face, "I've only got twenty, Tyra wants me to overhaul the Secondary Plasma Coils before we get to Atlanka City." Korvin stood weighing the options, "oh sure I could use a break, it's not like I'm guarding anything anyway. Nobody on this Ship is going to break in." Josephine nodded and flashed a look back to Persephone who was half-hiding around a corner down the hall. Korvin turned and he and Josephine walked down the hall turning to the left. Persephone could hear small snippets of their conversation, as she approached the Armory door the last thing she heard was, "so how's life on the Jovus. Are you missing the modern Sirian Star Ships yet?" Persephone checked up and down the hall for any witnesses. She then took a file from her vest pocket and slipped it between the wall and the panel. She popped it out and clicked a few rocker switches inside. The door slid up and she replaced the panel gently. The Armory was brightly lit, and groups of Plasma Emitter Rifles lined the walls. Several styles of both Personal Weapons and Assault Cannons were lined up in crates along the sides. It was standard procedure, while the Sirians never attacked first, they were well equipped to handle any violent attack aboard any Star Ship or Land Base. Not everybody respects peace, sometimes force is required to defend yourself. The room itself was standard Sirian architecture, brushed gold with marble flooring. This room was plainer than others, but it was a functional room that wasn't often used. There was a door on the facing wall, Persephone wasn't sure what was back there, but she surmised it could be additional equipment storage. She was down to about two minutes, so she walked quickly towards it, tapping a control she received an erroneous note in response to her attempted entry. She pulled her tablet from her pocket, "there's more than one way to skin a cat, let's see how you like this." She popped the stylus out and began tapping away on the interface. She quickly looked up as she thought she heard a noise from behind her. Persephone hit a couple more controls and the door mechanism shorted out, the door raised up and stopped halfway. Persephone tucked her tablet back into her vest and her stylus behind her ear. She tossed her hair back in satisfaction, "never impede a brilliant Scientist!" She walked into the sealed room and immediately to her left along the wall was a crate of PSG's. Persephone grabbed an equipment pack from the wall closest to her and filled it with several devices, enough for the Officers who had been accused by Ben'veh. As she put the last PSG gently in the pack, she heard a ruffling noise from outside, "hey, who's in there?" A muffled voice called from outside, and was rapping on the door. Persephone panicked, she looked frantically for a way out. The door was still stuck open. She had to think fast or she was going to get caught. She looked around, "umm...umm..got it!" She grabbed two Micro Explosives from the crate behind her, and she placed one on each side of the top of the door. She grabbed her tablet and entered the command to detonate the explosives, she set just enough yield to blow the door's interlocks. Persephone moved to the back of the room and closed her eyes, she'd never done this before. She hesitated for a split second, then hit the initiate button. A slight explosion sparked around the top of the door. It creaked as the sparks went down the sides of the door and then then it slowly slid down. Persephone breathed a sigh of relief, she was standing amongst Power Clips, Grenades and Plasma Bombs, not exactly the kind of hardware you want to be near an explosion. She heard the forward door slide open and boots clanking across the floor. Persephone pulled her tablet out again, talking to herself she frantically selected the Transport System. "Come on SARA, please tell me you can get a lock in here." Her tablet scanned the area, she could see the progress indicator. Green text printed across the top of the display, then flashed several times, a line appeared below it, then a second line. Persephone breathed easier, the Transport System had locked onto her co-ordinates. She could hear hands rubbing against the door and saw it start to slide up, "sorry fella's, I'd love to stay and chat, but I have a City to rescue." She tapped the initiate key on her tablet and tucked it back in her pocket. Lightning struck, and teal ribbons of energy surrounded her as she started to dematerialize. She caught sight of the door sliding up as two very large security officers walked in. She blew a kiss to them as the transport sequence ended. The two officers couldn't get a clear picture of who it was that had been transported, they knew it was a woman, but couldn't see clearly enough to identify her. The lead officer moved over to the Comm Panel and called up to Tyra who was on the Bridge, "we've had an incursion into the Armory." Tyra's voice crackled through the Intercom, "any idea who?" The officer shook his head, "No she was mostly phased out matter by the time we got in, it looked like she had an equipment pack on her back." Tyra's voice was silent, then crackled through the Intercom, "is anything missing?" The officer checked around, "it looks like a few PSG's have been taken." Tyra's voice was stern as she responded, "forget it, list those as defective and had to be destroyed." The officer scratched his head, "Captain?" Tyra's voice once again came through this time sterner than the last, "you heard me, Sergeant, this never happened." The officer nodded in acknowledgement, "understood Ma'am". Tyra's tone lightened, "thank you". The channel closed with an echoed pop, the Sergeant's companion raised his arms, "what was that all about?" The Sergeant responded, "I don't know Stevens, but when the Captain says forget it, we forget it, back to our post." His subordinate nodded, "mmm hmm".

Persephone materialized in Tyra's office, off of the Bridge, she put the pack down on Tyra's desk and tapped her Communicator. "Seph to Bridge, Tyra can you come to your office for a minute." Tyra was sitting with her head resting against the back of her chair as Persephone's message came in, "just five minutes, all I want is five measly minutes." Tyra tapped the Comm Channel, "on my way". Tyra got up and walked over to her Office, she tapped the door control and the door slid up. She found

Persephone sitting on her desk tossing a PSG up and down in her hand. The Sirian Personal Shield Generator was a relatively small device. It was an oval design in the shape of an eye, one large amber stone was set in the centre of the device, with an artistic design surrounding it in the shape of a cornea and eyelid. The device could be placed anywhere on the body, or as Persephone's plan was turning out, concealed. Tyra moved over to the desk, "you know I got a call not too long ago from the On-Duty Sergeant-At-Arms. He said there were some PSG's missing from the armoury, well now I know why." Persephone grinned, "that was fun, a little more intense than I planned but it sure got the blood pumping". Tyra shook her head with a smile, "so what's your plan?" Persephone held the PSG she'd been tossing in the air in her hand by one of the corners, "well, we can't set up a safe zone, the way the system is built it's all or nothing. While we can reduce the area affected, we cannot manipulate the field in that area." Tyra nodded towards the PSG in Persephone's hand, "so what's with the Shield Gen's?" Persephone put it down on the desk, "Josephine is going to modify one to turn it into a Transport Repulsion Field, then upload the changes to the network to modify the others." Tyra crossed her arms, "tricky, think she can do it?" Persephone bit her lower lip, "well, we don't have a lot of options, if she can't we're dead anyway. So whether we're dead out here or dead in the Bio-Storage Core, I can't see as it makes any difference." Tyra nodded, "good point". Persephone turned her head towards the ceiling slightly. "SARA, locate Josephine Vorn." SARA was silent for a moment before responding, "requested individual is in motion on Deck Three Section Twenty-four L." Persephone snickered at Tyra, that mischievous smile she was famous for, "SARA override standard procedure and lock onto Josephine Vorn, transport her to my location." SARA was quiet for a moment while she processed the request. "The requested function will cause momentary disorientation to the transported individual, do you wish to proceed?" Persephone looked at Tyra, Tyra raised an eyebrow at her in a, "you're not serious" manner. Persephone turned back to face the wall, "execute the instruction." Lightning struck and energy ribbons coursed through the centre of the room, so skinny you could barely see them, then filling out and rippling up until Josephine emerged mid-stride and stopped short of walking into the wall, "what the...?" She turned to see Tyra and Persephone sitting on the desk, "Persephone Analise!!! I hate it when you do that!."

Persephone laughed, "well it was the only way to get you here quicker." Josephine walked over to the desk, "uh huh, and the fact that you enjoyed it counts for nothing, right?" Persephone grinned mischievously, "of course I enjoyed it." Josephine shook her head and noticed the bag on the desk, "are those my PSG's?" Persephone picked up one and tossed it to her sister, "yep, do you think you can finish the modifications before we reach home?" Josephine popped open the back to access the circuitry, "well I kind of have to don't I". Tyra patted Persephone on the shoulder, "come, let's let Jo work in silence so she can concentrate." Persephone and Tyra got up and walked towards the door. Persephone turned around momentarily before they left, "love ya Jo." Josephine waved her Micro Fusion Conditioner at her sister, "yeah, yeah, now get out I'm trying to work here." Persephone nodded, a smile beaming across her face and headed out the door. Tyra moved towards the centre seat and put her elbow on the headrest. She was obviously in thought, Persephone moved over to see what she was thinking about. Tyra rested her head on her closed hand as Persephone moved toward her. "You know with all that's gone on, I totally forgot about the Jovus, she's still moored in Star Dock Three. Virtually no repairs have been done, her Engines are still out." Persephone ran her hands through her hair, "ugh, that means we've got six hours maybe eight maximum to get her Engines operational." Tyra looked behind her and then back at Persephone, "our power systems have taken a pretty significant amount of damage, and I've lost the Port and Starboard Wing Emitters. I don't dare tow the Jovus out of Dry Dock with the current state of my Ship. Juice is affecting repairs, but it's going to take a while, longer than we have to get Atlanka airborne and out of the path of the asteroid." Persephone rested her arm near Tyra's, "so we need to get the Jovus' Engines online?" Tyra nodded, and the only way to do that is to get an Engineering detail on board with Supplemental Power Units to power her Fabrication Plant; otherwise, they won't be able to replace the damaged Power Conduits." Persephone rubbed her neck, "was it only the Conduits that suffered damage?"

Tyra moved her arm off the chair and took a tablet out of her vest pocket, she tapped the display with her stylus calling up the most recent information on the state of the Jovus. "Thankfully yes, some of those systems are so outdated, that fabricating parts would be difficult and require specialized production facilities." Persephone nodded towards the tablet, "what about her Power Core, are her Reactors stable?" Tyra tapped a few more instructions into the tablet and the image swept from an overview of the Jovus' exterior to an internal dissection of Main Engineering. She tapped the Reactor Control Console and a plethora of text printed on the side. "One is, the others are a lost cause. They reported some searing on the outer casing of the unit from the surrounding fires before they were put out, but according to the internal diagnostics, the Reactor's Shielding and Power Stabilization Routines look intact. We won't really know until we power it up and run a few tests." Persephone pointed at the tablet, "okay so how do we get a team aboard the Jovus." Tyra motioned for Persephone to follow, she led her into the adjoining meeting room and waited for the door to close. "We can't beam in from the Helia, my Transporter's signal has been blocked; however, we can commandeer a terminal inside Atlanka City from one of the civilian areas and reprogram it to send us to the Main Transfer Bay on the Jovus." Persephone crossed her arms, "how do you plan on clearing the area so we're not discovered?" Tyra thought for a moment then leaned close to Persephone, "can you simulate an Ion power leak from the old Ion Thrusters, not actually create one but make SARA think so?" Persephone leaned back, "why not just ask SARA if she's willing to assist us?" Tyra stepped back, "I hadn't thought of that,

SARA...may I speak to you for a moment?" SARA materialized from a swirling white flash, "Of course Captain, how can I help?" Persephone leaned against the wall, "can you help us gain entry to the Jovus? We need a distraction so we can transport a crew aboard to repair the engines." SARA looked at Persephone and then to Tyra and back. "of course I will, anything you require of me to accomplish our shared goals, please ask me." Persephone scratched her cheek, "we need a malfunctioning Ion Injector to create a leak alarm, but not create an actual leak in the process." SARA smiled, "I think I can handle that." Persephone nodded, "now, it wouldn't give us much time. The system summons an immediate chemical containment unit from Emergency Services. We'd have about twenty seconds at most." Tyra nodded, "good, I'll only need ten". Persephone began to walk back towards the door, "You know this all hinges on us pulling off Jo's little trick with the Council." Tyra stopped at the door, "Jo's never let me down before, I don't expect her to now." Persephone nodded, "she wouldn't accept less than success." Persephone turned towards SARA who was still standing in the middle of the room, "thank you SARA, your help is going to save all our lives." SARA nodded with a radiating warmth, "that is my primary responsibility." She was surrounded by a whirl of white light and then vanished. The two women walked back out onto the Bridge and gazed at the Screen, Mesira's normally soft blue globe was tinted a bright crimson red. Tyra and Persephone were both disgusted by the gross pollution of the planet's upper atmosphere. Persephone shook her head, "Ben'veh had no right, it's going to take years to undo this damage." Tyra looked at her, "this planet has hours to live." Persephone's face was suddenly awash with concern, "Tyra, what about Terra or Laana? Laana has no atmosphere, but Terra supports a primitive civilization and extensive plant and animal life. That asteroid is a flaming ball of superheated plasma and when it hits Mesira it's going to explode. Could Terra's atmosphere be burned away by the subsequent plasmatic ring?" Tyra's eyes went wide, "I hadn't thought of that, quickly to Science Lab Two, we haven't much time." The two women rushed off the Bridge and into the ISTiS. Persephone didn't even bother with the control panel. "SARA override standard transit procedure and transport us directly to Science Lab Two." SARA's voice filled the ITSiS, "the requested function requires command clearance."

Persephone looked at Tyra confused, "Command clearance?" Tyra looked just as perplexed, "looks like our friend Ben'veh has been busy altering subroutines both in the City and aboard my Ship." Tyra hit a control on the ISTiS panel and the door slid up, Tyra leaned her head out, "Kiana, take the Long Range Data Communications System to Sirian High Command offline." Kiana looked at her strangely, "okay, but do you mind if I ask why?" Tyra looked up, "I think someone's getting into the Ship's systems without authorization." Kiana's eyes widened. "Amber alert, unauthorized data communications have been discovered in the ships systems, secure all communications and terminate all link-ups to Sirian Star Bases without command clearance." Tyra nodded, "thank you Kiana, as you were." Persephone smiled, "she didn't waste any time did she." Tyra smiled, "that's why she's on my Ship, top of her class and the best ears I've ever seen in action. Now then, let's try this again." Tyra lifted her head slightly out of instinct, "SARA recognize Command authorization. Tyra, Captain, Isis Isis two six four dash seven Mahte, enable." SARA's voice was silent for a moment, then she sent out the standard alert, "transport in progress, standby." The two women were engulfed in a large swirling vortex of energy ribbons, a pair of white lines scanned across them and as they electrified a rumble of thunder could be heard.

The colours danced around Tyra and Persephone as they were whisked through the Computer's Pattern Buffer. Science Lab Two was darkened, it had not been used for a while and as such had gone into power conservation mode. Its displays were dark, save for a few amber flashes. The lights were almost completely off. Sensing the inbound travellers, the lights began to raise their illumination, and the displays around the room flickered then sprang to life in an almost domino-like pattern. As the room returned to normal illumination, energy ribbons echoed into the room, then took shape and swirled into a twisting vortex. The entire room glowed teal from the materialization sequence, a strip of white light emerged from within the vortex, stretching out it revealed Tyra and Persephone. As the ribbons reduced in number, the last of the energy matrix raised up into the ceiling and the women emerged from transit. The two women made their way over to the Main Science Console in the centre of the room. Persephone looked at Tyra, "got any brilliant ideas?" Tyra nodded without breaking her stride, "one, but it's a long shot." As Tyra came up to the console, she tapped a few amber keys on the panel and a hatch retracted revealing a keyboard which rose up out of the console. Tyra bent over typing quite rapidly which was unusual for her. "SARA, I need a defence solution for a Class Four planet with tidal influence from its primary moon. Question, there is an asteroid on a collision course with the secondary moon, project planetary impact and extrapolate probable solutions to this event." SARA replied from the shadows in the room, "the requested function will take five minutes to complete." Persephone looked at Tyra, her normally soft features lined with concern, her forehead tightly knit in thought. Persephone tapped her with her elbow, "you know you shouldn't do that, you're just going to give yourself another headache." Tyra looked at Persephone, "what? Oh, yeah, Rachel's told me a thousand times not to, I guess old habits really do die hard." Persephone's face cracked a smile, leaning against the console with her backside, she nodded towards Tyra, "any ideas what SARA's going to come up with?" Tyra looked at her, then out the window at Mesira's red horizon, you could almost cut the tension with a knife, it was so thick around her. "My worst fear is that the entire atmosphere will be compromised and without direct intervention, Terra won't survive. I just hope we haven't waited too long."

As Tyra finished her statement, SARA's voice cut the air like a hot knife through butter, "analysis complete, the projected impact of Terra's atmosphere is measured at a 76.387 percent loss.

Possible outer skin rupture of Laana 87.546 percent." Tyra's face sank, and her head dropped. "SARA, is there any way to counteract this?" SARA was silent for what seemed like an eternity, Tyra's heart sank under the strain of the moment. After what seemed like forever, SARA finally responded, "yes, an Energy Shield Grid consisting of twenty-seven satellites in geosynchronous orbit could be used to deflect the plasma wave and redirect the energy into open space. The wave would then dissipate and burn out." Tyra looked at Persephone, "SARA what is the projected condition of Mesira after impact?" SARA processed the request, "Mesira is classified as a total loss." Tyra caught herself as she lost her footing slightly, "no!" Sniffing and fighting back her emotions, she cleared her throat, "describe the scenario, authorization Bastet One." SARA was silent for a moment then responded in the most chilling analysis both women had ever heard. " After impact, a major plasmatic shockwave will be emitted from the planet, the entire ecosystem will be engulfed in a global plasma fire. Within the first five seconds, the atmosphere will be burned away, within ten seconds, the entire ecosystem including all plants and animal life will be vaporized. All that remains will be plasma fires engulfing the entire globe. The force of the impact will destroy Mesira's orbit, the planet will be knocked clear of Terra and hurtled towards the Star in this system. Projected analysis indicates that the planet will catch the sun's gravity and swing around, evolving its own orbit. Projected orbital trajectory on screen now. Projected orbit will be highly erratic and Mesira will no longer be capable of ever supporting life again." Persephone gazed at Tyra with deep sadness, "our home, my life, my family, everything I know and hold dear." Tyra placed a hand on her arm, "that's why it's so important that we succeed." Tyra nodded to the sky out of instinct, "SARA is it possible to save any of the animal species from Mesira and transplant them to a favourable ecosystem?" SARA's voice chilled the air, "it is not, City Transport Protocols dictate that only individuals within the influence of Atlanka City will be affected by the dematerialization routine." Tyra was getting frustrated,

"SARA can the system be disabled to allow for transport of items or individuals outside of the City?" SARA's voice was cold which was so very unlike her, "no, there is insufficient memory for any external pattern storage." Tyra's head sank again, "that's it, we are at our limit, there's nothing we can do for them." Persephone looked at Tyra, "but all those animals, all the plants..." Tyra shook her head, "there's nothing we can do". Persephone's eyes went wide, "what about the pets in the City, some tend to wander." Tyra nodded, "I should be able to send a City-wide text message alerting people to find their pets." Persephone nodded, "let's do that, then get to Engineering." Tyra began to type on the keyboard, "I'm already on it".

From: Atlanka City Weather Control
Re: Weather bulletin for pet owners as per Humane Services Act

Message Follows:

All citizens of Atlanka City, please be advised that a major plasma storm is approaching the City and will hit within the day. If you have pets, please ensure that they are secured inside your dwelling. If they are not, please take the time now to use your pet trackers to find your animal and make sure they are inside within two hours. Please note that small cats are a top priority as they are endangered and neglect of any endangered species is a serious offence punishable by the Council of Thirteen.

Regards,

Persephone Vorn
Director of the Sirian Institute for Science and Technology.

Persephone slipped her tablet into her pocket, "a weather bulletin huh? Very nice, Ben likely won't pay any attention to that on his tablet, he'll just cancel the message, I've seen him do it a thousand times." Tyra motioned towards the door, "my thoughts exactly, I thought it was more convincing coming from you. My main concern is the cats, we can't afford to lose them, they're too important. The Institute of Preservation and Propagation is counting on our efforts in the City to save the species from extinction." Persephone stopped short of the door and tapped the control to open it, "we should be fine, those in the City who are caring for the small cats are very passionate about their safety and take great care of them." Tyra pointed down the corridor. "The ISTiS is just down there." Persephone nodded, "Then let's get moving."

The two women walked towards the ISTiS, as they did the doors opened and Kiana emerged. "Captain Tyra, hold for a moment." Tyra stopped short of the ISTiS and crossed her arms, "yes, Lieutenant?" Kiana handed her a tablet, "First Minister Ben'veh is on the Emergency Comm Channel and he's quite insistent. He's demanding that you and your accomplice's transport to the Council Chamber immediately". Tyra looked confused, "the Emergency Comm, why is he on the Emergency Channel." Kiana bounced on the pads of her feet slightly looking at Persephone, "because, we had a major failure in the Communications System, I thought Josephine told you." Tyra looked down at the tablet, "uh huh, well tell the First Minister we'll be there shortly." Tyra handed Kiana back the tablet and as Kiana spun around and walked away Persephone leaned over to Tyra, "we must make haste, he's getting suspicious." Tyra leaned over in response, "first things first". Tyra hit a control on the panel and as the door slid open she and Persephone walked in. Tyra tapped in the key sequence for Engineering and the two women vanished in a hail of swirling teal energy ribbons. The door slid open and Persephone and Tyra walked onto the Engineering Deck of the Helia, it was one of the larger decks partly because the walls were lined with Hyper-Conductive Power Conduits and Thermal Shielding. All that bulk required plenty of breathing space to keep the system cool. The corridor was an atypical design for Sirian Starships. It was large and round like a tunnel, Juice had described it to Tyra once as being like a cylinder core and the entire ship surrounded that core like a large skin. As they continued down the tunnel, it opened up into a vast chamber with multiple pulsing cores hanging above their heads, the entire chamber's lighting pulsed with the heartbeat of the Ship. Tyra looked around before sighting her target, Juice was waist-deep under one of the Main Power Transfer consoles. Tyra tried to walk up as loudly as possible. Tapping on the console, she tried to be as soft as she could, "Juice, you busy?" A sudden and unmistakable thump was heard followed by Juice moaning some unintelligible slur, "must you go around sneaking up on people like that?!"

Tyra giggled, "well I walked over here as loudly as I possibly could." Juice slid out from under the console, "it's this Junction Box, I can't seem to get the Main Power Flow balanced. It's these new-fangled tools, give me an old-fashioned spanner any day." Juice wiped his hands and put the cloth down on the disabled console. "Now then Captain, since my head's stopped ringing, what can I do for you?" Tyra pointed to the Main Engineering Office, "can we?" Juice nodded, "sure". Calling to a crew member behind him, "Moran, mind the shop for me will you?" Moran looked up from his work, "sure thing boss." Juice motioned towards the office and the three went in, Tyra touched the door panel as Persephone walked in and locked the door.

Juice's lip curled, "well it's not every day a man's locked in with two lovely ladies, not that I'm not flattered and all, but what did you need to see me for Tyra?" Tyra moved over to the window and gazed at the stars. "Juice you have Command experience correct?" Juice was surprised by the question. "You mean Star Ship Command or Engineering Command?" Tyra's gaze didn't falter, "Star Ship". Juice stammered visibly shocked. "Uh, yes but only so much as was necessary to graduate from the Engineering Corps Command School." Tyra turned around, "good enough, I need you to take command of the Helia while I'm gone to implement a backup plan. I'm concerned that our attempts to save ourselves may have inadvertently put a lesser civilization at extreme risk. I need someone in Command who can anticipate problems and create on-the-spot solutions. You're also the only Flag Officer left on board with Command Status. The rest of us will be reporting to the Council, I want you to be conspicuously absent." Juice looked not unlike a deer caught in the headlamps, the stunned expression almost made Persephone burst out laughing. Juice caught himself gawking and squinted a little as he asked his next question, "what exactly do you need me to do?" Tyra moved over to his desk and sat down, interlocking her fingers she looked at Juice. "I need you to fabricate and deploy twenty-seven Standard Defence Satellites rigged with networked Shield Grid Emitters." Juice leaned forward, "to what end?" Tyra got back up from the chair she'd been seated in and gazed back out the window, sighing heavily she rubbed the back of her neck, "we're going to shield Terra and its primary moon Laana." Juice sat back, "that's no small challenge, and you know I rarely turn down a challenge." Tyra moved over to Juice and looked out of the window passed Mesira at Terra, "that planet and its entire inhabitants are now your sole responsibility." Juice grinned, "so, no pressure then?" Tyra patted him on the shoulder, "none at all." Persephone had been standing in the corner watching the conversation quietly. As Tyra got back up and nodded toward her, Persephone pulled out her tablet and input a few commands into it. "SARA access Script File Wesheb 3764. Please read current input path on this interface device and bind Script Wesheb 3764 to this control." Tapping a key on her tablet SARA's voice piped up, "key has been bound, control is authorized, all Subsystems to standby mode, The Main Transfer Resolution Matrix undergoing reconfiguration. Estimated time to completion - ten minutes." Persephone raised her head slightly, "SARA perform all functions from this point in Silent Running Mode." The control panel blinked SRM (Silent Running Mode) and then winked off." Persephone tucked her tablet in her pocket, "okay, only one more stop." Persephone tapped her Comm Badge on her wrist, "Taven, Josephine, Clinch please meet me in Requisitions." Tyra raised an eyebrow, Persephone wiggled her finger motioning at her to follow, "come on." Tyra waved at Juice, "wish me luck." Juice called after her, "good luck".

As the door slid down Juice finished his sentence, "you're gonna need it". Tyra and Persephone walked into the ISTiS, as Persephone keyed in the sequence for Requisitions, Tyra looked at Persephone, "so why are we going to Requisitions?" Persephone's back straightened, "well, we need to conceal those Shield Emitters correct?" As the transport sequence bathed them in energy ribbons, they materialized nearby their destination and Persephone continued her explanation, "so we need something that nobody is going to search." Tyra and Persephone walked out of the ISTiS and into an adjoining room down the corridor, Tyra looked confused, "I suppose." Persephone walked over to one of the Main Consoles, this was the room where everything from clothing to weapons, tools, even parts were fabricated for this vessel. There were rows of Interface Consoles and Materialization Trays. They were all glowing a soft amber and the Consoles blinked with readouts and item explanations. Persephone walked over to the closest one. "Okay, something that's not going to stand out and make people think we're up to something, but will give them pause to think about searching us. SARA, craft me three brown suede pencil skirts and tailor them to the patterns for myself, Tyra and Josephine. Also craft me five jackets, double button, brown suede, flare business style. Tailor them for myself, Tyra, Josephine, Taven and Clinch." Tyra was nodding as she was getting an idea of what Persephone had in mind. As the items materialized Taven, Josephine and Clinch walked in, Josephine carried with her a cloth bag under her arm. Persephone caught sight of Josephine and put down the pile she'd gathered. She moved over to hug her sister, "Jo, are you okay?" Josephine nodded, "yes, it was just a minor scratch, it wasn't nearly as bad as it looked. A couple of passes with the Cellular Regenerator and it was fixed. I had actually just got out of the shower when you paged me. I caught Taven on Deck Three on my way down, what's all this?" Persephone separated the clothes. For us, three jackets and three skirts and for the gentlemen, the same jackets." Taven picked up his jacket and turned it around, "not bad." As he slipped it on he pulled at the cuffs, "ever think of taking up tailoring Seph...Seph?" Taven turned around as the three girls were pulling up their skirts, "wooookay!" Turning back around he heard Tyra's voice from behind him, "honestly you'd think he'd never seen a pair of legs before." Persephone's giggle echoed through the room. Persephone's voice came from behind, "Jo, can you give me a hand I can't quite reach, Taven you can turn around now." Clinch was snickering at Taven, who had moved to the other side of the room and now started to drift back to the rest of the group. As Taven turned around, the three girls were putting on their jackets. Persephone tossed her hair out away from the collar and it hit her back with a fairly loud slap. Tyra and Josephine were tidying themselves up as Persephone grabbed her hair band from her arm, pulling her hair into a ponytail she twisted it round and round and folded it into an interesting bun, "Jo, the Shields." Josephine reached into the bag that she'd brought with her. Handing the Emitters to the group, she reached down and attached the Shield Emitter to the inside of her skirt, Josephine and Tyra did the same. Taven scratched his head, "well that's all well and good but, what are we supposed to do?" Persephone shook her head, "Men, where would you be without us women to figure things out? Give me your shield!" She reached inside Taven's jacket, felt around a bit and latched the device on just below his inside vest pocket. Tyra was busy doing the same for Clinch, "stop fidgeting, honestly."

Gazing over the group, Persephone picked up her tablet from inside her vest which was lying in the pile with the rest of the clothing. She tucked her tablet inside her coat pocket making sure the intelligent display was fingertip ready. Josephine stepped forward, "now all of these Shields have been fine-tuned to repulse the Transport Energy Signature. This takes an extreme amount of energy and each cell will be depleted within ten seconds, so don't hit your shields until I tell you." Taven looked confused, "so how do we activate them?" Josephine held out her arm, "just tap your Comm Badge twice quickly and the Shields will activate. A confirmation tone will tell you that your system is online." Taven nodded and straightened his jacket, "simple enough." Persephone gathered the group, "we all know the risks and the consequences if we do nothing. We all go or we all stay, but from this moment there is no turning back, so I need each and every one of you to tell me you're ready to go." Taven stepped forward, "I'm always at your side Seph, no matter what." Tyra followed him, "as am I". Josephine stepped forward, "I've been looking after you since you were a little girl scraping your knees on the sidewalk, I'm not about to stop now. Clinch sauntered forward, "who am I to fly in the face of adventure, let's go to work!" Persephone nodded "right, to the Main Transport Bay. Oh, Tyra, you know what we discussed earlier?" Tyra nodded, "yes?" Persephone tilted her head slightly, "are you ready?" Tyra nodded again, "as soon as you give the word." The group walked out of the Requisitions Hall and into the ISTiS. Tyra called out to SARA, "Main Transport Bay". The group was washed in a flurry of swirling energy ribbons, zigging and zagging through the Internal Transfer Conduits, they emerged on Deck Five near the Main Transport Bay. It was a fairly small area, just enough for a small armoury, which was there in case they were boarded and the Transporter Bay itself. The system was automated, and the room was very general in design. Several teal energy currents crackled along the ceiling. The room itself was lit by the rippling energy currents that were coursing through the roof of the room. A large panel was embedded in the wall, Tyra tapped a few controls and a panel recessed and slid up, revealing a keyboard that slid out from the wall. Tyra tapped in the coordinates for transport into the Main System. The condition light blinked amber three times to signify standby mode. Tyra looked back to the group, "Is everybody ready?" The group nodded, Tyra tapped the ignition key and the amber standby lamp flashed teal, "here we go". As Tyra walked back to the group, Persephone reached for Taven's hand, "I'm nervous." Without breaking his forward gaze, he simply responded, "me too." A series of teal lightning strikes struck near the group, from the ceiling, ribbons of coursing energy showered over Tyra and her team, encircling them, they were scanned by white beams of light moving over the entire length of the group until they met, electrifying and rumbling with thunder. The room now vacant left an empty feeling, a lone console in the corner blinked slowly as the lights returned to standby mode and the system went dark.

OUT OF THE FRYING PAN...

A wave of teal light washed over the Waiting Area for the Council, lightning struck the ground and ribbons of dancing energy poured in from the ceiling. Forming a shape, the energy ribbons began to circle rapidly and a white strip of light shone from within the tempest. Spreading outward, Tyra and her team materialized into the room as the swirling vortex ebbed and retracted into the roof. It was night in Atlanka, the Hall was dark, which was quite odd. Normally the illumination in this area was quite high. The room itself was sandy-coloured marble by design, columns lined the room in staggered numbers. The walls glowed a soft amber from the sconces and the entire room felt somewhat smaller. Persephone's throat began to tighten, "Taven, this doesn't feel right." Taven looked around, "stay calm, everybody stay calm." As they sat down, the door towards the end of the room opened. A guard called from inside, "they're ready for you." Persephone got up with Taven, but fell back for a moment clutching Taven's hand. She reached up on her toes and kissed him gently. He hugged her quickly and motioned towards the door, "come on." Clinch called from in front of them, "hey Seph, so long as you're handing those out..." Persephone grinned, "sorry fresh out!" Tyra and the group walked through the door, Taven and Persephone quickly bringing up the rear. The Council sat around them, Ben'veh looked ominous, almost evil. It was not the man Persephone had worked so closely with for so many years, there was something very wrong.

Ben'veh crossed his arms, "well, well, well, you must think you're quite the heroes hmm?" Tyra's back straightened, obviously offended, she retorted "your brilliant plan to destroy the asteroid with torpedoes not only failed miserably, but you managed to completely pollute Mesira's atmosphere in the process. I can think of at least fifteen different violations of the climate integrity laws in that act alone." Ben'veh slammed his hand down, "silence". Persephone and Josephine jumped. Neither of them had ever seen this kind of behaviour from him. Fourth Minister Kelveena tapped at the console near her seat calling up information. Lightning snapped from the ceiling and arced into a holographic display. "These images were taken of a mysterious large object that resembles a Sirian Support Star Ship, passing close to the City about ten minutes prior to your theft of the Solaran, can we assume this is you?" Tyra put her hands behind her back, "yes". Kelveena tapped her stylus on the desk, "not only am I left scratching my head as to how you managed to get the Ship's power signature below the detection threshold without crashing it, but your manoeuvres are also most interesting. It appears the Ship itself is anchored to the terrain. If you weren't being cited for gross violations of conduct, I'd award you a medal simply for pulling off such a feat." She tapped the console and a security recording of their theft of the Solaran began to play. As Tyra watched the entire episode over again, she couldn't help a smile creep over her lips. Ben'veh cut short the recording. "Something about this amuses you Captain?" Tyra shrugged, "just a Captain's pride at seeing her crew perform the impossible." Ben'veh got up, "I don't think you realize the seriousness of your situation, do you think this is a joke?!" Persephone had heard enough, she burst forward walking straight to the table and placing her hands down. She was almost nose to nose with Ben'veh. "What is wrong with you! You'd prefer to grill us, we who are trying to do the right thing and you'd let your entire City, who you are responsible for die just to satisfy your own pride. What kind of twisted monster are you?" Ben'veh sneered at her, "don't you dare talk to me in such a manner." Persephone glared right back at him, "I'll talk to you how I please, respect is earned not bestowed and you've lost every last ounce you had." Ben'veh breathed heavily, "back off right now or I'll have you locked away and executed for treason." Kelveena who'd been watching the entire exchange gaped. "First Minister you can't do that, the laws regarding capital punishment were repealed centuries ago." Ben'veh snapped his head to fire a menacing glare at her, she was so shocked she visibly jumped backwards. Second Minister Terrance looked up at Ben'veh who was standing next to him. "Ben, you can't hurt her or any of them, it's against our highest laws." Ben'veh backed up looking from side to side, "you've turned against me, all of you. I won't be cornered so easily, I still have allies, you'll pay for this, all of you!" Persephone moved back to the group, tapping the control on her tablet, the shrill screech of a falcon's call was heard through the halls. Kelveena got up, "what on earth?" SARA's voice broke through the drone of the alert tones. " All systems green, patterns will be stored in ten seconds." Kelveena looked at Persephone, "what have you...?" Persephone shook her head, "I'm sorry Minister, we'll discuss this later". SARA's voice carried through the halls as all the doors slid down and locked. "Pattern storage in five seconds, please refrain from moving." Ben'veh shot a look at Persephone, "you!! I'LL KILL YOU!!!" SARA began a countdown, "four, three..." Ben'veh began to charge at Persephone as Taven and Clinch stepped in front of the three women. SARA's voice continued, "two, one..." Josephine screamed, "now!" As Ben'veh leaped at the group, Taven, Clinch, Josephine, Persephone and Tyra all hit their Comm Badges and a series of soft tones was heard, the entire room lit up in teal light. Lightning struck everywhere, coursing energy ribbons encircled everybody except their group, in rapid succession every unshielded person in the Council Chamber was decompiled and stored in the Pattern Buffer. As Ben'veh was dematerialized in mid-air, Persephone's Shield died. She looked at Taven in terror. The teal glow subsided and Persephone stood panting, so short of breath, she could barely breathe. Taven caught her as she fell to her knees, "Seph...Seph!"

Josephine knelt beside her and grabbed an emergency injector from her pocket, as she pushed it into Persephone's neck her breathing slowed. Her eyes fluttered open, "I'm not...?" Taven shook his head, "no you're still here." Persephone threw her arms around his neck, in the moment she didn't care. She was just thankful that he was there and that she hadn't been stored. Taven looked at Josephine, "do you always carry an injector in your pocket?" Josephine smirked, "one of the first rules of being a fantastic Engineer, be prepared for anything." Taven sat Persephone up, "there, catch your breath, you're okay for now." Persephone tried to speak in between breaths. "We, we need to, we need to board the Jovus and get her Engines online." Taven held her shoulders, "you settle first." Persephone breathed deeply in and out. Clinch squatted down and moved her hair onto her left shoulder, he pushed on a pressure point near the base of her neck. Her breathing slowed and she calmed down. Taven looked surprised, "where did you learn that?" Clinch dusted his hands off, "you know that week-long course in Stage Four Advanced Martial Arts that I took two years ago?" Taven nodded, "yes?" Clinch smiled as he got up and extended a hand to both Taven and Persephone, "it's amazing what you pick up while learning to defend yourself." Taven touched Persephone's arm, "are you okay now?" Persephone tucked a lock of hair behind her ear, "yes thank you. Thank you Clinch that was amazing." Clinch shrugged, "like always." Persephone walked over and extended a hand to Josephine who was checking the cell status on her Emitter. "Jo, my big sister, always coming to my rescue." Josephine took her hand and Persephone got up. "You'd be right there if the roles were reversed." Tyra nodded towards the Emitter, "how did we fare?" Josephine tapped the crystal and threw the unit behind her. "the cells are completely spent, the units are useless now. Discard them we don't want anybody to trace us." Persephone and Tyra reached up inside their skirts and dislodged them, while Taven and Clinch pulled them from inside their jackets. Tossing them on the floor, Persephone's gaze turned towards where Ben'veh had been. Tyra looked at her, "Seph, what are you thinking?" Persephone looked at Tyra, "I know he's sick and needs help. I confess though, it was nice to finally have the last word with him."

Josephine spoke from the back of the group, "what are we going to tell the rest of the Council when they ask why we did what we did?" Taven looked at Clinch and then to Persephone, "the truth." Josephine tapped her Comm Badge, "SARA override transport settings and transport the remaining life signs in this room to downtown block A64, Transit Station 762. SARA commented, "initializing." Teal energy ribbons swirled around the group and again they slipped into a thin band of light, which electrified and rumbled with thunder leaving nothing but the soft glow of the amber sconces and a low echo from the Hall.

The downtown core was quiet, it was a fairly common night in Atlanka City. The Transit Station was lightly manned, just a simple transfer clerk on duty. The station itself was located on the corner of a normally busy street. The Tower for the Sirian Galactic Bank was nearby, as was the Spire for the Telecommunications Infrastructure. A gust of cool air hit Persephone's face and caressed her hair as it passed. Her eyes closed taking in the moment, fleeting as it was, she wouldn't get many more like it. Mesira's sky was normally a deep indigo blue with Terra's soft sphere glowing in the background. Now the entire sky was a dark blood red and Terra's sphere along with Laana was blurry and hard to see. Tyra motioned towards the Station, "over here". Taven moved over to distract the clerk. Tyra snuck towards the Control Interface Panel near the Rear Transport Coils. It was a secondary console that was rarely ever used. Persephone moved near her, Tyra whispered, "get everybody into position, this will be over in twenty seconds." Josephine moved over near Taven standing just out of eyesight. Persephone nodded as Tyra tapped her communications badge and whispered to SARA, we're ready, create the distraction." SARA responded quietly, "understood, sounding Ion Alert now." Teal lights flashed everywhere, vibrant against the dark golden towers. The clerk snapped his head around and screamed, "hey!" Josephine caught him mid-stride and hit him with an injector. He fell limp and Taven caught him, "prepared is right." Josephine grinned as they shuffled and laid the man down on a bench nearby. Tyra motioned, "come on, come on, we have less than ten seconds." Persephone ran to the Main Console and her fingers flew across the keypad. SARA's voice snapped over the Intercom, "SIV Jovus on lockdown procedure, Command level authorization is required to override restrictions." Taven moved over to Persephone, "oh for the love of... SARA, override interlocks on SIV Jovus, Authorization Code Seti Isis nine seven two." SARA's voice crackled again as spotlights appeared in the distance, Josephine screamed to Persephone, "it's now or never." Persephone hit the control and the shrill call of a hawk was heard to register a transport was in progress. A Taeer-altnan Escort Shuttle slipped passed the closest spire, as the system engaged and the team was encircled in a swirling energy vortex; the door of the Shuttle opened as the Shuttle turned and hovered in mid-air. Persephone waved at the occupant as she and her team phased out and entered transit mode.

The Jovus sat dark in space, only basic Life Support was functional. All repairs to the Ship had been halted, pending a review on the possibility of simply scrapping the Ship and christening a new vessel in her name. The Main Transport Bay sparked slightly, some of its panels were shattered, others only half-functioning. The lights were almost non-existent and a piece of conduit hung from the black ceiling. A warm teal glow lit up the darkened room, brightening the surroundings and giving life to a sad lonely vessel. Once home to a vibrant crew and a loving Captain, she how faced destruction. The transport sequence began and the room was strobed and lit by swirling ribbons of energy. A single beam of light appeared in the storm, flashing and then expanding to reveal Tyra and her group. As the energy matrix finished the transport sequence, sparks flew from the damaged conduit. Taven ducked and covered his head from the shower of sparks above him. He walked off the pad and shook his head in dismay as he looked at his home, "what a mess." Tyra stepped over a couple of pieces of debris, "it can all be fixed." Taven nodded, "if they don't scrap my Ship first." Tyra grabbed Taven's arm, "hey, I won't let that happen, neither will you. The Jovus will fly again and under her own power. Now we have work to do, Jo, Taven you're with me, Clinch, Seph, head to the Bridge, see if you can power up the Secondary Generators and get the lights on, what's left of them." Persephone and Clinch nodded, "right." As the ISTiS was offline and damaged, they had to walk the corridors and use service junctions to access the higher decks. The deck they walked along had been so beautiful not so long ago, shining in brushed gold and marble floors. Columns sank into the wall, curved and contoured to the shape of the exterior windows. Now those same windows were cracked, some were non-existent instead, replaced by teal rippling Force Fields to keep the atmosphere inside. The floor was heaved in places where the plating had buckled from the explosions. Stray pieces of conduit and internal structure dangled from the ceiling. The Jovus groaned sadly, she was a mess, but not without hope. Such had been a recurring theme for the past week. So many times Persephone had thought those words, disturbing to her that those same words were now beginning to not affect her. She refused to allow that to happen, this kind of situation should be the exception, not the rule, and she wanted her life back to how it was before all of this happened. She yearned for quiet, sitting on the balcony of her apartment, listening to the waves crash against the shore at night, with a cup of tea in hand and reading a good book. Such memories now seemed so distant, so much had happened in such a short span of time. Piercing her daydream, Clinch was strolling along beside her, "Seph, psst, Seph?" Persephone turned her head to him, "oh sorry, what?" Clinch smiled, "daydreaming?" Persephone brushed a lock of hair out of her face as she moved aside a fallen tube, "something like that." Persephone stepped over a heave in the flooring paying attention to not get her shoe stuck, "you know when you use the Transport System all the time, you forget the sheer size of these Ships." Clinch grinned, "It certainly is easy to take for granted isn't it?" Persephone nodded, "mmm hmm". Clinch pointed to a doorway coming up on their right. "Okay, we're almost there. This junction should lead us to the corridor behind the Bridge. We can force open the door from there and get in that way." Persephone nodded, "good, because heels and large distances don't mix." As Clinch popped open the Manual Release Hatch to the door beside them he looked over at Persephone, "yeah, I meant to ask, why are you wearing those anyway?" Persephone pulled a shoe off and rubbed her aching foot while Clinch tried to get the door open, "oh, I've been wearing them since I first boarded the Jovus. With everything that's happened, I guess I haven't paid much attention to my footwear." She stated it so matter of fact that Clinch couldn't help but laugh a little, "footwear huh?" Persephone slipped her shoe back on, "ugh, yeah, is that door open yet?" Clinch reached his hand up inside the wall, "not yet," he winced as his arm stretched up into the wall and felt around. "I'm having some trouble with the Secondary Bypass, looks like this one wants to be more difficult. I'm going to have to pull the Fiber Optic Connections." Persephone tossed her ponytail behind her head, "I'll add it to the list of things to fix." As she said that, the door moaned and slid up halfway. Clinch shook his head, "poor old girl, come on, let's go, Seph, grab the other side would you?" Persephone leaned down and grabbed the opposite side of the door. Clinch, with his knees bent to brace most of the weight, looked over to Persephone, she returned his gaze with a nod and together they lifted the door up the rest of the way. Clinch held it in place, "Seph, there should be a latch or catch up near the top to manually lock this in place, find it and pull it out." Persephone felt around the top of the door, "you okay?" Clinch winced clearly having trouble with the weight of the door, "yup, I'm fine, take your time." Persephone's index finger crossed a plate, she pushed it and it popped loose and slid it across, "got it!" Clinch lowered his arms and rubbed his shoulders, "well now, that was an adventure wasn't it?" Persephone smiled, "yes we shall be remembered famously." Clinch shook his head, "this way, we climb from here." Persephone looked up the dark shaft, "it's little long don't you think?" Clinch grabbed hold of the ladder, "normally I'd say ladies first but circumstances being what they are..." Persephone squinted at him, "you have a dirty mind, get going." Clinch started to climb, "I'm going, I'm going." Persephone grinned and shook her head, "they never change." Clinch called back down, "what was that?" As Persephone began to follow him up the shaft she called back, "oh nothing." Clinch climbed ahead of her, "uh huh."

Taven, Josephine and Tyra emerged onto the Main Engineering Deck from the adjacent corridor. Amber displays flashed erratically throughout the almost pitch-black room. Taven slid down a panel on the wall near him and grabbed a beacon. Holding it in his hand he turned it on. It was a small oval device, designed to fit into the palm of a person's hand, quite normal in all respects. The light was a brilliant blue/white colour and the exterior was brushed gold. Tyra and Jo reached into the storage bin and grabbed one too. The three scanned the room with what little light they could throw from their hand-held Emitters. Josephine walked up just behind Taven, "I'm glad Fyar isn't here, his heart would break if he saw this." Taven nodded, "he would be the first one spearheading the reconstruction effort." Josephine stood close to Taven, her shoulder brushing against his arm, "don't worry, we'll get her flying again, but for now, I would settle for some light. Shouldn't Clinch and Seph have reached the Bridge by now?" Taven shook his head, "I don't know how much damage there is between here and there, they may have run into a few obstacles." Josephine nodded, "mmm, well!" She scanned the nearby wall, "the Interface for the Secondary Generators is right...over...there." She shone her beacon lamp on a specific Console that didn't look as damaged as the others. "It doesn't look nearly as beat up as some of the other systems, let me see what I can do." Josephine walked over to the console stepping over several pieces of destroyed conduit and various hunks of metal and plastic. Finally coming up to the console, she hit a few keys and brought up the Diagnostic Screen. Flickering and stammering, the display was erratic at best. Josephine frowned, "I know you're not feeling the best honey, but I need you to co-operate." Taven raised an eyebrow as Josephine dropped to her knees and pulled off the panel below the console, exposing the five Crystal Memory Sheets. Josephine pulled her tablet out of her jacket pocket, "mmm hmm, I thought as much. Taven, toss me a Sub-quantum Fusion Emitter please." Taven looked around, moving over to the Main Console he tapped a control and a drawer slid open with several small tools inside. Finding the Emitter he walked over to Josephine. Taven kicked the debris out of the way as he made his way over, "here." Josephine nodded, "thanks, it looks like there's a short in the Secondary Asynchronous Data Transfer lines, Taven, hold your beacon steady." Taven steadied his hand as Josephine activated the Emitter and aimed it into one of the Amber Crystal Sheets. Tracing randomly a little way down the side of the sheet, the console flickered randomly and suddenly the power steadied. It whined as the system stabilized and chirped slightly. Josephine replaced the panel and Taven held his hand out to help Josephine back up. She leaned over the console tapping in commands and reading reports. Taven rubbed his five o'clock shadow, "well, how does it look?" Josephine read the readouts, flipping through about four screens, she finally tapped a few keys bringing up the restart sequence. "The system reads green for a restart, but I don't know how much I trust these Sensors. If we have any kind of overload, I'm aborting the restart immediately." Taven nodded at the console, "go ahead." Josephine tapped a keystroke and the tray in the console shrieked as it recessed. Squealing a high-pitched metal grinding sound it slid inside and the keyboard slid out. Josephine was about to begin typing when several sparks flew from the keyboard. She jumped back as Taven caught her, "damn, it looks like there's another short in the Interface Panel." Taven called to Tyra who had moved over to the Main Control Array and was brushing debris off the console. "Tyra, can you find the Control Interlock over there and reduce the power flow to this console by fifty percent?" Tyra cracked her knuckles, "it's been a while, let me see if I remember." Tyra hit a few controls, scratching the side of her head and obviously unsure of the next step, she stood for a moment, her eyes lit up, "ah hah!" She leaned over the console and found the menu for Power Flow Adjustment, "how's that?" Taven watched as the console illumination dimmed, "that's good, hopefully, that will pad any more breaks in the line." Josephine moved over to the console, "okay, beginning Reactor Four's startup sequence, running prestart checklist and priming the Main Injectors." The main Reaction Chamber recessed into the far wall of Engineering, which had been pitch black, began to glow a very dim amber. This class of vessel used four smaller Reactors to feed stable power into a Main Chamber where the plasma was compiled and fed to every system from Communications to Warp Propulsion. "Looking good, reactants are stable, the plasma flow is settling down. Okay, I'm ramping up the plasma flow to fifty percent of normal." The chamber's hue glowed brighter, the entire compartment now was the colour of a summer sunrise. Josephine read the status readouts, calling to Tyra. "Tyra, double-check the instrument readings on Injector Port Thirty Four." Tyra tapped the console and took a moment to read, "it looks fine over here Jo". Josephine shook her head, "I don't trust it, I want absolute certainty. Just a minute, Taven, can you give me a hand?" Josephine motioned over to an access panel on the wall to the left of the Main Chamber, "we need to get that panel off." Taven and Josephine walked over to the wall, "now, there should be a button to dislodge the panel, but the system may be damaged so we might have to force it."

Taven felt around the plate as did Josephine, finding the switch to disengage the lock she turned to Taven, "okay, here goes." Josephine slid the button into the chamber casing and she heard a loud click, "hmm." Josephine grabbed the panel from either side and pulled it clear, "well what do you know, something worked properly for once." Josephine pulled her tablet from her vest pocket and a fiber optic line from one of her side pockets. Connecting the line both to her tablet and the Interface socket for the Reactor System, she ran a scan. "This tablet is set up to work as a stand-alone scanner for Engineering components. If this says the system is running clean, then I'll ramp up the power.

I just can't afford any mistakes, I have to be sure." Taven nodded, "no harm in being thorough." Josephine paged through the information being presented to her on the tablet, pulling her stylus out of her pocket, she tapped several key sequences into the device. Taven stood waiting patiently as Josephine held the device higher and squinted at it. "Reactors One, Two and Three are unsalvageable. Four looks to be running properly, I need to shut down One, Two and Three immediately, that's what's causing the variations in power flow. One is a complete disaster; otherwise, everything looks good from here. Core temperature steady, Coolant System normal, Injectors normal, Reactants Processing normal. Reactor Four looks to be intact. I think we're okay, it must be a faulty Sensor." Taven shook his head, "one of how many hundred on this Ship." Josephine waved her hand down, "pah, Sensors are easy, asking me to rebuild a Warp Core with nothing but a toothpick and wire, now that's more of a challenge. Just a minute while I disable the other three Reactors." Josephine tapped a couple of controls on her tablet and the room's illumination dimmed slightly. The teal pulsing light which was encased in the wall normally shone brilliantly and pulsed with the heartbeat of the Ship. Now it was dimly lit and pulsed ever so slowly. Josephine moved back to the console she had been working at before, "ramping up Plasma Flow to ninety-five percent and locking the system at that level." The teal ball in the centre of the glowing Reactor that had been dark, began to pulse gently with teal light. Josephine motioned to Tyra, "Tyra, hit the lights, internal only, limit illumination to the Bridge, Engineering and any other areas where we need to work." Tyra's hands tapped along the console, she turned around behind her and reached above her head, to input more command sequences into the Energy Transfer Array. Turning back to the Main Console, she input the last of the Command Protocols, "okay, here goes, lights coming on...now." The clicking sound of the internal lights turning on echoed through the Ship. Clinch was just helping Persephone out of the shaft when from below her, light racks switched on one after another. As she climbed out, all the lights in the corridor clicked on and the displays lit up. Clinch could see the devastation, most of the walls had been blown open. Several areas of the floor were heaved so badly, that if he moved over them the gravity became unstable. Persephone's mouth hung open, "Taven's right, she is a mess." Clinch flicked her shoulder with the back of his fingers, "she may have taken a beating, but she's a tough old bird, she isn't down for the count yet." Persephone smiled at his enthusiasm, it was infectious. Clinch pointed to the door to the Bridge, "over here, you know they have impeccable timing." Persephone nodded as they walked up to the door, "that was probably Jo, she's one of the most impatient people I've ever known." Clinch tapped the control and the door didn't move. "Yeah, if she can get something done, she almost always does it herself rather than wait." Clinch put his hand on his hips and stared at the door, "hmm, well we have power and the circuit is stable, I wonder why it won't move?" Persephone looked around the frame, then when she looked down she noticed some melted plastic leaking out from behind the door. Persephone pointed down, "likely something to do with that, Clinch give me your Plasma Pistol." Clinch pulled his weapon out and handed it to Persephone, "you sure you don't want me to do that, it's pretty fine work." Persephone squeezed the weapon gently and a beam of directed plasma energy shot out from the pistol. "I'm fine, I do this all the time." Clinch watched as she neatly seared a break between the melted material and the door, "well, I'm impressed, where did you learn to shoot like that?" Persephone pressed the door control and the door groaned and began to slide up, "my kitchen." She handed Clinch back his pistol and as he holstered it, the door slid the rest of the way up. Persephone walked through, Clinch followed scratching his head, "wait, your kitchen...I'm lost?" Persephone turned her head and smiled at him, "how else am I supposed to get off pancakes that are stuck to my ceiling."

Clinch looked at her oddly, "you plasma cut pancakes off your ceiling?" Persephone winked, "they're very sticky pancakes!" Clinch looked at her strangely, "uh huh. Okay, well it looks like most of the Secondary Systems are running, why don't you take Science and do a complete Systems Sweep and I'm going to check Navigation and Propulsion." Persephone began to move over to the Science Console. Clinch sat down at the Navigation Console, brushing debris onto the floor he began to run a systems check. Persephone walked over to the Main Science Array. The devastation of the Ship was such a shock she wasn't watching where she was going and a blown piece of Fiber Optic Cable smacked her in the face as she turned around. Pulling it out of the ceiling and brushing the debris off her console, she mused to herself, "remind me to dock the Maid's pay." Clinch grinned, he was happy to see her more like her normal self. The strain of the issue with the Council had been pulling her spirits down hard. Now with them stored safely in Atlanka's Memory Banks, she could focus on finishing the job they started and not worry about reporting to anybody. He tapped a few controls and after scanning the results he spoke without breaking his focus. "Well it looks like the Engineering Corps Team that was here managed to get the Propulsion Systems fixed; it looks as though the Power Flow Conduits for both Sub-Light and Warp are in good working order. I wonder why they didn't file the job completion report. The last news I received said that very little work had been done. Odd that they would deliberately violate procedure." Persephone was working away at her console but responded to him without breaking her gaze at the monitor, "perhaps simply an error in our favour." Clinch smiled, "maybe, in any case, the work was done. Now we just need to power the system up." Persephone's diagnostic program wasn't even halfway through, but she didn't like what she saw. "I've only got partial readouts, but from what I'm seeing this isn't good. Shields, Weapons, Sensors, Internal Transport and Communications are destroyed, they need to be completely rebuilt. Reactor Three is a hopeless pile of junk, number Two looks to have coolant problems and possible core damage. Reactor Four looks to be intact and Reactor One is a melted pile of titanium ooze. I'm getting some odd readings from the adjacent power relays, some interesting fluctuations in the power curve, it could just be a blown Sensor Relay." Persephone tapped her Comm Badge, "Taven, could you take Josephine into the deck below you and check on Reactor Four. It looks good but I'm getting some odd readings from the Relay Sensors." Josephine tapped her Badge and chimed in, "what about Two and Three?" Persephone's voice crackled, half distorted by the weak signal. "Nu..ber Two is a...total mess, possi...le cracks in the Reactor casing. Number Three is a...complete wri...off, the system is totally destroyed." Josephine shook her head as the Comm Channel closed, "that's going to make my life so much more difficult." Taven scratched his arm, "with one Reactor..." Josephine tucked her hair behind her ear, "we'll only be able to sustain twenty percent nominal thrust and our Manoeuvring Jets will be severely hampered. That's if number Four continues to function without problems. Even so, considering the condition of the other three, I'm hesitant to bring the remaining Reactor up to full power. They have all suffered extreme overheating stress, the whole set needed to be replaced before we left Space Dock. I'll never understand Sirian High Command sending us on a mission, knowing that our power systems were severely compromised." Taven motioned to the hatch near the wall to the deck below, "I trust your judgement." Taven and Josephine moved towards the hatch at the far Port side of the compartment. It was neatly nestled between two now-destroyed consoles. They normally regulated power flow to Science Labs Two, Three and Seven, Engineering Labs One, Three and Five and Supplemental Bridge controls. As Josephine was nearing the hatch, she spun around on her heels her ponytail whipping around behind her and she stormed over to Tyra. "Oh this is ludicrous, Tyra isn't there any way to get Internal Communications online?" Tyra tapped a few controls and brought up a diagnostic of the Communications Grid, "not that I can see, the power flow from the primary supply is severed at all points, any attempt to route secondary power will cause a cascading plasma flood into the adjacent corridors." Josephine was on a mission, "blast, let me take a look." Josephine moved beside Tyra and called up the same schematic, then she brought up a second schematic of the Internal Security Net beside the one for Communications. "Well, the one thing that doesn't seem to have suffered any damage is the Security Grid." Taven put his hands in his pockets, "likely because of the Shielding around it to prevent intentional overload by prisoners being confined." Josephine nodded, "that's a safe bet, hmm, I wonder...what if we dumped some energy into the Field Emitter Coils. Okay, they seem to be stable, now where was that...? Okay, here's what I'm doing. I'm sealing the broken conduits with Force Fields, this is by no means safe or sure to work. The only thing in those sections is the Primary and Secondary Armory right?" Taven nodded, "yes but if a plasma leak hits those weapons..." Josephine looked back at the console, "right, Taven, feel like taking a walk?" Taven moved over beside Josephine, "sure what do you have in mind?" Josephine switched the overview to a cross-section of the wall which housed the Main Control Array for the Armory door. Pointing to the diagram she began to explain, "okay, this is obviously an internal diagram of the wall control panel." Taven shrugged, "oh, obviously." Josephine squinted at him, "pay attention, now if you remove it, you'll find a red crystal slotted into the wall, it's oval and high gloss. That's the Primary Backup System for the Door Interface. Now the system is shielded from weapons fire, it will take a sustained burst at the highest setting to burn out the control pathways. Once you see the crystal burst, you can stop firing and the door should only be able to be opened by being cut open and removed." Taven pointed to the crystal, "just how long of a burst are we talking." Josephine looked towards him, "about a minute of constant fire." Taven nodded in response and started to walk towards the entrance to the Engineering Section; he was almost out the door when Josephine called after him, "oh Taven, use a Dual Cell Plasma Rifle, Second Generation." Taven nodded once and moved out the door. This was his home, his life for the last ten years. When he first took command of the Jovus, she seemed old and outdated, but as he got to know his Ship, he realized that old sometimes carries much more feeling than anything new could evoke. His bond with this Ship had grown strong over time and it tore him apart to see her in such a horrible state. He walked over to a Primary Access Hatch and stopped for a moment to run his hand along the wall, he could feel the scrapes in the gold plating and his heart sank. He vowed then and there that he would repair her, even if he had to do it with his bare hands. This was his home, and he would fight to keep it. He opened the hatch and dropped down to the next deck. It was dark, and most of the lights were blown out from the major explosion that had rocked this section. Thankfully, the Hull hadn't been breached, although it had been close. Taven pulled his beacon out of his vest pocket and holding it in his hand, it switched on. The entire deck was a complete disaster, panels from the wall lay across the hall, half-melted by the intense plasma fires before they were contained. He looked around, squinting in the dim light he caught sight of the Armory door. Walking over to the Armory he tapped the open control and the door buzzed and groaned. It moved a small amount, stopped, jittered a little, some dust fell from the side of the moulding and the door slid the rest of the way up. Taven walked in, this area wasn't nearly as badly damaged, the lights were mostly blown but the walls were intact. He wondered why the rest of Sirian Architecture wasn't so well shielded from explosions and fire. He shrugged at the idea and moved to a case in the far left corner of the room; unlatching the clasp he opened the top. Several Plasma Rifles lay before him. His ship carried several cases such as this and many others containing various kinds of ordnance. This was one of the most powerful beam-based handheld weapons they had. He pulled the rifle out; most Sirian weapons were very much designed like a normal gun. They had a butt, a handle and a barrel. This weapon was very different. It had a butt and handle; however, the normal barrel that on most Sirian weapons was just a straight piece of tubing with an Emitter at the end, was instead replaced by a sweeping arc which took the shape of a falcon at the tip; the wings swept out and then backwards, shrinking towards the back of the rifle and folding in near where the Optical Sensor Sight rested. Taven turned the weapon over and took a good look; he had to appreciate its design. As much as it was a very powerful weapon, it was almost a work of art in its own right. He took a Sensor Sight out of the case and slid it onto the top of the Rifle until he heard a click. The sight blinked on and an indicator light flashed amber, signifying that the modification had been correctly installed. Taven picked up four cells from the case and put them in his pocket; he hadn't used one of these weapons before, but he'd heard they were energy-hungry devices and burned through cells fast. He took two more cells and flipped open the compartment in the handle, sliding the two glowing teal cylindrical cells into their sockets in the weapon, he flipped the compartment closed and he heard a gentle whine to alert him that the weapon was now armed and ready to fire. Since he hadn't used a weapon of this grade before, he decided before he shot at such a delicate target, he'd better figure out exactly how to fire it. All Sirian weapons followed a standard design, the trigger was built into the handle, and you simply squeezed firmly to fire. Taven moved out into the Hall and found a fairly large piece of debris that was decently thick. He set the weapon to half-power and knelt on one knee. Looking down the scope he lined up his target, he squeezed the trigger and teal lightning rippled along the top of the rifle, energy swirled around the bird's wings, two white strips of light swept from the outside of the bird's wings to the centre, as the two stripes converged, the entire barrel glowed a brilliant teal and the weapon sounded a buildup. Within half a second the entire chain of events was over and the weapon discharged at the piece of wall plating. The beam from the barrel was a flat spread of multiple teal lightning forks. They focused shortly after firing and the entire series of discharges began to coil and spin hitting the target so hard, that it flew across the hall and slammed against a door. Taven released the trigger, astonished by the immense power of this particular rifle. He was particularly impressed by the complete lack of any kickback from the Discharge Emitters. He fired once more checking his aim, then moved back to the door. Kneeling across the hall from the door, he tapped his Comm Badge, "Taven to Engineering, I'm ready to seal this door." Josephine's voice crackled through, the signal was a little better as Taven was far closer to her location. "Okay Tav, pull the Control Panel out from the wall and let it dangle on the Fiber Optic Wiring." Taven placed the rifle on the floor and went over to the door, gently pulling the panel out; he didn't want to inflict any more damage than was needed. He gently tugged on the cable and left the control box to dangle on the wires as instructed, "okay Jo, the panel's out, it's this dark red crystal?" Josephine's voice crackled through the system, "yes, it needs a sustained burst from the weapon you pulled from the Armory. About one minute should do to burn through the shielding and melt the crystal." Taven walked back to the rifle and picked it up, "right, let's do this". He braced the butt of the rifle against his shoulder and aimed down the sight, finding the target, the Sensor Crosshairs flashed white to indicate the weapon was locking on, then a solid teal to indicate a confirmed lock. Taven held the weapon steady and squeezed the trigger. Again the weapon charged as rings of energy swirled around the Emitters and lightning arced up the barrel. Two lines of brilliant white scanned from the tip of the wings to the centre, when they met, a blinding stream of lightning arcs exploded from the front of the rifle. From a flattened line to a swirling vortex, the teal bolts of lightning twisted themselves around and around smashing into the crystal in the wall. Taven breathed a sigh of relief but controlled his outburst as he did not want to lose his aim. The wall began to glow as Taven held the weapon steady. A large burst of sparks flew out from the Control Pad area. Taven continued his fire a few seconds longer, then let go of the trigger. Taven let out a heavy breath as he tapped the Comm Badge on his wrist, "alright Jo, try to raise the door remotely." Josephine was in Engineering at the Main Panel, "running entrance script, getting a neken three six four error, it looks like the door mechanism is fried. Do that for the other door as well and we can jury-rig Communications back online. Taven got up and moved down the hall and around a corner, "right." Josephine was bent over the Primary Engineering Console, while Tyra was behind her and to the right working on the Initialization Algorithms for the Engine Startup Routine. Tyra tapped a control holding the input paths and moved over to Josephine, "how's he doing?" Josephine tapped a control bringing up a hallway schematic. "He should be just about here if he's moving at a good pace." Taven's voice crackled through the Intercom and Tyra moved back to her console to finish her preparations. "Okay Jo, I'm almost there, same deal as before?" Josephine tapped her Badge and adjusted its position, "should be, just burn out the crystal and head back here. We still need to inspect that Reactor." Taven was walking down a fairly long corridor and turned a sharp right towards a dead end. This area was heavily damaged. The window in the far wall was gone, a rippling teal force field stood in its place. Most of the doors and walls had intense plasma burns. The rug was completely incinerated and yet, near the window, a single potted plant stood out amongst the devastation. It was a simple rubber tree tropical plant, not unlike so many others on board. This plant had seemed to survive. Taven was mystified, he could not understand why this plant had not perished with the others. He stood there observing it momentarily, then he turned towards the door and knelt down on one knee. Turning the rifle over he popped open the Plasma Cell Compartment. The Cells inside weren't spent, but he didn't want to take any chances. Turning the rifle right side up he tapped the handle gently a couple of times on his hand so that the cells would slide out of their housings. He placed the two used cells on the floor and reached into his pocket for two fresh ones. Sliding them inside the handle, he tapped the panel shut and checked the power gauge. Reading a full charge, he placed the weapon on the floor and once again removed the control panel from the wall; pulling on it gently he let it dangle on its cord. Taven looked inside and noticed some charring around the crystal. He tapped his Comm Badge and ran a finger along the edge of the burned area. "Jo, the right side of the crystal looks like it's been seared by heat, is that going to cause a problem?" Josephine looked up from the console where she was working, "seared, inside the panel housing?" Taven nodded, "yes, it's burned around the crystal and I can make out fractures in the metal." Josephine looked at Tyra and Tyra looked back at her. "I honestly don't know, I don't think so. My best guess is, burn it as quick as you can to avoid secondary issues." Taven looked down towards the deck plating, "are you're sure?" Josephine shook her head, "not really, but at this point, things can't get much worse." Taven placed a hand on his knee as he got up, "alright." He moved back over to the weapon on the floor and picked it up. Bracing the butt against his shoulder, he raised the weapon up and took aim through the sights. As the Sensors locked onto the target he took a deep breath in and thought of an ancient prayer. "By the Five Gods, I pray for good fortune and a good life. May I give and receive nothing but happiness and love. When my time is over and my day has come, may I look back upon my life knowing that I was the best I could be and those around me valued me as much as I valued them." As the Sights locked and the tone sounded confirming a hard lock on the target, Taven looked sharp and squeezed the trigger. Teal lightning arced along the barrel, energy ribbons encircled the wings and two white strips of light moved from the wingtips to the centre. As they met, a swath of teal energy erupted from the rifle, twisting and coiling until it was a tight cylinder of shimmering energy and the discharge slammed into the wall. Random arcs of electricity sparked up and down beside the door. Taven moved his arm to activate his Comm Badge, "umm, Jo, we've got random electrical discharges here. I don't know if I like the look of this." Josephine tapped the Comm Channel on the panel in front of her; she'd been working on the station directly across from the Main Console and it was giving her trouble. "Taven, just keep up the fire, you only have twenty seconds left before burnout." Taven looked up and down the door, the arcs were growing in both intensity and frequency. "Jo, it's getting a little crazy here. I think there might be some residual power left in this....Aggh!". Josephine went into a panic, "Taven... Taven!?" She looked at Tyra, "stay here." Josephine ran out the door, she hadn't thought of any power being left in the system. She blamed herself, how could she not have considered that. Running through the halls towards Taven's location all she could think of was if he was hurt, Seph would never forgive her. As she rounded a corner, she could smell burned electronics and see smoke. She ran towards the smoke and found Taven dazed but otherwise unharmed. "Thank the Gods, are you hurt?" Taven coughed as he caught his breath, "damned thing exploded, good thing I was back here or I'd have received more than just a little toss." Josephine struggled to catch her breath, she was so relieved to know that he was alright. His safety by Sirian Naval Law was her responsibility as Executive Officer. She couldn't imagine trying to explain to a Tribunal that her Captain had been killed trying to seal an Armory door on a derelict Ship. Still, the moment had passed and no harm had been done. She grabbed Taven's arm and helped him to his feet. She dusted off his shoulders, "don't scare me like that". Taven smiled, "I never do intentionally you know." Josephine rolled her eyes, "come on, we still have to check the Reactor." Walking back down the Hall towards Engineering, Taven stopped at what used to be the Primary Crew Lounge. The door had fallen in and most of the plating was heaved. The walls were a mess of conduit and Fiber Optic Cabling, much of the room was uninhabitable. Still, Taven felt drawn and he stepped inside. Looking back to Josephine, he turned back towards the window and gazed out at Mesira. "You know before this all happened, I'd planned this wonderful dinner for Seph and I. I was going to transport her aboard when she least expected it, and she'd have materialized amidst soft candlelight and an empty room with a simple table set for two. I'd been thinking all week about how to make it a memorable night." Josephine walked over towards the window and stood beside him, "I think you must have asked every woman on the Ship what she found romantic." Taven's gaze rested on the asteroid moving silently towards Mesira, now easily visible. "Then that happened, Jo, do you think I'll ever get the chance to have that dinner the way I wanted to with Seph?" Josephine looked at Taven, "Tav, if you haven't figured it out by now, let me spell it out for you, she loves you. I think you have many more opportunities ahead of you. This isn't the end, not for you or I, not for the Jovus or Seph, and not for Atlanka. This is just the beginning, everything happens for a reason. You both are supposed to be together for a reason, trust me." Josephine tapped his shoulder, "now come on, the repairs can't wait. If we don't get this old rust bucket moving, we won't have a Ship to repair." Taven took a last look, "then let's get this old bird flying." They walked back out into the Hall and returned to Engineering.

Taven and Josephine walked into Engineering, Tyra's back was turned but she heard the door open and rushed over, "Is everything okay?" Taven rubbed the back of his neck, "Yeah, I just got a little tossed around, other than a couple of bruises, I'm fine." Tyra nodded, "good, Jo while you were gone, I set up the script for the Comm System. I need you to double-check my commands, but it should seal the system and let us channel enough raw plasma into the system to get Communications back online." Josephine motioned towards the console, "let's have a look." Josephine and Tyra moved over to the console, while Taven walked over to the plate which allowed access to the Reactor Pit. Josephine scrolled through four or five pages of command sequences, "it looks good. We won't know until we run the program though." Tyra looked over to Josephine, "that's your next miracle, get the Main Power back online." Josephine nodded, "one miracle at a time." She turned to Taven and called over to him, "Tav, do you have that hatch open?" Taven reached down and pulled up a retracting handle. Turning it forty-five degrees clockwise and ten degrees counter-clockwise, he pushed it back into the deck and the hatch's locks clicked as the hatch slid into the floor. Taven pointed down towards the Reactor Pit, "it's open." Jo looked at Tyra, "do you still have your Beacon?" Tyra reached into her pocket, "right here." Josephine nodded, "thanks." Josephine tossed the beacon to Taven, "Tav, catch." Taven caught the beacon and placing it in his hand he peered down into the Pit. It was an unbelievable mess, the floor had sunk in several places into the Hull. He found a good spot to put his feet down and tapping a button inside the hatch-casing, a ladder lowered from the roof of the Core to the floor. Taven got a grip and as he did the Ship creaked. He looked up at

Josephine, "are you quite sure this area is safe?" Josephine finished walking up to him and crouched down, "well the system says it's structurally sound, I can't say much as to the flooring or decor, but we won't get blown into space." Taven looked at her from the top of his eyes, "that's a reassuring thought." He started to climb down, as he did the area around him groaned and creaked. Most of the floor had sunk into the Primary Hull but along a Support Beam, there was enough left to walk over to Reactor Four. Josephine followed him and halfway down the ladder, she scanned around with her beacon, "by the Five Gods. The devastation is almost unimaginable." Taven took her hand to steady her as she reached the bottom of the ladder. "I'm surprised anything left down here works at all." Taven nodded in the bleak light, "over there." Josephine shone her Beacon towards Reactor Four, the light hit a few unseared spots and shimmered in the distance. The Reactor was a beehive shape. A wide base with a Reactants Monitoring Display, two control panels on either side and several lines running up to the top of the Reactor, which normally gave off a bright amber almost white light. Josephine squinted, "well it looks alright, at least visually, here keep me steady." Taven walked behind Josephine along what was left of the flooring. The beam they stood on creaked and moaned, Taven couldn't help thinking the Jovus was calling out to him in pain. They got close and Josephine pulled her tablet from her pocket and plugged it in. Calling up an internal schematic of the Reactor's Main Core she ran a full diagnostic. "According to the Reactor's Primary, Secondary and Tertiary Sensors this Reactor is intact. The Power Conduits that lead from it as well are showing a green light. Wait, it looks like the Automatic Power Flow Controls are offline." Taven spoke from the blackness, "can you compensate?" Josephine shone her Beacon on him, "I'll have to manage the power and control the Engines from Engineering." Taven motioned towards the reactor, "first things first." Josephine nodded, tapping her Comm Badge she called up top. "Tyra, run that initialization script. I will monitor the entire system from down here." Tyra's voice crackled over the Intercom, "I'm executing the start-up routine now." A sudden clank and hum emanated from behind them as well as a loud buzzing sound. Starting softly and growing with intensity, the Reactor began to emit soft amber light. It had already been providing partial power to the Secondary Systems. Each Reactor casing contained a Secondary Battery that could power the Secondary Systems of a disabled Star Ship for several days until help arrived. Pulsing slowly, the light grew steadily until it was sufficient for Taven and Josephine to turn off their Beacons. Tyra's voice crackled back across the Intercom, "Reactants primed, the System Board shows green and ready for primary start-up." Josephine tapped on her tablet reading primary data from the Reactor itself, she couldn't afford a mistake. Their lives depended on it, "okay Tyra, the Reactor's Internal Diagnostics are showing the same as the Sensors. I think we can trust them, bring the Primary Injectors up to twenty-five percent power and hold it there. " The window in the front of the Reactor which had been dark sparked to life. Teal plasma crackled and sparked with a wash of colour. The lines on the top of the Reactor grew significantly brighter. Josephine continued running constant diagnostics, "okay, now to fifty percent." The plasma wash in the front of the Reactor changed to a more solid form, it began to spin, still unable to be made out completely; however, the form was definitely a spiralled shape. The lights grew much brighter and Josephine still tapping away on her tablet, called up one last time, "okay Tyra, it looks good, bring it up to seventy-five percent and hold it there. Keep the power curve soft and prime the Engines. Watch for any sudden spikes and compensate with the Tri-variance Surge Buffer." Josephine walked back over to the ladder and climbed up, Taven trailing after her, they emerged back out of the Pit and Taven straightened his jacket. Josephine moved over to Tyra and tapped into the Main Control System accessing the Power Initialization for the Comm system. "Well we have power, let's see if we can get some Communication." Taven nodded as Josephine fed in the instructions for the Power Transfer into the Communications System. Taven reached for his ears as a sharp piercing screech deafened the entire Ship. Josephine screamed above the noise, "one second, there...ouch, that hurt." As the screeching subsided, Josephine nodded her head in a positive manner. "There, Communications are online." Taven stuck a finger in his ear and wiggled it around, "what?" Josephine grabbed his arm and pulled his finger out of his ear. "Very funny, let's see if this works." She tapped the Comm Panel. "Engineering to Bridge, Seph, Clinch, can you guys hear me?" The Comm Channel was silent for a moment, enough to make Josephine shake her head in disapproval. Persephone's voice then crackled over the Intercom, it was garbled with static and fuzzy but she could hear her. "We're here, hey the next time you want to send a ten-decibel signal throughout the Ship, you might want to warn someone. I fell out of a chair and Clinch had his head underneath a console." Josephine snickered, "is he okay?" Persephone's voice crackled through, "laugh all you want, yes he's fine, he's sitting next to me holding his head and muttering something under his breath about getting even." Josephine giggled, "well tell him he can nurse his head later, I need him to bring the Main Engines online." Clinch slid off the Console he'd been sitting on and moved towards the Navigation Station. He dusted off the remainder of the debris from the top of it and keyed in the main start-up sequence for the Primary Drive Coils. An amber warning light blinked and he pointed it out to Persephone, "I can bring the Primary Coils up to power, but I have no control over Thrust Vector or Course Assignments. Are you sure the Main Bus is intact between the Bridge and the Primary Control Computer?" Josephine leaned over the Main Console, "it should be, wait, damn, it's shorted out. I don't have time to crawl through over a fikan of conduits to get to the junction, I'll fix it later. Okay infusing the primary coils with twenty-nine Kordans of Drive Plasma, adjusting the power flow, synchronizing the Main Exhaust Manifolds, opening Rear Space Screens and rolling back Protective Housing. Running plasma through Secondary Coils and feeding coolant. Just a little more, running up the pressure and...got it, powering up Engines to standby." The Jovus's great tail flashed sporadically and then slowly glowed soft amber. The lights, what was left of them, blinked on inside and the external illumination came on. Josephine rested her hands against the console and her head sank as she let out a massive breath of relief, "thank you". Taven walked over, "it seems the old girl's still got some fight left in her." Josephine nodded, tapping the controls she brought up the Manual Reactor Power Flow Monitor and beside it, the Main Navigation readouts. "I can both manage Power Flow to ensure we don't have any unfortunate issues and pilot the Ship from here. Taven motioned to Tyra, "let Tyra take the Helm and you focus on keeping that Reactor under control." Josephine nodded as Taven started to make his way to the door, "where will you be?" Taven spun around on his heels, "where the Captain belongs of course, on the Bridge." With that Taven walked through the door and out of Engineering.

Taven walked onto the Bridge, looking around he hardly recognized it. The screen was blank, conduit and piping dangled from the ceiling and the stations around the Bridge, which normally were a dance of light and flashes, sat dark and silent. He walked over to the Science Station and ran his hand along the soft metal and smiled, he was home, he'd never leave this place again. Persephone had been leaning over the Aft Engineering Station and hadn't noticed him walk in. Clinch likewise, had been leaning back in his chair with his head tilted back and his eyes closed. Taven walked over to Persephone and lightly touched her back, she turned her head and smiled, "hey, I didn't hear you come in." Taven nodded towards what she was working on, "I'm not surprised, you look completely engrossed in your work." Persephone shook her head, "it's a mess Tav, but she's not without hope. I was tossing around this idea, it's something the Ministry has been working on for the last several months. They're experimental and if they malfunction it could cause more problems than it solves." Taven raised an eyebrow, he was intrigued. Usually, when Persephone got vague, it was a prelude to a revelation. "Okay, now you've got me curious, what have you been working on?" Persephone tugged on Taven's arm and motioned to the Conference Room. They walked across the Bridge and Clinch heard Persephone's heels clacking against the deck plating and opened his eyes. "Taven, hey, so who's driving." Taven put a thumb behind his head, "Tyra's at the Helm from Engineering." Clinch shrugged, "so what am I supposed to do, I scarcely have a station left." Taven grinned, "just enjoy the ride, my friend. Wait, actually, can you see if you can get the screen working? If we're moving, I'd like to be able to see where I'm going." Clinch nodded, "alright." Persephone and Taven ducked under the half-raised door, the control circuit to this room had been completely destroyed and any movement of the door would cause it to drop and the room to be inaccessible. Persephone moved over to a cracked window; gazing out at the stars she could see Jepatira's soft golden globe in the distance, like a speck of brown against the night sky, she got a sharp shiver down her spine. Taven moved over and stood beside her, "so what's your idea?" Persephone looked out into the night sky, "what makes you think I have an idea?" Taven turned to look at her, "I know you." Persephone let a smile slip out, it felt good. Her head dropped slightly and a lock of hair fell against her face, "that you do, I didn't want to mention it in front of Clinch, but I think I might have a way to get a couple of systems back online." Taven's eyes popped out, "you can't be serious, the Jovus needs a massive overhaul." Persephone nodded, "yes she does, but I might be able to get Shields and Weapons back online." Taven, astonished, crossed his arms, "okay, I'll bite, how exactly?" Persephone walked over to the terminal on the wall, it had a large crack through the screen but it looked to still be operational. She keyed in the transfer sequence to what she'd been working on at the station on the Bridge. The screen flickered and sputtered, Persephone's brow furled and her mood soured. She curled up her fist and hit the wall, "oh just work already". The screen cleared and an image of what she was thinking about appeared on the screen. It looked like a robot, several Manipulator Arms extended out from the body. Two large eyes were located on top with another Manipulator Arm extending from the head. The body was a one-piece design with what looked like thruster jets around and on the bottom of the device. Taven looked curiously, "what on earth is that thing?" Persephone crossed her arms and walked back to Taven slowly, "this is what we've been working on for the past year or so, it's called a Micro Fabrication and Repair Device, we call them MFARD's". Taven walked over to the screen, "how big is it?" Persephone followed him, "it's no bigger than the thickness of a Sirian hair follicle." Taven turned to her, astonished, "what is it capable of?" Persephone reached across him and tapping a few controls she brought up the design schematics. " Quite a bit actually, it was originally designed to augment standard Hull Repair Systems. These machines travel along the Hull and then build up the damaged portion with Micro Fabrication utilities built into the chassis. They can rebuild an entire Star Ship Hull within a few days." Taven rubbed his chin, "you said getting systems back online, the Hull isn't damaged." Persephone tapped another control and it brought up a cross-section of the Droid's Micro Core. "I've been working to implement the design across a broader platform so that it is a widely versatile instrument for all manner of repairs aboard a Star Ship. If I can just nail down the Shield failure issue, these devices could enter environments that are hazardous or possibly deadly to standard Crew. It would increase the safety factor aboard Star Ships ten-fold." Taven nodded, "and you want to try your experiment aboard the Jovus?" Persephone shrugged, "we're stuck, I don't see any other way, we don't have the time to rebuild the systems ourselves and the Star Dock has us locked in with Cross Beams. If we want to free the Jovus, we need our Weapons back online to melt the Beams." Taven walked over to the window, "what is the worst-case scenario?" Persephone pulled on a lock of hair and twirled it around her finger. "The coding goes haywire and instead of repairing the systems, they bore a hole through the Hull." Taven looked back with an expression that just made Persephone burst out laughing, like a Forkati deer which has been caught on the road, his face was priceless. "Taven, it won't get that far, if I notice any abhorrent behaviour, I'm immediately shutting the lot down." Taven's expression relaxed if only slightly, "are you trying to frighten the living daylights out of me?" Persephone grinned, "is it working?" Taven nodded, "yes, you're evil!" Persephone moved over and kissed his cheek, whispering in his ear, "and you wouldn't have me any other way." She tapped his arm, "come on, let's see if my little science project pays off." Taven followed her, "oh, I hope I don't regret this." Persephone crouched under the door, "stop being such a pessimist, it's unbecoming." Taven crouched behind her, "yeah yeah." Persephone walked over to the station, she was halfway there when she noticed that the View Screen was on and showing a progress report of the asteroid's impact, a countdown if you will; it made her stop dead in her tracks. Her good mood bled out like an ancient ritual to appease the Gods. The reality of everything hit her full force. In less than twelve hours, everything would be destroyed. Her face darkened, and she glared at the asteroid daring it to defeat her. This put her into a frame of mind that would last for the rest of the day, I will not fail, I will not relent and I will prevail. Persephone walked quickly over to the Science Station and called up the Control Program for the MFARD's. Taven walked up behind her, "how long until we notice a change?" Persephone pointed to a predetermined schedule. "The first item is the Power Distribution System, then Shields and Weapons followed by Sensors and Navigation. The internal structure can be repaired by Atlanka Star Base with a proper team." Taven nodded, "just the basics." Perspehone breathed in; closing her eyes she mumbled something under her breath. Staring down at the panel she hit the run key and a light buzzing sound could be heard. At first, that was all there was, this slight hum, but a few moments later Taven caught something out of the corner of his eye. A piece of wall shimmered, he thought it was odd and moved over to take a look. The conduits in the wall were being destroyed and reconstructed by this shimmering light. The wall was being repaired as this wave of sparkles moved across the wall.

Persephone moved over to him, "so far, so good." Taven turned to her, "how are they doing." Persephone looked over, "they're about thirty-eight percent done with the Power Grid. Taven watched in astonishment, "I can believe it." The swarm moved out from the wall and up the ceiling, shimmering down a long piece of dangling conduit near Taven; he watched as the item disappeared from the tip of the damage all the way up into the ceiling, the conduits were fabricated and the roof closed off as the buzzing seemed to disappear. Persephone smiled, "they've moved on, they should be heading to Engineering and the Reactor Pit." Taven hit his Comm Badge, "Taven to Engineering, Jo, Tyra, put down whatever it is you're doing and step away from the consoles, you're about to have some small visitors." Josephine's voice crackled over the Intercom, "umm, Taven, what are you talking about?" Just as she asked the question the shimmering swarm washed over the walls, sparkling across the damaged sections, Josephine was awed by what she was witnessing. "Taven, what is this?" Persephone responded, "they're Micro Machines, designed to repair systems we can't reach." Josephine watched the spectacle as the disaster that was Engineering was restored to its normal condition. "Seph, is this your creation?" Persephone smiled, "to an extent, it was a team effort and a lot of long nights by the coffee machine." Josephine couldn't take her eyes off the progress of these tiny engineers. "Spectacular, you may even put me out of a job." Persephone grinned, "that's never going to happen Sis." Josephine grinned as she watched the last of the wall repaired and the shimmering swarm broke into two. One set went down into the Reactor Pit, the other traversed the floor and moved up into the Main Control Console and the surrounding consoles around Josephine and Tyra. They shimmered with a soft white light. Where once damaged and inoperable systems sat, they were now fully restored, even the gold shined in the soft light of Engineering." Josephine ran her hand along the panel, it was smooth, without so much as a scratch. "Seph, you've outdone yourself, that was something else to behold." Persephone moved over to the

Engineering Station, "you haven't seen anything yet." She called up the start-up routine for the Internal Power Grid and activated the internal illumination. All over the Ship, clicking sounds could be heard, as the power flowed into the Control Conduits and the lights switched on. The Jovus sang a percussive chorus of clicks and whooshes. All over the Ship her once destroyed interior was reborn. Her Halls once again shimmered gold and her floors were lined with marble. The columns that surrounded each door and the long windows that looked out into the great unknown, once again shimmered with a peaceful softness. Persephone beamed a smile, "Internal Power Grid and Superstructure has been repaired. The swarm is moving into the Shield Power Coils and the Weapon Pre-Fire Chamber." Taven moved over to Persephone, "already, what's online?" Persephone smiled at him, "why don't you head out into the Hall and take a look for yourself?" Taven looked at her curiously but decided to take her advice. He walked towards the door that had been forced open by Clinch and Persephone not so long ago and as he approached, it slid up. Taven stopped dead in his tracks, he had not expected that. Cautiously, he moved out into the corridor and a spectacle greeted his eyes. The Hall shined soft amber, the walls a brushed gold. Even the internal Computer Panel Network blinked status lights along the wall. He felt lightheaded and dropped to his knees. He didn't notice Persephone when she walked up behind him, crouching down she rested a hand on his shoulder. All Taven could say was, "how?" Persephone knelt down beside him and rested her head on his arm, "when I sent the command to repair the Power Grid, I slipped in an algorithm to repair the Internal Structure." Taven turned to her, "but that wasn't needed for the ship to function." Persephone looked into his eyes, "it was needed for you to function." Taven wrapped his arms around her, "you're far too good to me." She enjoyed the embrace and whispered, "you deserve nothing less." Fighting the urge to just stay in that moment, she straightened and adjusted her jacket. Tucking a lock of hair behind her ear, she looked up at Taven, "we should, um, check the progress of our team." Taven nodded, "agreed."

The glittering swarm danced across the destroyed Coils, with each one restored it began to glow a soft teal. Diving from the Shield Power Chamber, the swarm went clear across the Ship and into the lower decks to the Weapons Control Room. Where a once-charred and destroyed ruin lay, it was quickly transformed into a shining beacon. Amber displays lined the walls, and a large Console, once shattered and broken, now blinked happily with status lights and readouts. The large cylinders in the back of the room, behind a honeycomb-shaped cage, which covered half the room, began to shimmer and sparkle as the swarm set to work. Within seconds, they flashed erratically and then a hum could be heard as they began to glow a soft amber, warm and inviting. Persephone walked onto the Bridge and headed over to the Science Station, which had been repaired while the swarm was on the Bridge to its original state. In fact, most of the systems had been repaired, at least the crucial ones. The only thing Persephone hadn't included were the Science Labs, Engineering Labs and Crew Quarters. As there was no Crew currently aboard and no projects being done, those areas could be rebuilt by the Sirian Engineering Corps. Persephone's hair had once again decided to be difficult. She leaned over, tucking a lock of hair behind her ear and began to check on the progress of her little workers. As she typed, her hair repeatedly fell in front of her face; frustrated she pulled a hairband from her vest pocket and pulled her hair up into a rather dishevelled ponytail. She finished checking her helpers' progress and motioned for Taven to come over. He'd be running a diagnostic of the Main Systems from the Secondary Engineering Console; Persephone hadn't even noticed him break away when she walked back in. He moved over leaving the system to finish it's diagnostic and walked up beside her. Resting a hand against the Console, he nodded towards the display, "so, how are we doing?" Persephone pointed towards the last notes on her checklist. "They're just about done, only minor repairs left." Taven looked around the Bridge, perplexed he looked back to Persephone, "say, wasn't Clinch in here with us?" Persephone turned around, "he was, I wonder where he's gone?"

Taven shrugged, "maybe he headed to Engineering to help Jo and Tyra." Persephone snickered, "well there's an easy way to find out, Bridge to Lieutenant Zozen, where are you?" Clinch was just walking up to the Bridge, as he entered the room he responded, "look behind you." Persephone spun around to see him carrying a tray with three cups of coffee. He smiled and handed Taven and Persephone theirs. "By the way the Replication System is online, I just grabbed these from the Officers Lounge." Persephone held the cup and inhaled deeply, she hadn't had anything to eat or drink for hours. She had been so busy with everything going on, that she'd completely forgotten to eat. A thought flashed across her mind suddenly, if things went badly and they lost communication with Siria Prime, she would be unable to renew her Personal Enhancement vaccine. The Personal Enhancement system had been implemented by the Sirian Navy to be used by its Star Ships and Star Bases as a matter of convenience. The injection fortified the body and slowed it's consumption of food and other similar body functions. The justification for the serum was that when you're in space, there are times when you simply can't eat or use the restroom. This injection was designed to make those needs seldom so that they could be managed easily. Persephone didn't like the prospect of returning to a normal diet, but at the same time, she didn't particularly like being on suppressive medication either. She let the thought pass, took a long sip of coffee and enjoyed the moment. Taven took his cup from Clinch, "you know this kind of behaviour won't get you promoted." Clinch beamed a big grin, "you say that now." Taven chuckled as he took a sip, "mmm, not bad, but it still doesn't come close to the real thing." Persephone took another sip and leaned back against the console, "one of the things about being on a Star Base, you're spoiled with real food." Clinch nodded, "after being on exploration duty for six months straight, coming back home and having a hot cooked meal is something you really look forward to." Persephone stood up, put her coffee down and turned around to check the final readouts for the MFARDS. "Speaking of which, how did you get Jo to cook you that dinner anyway?" Clinch finished his coffee, "I told her I'd take her Engineering shifts for three days." Persephone turned around and looked at him with a raised eyebrow, "that's a big payment for a meal." Clinch nodded, "it was a fantastic meal!" Taven stifled a laugh, "always thinking with your stomach." Clinch moved back over to the Helm, "of course, is there a better way?" Taven pointed to the Helm Console, "do you have Flight Control Access?" Clinch turned towards his station and ran his fingers along the console, tapping keys as he went. "It looks like the little guys were able to salvage Reactors Two and Three but One was beyond repair, it will have to be replaced. Power control readouts look good, Ion flow is steady, Power Flow Control system is...wow, completely restored. Seph, you should write a paper on those little guys." Persephone unbuttoned her jacket and put it on a chair nearby, "I'm just glad it worked, how are Shields and Weapons?" Clinch tapped a few more controls. Weapons are online at fifty percent nominal power; shields are available to a maximum of seventy-five percent standard throughput, so not perfect, but good enough. Those, what did you call them?" Persephone pulled the chair with her jacket on it over and sat down, "MFARDS." Clinch turned around, "well whatever the name, they're a great emergency measure. You should ensure that the research continues and they are implemented as a safety system for disabled Star Ships." Persephone pointed to the screen, "one thing at a time, we've still got to get out of here, what are the readouts on the Star Dock. I'm sure they're aware we're here by now, have they locked down the clamps?" Clinch tapped a few controls on the console as Tyra walked onto the Bridge. "Yes, Star Dock Control Systems are in independent running mode. I cannot gain access to the network to disengage them." Taven walked over to Tyra, "think you can take the Weapons Station?" Tyra raised an eyebrow, "hi Tyra, nice to see you, how have you been?" Taven rolled his eyes, "hi Tyra, how was Engineering? Now can you take the Weapons Station?" Tyra beamed a cheeky grin, "but of course." Persephone was tapping away at the Science Station, "you know, normally, I'd go out of my way to find a solution that wouldn't damage anything, but considering these Dry Docks are going to be obliterated and us along with it if we don't get this tub moving..." Taven nodded, "right, Clinch bring the Engines up to standby and hold the thrust coefficient at seventy-five percent. When we're ready to go, I want to be away from this Station as fast as possible." Tyra turned around from the console, "you know these stations have automated defences and will return fire if attacked." Taven nodded, "why do you think I want to put as much distance as possible as quickly as we can." Tyra turned back to the Weapons Array, "running a full diagnostic on the Primary Weapons Coils. If we're going to try to shoot our way free, I'd rather know that we won't have a misfire and end up locked into a Station that's pummelling us." Taven nodded, "okay, Seph can you run a full diagnostic of the Primary Shields from over there." Persephone tried keying in the sequence. "No, most of the damage is repaired, but there are still some broken links." Persephone tapped the Comm Channel, "Bridge to Engineering, Jo, can you run a quick diagnostic of the Shield Coils and Energy Dampening Systems?" Josephine's voice crackled over the Intercom, "running diagnostic, just a few seconds, readings coming in now. Okay, I can give you enough power to absorb about five or six shots, beyond that I can't make any promises. I highly recommend that we get out of range fast, the power systems are stable, but they're by no means in proper working order. I'm still having to cross-correct fluctuations, the Automatic Reaction Control Matrix is missing." Taven leaned over the Console Persephone was standing at, "just hold us together Jo." Persephone was about to tap the Comm Channel closed when her eyes opened wide, Taven knew that look. Persephone was about to have an epiphany, this was a fairly common occurrence, but it was always a little funny to see her reaction. Persephone tossed her ponytail aside as she thought out loud, "Jo, can we disable all the internal power to the decks except for Engineering and the Bridge?" Josephine was silent for a moment then responded in a confused voice, "you mean turn off the

Power and Climate Controls?" Persephone scratched her cheek, "yes, it would allow us to channel the power that is being fed to those areas which are unoccupied at the moment." Josephine walked over to the Main Power Junction Relay Control Interface across the room and called up a readout of the current configuration. "I don't see how, the system is designed as a single unit, turning on the power to one Deck turns them all on. It's designed that way to protect the crew, as there are several redundant Power Junctions in case any one system fails." Persephone bit her lower lip in thought, "the system was never designed with a situation like this in mind. Can you lock off the power feeds with a Security Field similar to how you did with the Communication System?" Josephine blew a long sigh of air through her lips, "I can try, If I'm going to do this, that door on the Bridge needs to be sealed and air-locked. I'll be initiating a Hull puncture warning, which will seal all those decks totally off from each other. I just hope the seals weren't damaged." Persephone shook her head, "you're filling me with confidence Jo." Josephine put her hands up to the Power Control System Interface, "if this doesn't work, I'm going to have to drop the fields or you'll all asphyxiate." Taven had moved towards the centre seat. He nodded towards the Comm Array near the Science Console, "we know the risks Josephine." She took a deep breath, "alright, initiating Hull Breach Containment Procedures, activating Security Fields, siphoning Plasma Flow and diverting it to the Shields." Taven's eyes lit up, he had an idea. He moved back over to Persephone. "Seph are the Tractor Beams repaired?" Persephone keyed in a sequence and checked, "they are, but what good will pulling on the beams do us?" Taven shook his head, "set them to Repulse Mode and run a phased coherent pulse through them at two-second intervals." Persephone's lip curled, she knew exactly what he was thinking, "deploying Tractor Emitters and running plasma to Emitter Power Coils." The Jovus was stuck like a fly in amber. She was running under her own power but two large beams were piercing her Hull, holding her in place. Normally this was a good thing, as it stabilized the

Ship for Crews while they affected repairs to a disabled Star Ship. Now they were an inconvenience, more alarming was that the Star Docks were armed with four Plasma Pulse Cannons. They weren't exceptionally powerful, but they were meant to deter anyone who attempted to commit an act of piracy and steal a docked vessel. The Jovus' swept wings shimmered in the sunlight; underneath her soft golden body, the asteroid could be seen. It was getting far too close for comfort, they were running out of time. A square plate recessed on the Wings near the tips, retracting and sliding into the Hull, a pair of golden Emitters lowered with teal illuminated cubes at the centre of them. Locking into place, the Emitters began to pulse brighter and darker. It was caused by the plasma being routed to the Emitter system, they were now ready for use. Persephone, who had barely moved a muscle called out from the Science Station, "Emitters locked in place, online and in Repulse configuration." Taven called down to Engineering, "Jo, how much more power can you give me to the Shields?" Josephine, who'd moved back over to the Main Control Console, checked the power reserves, "you've got eight shots before total Shield collapse, I hope Clinch is ready." Clinch called over from the Navigation Console, "I've weaved asteroid fields and dodged lightning bolts, this will be a cakewalk." Josephine hit a few more controls, "we're ready here. Make this fast, I can't make any guarantees, this Ship is being held together with spit, polish and a lot of hope." Taven sat down, "what's the fire interval on those Pulse Cannons?" Tyra turned her head around, "once every fifteen seconds. They're fairly low power and meant to ward off would-be thieves, but in our current state, they could be very destructive." Taven sat back, "then we'll just have to outsmart the computers, Shields up!" Electricity arced across the Jovus' Hull as her Shields engaged. Settling into a formfitting bubble of charged lightning, the station's automated warning filled the Bridge, "attention, this vessel is property of the Sirian Imperial Navy, cease your actions immediately or you will be fired upon." Taven grunted, "great, just what we need. Tyra, target those beams and fire when ready, Seph, augment the Plasma Beams with Repulse blasts from the Main Tractor Emitters." The two women spoke in unison, "on it!" Two plates on each side of the Nose and Tail of the Jovus retracted and slid inside the Hull. Glowing teal half-spheres rose out and locked into place; crackling with energy and culminating in a massive lightning storm, shooting both from the Nose and Tail into the Beams locking the Jovus in place. Persephone was just half a second behind Tyra, "Repulsors firing!" Arcing forks of teal lightning shot out from the Tractor Emitters slamming into the Beams. White streaks moved rapidly down the Repulsor Beams, shaking the Station with each impact. The station's warning repeated, filling the Bridge once again. "Alert, Station defences responding with all necessary force. Stand down or you will be disabled and incarcerated." The Jovus was being shaken fairly strongly with the impact of the Repulsors. Persephone's cup, which she had forgotten was on the console next to her, shook so hard it fell off the display and shattered against the marble floor. Taven called over to Persephone, "how are we doing, that thing is going to start shooting at any moment." Persephone called back, "halfway through, just a few seconds more." The station's automated warning filled the Bridge again, it sounded cold and angry. "Engaging target, firing to disable." From the Star Dock's overhead roof, four large plates recessed at the corners and slid into the Hull. Four fairly large cannons lowered down and locked into position. Turning towards the ship and locking the target, they fired a single burst from all the cannons simultaneously. The blast hit the Shields hard, a shower of sparks ignited over Taven's head and sparks shot out from the Engine Couplings in Engineering. Josephine called up from Engineering, "we don't want to take another one of those. We just had massive power fluctuations across the board." Taven called over to Tyra, "full power to the beams." Tyra called back without breaking her gaze at the screen, "full power will overload the Primary Weapons Coils. We'll have less than twenty seconds before we burn out the Power Transfer System." Taven looked around as his Ship shook around him, "do it, or in twenty seconds we'll all be dead!." Tyra hit the controls, "full power!" The Plasma Beams went from a brilliant teal to a searing red colour. The Repulsors smashed into the Beams holding the ship in place and they began to give way. The cannons from the facility glowed teal and once again hit the Ship hard, this time puncturing the Hull through the Shields. The blast rocked the Ship, Persephone yelled over the noise, "Hull breach on Deck Three Subsection Twenty-Four, Crew Quarters." Clinch called from the Navigation Console, "that blast finished the job, we're free." Taven leaned forward, "what are you waiting for, get us out of here." The Engines on the Jovus flared a brilliant teal and she moved out of the Dock. Taven got up and moved over to the Helm, "Floor It!" Clinch slid his finger up the Throttle Gauge to the top and the Jovus' Engines went from a brilliant teal to a bright red as she quickly moved away from the Dock. The cannons on the facility began to glow teal again; Taven seeing the pre-fire sequence fought back his fear, "hard to Port, Spiral Pattern, head for Terra." The Jovus spun on her axis as the cannons fired and turned sharply to port. As the plasma bolts screamed towards her body, she pulled away and they barely escaped hitting her Tail. Twisting and spiralling in the night sky in a bizarre dance, the cannons of the facility fired one last time. Tracking their target, they were on course for the Jovus' Starboard Wing. Clinch knew his adversary all too well, he dove the Jovus straight down and spun her one-hundred eighty degrees horizontal. The plasma bolts soared passed her Wing and continued out into space. Taven dropped back into his chair, his heart in his throat, he caught his breath, "are we out of range?" Tyra, whose hands were stone white, turned around, "yes." Clinch blew a sigh of relief, "oh I'm glad that's over." Taven stood up and walked over to the Helm and tapped him on the shoulder, "nice flying, set the Autopilot to bring us alongside the Helia. Seph can you open a channel to Juice?" Persephone keyed in a sequence, "got him, onscreen." Tyra stood up and looked at the view screen as arcing waves of electricity sizzled and brought up the image of Juice in the centre chair of the Helia.

Tyra moved near Clinch, "Juice, how goes deploying the satellites?" Juice rubbed his cheek, "we'll be done in time, how are things progressing on your end?" Tyra motioned to Persephone, she got up and moved over to the screen, "we've got the Jovus free but we're still unclear on the state of Atlanka's Engines, we'll only know once we get back down there." Taven spoke up from his chair, "Juice, mind keeping an eye on the Jovus while we finish up?" Juice raised an eyebrow, "we don't have the power to tow her." Taven shook his head, "no need, she's under her own power. I'm just going to set the Autopilot to keep the Ship at close range to the Helia. Auto Navigation can handle the rest." Juice nodded, "we'll take good care of her." Taven got up, "right, to the Main Transporter Room then?" Persephone shook her head, "no, I can override and take us directly to the Main Engineering Hold of Atlanka City." Taven motioned to Persephone, "whenever you're ready." Persephone bent back over the terminal near her and keyed in a transit sequence, "alright hold still." The ISTiS began to cycle and teal lightning bolts struck around the Bridge and in Engineering. Teal energy ribbons twisted and spun around the team and two strips of light slowly scanned closer together. Connecting, they electrified and with a resounding rumble of thunder, the Bridge was empty. All that could be heard was the gentle hum of the Engines and the occasional beep from the Consoles.

BREATH OF ION

Atlanka's Main Engine Room was softly lit with gentle amber light. Most of the systems were still on Geo-thermal energy. Rachel was milling around near the Systems Control Network Console which sat in the middle of the room. It was a fairly large display panel with Integral Holographic Screens for simultaneous control of all City networks and Propulsion Systems. Atlanka City's Star Drive was powered by one very large Ion Propulsion Unit and two smaller support drives. The Engines had last been in use when Atlanka City settled on Mesira's surface hundreds of years ago; at that time, they were evacuated of any fuel they contained, the Geo-thermal Power Feeds were driven into the ground and the City ceased to be under the power of the Main Reactors. As a direct result, the Drive Systems and Inflight Power Transfer Feed Network had suffered not only age, but degradation from lack of use. Rachel looked around the room, still somewhat in awe of its size and complexity. Black glass panels lined the walls, each displaying a different Subsystem and its condition. Near the far side of the room opposite the door, behind a wall of brushed bronze pillars, sat a massive oval inset into the wall. Around the radius, fingers of pulsing light illuminated down the lines encircling the Main Drive Chamber. The centre, a brilliant teal, which normally shone in the centre of the housing, pulsing with the gentle heartbeat of the Engines, was now dark with just dim amber light surrounding it, the Engines were clearly in standby mode with the Drive Chambers offline. Rachel began to make her way across the room and was near the Main Systems Console in the centre of the room on the subfloor, when in front of her a fork of teal lightning struck near the door. Ribbons of teal energy began to spin and whirl, electrified lines of white energy moved closer together and when striking, a clap of thunder could be heard as the dancing ribbons of energy sputtered and spun up into the ceiling. Tyra, Persephone, Taven and the rest of the Crew materialized in, as Rachel pulled her tablet from her pocket and shook her head. Persephone walked over to Rachel. Rachel tucked a lock of hair behind her ear, "it took you long enough." Persephone motioned for the rest of the group to join her. Taven and Josephine moved over to her location as Tyra and Clinch moved over to the Main Drive Console and Molecular Pattern Storage Array. Persephone nodded towards the Primary Console, "how are we doing?" Rachel tapped a few keys on her tablet and returned it to her vest pocket, "we're doing fairly well, the Main Pattern Storage Matrix is in good order. I'm not entirely sure about the backups, I'm getting some anomalous power spikes from the network surrounding the primary backups. I'd prefer not to have to do a mid-flight shunt into them, in other words, don't damage the ship when you decide to take off." Josephine shook her head, "well, nothing has gone smoothly up to this point, but we'll do our best." Rachel looked towards the Engineering team, "they'll know more about the state of the Engines than I do. Every indication I get from them is while the Medical Systems are stable, the Engines are far from ready." Josephine bit her lower lip and Taven looked to Persephone with evident worry. Rubbing his neck he looked towards the Main Engine Housing, "oh that is not good, do you have any idea what the issue is?" Rachel pointed to her Insignia, "not unless this has changed from Medical to Engineering. You're best to talk to Ferus, he's still got his head buried back there, never heard someone curse at inanimate objects so much in my life." Josephine looked at Persephone, "I'd better go see what the problem is." Persephone nodded, "I'll go with you." Taven threw his thumb behind his head, "I'm going to go check in with Clinch and Tyra, they seem to have wandered off." Persephone and Josephine nodded at Taven as he moved off to try to find Clinch and Tyra. Persephone turned to Josephine, "where's Ferus?" Josephine pointed towards a door near the Main Drive Housing along the wall, "he should be in there, that's Primary Systems Access". Persephone and Josephine walked over to the door; as it slid up, they walked into the room and it was quite dark. Most of the ambient light came from an open hatch in the wall. Josephine pointed towards the opening, "it looks like they're in the Main Drive Chamber using the illumination mode to repair any fissures or cracks." Josephine moved over to the hatch and putting a leg inside began to duck down, "you know I'm really not dressed for this kind of work". Persephone giggled, "you've never cared what you wore so long as there was polymer grease involved." Josephine tied her hair back, "it's just these cursed heels you had us put on. Hang on, I can't work like this." Josephine sat down in the opening and resting her ankle on her knee she pried the heels off her shoes. "Much better, don't feel like getting stuck in a plasma groove." Persephone shook her head, "after you." Josephine ducked down and entered the Main Thrust Chamber for the Main Ion Engine. Persephone followed her through but was quickly shocked by the sheer magnitude of the size of the area. "They weren't kidding when they said these things were massive." Josephine nodded, "you need a lot of power to push something as heavy as a Star Base." Persephone looked down the Chamber and saw a light shimmering in the distance, it was a plasma torch. "Looks like they're still sealing the Chamber." Josephine nodded and began to walk towards the team in the distance. Persephone kept an eye on where she was going, wavy grooves inundated the surface of the Primary Drive Chamber, meant to guide charged plasma as it ignited, just before exiting the Coils which provided Atlanka's main thrust. She now realized why Josephine had removed her heels. Navigating this area was considerably more challenging in heels. Josephine walked up to Ferus, who was kneeling beside one of his team members as he sealed a weak spot in the Main Drive Chamber. Josephine looked back to Persephone as she finished making her way down and then back to Ferus, "what's the situation?" Ferus got up and moved over to Josephine, putting his hands in his pockets he shrugged, "we've got just about all the areas that were breached sealed up. We tried a startup about six hours ago but the system stalled and didn't get past Phase Four of the initialization. Josephine looked towards the man who was still sealing the crack, "let's try again, how long until he's done." The man who was sealing the fissure stood up, "just finished." Josephine turned to Ferus, "right, let's see if we can get these Engines online. Everybody clear out unless you want to be a crispy critter." Persephone tossed her arms out in a gesture of exacerbation and shaking her head began to walk back to the hatch. Coming up on the hatch Josephine bent over and walked through, Persephone and Ferus' team followed. Josephine grabbed a handle on the hatch and pulled it up and then pushed it forward, closing it. Pushing two pins in at the top and keying in a sequence on a nearby control panel, a loud clack could be heard and a Teal Energy Field energized around the hatch.

Josephine moved back into the Main Engineering Section, Persephone and Ferus closely followed her. Josephine walked up to the Main Engineering Control Console, tapping three keys, the Holographic Screen's Rails slid out of the top of the panel and energized, forming a half-transparent information screen. Projected was a cross-section of the Engine Core. Josephine pulled a stylus from her pocket and tapped several sections, muttering softly to herself as she did. Looking back down at the Main Panel, she tapped a key to raise the Programming Keyboard and another key to confirm the request. A piece of the touch panel which was encircled by a gold square recessed, and a brushed gold keyboard slid out, back-lit by amber symbols it locked into place and Josephine leaned over to key in a set of instructions. Rubbing her neck, she looked at Persephone, "you know this is way more complicated than trying to restart the Jovus. I can't find a startup script anywhere. I'm having to manually write one." Ferus nodded, "that's because there isn't one, the system is so complex and interconnected, that a fresh script has to be written each time the Engines are powered up because no two situations are the same." Josephine blew a stream of air through her lips in frustration, "you'd think they could write a program for that wouldn't you." Ferus grinned, "where would the fun be in that?" Josephine looked at him and shook her head, "alright, the sequencers are primed, Reactants are running at nominal pressure and Plasma has been shunted into the correct fuel lines for start-up, let's see what happens." Josephine tapped a control and the keyboard slid back into the panel; moving slightly to her right she was in front of a fairly large section with many amber lights both steadily lit and blinking. Leaning over, she held her finger over the Initialization Icon briefly in hesitation. Then, with a breath in, she tapped the control. A loud clunk and a fuzzy resonating hum could be heard, low and grumbling at first. Persephone looked around, pulling on Josephine's jacket she nodded towards the Main Drive Core. The expansive fingers that shone out from the centre, which had been dull and barely lit, were becoming brighter with pulses of white light streaking out from the centre. The tone in the Engine Room took on a more solid sound and the fuzz faded from the noise as the pulses from the Core became more constant. The plasmatic ball of energy which was in the centre began to illuminate, lightly shimmering a teal glow. Suddenly Emergency Klaxons sounded, teal lights blinded the Engine Room and the displays turned from soft golden amber to a hard teal. It was a warning of potential overload and explosion. Josephine screamed over the noise... "Shut it Down!! Shut it Down!!!" Ferus was already three quarters of the way through cutting off the Drive Plasma. As the Core destabilized, a resonating thud could be heard and a low and fading groan echoed as the power drained from the Ion Engines. Josephine, who had lost her breath due to being caught completely off guard, and scared by the sudden explosion of noise, regained her composure and tried to catch her breath. "What was that?" Ferus was running his hands over the control console, "I have no idea, the Sensors say there's no flaw, but the System registered a sudden uncontrolled spike in power flow." Josephine raised an eyebrow, "what?!" Ferus looked at her strangely, "the information is contradictory, it's like the Internal

Sensors are confused." Josephine ran her hands over the array, "no fissures, no faults, not even a break in a fuel line. Could the overall condition of the system be responsible?" Ferus shook his head, "I don't believe so, while the Engines themselves are quite old and very degraded, the system registers as stable and shows a green light on power-up. If there was any catastrophic problem, the Sensors would disallow the startup procedure and alert us to where the issue is." Josephine crossed her arms and stood motionless for a moment clearly in thought, then tapping her foot, she gazed first at Persephone then back at Ferus, "then I guess we'll just have to rely on our eyes and ears and put the technology to the side for a little while." Ferus looked at her sideways, "you've lost me." Josephine nodded towards the Core, "I need your Team to do a complete sweep of the Thrust Chamber and surrounding fuel lines, I want to know whether it's a Sensor malfunction or if there is an actual flaw in the Core." Ferus nodded and walked into the other room, where the rest of his Team had stayed behind and were chatting amongst themselves. " Alright fellas, I need a full inspection of the Drive Chamber and surrounding lines. I also want a structural analysis done of the tolerance stress of the material making up the Ion Chamber. Use standalone equipment only, Internal Sensors are possibly malfunctioning." The team groaned, but got up and reopened the hatch. Ferus looked back at Josephine and after giving her the thumbs up, he disappeared behind the door as it slid closed after him. Persephone's brow was wrinkled. Josephine looked over to her sister, she knew that look, something was bothering her, "Seph, what are you thinking?" Persephone gazed hard at the Engine Panel, "well I'm no Engineer, but with a system of this magnitude, there must be backups and redundancies for the backups and then backups for those. Surely, if one system should fail, another would pick up in its place to avoid such a catastrophic reaction. It would be irresponsible to build such a massive structure which housed so many individuals without that kind of redundancy." Josephine's eyes grew wide, "you know something, your right. Working on the Jovus and the Serus for so long, the number of backup systems in a facility like this slipped my mind, what are you thinking?" Persephone turned and leaned against the console running her hand beside her head and crossing her arms afterwards, "well, why didn't the backup systems take over; moreover, why didn't the Sensors warn us of an impending Systems malfunction before it happened." Josephine scratched the side of her head, "I have Ferus doing a manual structural confirmation now to find out if we have an issue with the onboard Sensors." Persephone looked from side to side, shaking her head, "I don't know Jo, something about this doesn't sit right. Those Engines should have started, everything was perfectly fine and then suddenly, it wasn't fine. Sirian Systems don't operate like that, not natively anyway. It's almost like it was tampered with." Josephine shook her head, "the Council is in Bio-Molecular stasis. There's nobody to tamper with anything." Persephone looked towards the now dimly lit Engine bulkhead. "Then how do you explain the sudden destabilization of the entire Plasma Stream, so much so, that it started a Sub-nuclear Reaction within the system itself. If we hadn't shut the Drive down, it would have exploded." Josephine gazed towards the bulkhead as well, "I can't, but before I start spinning conspiracy theories, I want to know it isn't something mechanical that's wrong with the Drive System." Persephone nodded, "logical, but let's do a little hunting of our own." Josephine nodded in agreement as Persephone turned to the console. "SARA, do you have a readout on the conditions of the overload from the startup attempt on the Main Ion Propulsion System?" SARA was silent for a moment as she thought, "I do, I'm displaying the primary sensor data on the Main Screen." Josephine and Persephone turned around to look at the massive screen that hung above them and across the room. It was a Primary Display for both Ship's systems and operational data concerning the City. Built as a multifunction display unit, it was capable of displaying multiple simultaneous data streams at once in real-time. Persephone tilted her head slightly sideways and Josephine scratched her cheek, this wasn't

Persephone's area of expertise. She couldn't help but notice the large sudden spike in plasma to Ion Drive conversion just before the alarm sounded. Persephone pointed to the screen, "I assume that isn't supposed to happen." Josephine stood dumbfounded, "no it's almost impossible, just about everything has to go wrong for that kind of uncontrolled spike to occur. Unless the entire system is completely inoperable, that kind of spike just shouldn't happen." Persephone turned to face her sister, "so what does that tell us exactly." Josephine looked at her sister in obvious distress, "it means that if Ferus confirms what I suspect, then we have a very large problem on our hands. Someone, somewhere, doesn't want this City to move and is actively working against us." Persephone squinted, "but who would be so stupid as to hamper our efforts, for that matter, who among the general population even knows what we're up to." Josephine shrugged, "that's just it, the only people that even knew of our efforts are those aboard our own Star Ships and the Council. The Council is in stasis and I just can't believe it's one of our own." Persephone rubbed her neck, "so who does that leave as suspects?" Josephine was without an answer, all she could do was shrug, "I don't know, but whoever it is, we'd better find out and fast. Tracking a saboteur in a City this size could take hours, even days to locate." Persephone tapped her foot, "we don't have days." Josephine blew a strand of hair out of her face, "of that, I am painfully aware." Persephone placed her left elbow on her right hand, and put her finger in the air, "so we have a possible malicious force standing against us in a massive City, somewhere, who has access to the Main Star Drive and is willing to destroy a good portion of the City to keep us from moving it." Josephine's head dropped, "if we try we fail, if we don't we fail. Talk about a no-win situation." Persephone placed a hand on Josephine's shoulder, "there's always a way out, we just have to find it." Josephine nodded, "okay but where do we look?" Persephone stood in thought for a moment, "the system tracks all incoming and outgoing commands and communications for the given day, before purging the Database and starting fresh for the next, correct?" Josephine nodded, "it does, but wouldn't you think anybody who is smart enough to overload the Ion Power Core remotely, would be smart enough not to leave a trail?" Persephone shook her head, "criminals, as history has shown, are notoriously clumsy when it comes to covering their tracks. There's almost always something to follow. Jo, call up the transit logs for the Engineering Section, ruling out our own work, see if there's anything that pops up which we can't easily explain." Ferus walked up behind the two women, "well, it's not a flaw in the design or mechanics, while the system is stressed and really should not be in any sort of use, it is stable and functional, all mechanical devices are confirmed operational and reasonably safe for use. There is no mechanical reason for any sort of overload or spike, here's my confirmation." Josephine took the tablet from Ferus and read the information it contained, "I was almost hoping you would find something. You took these readings without using the Internal Sensors, correct?" Ferus nodded, "I used the Integrated Suite in the tablet, it took twice as long, but unless the Sensors in my handheld unit are faulty, which I highly doubt, then those readings are accurate to within one trillionth of a percent." Persephone looked at Ferus and Josephine, "then we have a saboteur who's trying to keep the City grounded." Ferus shook his head, "the fool." Josephine turned to the console, "a fool who will kill us all unless we find him and stop him before we're out of time." Persephone was watching the Holographic Display as Josephine paged through information. As one page slipped past, she noticed something out of place, "Jo, go back two pages, there you see that transfer point, what is that?" Josephine zoomed into the diagram and attempted to isolate the anomalous readout. "The Sensors say it's a power spike from a Matter Replication Unit." Persephone shook her head, "nuh uh, I'm not buying it. There you see that power curve, that's no Replicator, it's more like the trace from a plasma diversion being fed from an Optical Targeting Sensor." Josephine looked at her, "this City isn't fitted with such devices, the only Ship that contains them in this region is the Solaran which is a wreck and the Koltanastra which is six light years away, patrolling the perimeter of the Sesmet Nebula. That sort of device couldn't be in Atlanka, as they're integrated into Saqr Class Star Ships." Persephone wrinkled her brow, "alright so whatever it is, it's masking itself intelligently against any scans at it or nearby." Josephine nodded, "makes sense, so we're dealing with someone who can alter the electronic signature of a given system with ease and on a moment's notice." Persephone tapped her foot, "SARA, how many people currently residing in Atlanka have stage seven technical training?" SARA was silent for a moment before she responded. "twenty-two, would you like a list?" Persephone nodded to thin air, a simple habit many Sirians developed when working with artificial intelligence, "yes." SARA complied and after a brief silence responded, "the information is now being displayed on the Main Screen." Persephone and Josephine looked over the names. Their's were at the top of the list, as well as Juice, Clinch, Fyar and First Minister Ben'veh. Persephone turned to Josephine, "you don't think...?" Josephine shook her head, "not a chance, he got stored with the rest of the Council." Persephone read the rest of the list. "Most of the rest of these people are in technical or logistics positions, some I know, most I don't. I can't see them having any connection to what's going on." Josephine stood motionless, clearly in thought, "you know, the easiest way to trace where the interference is coming from, would be to try another Engine start." Persephone looked at her in shock, "you're not serious? We barely contained the last one." Josephine motioned to the console, "that was before I knew what to look for, I'd lay odds they use the same tactic to interfere with the Power Flow again. When they do, I can do both a controlled shutdown and trace where the signal came from." Persephone took a long look into her sister's eyes, searching for any sign of doubt and she found none. The look on Josephine's face was cool and confident," alright, but don't take any chances. Trace or none, that Drive needs to be shut down before any damage can be done." Josephine smiled, "I've already got it all planned out." Turning back to the console, Josephine reached into her vest pocket for her stylus. It wasn't there, she checked a couple of other pockets. "Now where on earth did I put that?" Persephone looked on the console, picking up Josephine's stylus, she wiggled it in front of her sister's face. "Right in front of you, where else?" Josephine giggled, "hiding in plain sight as usual. Alright, here goes nothing, Initializing startup sequence. Seph, keep an eye on the Dynamic Power Converter, if anything spikes, hit the big red abort button." Persephone had to laugh at the obvious programming that at times went into Sirian technology. When you really needed to make something clear, nothing said, hit me if you're in trouble like a big red button with white lettering." Josephine was watching the screen intently, she tapped her stylus in several places, turning the dark blue sections on the screen to teal. One by one, she infused the Ion Nodes with Plasma. Things were going well, over half the Drive Systems were online, then the calm was pierced by a shriek from Persephone, "it's spiking, aborting startup." Josephine's hands flew across the keypad, "the Auto-sequencer isn't responding, I'm going to have to dump the plasma into the ground." Persephone's eyes went wide, "we have precious little to spare, barely enough to get into orbit." Josephine looked up briefly, "either I dump it, or it's going to dump us. Personally, I prefer not to die in a raging inferno." Persephone nodded, "good point." Josephine was watching the gauge, praying desperately, hoping she could get the system back under control. The system levels spiked hard and the Engineering Room began to shudder; sparks flew from behind Josephine and a piece of deteriorated metal fell from the ceiling stopping only two inches from her head. Ducking and covering her head, she looked up as the power levels began to drop, a resonating clunk was heard and a vacuous whistle filled the room. As the whistle died out, Josephine stood up beside the now dangling piece of conduit. Persephone's eyes were glossing over, "Jo!" Persephone looked at the conduit now dangling close to Josephine's head, "don't do that again!" Josephine looked at the conduit that just about knocked her out, "no, I think I have my incentive to not attempt that again." Persephone looked down and breathed deeply, calming herself," please tell me that was worth it." Josephine brushed the dangling piping aside "actually it was, look here." Persephone looked at the screen but didn't quite understand, "what am I looking at?" Josephine pointed to the spike in power, "if I can trace this..." Josephine walked over to the Secondary Systems Array, which was along the edge of the room and up a set of two stairs, near the door to Engineering. She leaned over the console and ran her hands along the symbols. Several began to blink in an asynchronous fashion, "there, got him!" Persephone looked down, "where?" Josephine ran her hands along the console again and the screen behind them lit up, scanning the City and zooming in as it found its target in stages. The display lit up with crosshairs flashing in teal on a black and white image of the City from a bird's-eye view, "there, in that house." Persephone looked around the target, "that's in the residential section. We can't simply barge in with disregard for the populace." Josephine nodded, "good point, the last thing we need is someone getting in the way. I'm going to feed a false image into the Emergency Services System. The residents should very shortly be under an evacuations order due to a Geo-thermal Induction Coil rupturing." Persephone nodded in approval, "good enough, let's go find out just what's going on". Josephine agreed and the two women walked towards the door; as they walked through and out into the hallway, Josephine stopped dead in her tracks, Persephone turned around and walked up to her, "what is it?" Josephine looked back behind her and then towards Persephone, "there's no reason to assume this individual is going to refrain from further interference by us simply talking to him or her." Persephone put a hand on her hip, "and?" Josephine looked towards the floor in thought for a moment and then back up at Persephone, "and I think it's only prudent that we take along something to defend ourselves if things go badly." Persephone stood in shock, "you don't actually think a resident of the City would shoot at us?" Josephine shook her head as she walked towards the ISTiS, "at this point, I'm not prepared to assume anything." The two women walked into the

ISTiS and as the doors shut, Josephine tapped in the sequence for the Armory. "I really don't want to have to fire on a citizen of the City." Persephone turned to her as the matter stream began to form, "let's hope you don't have to."

Colours danced around the sisters, twisting and spinning in an elaborate ballet of wonder. Fading away, Persephone and Josephine emerged from the ISTiS in the Sirian Central Headquarters for this region of space. Josephine looked over to her sister, "keep your head about you, we don't know how far this goes and what has been told to the Defence Teams here." Josephine and Persephone walked down the hall and stopped just outside the Armory, a single guard was standing watch. He noticed the women approach, "ladies, can I help you?" Josephine stood a little more stiff than normal, "Executive Officer Josephine Vorn of the SIV Jovus, I'm here to requisition two plasma pistols." The guard shook his head, "sorry ma'am, but the Armory is sealed by order of the Council." Josephine scratched her head, "did they tell you why?" The guard shook his head, "no, I wasn't privy to the information, I was simply told to keep the doors shut." Josephine nodded and moved up closer to him, "good, just one thing," the guard looked over to her, confused, "and that is?" Josephine hit his side with an injector, as he succumbed to the sedative Josephine finished her statement, "I'm sorry, you'll be fine in a few hours." The guard's eyes closed and his body fell limp. Josephine grabbed his key pass and tossed it to Persephone, "quickly, get the doors open." Persephone slipped the key into the wall socket and several beeps could be heard. The light around the socket illuminated teal and the card slid out. After a moment the door slid up and Josephine grabbed the now unconscious guard underneath his arm, "give me a hand here." Persephone grabbed the other side, "what did you give him." Josephine reached into her pocket as they let the man down gently inside the room, "just a light sedative, the only side effect he should have is a good night's sleep." Persephone shook her head, "alright, so what are we looking for?" Josephine scanned the room; it was a room very much like the Armory aboard the

Jovus; however, it was significantly larger with far more storage inside. Finding the right case, she moved over to it and popped the locks on the front, "here." Persephone moved over to her sister and looked inside. The case housed several Sirian plasma pistols. They were a fairly standard design, with a handle that was ribbed for control and a barrel with a Teal Emitter at the end. As with all Sirian weapons, simply squeezing the handle would fire the weapon. Josephine tossed one to Persephone and a holster to go with it. "I assume you know how to use one of these?" Persephone pulled the chamber's primer back and turned the safety off, the weapon made a high-pitched hum to indicate it was charged and ready to fire, "yes." Josephine finished tightening the belt around her waist, "I just hope we don't have to use them." Persephone nodded, "so do I." Persephone moved over to a panel inset into the wall and called up a screen, "I assume walking through the City with weapons on our hips is a bad idea, correct?" Josephine grinned, "only slightly." Persephone finished keying in the command sequence and moved back over to her sister. "I thought you might say that." A soft hum could be heard and a wash of teal light blanketed the room, lightning struck the two women and spirals of teal energy spun around them from the ceiling. Energized strands of white scanned across them as they vanished slowly from sight; as the white lines met a resonating clap of thunder was heard and the room was left empty, save the guard, napping in the corner.

Persephone and Josephine materialized at a transit terminal, some distance down the street from the house that was responsible for the signal. Josephine looked around, the wind softly tossing her hair in front of her face. The street was silent, an eerie silence not unlike the calm before an extremely violent storm. The street was not unlike a residential street on a hundred other worlds. Houses lined both sides. Lawns filled with Mesirian Kaigrass lay in front of most of the properties. The homes themselves were made from polished limestone and had artistic roofs. The homes themselves were powered by a small Fusion-Ion Generator. As much as the City was powered by Geo-thermal energy, every home had its own power source so as to not put undue pressure on the Geo-thermal Processing Plants and Generators. Persephone squinted in the light, dawn had broken sometime earlier and the sun was low in the sky. The sky, which normally was a deep blue, the colour of the most majestic oceans she could remember, was now stained in red. Such a terrible atrocity that it made her blood boil, this kind of environmental damage went against everything she believed in and had fought so hard for. Raising a hand to her face and shielding her eyes from the light while they adjusted, she pointed down the street, "that way." Josephine walked beside her, the wind rustled the trees which stood on most of the home's lawns, a vehicle sat running, it had been left running when the evacuation order sounded. Persephone and Josephine walked in front of the house. Persephone looked down the street and back to the house, "it looks completely deserted." Josephine loosened her holster, "yeah, well looks can be deceiving." Josephine moved closer to the door with Persephone hanging back to let her sister deal with any threat that may lie inside. Josephine pressed the door chime, "Sirian Defense, open up, there's an evacuation order for this section; you need to leave for your own safety." There was no answer, nothing. Josephine put her hand up in a stay-put gesture and pressed the entry icon. The door slid up and she peered inside. The house was dark, except for ambient light from the windows, in the room was a couch, a chair, potted plants and a plasma display. Everything looked as it should be for any Sirian home, but then something caught her eye, an anomalous console in the back of the room in front of a large window. It was brushed gold with a black glass top, it was not unlike any other Sirian console you would find in a thousand other places; however, this one belonged in a Sirian Defense Post and was Imperial property. Josephine's throat began to close up, she called out again, "hello?" She pulled her pistol out, there was something not right here. Persephone walked slowly through the door. She had, as well, drawn her weapon; this situation was in no way normal and something very ominous was happening.

Josephine scanned the corners and searched the rooms; beds and nightstands stood silent in the rooms. Josephine was satisfied there was nobody in the home, she sheathed her pistol and moved over to the console, Persephone followed her lead, "well, any ideas Jo?" Josephine looked over the console, but none of the readouts made sense. Many of them were random and none seemed to follow any pattern. "This station, it makes no sense, here it goes from Power Core Status to Life Support. Again, here it jumps from Recycling to Weapons Status." Persephone looked over the console, "think it's a cover, so someone thinks it's just a regular console?" Josephine nodded, "that would be my guess, hmm, let's see what happens." Josephine hit a control and the screen cleared, it asked for a passkey. Josephine stood for a long moment, "passkey, why on earth would it want a passkey?" Persephone looked at the console, "I think we've clearly found the source of the problem." Josephine put a finger in the air, "let's not jump to conclusions. I'll just enter something, let's see what it does." Josephine typed in the Hieroglyphic equivalent of "let me in". The display flashed red, printed there on the screen was a timer with a countdown. "Enter the correct code within twenty seconds or else!" Josephine turned to Persephone, "umm...hide now!" As the two women ran across the room, two turrets materialized out of thin air and lowered from the ceiling. They barely got around the corner before the turrets fired on them. Persephone was short of breath, "well so much for them not shooting at us." Josephine pulled her pistol and put the setting on high, "it's not a who, it's a what. Those things are being computer-controlled." Persephone grabbed for her gun, "oh, so not the source of the trouble after all." Josephine peered around the corner, as she did two teal lasers shone in her direction and she barely got back behind cover, as a barrage of plasma bolts hit the wall near her. Josephine nodded towards the wall across the room, "think you can make it over there?" Persephone looked at her wide-eyed, "you want to use me as bait?" Josephine looked at her with an exacerbated expression, "I need someone to draw their fire, so I can destroy the turrets. I don't see any other volunteers do you?" Persephone peeked around the corner and the two turrets again locked onto her position quickly. Lurching back around, another barrage struck the wall and shot out a window nearby. "Any brilliant ideas?" Josephine looked around, "see that couch, run towards it and drop to the ground, that should give me enough time to take out one." Persephone shook her head, "if you're wrong, I'm going to haunt you." Josephine grinned, "trust me!" Persephone nodded, "uh huh, right, on three - One, Two...Three!!" Leaping from the corner, Persephone ran across the room diving behind the couch, Josephine spun around the corner as her sister hit the floor, aimed and fired a single blast which caused a shower of sparks and a modest explosion." Persephone coughed on the smoke, "that's one!" Josephine pointed to the wall, "run to that corner, I'll cover you." Persephone got on her feet and crouched, "oh what a tangled web we weave, I swear I'm going to kill whoever is responsible for this! NOW!!!" Persephone ran for the corner, Josephine spun around, dropped to her knee, aimed the pistol along her arm and fired another blast as the turret got a solid lock on Persephone. It fired one burst before Josephine's plasma discharge hit it, blasting it into tiny pieces. That one burst flew through the air, out of time, the air behind it rippled with heat; in front, Persephone was frantically trying to reach the corner. The blast was in perfect alignment to hit her head. Persephone was in a serious situation, the blast had nothing to impede it striking her down. In that moment, her shoe slipped out from under her, her ankle twisted and she fell to the ground howling in pain. The bolt which would have been her death flew passed her head barely missing her ear and burning strands of hair as she fell. Josephine saw Persephone hit the floor and the plasma bolt impact the window behind her sister. Sliding across the wood, Persephone's back hit the wall and she cried out in pain. Josephine spun around the corner, checking for anything else that would try to kill them. When she was satisfied she ran over to her sister who was clutching her foot rocking back and forth, tears streaming down her face. Josephine ran over and dropped to her knees, "hang on Seph." Josephine pulled an injector from her pocket and hit Persephone's neck with it. It was loaded with a drug that acted as a pain killer, a sedative or a muscle relaxant. The drug itself intelligently affected what needed to be done. Josephine took her sister in her arms, as the pain lifted Persephone's face eased. She sat up, still holding her ankle, sniffing, she turned to her sister, "thanks." Josephine nodded towards her foot, "how's the ankle." Persephone let go of her foot and moved it around, "no damage and the pain is easing off." Josephine sighed heavily and clutched her sister. She wiped the tears from Persephone's eyes, "that must be the first time someone has tripped over their own two feet and it saved their life." Persephone looked at the window behind her, "how close..?" Josephine's eyes darkened, "you don't want to know." Persephone threw her arms around Josephine and gave her a strong hug, "I love you". Letting go she got that look, Josephine knew she'd gone from agony to anger. "Nobody shoots at me and gets away with it." Josephine shrugged, "but where do we look now, this was the only real lead we had." Persephone put her arm out and Josephine helped her to her feet. "No we have a solid one now, the power for those turrets had to be fed from somewhere. You can't hide a Weapon's Grade Plasma Transfer, there's a hardcoded file of everything to do with defence or offence." Josephine nodded towards the console, "you think whoever is doing this was taken off guard by our arrival and tipped their hand?" Persephone nodded, "that's my guess, we would have had exact co-ordinates but it seems in your flurry of fire with those turrets, a stray shot hit the console, it's toast." Josephine looked at the console, "well it was the console or your head, shame that it had to be the console." Persephone turned around and glared at her, "very funny, come on." Josephine followed, "where are we going?" Persephone pointed to the downtown core, "my office, I can track the Power Transfer from the Science Ministry." Josephine and Persephone ran towards the residential Transit Station. Stepping on the pads, Persephone keyed in their destination, teal bolts of lightning struck the two women, teal swirling ribbons of energy entwined around them. Two beams of white light scanned from the edges of the pads closer together, touching, they electrified and resonated with a rumbling clap of thunder.

It was early morning in Atlanka City, the sun hung low in the sky, its beams glistening off the City's golden spires. The City itself was calm; most people who began work today started later than this and many of those who did start at this time had the day off. The downtown section was light with traffic, the Transit Station outside the Science Ministry softly hummed among the white noise of the City. A few vehicles floated past now and then and a soft breath of wind echoed through the trees. At the Transit Station, lightning struck as twisting energy ribbons encircled two of the Transit Pads. As Persephone and Josephine materialized, Persephone wasted no time in getting inside the building. Josephine had to half-run to keep up, her sister was searing with anger. Josephine knew being shot at was only part of it, she would have bet her last credit that what was really driving Persephone's rage was that someone would be so foolish to try to hamper their efforts. They might as well have been asking to commit suicide and they didn't even realize it. Persephone walked over to the ISTiS inside the Science Ministry. Nothing much had changed, it was much as she'd left it. Fewer people, as it was for many in the City, a day to be with their families. The desk clerk nodded as she passed, "hey Seph, how is it....going?" Persephone walked right by and didn't even acknowledge him, making a bee-line for the ISTiS, she walked in and barely gave Josephine enough time to make it in before the door slid down. Josephine looked at her sister. "Listen, Seph, I know you're angry, but you can't let it affect you like this." Persephone shot a look at her sister, "oh no?" Josephine tapped a control on the panel locking the system, "no, look at yourself, storming around, anger pouring from you. You need to step back a moment and get a handle on yourself." Persephone hung her head, "you're right, if I let my emotions affect my judgement, then I may do more harm than good." Josephine put a hand on her shoulder, "I don't think much more harm can be done at this point, but you get the idea." Persephone nodded, "yes, thank you". Josephine reached forward and unlocked the system. Persephone leaned across Josephine and tapped in the key combination for the Executive Level. As the two women were enveloped in the transit sequence, they found themselves near Persephone's office. Persephone walked out of the ISTiS with Josephine closely behind. As she made her way to the door, it slid up and the lights flickered on. SARA's voice echoed through the room, "good morning Director, you have three new messages and one conference call requested, Shall I put them through to your office?" Persephone tilted her head up as she crossed the first room, "no thank you SARA, I'll take them later." SARA's voice filled the room once again, "as you wish, storing messages." Persephone walked into her office and moved around behind her desk. Tapping a control, two silver rods slid out from the top of her desk and rippling teal currents of energy coursed between them. Her screen winked on and showed a status display of all current projects being performed by Research and Development, Archaeology and Societal Research. Persephone pulled a stylus from her coat pocket and she ran her hands down her jacket. With everything that had gone on, she hadn't even had the chance to change, she felt positively filthy. Josephine was accustomed to extended periods where you just didn't get the opportunity to change your clothing. Persephone simply found it unclean. Shaking the thought from her head, she sat down and tapped the clear screen icon on her display. She looked up at Josephine who had taken a seat across from her. "Now, there should be a record of where that transfer was initiated from and who authorized it." Josephine put her hands on the desk, "you don't think whoever it was would be foolish enough to use their own name?" Persephone tapped a few icons and brought up several windows overlapping one another. "Well, they would have to use a Level Eleven Clearance Code to transfer Weapons Grade Plasma from the reserve tanks into another system, aside from the Main Defence Batteries. There are only so many people with that level of clearance." Josephine nodded, "so, where do we look?" Persephone looked at the screen and her brow furled. "The best place to hide is in plain sight." Josephine raised an eyebrow, "you've lost me." Persephone pointed to a list on the screen, "think about it, if you didn't want to get caught, you would put something in the most obvious place possible, because nobody would think you were stupid enough to not cover your tracks. Look here, there's an anomalous command sequence coming from the Sirian Command Centre." Josephine stood up and moved around the desk, "I don't recognize the format, it looks like gibberish." Persephone looked closer, "you know, I'd bet that's Type Six Code." Josephine looked over at her sister, "that hasn't been used in six-thousand years." Persephone tapped several areas of the screen, "exactly, anybody looking at that, who didn't know about ancient Codes and security, would simply think it was background noise put out by the Geo-thermal Chambers." Persephone opened up the Decryption Database and ran the sequence of symbols through the system, "Got him! Whoever he is, he's on the Third Floor of the Sirian Defence Building." Josephine stood up, "you want to transport directly in?" Persephone looked at the screen, then her gaze dropped to her foot momentarily. "No, I think we had better go in from the door, considering the last place had automated defences." Persephone tapped a key on the desk and the screen crackled and blinked off. The two silver rods retracted back into the desk and Persephone stood up. "Wait, if there are automated defences, I don't want a repeat of what happened before." Persephone looked towards Josephine, "SARA, are there any Electromagnetic Pulse Grenades in the Armory." SARA was silent for a moment then replied, "one case of eight grenades located." Persephone grinned, "SARA transport four to my office." An alert sounded, SARA's voice filled the room, "alert, transport of hazardous or explosive materials requires Level Nine clearance." Persephone raised her head slightly, "Isis, Bastet four seven two amber." SARA responded, "clearance approved, commencing transport." Four tiny lightning bolts flashed on the desk followed by dancing ribbons of energy. As the four grenades finished the transport sequence, Josephine picked them up, "insurance?" Persephone smiled, "something like that." Josephine began to walk out the door, "do you have a location for this guy?" Persephone pulled her tablet out of her vest pocket. Tapping the screen, she brought up an overhead map that both tracked them and the target. "Sirian Defense Building Third Floor, East Wing, near a Transit Station." Josephine looked at the handheld unit, "nothing more specific than that?" Persephone shook her head, "not at this distance, once we get closer I'll set my tablet to track the emissions of that Console we encountered. Hopefully, he or she is using the same one." Josephine rubbed her neck as the two women exited Persephone's office and walked towards the ISTiS, "and if they're not?" The door to the ISTiS slid open and they walked in, "think positive Jo, think positive!" The door to the ISTiS closed behind them and the transport sequence began.

Persephone and Josephine walked out of the ISTiS, they were on the Third Floor of the Sirian Defence Building and on the east side, but Persephone's tablet was being frustratingly vague about the direction in which to go. Josephine watched her sister tap several keys trying to get a bearing on the Console's energy signature, " any luck Seph?" Persephone grimaced, "I've got a fragmentary reading but it's incredibly weak. It's only partially there and fades in and out." Josephine's ears perked up, "fading in and out?" Persephone handed her the tablet, "here look, there and there, the reading almost completely vanishes, then reacquires with no discernable pattern." Josephine watched the sequence repeat, all of a sudden a thought crossed her mind. She looked up and Persephone's eyes met hers. At the same moment, they both realized what was going on, "cloaking device!." Persephone shook her head, "but they're illegal unless installed in Defence Grade Star Ships. They are strictly prohibited for terrestrial use." Josephine pointed to the quantum dip in molecular cohesion, "Stage Two Fodajulsvi Cloaking Field, I recognize that fluctuation. It happens when the system cycles into phase two from phase one." Persephone keyed in a command sequence, "got it! I have a lock on it's direction, it's down this hallway, around a corner and at the end of another." Josephine pointed to the door nearest them on the right. "This time I'm taking a little insurance." Persephone looked quizzically at her sister, "say again?" Josephine moved over to the door and tapped the panel to open it. "They shot at us last time, no reason to believe this will be any different." Persephone nodded, "uh huh, good point, what's your idea?" Josephine walked into the room which was an overflow storage area for various items. Josephine pointed to Persephone's rather bulbous pocket. "Hand me one of those EMP grenades will you?" Josephine went on to explain, "every room is shielded from another in this building, so we can't affect anything that's not in that room." Persephone stood for a moment silent. "What if whatever is in there is shielded for EMP?" Josephine grinned widely, "think positive Seph, think positive." Persephone shook her head, "right." The two women walked out of the storage room and back into the hall. Persephone stopped briefly and tapped a control key on the door, as it slid down they made their way down the hall. Persephone was tense, she was scared. She was out of her element, this was nothing she had been trained for. She had never wanted to join the Military, she had always been a student of the mind. Her pursuits were always intellectual. Even as children, she was always the first to solve a conflict with wit and sarcasm, rather than brute force or physical restraint. Josephine on the other hand was a fair bit more hands-on than her sister. She had always been a little more hot-headed than Persephone. Her brown locks, Persephone sometimes thought should have been a flaming red, because there were times when Josephine went right off the edge. While she had never seen her lash out at another physically, she was fairly well known both in the Sirian Defence Force and in the City in general as somewhat of a loose cannon. Persephone took comfort in knowing that Josephine's outbursts had almost always been due to an injustice being exerted or in defence of someone who was innocent. Her heart was as pure as Calesteran meditation crystals, her methods sometimes, however, were a little unorthodox. Persephone recalled a memory from their childhood as they rounded a corner. In her mind played a visual of the children from their school making rather rude comments to her. Josephine came around the corner where these two girls were standing, with a bucket in her hands. As they continued to insult Persephone, Josephine poured ice-cold water all over both of them. While she had the effect of shutting them up, those two girls were off school for the next two days with chills and fever. Josephine got reprimanded for acting out and causing harm to fellow students. Persephone smiled, knowing that she was simply defending her sister from two people who thought just because she was shorter than them, they could be uncivil and cruel. Josephine caught her smile, "what?!" Persephone beamed a smile, "just remembering those two girls you drenched back in school." Josephine laughed lightly, "well, they had it coming!" Persephone's face changed, Josephine could see she was visibly frightened. She stopped her sister just before they got to the door, "Seph, stay behind me. After what happened before, I'll take point. I won't ask you to do that again." Persephone looked back at her sister, her eyes sharp as a knife. "I'll do whatever I must to get this City off the ground." Josephine put a hand on her shoulder, "as a Sirian Officer it's my responsibility to safeguard the lives of civilians. I know you mean that, but trust me when I say this has gone beyond anything you were taught in school. We've crossed into my training now, trust me." Persephone took a step back and nodded in agreement, her hands were trembling. She clasped them together to hide the horrible shaking she was feeling. Josephine looked towards the door, two doors away from them. "There it is." Persephone looked, it was just a door, nothing special, no obvious tampering, not so much as a scratch. Josephine motioned to Persephone across the hallway and on the opposite side of the door, "stay on that side and don't lean in. I'll let you know if it's safe to enter." The two women took up positions on either side of the door. Persephone's back was to the wall, her fear started to creep into her arms and legs, she'd never been so scared. Josephine pulled her pistol from its holster and turned off the safety. She breathed in deeply a couple of times and tapped the key next to the door to open it. Holding her pistol to her chest, she waited and waited but nothing happened. She leaned looking with just one eye in the door, it was dead silent. Inside, there was a console at the far end of a small room. Two unusual square pillars were set near the door on either side of it at the midpoint of the room. Brushed gold adorned the walls and soft amber light glowed from the lighting strips both in the ceiling and along the walls. It was hauntingly quiet. Josephine's hair stood up on the back of her neck, she waved her hand up and down at Persephone in a "stay put" fashion. Dropping low, she slowly moved into the room; as she passed the door she could see the console clearly. The same gibberish that was printing on the other one was apparent here as well. Standing up she looked around surveying the entire room. She called back to Persephone, "it seems clear, come in but keep your eyes open." Persephone slinked in, moving with extreme caution. Josephine pointed to the console across the room. "It looks like we're in the right place, the same garbage is being displayed here as there was last time." Persephone, feeling a little safer stood up looking from side to side, she could see no danger. She inched towards the console bit by bit. Josephine moved beside her, guarding her. "I don't understand why there weren't any defences." Persephone hadn't noticed the teal circles emitting an almost invisible stream of light between the pillars. Unknowingly, she stepped across the Trip Sensor. Teal lights flashed all around them; Persephone snapped her head around to the console. Blanking out and ringed in red it read "Deploying Defence Systems, rerouting to Council Antechamber." Josephine looked at her sister as four turrets uncloaked from the ceiling. "get out of here!" Josephine and Persephone made a beeline for the door. As the turrets got a lock on Josephine, she rounded the corner, the blasts struck the corner of the door and blasted several holes into the surrounding area. Josephine pulled one of the EMP grenades from her pocket, "I've just about had enough of this." She tapped the arm key on the top of the grenade, spinning around she flung the grenade into the room screaming the words, "enough I tell you!" Dropping to her knees she yelled at Persephone, "cover!" Both women covered their heads as a large teal pulse of electricity burst out of the grenade and ringed out a little way through the door, out of the room and into the hallway. Persephone was still holding her head, shaking like a leaf. Josephine looked around the corner, the turrets hung from a tether on the ceiling. Clearly destroyed she crawled over to her trembling sister. "It's okay Seph. It's over." Persephone looked up from her arms in which her face had been buried, still trembling but fighting to regain her emotional control. She looked at Josephine, "I'm not cut out for this." Josephine rubbed her shoulder, "I know." Persephone sniffed hard, still fighting back her fear, "Council Antechamber..." Josephine was looking into the now damaged and inoperable room. "Hmm?" Persephone's last bit of fear melted away as she began to boil with rage, "Council Antechamber!" Josephine looked at her, "that's where it went?" Persephone nodded, "the more I think about what we've experienced, the lack of any physical evidence, just technology and automated defences, I think we're dealing with an Artificial Intelligence." Josephine sat on her legs, " SARA wouldn't do this, she has been helping us." Persephone shook her head, "no, something different and much less sophisticated. This is running a prearranged program. I think we're fighting a failsafe someone wrote, in case they were unsuccessful in hampering our efforts and were incapacitated." Josephine's eyes went wide, "you don't think Ben...?" Persephone's gaze grew cold. "Can you think of anybody else who would have the expertise, training and knowledge, to design such a program to keep us from succeeding?" Josephine's hair fell in her face, "no and that's what frightens me." Persephone looked down the hall and then back to her sister. "If he's the one who wrote this, then he's not only guilty of severe damage to Sirian Military Property, but of Attempted Murder against two persons, twice." Josephine shrugged, "what now?" Persephone grabbed the wall behind her; standing up she reached down to her sister who grabbed her hand and stood up beside her. "We go to the Council Antechamber and see what's there." Josephine nodded, "we've gone this far. If we don't get the Engines up and running we're all as good as dead." Persephone pointed in the direction of the ISTiS, "let's go." The two women walked back down the hall and rounded the corner, Josephine, without breaking a stride, made a fairly obvious observation. "You know considering the last encounter was sufficiently harder to evade than the previous, we might want to consider that the next will be far more than we can manage." Persephone smiled as they entered the ISTiS, "I've already got that figured out. Let's see what we're up against first." Persephone called to SARA, "Council Building!" The transit sequence began and teal forks of lightning struck the women. As encircling ribbons of energy spun around them and two white beams scanned across them, they dematerialized and entered the Transporter Feed Network. Perceived by the user as a wash of colour and light, the system was a visual delight for any who used it. As the colours faded away and the swirls of energy left Persephone's line of sight, she was once again able to move. She and Josephine walked out of the ISTiS and stood just outside the door. Persephone once again pulled her tablet from her pocket. Clicking the screen on, she panned through a few pages of information. "There now, that's odd, I'm reading a significant power flow in addition to that Consoles energy signature, what is that?" Josephine pulled the tablet close to her so she could read it, "what on earth...?" Josephine took a good hard look, "they look like Hard Fusion Vortex Cores, nothing in Atlanka is powered by such things. The only thing I can think of is Burtanium Drills for mining, and Hazmat Droids for exploration. Everything else is fuelled by Single Mould Fusion Power Cores." Persephone tapped her tablet and read the information. "Well, the Sensors on board this thing confirm the readings. There's something down there drawing a lot of power off the grid, and apparently being augmented with supplementary power from illicit Cores, which should not be in use." Josephine looked down the hall just in front and to the left of them. The hall seemed to get longer as her gaze drew down it. She knew something dangerous lay at the end. Her own fear began to creep up her neck but she buried it. She would be afraid later, right now she had a job to do. Persephone held up her arm and chimed her Communicator. "Taven, you reading me?" Taven's voice crackled through, "yes, where are you? I've been searching all over the city, something about weapons fire in the residential area and an explosion in the Sirian Defence Tower." Persephone grinned, "that was us. I'm afraid we're about to bite off more than we can chew. We've been attacked by what I believe is an AI, buried in a series of consoles with instructions to not only surge the Engines if they were attempted to be started, but also defend itself from interference." Taven's voice was heavy, "where are you, I'm on my way." Persephone tapped a couple of icons on her tablet and ran her stylus over a section of white. "I'm sending you the exact location, we're in the Council Building, Antechamber Area." Taven's voice crackled through again, he sounded shaken and worried. "Stay where you are, do not proceed without me." Josephine yelled over Persephone, "understood Sir." Persephone and Josephine waited for what seemed like an age, legs folded and backs against the wall. Persephone found a game of Mahzrisha Solitaire on her tablet she had forgotten about. She was barely finishing her first hand when the ISTiS let out a gentle hum. Josephine got up, "here he is." Persephone tucked her stylus into her tablet and her tablet into her pocket, "about time." As the door opened, Taven, Tyra, Clinch and Fyar walked out." Persephone's eyes opened wide, "Fyar, where have you been?" Fyar smiled, "nice to see you too Seph. When I wasn't given any specific task, I returned to the Engine Room of Atlanka City and have been working with Ferus to get the Engines online and stable enough for transport." Taven picked up several rifles, they were all Dual Cell Plasma Rifles, the same one Taven had first used on the Jovus. Passing them out to Fyar, Tyra, Clinch and Josephine, Persephone stood there wantonly, "nothing for me?" Taven put his hand on her shoulder, "you've already done enough. We're trained for this kind of thing, I couldn't bare it if you got hurt, or worse." Persephone's head dipped in acceptance, "alright." Her eyes glazed over, "but if you get shot, I'll never forgive you." Taven smiled and looked back to his team, "Initialize Discharge Emitters and disengage safeties". The group collectively ran their fingers back along the top of the weapon to pump power into the plasma chamber. A light on the side of the weapon turned on indicating the weapon was now active and ready to fire. Taven waved in front of him, "let's go see what's going on." Moving slowly and as a group, Taven and the rest of the squad inched up to the entrance to the Antechamber. Waving at both sides of the door, Tyra and Clinch took up positions on one side, while Taven and Josephine took the other. Tyra looked at Taven, "do we have any idea what's inside?" Taven shook his head, "no, look sharp." Taven reached above his head and tapped the key to open the door. As it slid up, he could hear a strange whirr. Peeking around the corner he was puzzled by what he saw. "I thought you said this was the Antechamber to the Council." Persephone who had moved to a door nearby and was hiding half inside the room whispered, "it is." Taven nodded towards the door, "not according to what I'm seeing." Persephone peeked around the corner a little more and was perplexed by what she saw. The room which should have been a large area covered in marble and beautiful columns was instead, a medium sized cubical area surrounded by large what looked like stones. She shook her head, "stones?! What on earth are stones doing in the City? Those aren't part of the architecture." Taven peeked around, "we've got what looks like a Console, two turrets and two Exploration Droids." Josephine's left eyebrow went up, "Droids?" Taven pointed to the door, "that's what it looks like." Josephine shook her head, "no, no something is very wrong here." She looked at Taven, handing him the rifle she took off her jacket and hung it from the barrel of her rifle. "Taven if you wouldn't mind keeping an eye..." Taven nodded as Josephine slowly hung her jacket into view of the Droids. Their eyes suddenly flashed brilliant amber, then turned red. The backs of their hands raised up and a Plasma Emitter slid out from inside. Their eyes turned to lasers and as they looked towards the hung jacket, they raised their hands and fired a flurry of Blaster Bolts at the door. Josephine ducked back out of the way. Taven shrank back knocking Josephine onto the floor as they collided. She scampered back out of the line of sight and yelped, "Son of a...what the hell are those things?!" Taven looked back behind him at Josephine, "apparently, they've had a few upgrades." Josephine shot him back a sharp look, "you think!?" Taven sat for a moment in thought, looking back to Josephine, who was putting her finger through the now hole-ridden jacket she had on, he pressed his lips together, "mmm, wait. Do you still have an EMP grenade?" Josephine was caught off guard. "How did you...?" Taven grinned, "I noticed Seph's terminal was on and a Weapons-grade transfer to her office was logged." Josephine nodded, "I see, yes I have one left." Persephone held up the other two, "I have the others." Taven nodded to Persephone and sat with his back flat to the wall in thought, "toss it in there, I want to test something." Josephine ran her hand in a plus sign over the hawk and it glowed brilliant teal. "Duck and cover your heads." She flung the grenade into the room and ducked back behind Taven. Persephone scrambled into the room she was hiding in as the grenade detonated. Teal plasma washed over the entire room, the bulbs burst and the panels along the walls shorted out and melted or exploded. All was quiet, from the corner of his eye, Taven could see intermittent lights flashing irregularly. He peeked around the corner into the darkness and two sets of red beams locked onto him, he shrunk back around the corner as a flurry of Bolts flew out of the room striking several places, including just near the door of the room Persephone was in. Covering her head Persephone shrank away, "can't you just shoot the things?!" Taven looked back to Josephine, "shielded?" Josephine pulled her rifle close, "it seems that way." Taven's head sank and he sniffed through his nose, "alright, we do it the hard way." Persephone called out from the door she was hiding behind, "don't hit that console. Take out the defences but don't hit the console, I can delete the AI and ensure it doesn't jump again, but I need a clear path and that console needs to be intact." Taven looked back to Josephine, "remember Asteron IV?" Josephine shook her head, "I try not to." Taven nodded, "just like that." Josephine took up a position directly in front of Taven. Taven looked at Tyra and Clinch, "I need you to draw their fire. Be careful, they seem to have very good targeting suites installed." Tyra and Clinch nodded in agreement. Taven held up his hand, pointing to Tyra and then counting down, three, two, one... Tyra put her head around the corner, the red beams from the eyes of the Droids moved towards her. As they fired she ducked back around the corner and Taven whipped around with his rifle, aimed at the Droid which had been illuminated by their own plasma fire and discharged his rifle. Plasma energy arced up the barrel and the emitter at the front glowed with a brilliant teal colour. Lightning arced from all over the Emitter and streamed out of the weapon. Coiling and twisting into a condensed cone of supercharged plasma, the discharge struck the droid square in the chest, not only burning a hole right through the power system, but also sending it slamming into the wall behind it. Taven spun back around the wall and held his weapon vertically, "one down." Taven heard a click, but dismissed it as his ears playing tricks on him. Pointing to Clinch, he again raised his hand counting down, three, two, one... Clinch put his head around the corner, the red lights from the remaining Droid's eyes found him almost immediately, and sent a flurry of Plasma Bolts in his direction. Taven spun around and as before discharged his weapon. As the stream of plasma energy flew towards the Droid, all of a sudden Taven noticed a slight glint on the droid that hadn't been there a moment ago. Then it dawned on him, "shields!" He spun around the corner as the plasma discharge impacted, a large honeycomb Shield erected around the Droid's chassis. There was little time, while the Dual Cell's Discharge had been sailing towards the Droid, it had fired. Taven's head and upper torso hit the wall, but his arm was still in view as the flurry of Plasma Bolts hit the doorframe. As they flew passed, Taven almost got his elbow out of the field of fire and a stray shot grazed his forearm. Persephone watched him get struck in absolute horror. Screaming, he hit the wall, his weapon dropped from his hand and sweat beaded down his face. "So help me, I'll kill the maniac who did this with my bare hands, agh, god!" He lifted his arm with his other and rested the smouldering wound in his forearm in his lap. Josephine's jaw dropped as she watched the entire exchange take place. "By the Five Gods, Taven!" Persephone was halfway out the door and Josephine held up her hand, "Seph, stay back." Persephone, not one to argue with her sister knowing she was right, moved back into the doorframe she had been in." Taven clenched his teeth as Josephine searched the pockets of her perforated jacket. "The thing has Shields. It's going to take more than one rifle to break through them." Josephine's frantic search yielded a positive result. She found her injector in the one pocket that hadn't been obliterated by the firestorm earlier. Josephine tilted Taven's head sideways and hit his neck with an injector of painkillers. Taven winced with the injection, while it didn't hurt in itself, the plasma strike on his arm was excruciating. Plasma weapons not on low power settings, had a nasty habit of electrifying the surrounding tissue on a humanoid, and causing it to sizzle a fair time after the initial strike. It was why all Sirian weapons were on a low power standard-setting and only two weapons in the entire arsenal of Sirian Infantry weaponry were designed with a high power setting. Taven's face eased slightly, but he was still in a lot of pain, "the good news is, drawing that much power from the Core should increase the charge time on their weapons by one hundred percent. Drawing their fire should give you a clear three seconds of free fire." Josephine looked at Clinch, Clinch looked behind him, "me, you want me to be bait?" Josephine's head sank, "you're the only one who can. Tyra and I have about two years more experience with weapons training than you." Clinch shrugged, "well, we've all got to go some time, it might as well be in a blaze of fire." Josephine moved Taven off to the side. She looked at Tyra, both women were knelt holding their weapons vertically. They looked at each other, nodding, Josephine looked at Clinch, "you're on." Clinch leaned his head around the corner and put his hands up in a very mocking gesture, "hey ugly!" The droid's eyes fixated on him, and as he ducked back behind the wall, a trail of Bolts sprayed into the hallway, one hitting just above Persephone's head. Calling into the hall she remarked sarcastically, "any time now, my head is a rather vital part of me, I don't feel like losing it!" Josephine paid no attention to her sister's outburst, she was too busy giving the order. "now!" Josephine and Tyra spun around, their shoulders hitting one another. The Droid's head cocked sideways and both women fired. Twisting bolts of energy spun and coiled into two beams, one just barely short of the other. As the first impacted the Droid's Shields, they flashed erratically and the power failed. As the second hit, it slammed into the chest of the Droid, blasting a hole straight through its power Core. Josephine and Tyra's hair was a mess and hung over their faces, being pushed by the rapid breathing coming from their lips, as it dangled in their eyes. The Droid's eyes began to flash, growing faster and faster. Tyra screamed, "duck!" Josephine and Tyra shrank back behind the wall as the Droid exploded and dust and dirt flew everywhere, out the door and all over the two women who were at an almost panic level. Josephine peeked into the room, the Droid was obliterated, the turrets which had not activated were severely damaged from the explosion and the Console sat covered in debris and dust. Josephine called back to Persephone, "I think it's clear." Persephone muttered something under her breath and jumped to her feet. Running across the hall and into the now dust-filled room, she coughed as she inhaled some of the particles. "It looks like it hasn't been able to reroute." The console showed a display of the Engine Core and the Primary Power Line with a travelling image of fuel being fed into the system. "Oh no no no no no, I haven't come this far to let you outsmart me now." Persephone dropped to her knees and ripped off the panel covering the crystal sheets that both powered and configured Sirian technology, "oh to hell with it." Persephone pulled every single sheet from the housing and tossed them aside. As she pulled the last one out she reached for a crystal that was inset into the console's Main Core. It was the Power Configuration Module. She wrapped her hands around it, it wouldn't move. A signal beeped from up top, she knew what it meant, the fuel line was overloading. Persephone called out, "Taven, Clinch, somebody help me!" Clinch came in and dropped to his knees beside her, "what?" Persephone's eyes were starting to tear up, "that one, pull it or it's all over." Clinch wrapped his hand around it, the crystal wouldn't budge. "It's locked in, I can't remove it while the power is active." Clinch heard a second chime from the top of the Console, it read severe over-pressure warning. "Tyra, toss me your gun." Grabbing Persephone's jacket Clinch looked her in the eyes, "I'll apologize for this later." He threw her out of the room as Tyra's rifle sailed past Persephone and into Clinch's hands. Standing square with the Console, he discharged the rifle directly into the Power Crystal. As the console overloaded, Clinch dropped to the floor and covered his head. The console erupted in an explosion enveloping all that could be seen in the room. Persephone was the first to look into the room, as pieces of conduit collapsed and a beam fell to the ground. Tyra looked in, there was so much dust it was hard to see. Josephine gazed into the chaos, her heart breaking in half. A single tear fell from her eye, "Clinch...No!" Taven fought back his pain and got to his feet, staggering into the room he coughed on the smoke, thick as pea soup and twice as vile, he bent down and threw moulding and debris off the floor. Fyar ran in and assisted Taven's frantic digging through the conduit and debris. Josephine fell to her knees, her eyes welling up with tears. Tyra seemed to be in shock and simply stared into the room. Persephone reached over to her sister and pulled her close. The three women knelt in the doorway, sullen and shocked. Taven threw a couple of fairly large pieces of wall plating away from the floor and found a hand among the debris, assuming the worst, he put his hand on Clinch's not expecting anything. Clinch grabbed his hand hard and pulled on his arm. Taven, clenching his teeth and straining against not only the weight of the debris, but his own injury called to Fyar, "he's alive, help me!" Fyar rushed over, "you stubborn son of a..." Together the two men pulled their friend out of the heap of scrap metal. He was badly burned, with his hands seared along with his back, but he was alive. Taven and Fyar dragged him out into the hallway. Josephine scrambled to his side, tapping her Comm Badge, "Rachel, we need you up here right now, Clinch is badly hurt." Rachel's voice crackled through, "on my way, what are you guys doing up there, blowing up the entire City." Clinch coughed and wheezed as he strained to speak. The pain was great but his will was greater. "It didn't get a chance to migrate. The AI is destroyed." He coughed again, his face burying into Josephine's leg. Josephine reached for her injector and tried to ease his pain but the indicator flashed white. It was out of medication. Throwing it down the hall in fury, she reached down and pulled him close to her. Her arms around his chest, her eyes full of tears she sat with him for what seemed like an eternity. The door of the ISTiS opened and Rachel walked out into the hallway. "My God, what happened did a bomb go off?" Josephine looked behind her, "quickly, I could do nothing, my injector is dry." Rachel pointed down, "flat on the floor with him." Persephone sat on her legs, her arms crossed, worry draining the life from her face. Josephine laid Clinch down, pain resonating from his face, the agony flooding from every pore of his body. She could feel his pain, his agony seeping from his mind outwards. Persephone looked on powerless to do anything. Her mind dwelled on thoughts of her watching one of her closest friends die right in front of her. Rachel pulled a tablet from her pocket and ran it over Clinch's body. "Second Degree burns, it looks like some lacerations in the muscle tissue around the forearms. Some slight irradiation of the flesh on his back and a very large bruise on his ego, nothing I can't fix." Rachel touched an aquamarine gem on her bracelet and put her hand level with the ground and about a foot above it. A golden case emblazoned with a falcon and hieroglyphics on the side materialized from under her hand. She opened the top by touching two opposing half-scarab icons together. As the top opened a slight hiss was heard and she pulled out a handheld device that was simply a flat black square on a handle. She looked down at Clinch, "now hold him still, this will hurt." She squeezed the handle and a crisscross pattern of tightly knit bolts of lightning ran across the square. She moved the device over his back, and fingers of electricity arced out from it. Striking and running along his burned flesh it began to knit together and heal. Clinch's teeth locked and his face went bright red as he fought the pain. The Epidermal Rejuvenator restored his back and hands to normal. She reached and took out what looked like a flat golden trapezoid with a handle on the bottom of it. She squeezed the handle and energy charged along the edges of the trapezoid. An azure blue mist sprayed out and onto Clinch's back. His flesh began to illuminate as the mist covered his back, and then the glow dissipated and died out. Rachel put the devices back into the case and looked at Josephine, "he's okay, you can relax." Josephine looked at Rachel, "I don't know why I'm so upset." Rachel smiled at her and squeezed her leg, "I do, you'll figure it out soon enough." As Rachel finished with Clinch's back, she looked over to Taven and noticed his injury, "why didn't you say anything?" Taven nodded towards Clinch, "my crew is my first priority." Rachel moved over to Taven, "well he'll be sore for a few days but he's perfectly fine, now let me see that arm." She once again reached into the case for the Tissue Regenerator. Turning it on, she ran it across Taven's arm. His teeth locked as he fought the pain. As she finished healing his injury, he turned his arm over and moved his hand, "fantastic work as always Doctor." Rachel placed the Rejuvenator back into the box it came from and scanned them both with her tablet. "Your burns look good. The irradiation has been negated and the lacerations have been repaired, You be more careful, I don't want to have to do major surgery on any of you, understand?" Rachel turned to Clinch and waved a finger at him, "and don't stand beside exploding objects, it's bad for your health." Rachel knelt on one knee and placed her hand on the box, she touched a control on her wrist and the box her hand was placed on shone a brilliant teal. Electricity sparks encircled it and coursed around it until it vanished from sight. Rachel got up, "The Bio-Containment and Infrastructure Storage Systems are ready to go, just give the word." Persephone grasped Rachel's arm warmly, "thank you". Rachel shrugged, "what's to thank, it's my job, but in any case, you're welcome." Josephine was sitting on her knees beside Clinch as he rubbed the back of his neck and shook his head slightly. Josephine's head hung low, "I thought you were..." Clinch smiled as he rubbed his neck, "dead?...nah, it takes more than a little explosion to stop me." Josephine reached out and touched his face with her hand. She stared deeply into his eyes; he returned her gaze and touched her knee, "are you alright Jo?". She didn't blink nor move a muscle. She spoke without thought, but from pure emotion, "I am now." Josephine reached out pulling Clinch towards her and kissed his lips gently. Josephine didn't even realize that she had reached out to him and wrapped her arms around him until she was already in the embrace. Clinch returned her kiss and held her for a moment. He patted her back gently as he broke the embrace and cleared his throat. "Umm, shouldn't we be doing something, like getting off this planet?" Persephone walked over and helped her friends to their feet, "Indeed, let's finish what we started." Persephone looked to the sky, "SARA, override Primary Transit Interlocks and lock on Atlanka's Primary Bridge Section, flight configuration. Transport all persons in the current area directly to there." SARA's voice responded, "group transport safety Protocols prohibit the transport of groups anywhere other than the designated Transit Hubs." Persephone pulled her hair out of her ponytail and let it down, Josephine and Tyra did the same. Persephone looked out the window at the asteroid that was almost on top of them, a flaming ball of Superheated Plasma barely outside the atmosphere. "Override condition aqua, Code Verification Isis Bastet Emergency Override sequence 5624-3 Seth." SARA's voice once again echoed through the corridor. The requested function is not recommended, proceed at your own risk. Persephone took a look at her team, their last chance of saving over one million lives, "understood, initiate!" Electricity struck, teal ribbons of swirling energy enveloped the group and a set of white lines drew closer together. The energy vortex was utterly tornadic as the lines made contact. A resonating clap of thunder echoed through the halls as the group vanished. As they disappeared, a single piece of piping fell from the damaged room nearby and struck the floor.

THE GREAT ESCAPE

The Bridge of Atlanka was small by comparison to most Sirian vessels. Its systems were few but as it served strictly as a means to move the City from one location to another, it didn't need more than the most basic of Controls and Interfaces. The design was an ancient one, back from a time when the Sirian fleet was in its infancy. The Bridge was shaped in a rough triangular fashion. The Screen at the front was fairly small, columns were sunk half into the wall beside it. There were two Bridge Stations along each wall leading out from the front, with the Navigation Console and Captain's seat directly in the centre, behind were a set of handrails and along the back wall were three doors. The centre one led to the rest of the City's substructure. The two sides were a Conference Room and Living Quarters for those entrusted to move the City from one area to the next. It was dim, the lights were barely on. All the consoles were dark and the Screen at the front was black. A golden sheet was draped over the Centre Console and the chairs along with it. The room began to shine with teal light, lightning struck near the centre door along the back of the room, and a large swirling energy mass lowered from the ceiling. With the coils of plasma twisting and spinning, the team emerged from transport. Clinch's first reaction was an impressed whistle, "wow, you don't see this every day." Taven walked towards the Centre Seat, "she's old, but she'll fly." Taven looked towards Fyar, "head to Engineering, if things go south I'll need you there." Fyar nodded, "right!" Persephone walked towards the Navigation Console and ran her hand along the soft cloth that lay over it. She grasped a side of the cloth and pulled it from across the console, sliding it off. A Sensor on the top detected the movement and the lights came up. Consoles sprang to life one by one and the Screen flickered and finally settled on an image of the Mesirian afternoon sky. Taven walked over to the Centre Seat and pulled the cover sheet off. He took the opportunity to sit for a moment, "not bad for an old ship, not bad at all." Persephone giggled, "are you comfortable?" Taven smiled, "surprisingly yes." Taven leaned on the armrest looking at the Controls. They were raised glyphs embossed into the arms themselves. It was a very old design indeed, one that had not been used in a very long time. Taven smiled at Persephone, "you know, as old as the Jovus is, it's still easy for me to call up just about any information on Ship's Status at a glance from my chair. I sometimes forget that there are Ships far older that make you appreciate that ease of access, see here." He pointed to a few of the glyphs, "these access the Main Screen, which, when you think about it is fairly cumbersome. What if vital information was being accessed on the Main Screen and the Captain bumped the armrest. Not that it happens often, but even I've hit a control once or twice with my elbow." Persephone tapped his shoulder, "well you can't have everything." She looked around the Bridge and took in the antiquity. "You do have to appreciate the design though, very aesthetic." Taven looked up at her, "you would notice the art involved." Josephine called from behind him, she had called up the Main Systems on the Engineering Console. "We're ready here, standing by for Engine Preheat and Priming." Taven looked over to Rachel, who was on the far side of the Bridge, "Rachel, are you set?" Rachel didn't break her gaze from the Screen, "just a couple of minutes, this has to be done right the first time. This isn't like storing a document on a tablet and plugging it into a console elsewhere, this is precision work." Taven looked down at himself, knowing what little time was left. The asteroid was entering the atmosphere and they still hadn't managed to get the population stored. A bead of sweat ran down the side of his face and he began to feel a swelling in his throat. He could feel the unsettling signs of panic gripping him. He couldn't afford to be compromised now, he got up from his chair. He moved towards Rachel who was at the Medical Control Array.

Standing beside her, he placed a hand on her shoulder, "you'll let me know when you're ready?" Rachel looked into his eyes, she could see what was on his mind. Before transferring to the Helia, she had worked as a Primary Nurse and On-Call Doctor aboard the Jovus for three years after Taven took command. She had a certain familiarity with his looks and this one she understood. She took her hands off the console and leaned close to his ear to whisper, "Taven, go clear your head, you need to focus." He smiled and dropped his head in slight embarrassment, "is it that obvious?" Rachel turned back towards the Console, "only if you know where to look, I saw you through some rough spots when you first took command." Taven nodded his head and rubbed his nose as he moved across the Bridge. Tapping the open control on the keypad of the Captain's Office, he walked in and let the door slide shut behind him. A diagonal window was across the room. It was spartan, with a desk and a single chair. A small inset black panel along the wall and a small potted tree in the corner. Taven moved over to the window. Sirian architecture was always designed with windows. The psychology behind it was that nobody likes feeling like they're in an enclosed space, even when every side of them is a Bulkhead. To resolve this issue, every room aboard a Sirian Star Ship that did not include an actual window provided a holographic replacement. Sensors on the exterior of the Ship or Star Base scanned the view constantly and projected an image appropriate to whichever way the room was facing onto a holographic window. In this manner, no crew member, guest or resident was ever without a view of the horizon or a starlit sky. He took a long look out towards the Ubrean Forest. Not so long ago, he'd taken a walk through that wooded glade, trying to get up the nerve to ask Persephone out. Now he looked upon it for the last time. He was deep in thought, so deep he didn't hear the door slide open and shut behind him. Persephone walked into the room. Taven stood, feet apart hands crossed in front of him. He looked so distant, she walked up behind him and touched his back, "Taven, are you okay?" Taven stared out the window, "do you remember the day I asked you out for dinner?" Persephone smiled, "that was two days before my meeting with Sorvan wasn't it?" Taven nodded, his gaze still transfixed to the soft ruffle of the trees in the distance. "I took a walk in there, and I stopped by this old tree. It was gnarled and somewhat disfigured, but as I leaned against it, there was something so comforting, so soothing about it, its leaves covered the entire area in a sparkling light play of shade and light. The wind caressed the leaves and I felt so at peace, that I felt I could do anything, even have a chance with you." Persephone beamed a smile, "you always had a chance. Nothing would have ever given me a reason to not give you one. I think you've done remarkably well with everything that's gone on, and on a personal level, I couldn't have someone better at my side." Taven looked across his shoulder then turned towards her, "if something goes wrong, I'm going to be responsible for the deaths of over one million people." Persephone put her hand on his cheek, "Nothing will go wrong my love. You're strong, and I'm right here beside you. Trust in me, as I trust in you and this too shall pass." She leaned forward and kissed his lips gently. As she did the Comm chimed. Taven, without breaking the embrace, touched the Badge on his wrist while it was wrapped around Persephone. It was Rachel's voice, "Taven, we're ready, we have to go." Taven broke away, gazing deep into Persephone's eyes, he saw a sparkle, stealing one more hug he responded, "on our way." Taven nuzzled into Persephone's golden curls, "thank you." Persephone nodded, "that's what I'm here for." Taven walked over to the door and tapped the control, he followed Persephone back onto the Bridge. Rachel looked up from the console, "do or die time Chief, we all go or we all stay." Taven sat down in the Centre Seat. Taking a deep breath he closed his eyes, with a long exhale he opened them, "time to close up the store, initiate storage procedure." Rachel turned back to the console. Josephine ran her fingers across the controls, "Engines to Flight Configuration, Priming Injectors and loading Ion Discharge Buffers." Josephine looked up at the console, reading the Engine startup information, "Initializing Cascade Reaction, Throttling Ion

Accelerators to standby, initiating run start." There was a loud clunk and Atlanka shook lightly. A resonating hum could be heard throughout the City. Fyar's voice crackled through the Intercom, "Taven, no issues on startup here the Core Chamber is online and feeding power evenly. Main Thruster Quads are coming up...now. Engines engaging." There was a small indicator atop the Main Screen that Taven hadn't noticed before, as he looked at it, it changed from saying "Deployed" to "In Transit". Atlanka's Engines fired and a rumble was felt across the City. As it quietened and the Engines got their footing, Rachel looked at Josephine and Josephine to Rachel. Both women nodded. Rachel said from the Medical Console, "Initiating Bulk Storage of all Persons, Pets and items inside the City. Extending Storage Range to include all sprawling additions to the original landing site." A massive fork of lightning struck the highest tower. Ribbons of teal energy encircled the City. Two lines of blinding light scanned from the City's edges to the centre. As they touched and electrified, a deafening clap of thunder shook the City. The City was suddenly quiet, a haunting quiet, Rachel looked up from the console, "it will take SARA a few minutes to process and compile the Database." Persephone walked over to Josephine, "it's going to be a few minutes, I'm going to go stand on the Dock." Josephine nodded in agreement, as Persephone walked passed Taven's chair she looked over, "I just need to say goodbye, I won't be long." Taven nodded, "Atlanka won't leave without you." Persephone nodded and walked into the ISTiS. Josephine followed her and as the door closed, Persephone's emotions began to surface, "Docks". The transport cycle began and as Persephone and Josephine watched the colours of the matter stream dance in front of them Persephone grabbed her sister's hand as the transport sequence ended. The two women walked out to the edge of the Dock, it was late afternoon now, Persephone looked up and saw the asteroid. She hated it, if there was a way she could sling anything at it to destroy it, she would. She didn't want to lose her home. The late afternoon breeze caught their hair, Josephine's dark locks rustled in the

wind. She turned to Persephone, "do you think it'll work."
Persephone's eyes betrayed her, tears ran down her cheeks and
fell onto the brushed gold Dock as the waves gently lapped
beneath them, "it has to Jo, we have no choice." Josephine
turned to her sister, "no matter what happens, I want you to
know that I've always been proud of you and that I love you."
Josephine wrapped her arms around her sister and her emotional
barricades suddenly broke away. Her eyes welled up and both
women released a buildup of stress and anxiety that they had
been keeping suppressed for over a week. Persephone's words
broke through her sister's hair, "I love you too, Jo." Taven's voice
crackled through Josephine's badge, "we're ready ladies,
standby." Persephone and Josephine took one last look out over
the horizon. As they both ran their hands under their eyes trying
to hide their pain, the transport sequence started. Persephone
raised her hand and waved farewell to a place she'd known as
home ever since she was a little girl, "goodbye". As Persephone
and Josephine materialized onto the Bridge, Taven couldn't help
but notice Persephone and her sister looked a little shaken. He
waved them over, "are you okay?" Persephone shook her head
as another tear dripped down her cheek, "no, I'm not."
Josephine simply turned her head to the Screen and gazed
longingly at the horizon. Taven sat back in his chair taking a
Command posture. Persephone stood at his side. Taven looked
around the Bridge. "I just want to say no matter what the
outcome of this is, you have all done more than I ever imagined
possible. You exemplify the best of the Sirian Empire and the
heart of every Sirian across the Galaxy. Now, let's get the job
done, initiate pack down." Josephine rubbed her nose and moved
back to the Engineering Console. Josephine's hands danced
across the keypad and every Screen on the Bridge switched to a
random Sensor Feed showing a different area of the City.
Lightning struck every tower and building in the City. A tornado of
teal energy ribbons started from the top of every building and
moved down the structure to the ground. As it did, an outline of
the building arced in teal electricity, resonating briefly before the

lightning faded. A constant drone of thunder could be heard from the Docks to the Repair Pits, from the Residential Area to the Downtown Core. As the last buildings vanished into the back of the great bird Atlanka rested on, the whole City vibrated. Taven looked up and around him at the vibration, he wasn't used to this much shaking on a Star Ship. The Jovus, at her worst, never shook this much or this long. Josephine's voice came from behind him, "all tucked in, ready to go." Taven smiled, "very poetic. Alright Clinch, let's see if everything we've done has been worth it. Ventral Thrusters to full power, lift to ten Fika's above ground, then blow the Geo-thermal Lines." Clinch ran a series of commands into the Helm. Repeating the instructions to ensure everything was precise, "Main Thrusters to station-keeping, Ventral RCS to one zero zero percent." Atlanka shook first lightly then more and more until Persephone was having a hard time standing. She moved behind Taven's chair and held onto the headrest. The metal squeaked in the walls and overhead in the ceiling. Josephine called out over the noise, "external vibration exceeding design limits, if we don't move, we're going to shake to pieces." Taven called to Clinch, "give us a little boost with the Main Engines, try to shake us loose." Clinch ran his hands over the controls, as he did the City lurched violently. Persephone was thrust into the back of the chair. Taven called out, "again!" Once again, the City was rocked by a sudden lurch forward. Josephine called out from behind them, "one more like that and we'll bust the Main Fuel Lines, Tortional stress is red-lining, we've got to go, now!" Taven leaned over, "put it to the floor Clinch!" Clinch tapped a Control and the Rear Thrusters reduced by fifty percent, while the Forward Thrusters increased by one hundred percent. As the City shook violently the horizon began to drop from the Screen. Persephone pointed to the Screen, "the Nose is lifting." Taven nodded "I see it, equalize Engine power, get me some altitude." The Aft RCS engaged and the City began to rise out of the hole it sat in. Still shaking but now moving, Atlanka rose slowly from the deep impression she had left in the ground. Her Ion Engines rose up to where you could see the massive cylinder of amber resting on her underneath, flanked by two smaller Ion Engines on either side of the Main Thruster Assembly. As she rose, along the back of the City a series of rectangles stretching across the back of the Wings retracted and slid into the Hull, exposing teal Warp Initiator Strips which rose and locked into place. As Atlanka came to a hover, two large Umbilicals were connected to either side of the City underneath the centre of the great Wings. Taven was listening to the City, the shaking was subsiding quickly. Satisfied, he sat back in his chair, "blow the Geo-thermal Lines, get us off this planet." Clinch ran his hands over the Controls, "already on it boss, hold onto your butts this is going to get rough." As Atlanka hovered over its impression in the dirt, the Twin Umbilicals resonated and with a large bang, they dislodged and fell to the ground. The Geo-thermal Intake Valves retracted into the Hull and large square plates of shimmering gold lowered into place. Atlanka's Nose tilted slightly up, her Engines resonated with immense power. Turning from amber to a brilliant teal then almost pure white, they rumbled with energy. Slowly, barely, Atlanka began to move. Picking up speed she moved out over the ocean and then began to rise up into the clouds. Moving faster now she slipped into a cloud and rings formed behind her great Wingspan. As she continued to gain altitude and climb above the clouds, the sun glistened on her Wings, as if Mesira itself was wishing them farewell. The clouds shrinking behind them and the beach they'd all called home were now but a speck of dust on the Screen. Persephone walked over to the Screen, now looking at the Continent she grew up on as Atlanka broke through the upper stratosphere, Persephone touched the wall and her head sank". Taven wanted to comfort her, but he knew he had to keep his focus. Josephine called from behind him, "Initiator Strips Deployed but I'm getting conflicting reports from the Warp Engines." Persephone's brow furled, "what?!" She moved over to her sister and looked at the Screen, "the System registers no flaw in Mechanics or Function. The Reaction Chamber simply won't start." Persephone's eyes widened, "this is not good!" Josephine hit a key and the Fuel

Manifest came up. Josephine turned around, "the Reserve Tank for the Warp Drive is empty. I can't start the Engines without Drive Plasma." Taven spun around, "we don't have any?" Josephine shook her head, "the line must have burst when we were trying to get the City off the ground with all that shaking." Taven's face drained of all colour, "does anybody have any brilliant ideas of how we're going to do this without Warp?" Clinch spun around, "make for Terra, the Helia's been deploying a Shield Grid to protect that Planet, it will protect us too if we can get behind it before the asteroid explodes. Taven tapped his chair, "good idea." Atlanka banked towards Terra, her massive Wings shimmering against a dark starry sky. Josephine looked at the Sensors, horrified, she spoke without thinking, "time's up!" Persephone's head whipped around as the asteroid exploded in Mesira's atmosphere. Streaking through the sky, it made the water wake behind it as it raged through the atmosphere. Slamming into the Fortidan Desert, which was about one-hundred Fikans from where Atlanka had just left, a blast of teal fire flew up into the sky. A massive Displacement Wave destroyed every cloud it touched; following it, was a massive Teal Firewall. Persephone watched as the ring of fire washed over her world, the forest, the beach, the atmosphere. Everything was gone in a matter of seconds. Josephine looked over to Taven, "I realize this is probably a bad time to bring this up, but we have a massive flaming Plasma Wave that has ringed out from the planet, it's tracking directly for us." Taven got up from his seat, "no no no, it's too soon. Clinch can you get us behind the Shields before it hits." Clinch shook his head, "I doubt it, this City doesn't respond well to sudden course changes and we're still quite a ways out." Taven sat back in his chair, calling back to Josephine, "how long?" Josephine called out from her station, "less than ten seconds." Taven yelled, "secure all Systems, brace for impact." The massive wave of Teal Energy moved closer and closer to Atlanka City. Her Engines turned red from Emergency Thrust, but the wave just kept on coming. Josephine covered her head, "impact!" The wave slammed into the back of the City, washing over the entire length of the great bird and stressing the City's Auto-Deployed Shields. A beam from the ceiling shook loose on the Bridge and fell next to Clinch. The Console next to Josephine erupted in sparks and flames. Sparks shot out from the walls and overhead. As the wave crested the City's Nose, it dispersed. "Josephine looked over to Persephone, "didn't SARA say it was going to slam into Terra as well?" Persephone shrugged, "nobody's perfect I guess." Clinch piped up, "umm guys, we have a much bigger problem. I have lost just about all Navigational Control." Taven leaned forward, "how bad?" Clinch tapped across the Console receiving a series of negative tones and buzzes and threw his hands up in the air. I have fifty percent power on Central RCS, seventy five percent on Forward RCS, twenty five on Port and Starboard and zero on Aft. The main Ion Drive System is out, at this point, I can't change our course, nor can I avoid entering the atmosphere, we're going to crash into Terra." Taven shook his head, "do we have enough to establish a controlled entry?" Clinch checked his systems, "barely." Taven nodded, "I'll take barely, get it done." Clinch's hands ran over the Controls as Atlanka's belly began to glow from friction against Terra's atmosphere. The Shields were absorbing most of the heat, but a percentage still leaked through. The City was designed to withstand a controlled entry even with its Shields disabled. Taven was thankful the Shields hadn't been compromised; he was worried about the extent of the damage otherwise, though. Something felt "off" to him. Atlanka streaked across the morning sky like a brilliant fireball. As the City emerged from the flaming inferno, they saw the cloud tops and nothing but Ocean. Taven leaned forward, "Clinch, why do I see water. Water is bad, very bad." Clinch nodded, "I know, I couldn't get enough of an angle on our descent to bring us in closer, I'm hoping our sheer speed carries us across." Taven watched as the clouds slipped first under them, then around them, then above them. "Clinch, I'm still seeing water!" Clinch tapped a few Controls, "nudging us twenty degrees northeast." Taven raised an eyebrow, "why?" Clinch shook his head, "we'll never reach the mainland, we don't have enough Thrust or Altitude, but I think we have enough to make it to the Island we left the Solaran on." Taven sat back, "ETA?" Clinch tapped a few more controls, "forty-five seconds, it's going to be close, we'll be scraping the Deck as we hit the Island." Taven smirked, "don't hit the Island, please." Clinch grinned as he worked the Navigation Console, "I'll do my best. Contact in thirty seconds, the island should be visual anytime now." Persephone squinted and then pointed, "there!" Clinch made a few minor adjustments and Atlanka banked slightly as the ocean crashed beneath them. The City was so close to the ocean, that the waves almost touched the Ion Manifolds. They had levelled off from sheer velocity, but that would only hold so long, the island was coming up fast, Taven wiggled his finger, "ah ah, we don't want to overshoot." Clinch stared at the screen, "just a little more, just a little...there, deploying Breaking Thrusters!" Four large plates recessed on the front of Atlanka's Wings, two per side, and slid into the Hull. Massive rectangular devices rose out and locked into place. As they did, the ports on them began to spin around and around, faster and faster, suddenly all of them erupted in teal flame and the City began to slow. As they soared over the last of the ocean and just over the beach Clinch squinted, "forward motion to ten percent, Ventral Thrusters to Max Reserve Power."

Taven stood up, "let's find a place to park." As the City moved over the trees with a low rumble, Josephine watched the Monitor. Seeing a clearing she pointed, "over there. That looks like an open field it should serve nicely for a starting spot." The spot was a mere minutes' walk from the beach, it was covered in emerald green grass, red, white and yellow flowers dotted the area and there were wild deer grazing by a brook near the entrance to a forest. SARA's voice shattered the calm on the Bridge, "alert, planetary shift, alert!" Taven yelled above SARA, "what's going wrong now?!" Persephone called up the Science Station's alert message, "just what I was afraid of, Mesira has been knocked clean from its orbit. It's on a direct course for the Seba. Taven stood up as the City came to a hover over the meadow, "by the Five Gods!" The screen showed Mesira now a flaming ball of teal fire flying past Terra, hurtling towards the Sun. Tyra, who'd been somewhat in the background working on keeping the City's fragile Fuel System and Transport Interface balanced, looked up and tapped a Comm control on the panel, "Juice, Code Kem. Mesira's on a collision course with this System's Seba. Get the Helia and the Jovus to within twenty Fikans of Terra's surface, over land." Juice's voice crackled through, the channel was filled with static and distortion. "We see......on....way to.....surface now.....hover......contact when event.......end." Tyra breathed a sigh of relief and closed the Channel. Taven leaned over to Persephone, who had moved back beside him, "so what happens now?" Persephone brushed a lock of hair out of her face, "well, either the planet will impact the Seba causing a massive solar discharge, which could do almost as much damage as a Nova; or, the planet will get caught in the Seba's gravity and get swung around and thrown back out the other side, which would put it into a much more stable albeit somewhat erratic orbit. Taven looked at her, "what can we do?" Persephone shook her head, "this one's in the hands of the Five Gods. We're completely helpless." Mesira careened through space, passing the other planets as a flaming ball of plasmatic fury. As it approached the sun, it began to roll on itself, over and over and over. Spinning on its axis like a top at a birthday party, it ran over gravitational eddy's, the movements were erratic, with sudden shifts like the wind blowing from the south then suddenly and without reason, gusting from the north. Mesira hit a gravitational breakwater and was pulled into the overwhelming gravity of the Sun. Swinging around at nearly the speed of light, the entire exchange was shown as a blur. Mesira looked to be around both sides of the sun at the same time. Mesira was rocked by explosions as the subterranean magma was flash-heated to extreme temperatures. Every volcano and mountain on the surface erupted, every last trace of water evaporated away as Mesira rounded the Sun and was thrown out the other side. The planet that emerged was nothing like the planet that had been their home not a half-hour ago. Blackened, running with rivers of lava, still glowing with plasma fires, but they were quickly being replaced by the planet's own core, violently vomiting from the assault it had endured. Not one cloud, not one drop of water, not one plant. Persephone watched as Mesira slowed down from the pull on it due to G-Forces being exerted on its travel away from the sun. Josephine looked upon her home and she softly muttered to herself, "my home, everything, gone." Taven turned to her, "we're alive, and the City is intact, mostly, we succeeded." Taven was taken off guard by the shrill cry of a falcon. SARA's voice filled the air, "Critical Systems Failure Imminent, Primary Thrusters have exceeded design limitations and will disengage in ten seconds." Taven spun around, "Clinch!" Clinch's hands flew across the board, "taking us down." The City slowly lowered towards the ground. Taven watched, his instinctual reaction to stand won out and he moved and stood beside Clinch. "Can we descend any faster?" Clinch hit a few Controls and shouted over the drowning noise, "if we go any faster we'll blow the entire RCS Relay System." SARA's voice filled the Bridge again, "five seconds." Persephone, Josephine and Rachel found a seat, they knew without needing to be told. Atlanka was just barely ten Fika's above the surface when the RCS Thrusters cut out. As the City fell to the ground, Taven screamed out, "Clinch!" As the City hit the surface, the Primary Engine Chamber was flattened along with the Secondary Thrust Cores. A large ring of grass was flattened and thrown out by the impact and the subsequent burst of wind it generated. Taven lost his footing as the City struck the ground, slipping off his right foot he lost his balance and fell sideways, his head striking the side of the Navigational Array. As he lay on the floor, his vision blurring, blood seeping from his head, and his consciousness slipping away, he could only speak one word, "Seph...?"

The saga continues in

DAWN OF MAN
AFTERMATH

Printed in Great Britain
by Amazon

83700249R00163